Ready Player One

'Fascinating and imaginative . . . it's non-stop action . . . Readers are in for a wild ride.'

Terry Brooks, #1 *New York Times* bestselling author of the Shannara series

'This non-gamer loved every page of *Ready Player One.*'

Charlaine Harris, #1 *New York Times* bestselling author of the Sookie Stackhouse series

'I was blown away by this book . . . because Ernie Cline has pulled the raddest of all magic tricks . . . A book of ideas, a potboiler, a game-within-a-novel, a serious science-fiction epic, a comic pop culture mash-up – call this novel what you will, but *Ready Player One* will defy every label you try to put on it. Here, finally, is this generation's *Neuromancer.*'

Will Lavender, *New York Times* bestselling author of *Obedience*

'Completely fricking awesome . . . This book pleased every geeky bone in my geeky body'

Patrick Rothfuss, #1 *New York Times* Bestselling author of *The Wise Man's Fear*

'If this book were a living room, it would be wood-paneled. If it were shoes, it would be high-tops. And if it were a song, well, it would have to be *Eye of the Tiger*. I really, really loved it.'

'Imagine *Dungeons and Dragons* and an 80s video arcade made hot, sweet love, and their child was raised in Azeroth.'

'The pure, unfettered brainscream of a child of the 80s, like a dream my 13-year-old self would have had after bingeing on Pop Rocks and Coke . . . I couldn't put it down.'

'Pure geek heaven. Cline blends a dystopic future with meticulously detailed nostalgia to create a story that will resonate in the heart of every true nerd.'

Chris Farnsworth, author of *Blood Oath*

'*Ready Player One* is a fantastic adventure set in a futuristic world with a retro heart. Once I started reading, I didn't want to put it down and I couldn't wait to pick it back up.'

S.G. Browne, author of *Breathers and Fated*

'Cline has somehow managed to jack into the nervous system of some great warm collective geek dream nostalgia of the 70's and 80's . . . *Ready Player One* let me romp through some of the best memories of my youth.'

Paul Malmont, author of *The Chinatown Death Cloud Peril*

'Cline's novel is a nerdcore odyssey; engaging and fun, this Gen-X popcult thrillride drew me in like a *Galaxian* machine set to free play.'

James Swallow, bestselling author of *Nemesis*

'This is the best book of its type since *Neuromancer*; Ernie Cline is the new William Gibson.'

Joseph Delaney, author of *The Wardstone Chronicles*

Ready Player One

Ernest Cline

C

Century · London

Published by Century 2011

2 4 6 8 10 9 7 5 3 1

First published in Great Britain in 2011 by
Century
Random House, 20 Vauxhall Bridge Road,
London SW1V 2SA

www.randomhouse.co.uk

Addresses for companies within The Random House Group Limited can be
found at: www.randomhouse.co.uk

The Random House Group Limited Reg. No. 954009

A CIP catalogue record for this book
is available from the British Library

ISBN 9781846059377

The Random House Group Limited supports the Forest Stewardship
Council® (FSC®), the leading international forest certification organisation.
All our titles that are printed on Greenpeace approved FSC® certified paper
carry the FSC® logo. Our paper procurement policy can be found at:
www.randomhouse.co.uk/environment

Printed and bound in Great Britain by
CPI Mackays, Chatham, ME5 8TD

For Susan and Libby

Because there is no map for where we are going

Everyone my age remembers where they were and what they were doing when they first heard about the contest. I was sitting in my hideout watching cartoons when the news bulletin broke in on my video feed, announcing that James Halliday had died during the night.

I'd heard of Halliday, of course. Everyone had. He was the videogame designer responsible for creating the OASIS, a massively multiplayer on-line game that had gradually evolved into the globally networked virtual reality most of humanity now used on a daily basis. The unprecedented success of the OASIS had made Halliday one of the wealthiest people in the world.

At first, I couldn't understand why the media was making such a big deal of the billionaire's death. After all, the people of Planet Earth had other concerns. The ongoing energy crisis. Catastrophic climate change. Widespread famine, poverty, and disease. Half a dozen wars. You know: "dogs and cats living together . . . mass hysteria!" Normally, the news-feeds didn't interrupt everyone's interactive sitcoms and soap operas un-less something really major had happened. Like the outbreak of some new killer virus, or another major city vanishing in a mushroom cloud. Big stuff like that. As famous as he was, Halliday's death should have war-ranted only a brief segment on the evening news, so the unwashed masses could shake their heads in envy when the newscasters announced the ob-scenely large amount of money that would be doled out to the rich man's heirs.

But that was the rub. James Halliday had no heirs.

He had died a sixty-seven-year-old bachelor, with no living relatives and, by most accounts, without a single friend. He'd spent the last fifteen years of his life in self-imposed isolation, during which time—if the rumors were to be believed—he'd gone completely insane.

So the real jaw-dropping news that January morning, the news that had everyone from Toronto to Tokyo crapping in their cornflakes, concerned the contents of Halliday's last will and testament, and the fate of his vast fortune.

Halliday had prepared a short video message, along with instructions that it be released to the world media at the time of his death. He'd also arranged to have a copy of the video e-mailed to every single OASIS user that same morning. I still remember hearing the familiar electronic chime when it arrived in my inbox, just a few seconds after I saw that first news bulletin.

His video message was actually a meticulously constructed short film titled *Anorak's Invitation*. A famous eccentric, Halliday had harbored a lifelong obsession with the 1980s, the decade during which he'd been a teenager, and *Anorak's Invitation* was crammed with obscure '80s pop culture references, nearly all of which were lost on me the first time I viewed it.

The entire video was just over five minutes in length, and in the days and weeks that followed, it would become the most scrutinized piece of film in history, surpassing even the Zapruder film in the amount of painstaking frame-by-frame analysis devoted to it. My entire generation would come to know every second of Halliday's message by heart.

• • •

Anorak's Invitation begins with the sound of trumpets, the opening of an old song called "Dead Man's Party."

The song plays over a dark screen for the first few seconds, until the trumpets are joined by a guitar, and that's when Halliday appears. But he's not a sixty-seven-year-old man, ravaged by time and illness. He looks just as he did on the cover of *Time* magazine back in 2014, a tall, thin, healthy man in his early forties, with unkempt hair and his trademark horn-rimmed eyeglasses. He's also wearing the same clothing he wore in the *Time* cover photo: faded jeans and a vintage Space Invaders T-shirt.

Halliday is at a high-school dance being held in a large gymnasium. He's surrounded by teenagers whose clothing, hairstyles, and dance moves all indicate that the time period is the late 1980s.* Halliday is dancing, too— something no one ever saw him do in real life. Grinning maniacally, he spins in rapid circles, swinging his arms and head in time with the song, flawlessly cycling through several signature '80s dance moves. But Halliday has no dance partner. He is, as the saying goes, dancing with himself.

A few lines of text appear briefly at the lower left-hand corner of the screen, listing the name of the band, the song's title, the record label, and the year of release, as if this were an old music video airing on MTV: Oingo Boingo, "Dead Man's Party," MCA Records, 1985.

When the lyrics kick in, Halliday begins to lip-synch along, still gyrating: "All dressed up with nowhere to go. Walking with a dead man over my shoulder. Don't run away, it's only me. . . ."

He abruptly stops dancing and makes a cutting motion with his right hand, silencing the music. At the same moment, the dancers and the gymnasium behind him vanish, and the scene around him suddenly changes.

Halliday now stands at the front of a funeral parlor, next to an open casket.† A second, much older Halliday lies inside the casket, his body emaciated and ravaged by cancer. Shiny quarters cover each of his eyelids.

The younger Halliday gazes down at the corpse of his older self with mock sadness, then turns to address the assembled mourners.§ Halliday snaps his fingers and a scroll appears in his right hand. He opens it with a flourish and it unfurls to the floor, unraveling down the aisle in front of him. He breaks the fourth wall, addressing the viewer, and begins to read.

"I, James Donovan Halliday, being of sound mind and disposing memory, do hereby make, publish, and declare this instrument to be my last will and testament, hereby revoking any and all wills and codicils by me

---

*Careful analysis of this scene reveals that all of the teenagers behind Halliday are actually extras from various John Hughes teen films who have been digitally cut-and-pasted into the video.

†His surroundings are actually from a scene in the 1989 film *Heathers*. Halliday appears to have digitally re-created the funeral parlor set and then inserted himself into it.

High-resolution scrutiny reveals that both quarters were minted in 1984.

§The mourners are actually all actors and extras from the same funeral scene in *Heathers*. Winona Ryder and Christian Slater are clearly visible in the audience, sitting near the back.

at any time heretofore made. . . ." He continues reading, faster and faster, plowing through several more paragraphs of legalese, until he's speaking so rapidly that the words are unintelligible. Then he stops abruptly. "Forget it," he says. "Even at that speed, it would take me a month to read the whole thing. Sad to say, I don't have that kind of time." He drops the scroll and it vanishes in a shower of gold dust. "Let me just give you the highlights."

The funeral parlor vanishes, and the scene changes once again. Halliday now stands in front of an immense bank vault door. "My entire estate, including a controlling share of stock in my company, Gregarious Simulation Systems, is to be placed in escrow until such time as a single condition I have set forth in my will is met. The first individual to meet that condition will inherit my entire fortune, currently valued in excess of two hundred and forty billion dollars."

The vault door swings open and Halliday walks inside. The interior of the vault is enormous, and it contains a huge stack of gold bars, roughly the size of a large house. "Here's the dough I'm putting up for grabs," Halliday says, grinning broadly. "What the hell. You can't take it with you, right?"

Halliday leans against the stack of gold bars, and the camera pulls in tight on his face. "Now, I'm sure you're wondering, what do you have to do to get your hands on all this moolah? Well, hold your horses, kids. I'm getting to that. . . ." He pauses dramatically, his expression changing to that of a child about to reveal a very big secret.

Halliday snaps his fingers again and the vault disappears. In the same instant, Halliday shrinks and morphs into a small boy wearing brown corduroys and a faded *The Muppet Show* T-shirt.* The young Halliday stands in a cluttered living room with burnt orange carpeting, wood-paneled walls, and kitschy late-'70s decor. A 21-inch Zenith television sits nearby, with an Atari 2600 game console hooked up to it.

"This was the first videogame system I ever owned," Halliday says, now in a child's voice. "An Atari 2600. I got it for Christmas in 1979." He plops down in front of the Atari, picks up a joystick, and begins to play. "My favorite game was this one," he says, nodding at the TV screen,

---

*Halliday now looks exactly as he did in a school photo taken in 1980, when he was eight years old.

where a small square is traveling through a series of simple mazes. "It was called Adventure. Like many early videogames, Adventure was designed and programmed by just one person. But back then, Atari refused to give its programmers credit for their work, so the name of a game's creator didn't actually appear anywhere on the packaging." On the TV screen, we see Halliday use a sword to slay a red dragon, although due to the game's crude low-resolution graphics, this looks more like a square using an arrow to stab a deformed duck.

"So the guy who created Adventure, a man named Warren Robinett, decided to hide his name inside the game itself. He hid a key in one of the game's labyrinths. If you found this key, a small pixel-sized gray dot, you could use it to enter a secret room where Robinett had hidden his name." On the TV, Halliday guides his square protagonist into the game's secret room, where the words CREATED BY WARREN ROBINETT appear in the center of the screen.

"This," Halliday says, pointing to the screen with genuine reverence, "was the very first videogame Easter egg. Robinett hid it in his game's code without telling a soul, and Atari manufactured and shipped Adventure all over the world without knowing about the secret room. They didn't find out about the Easter egg's existence until a few months later, when kids all over the world began to discover it. I was one of those kids, and finding Robinett's Easter egg for the first time was one of the coolest videogaming experiences of my life."

The young Halliday drops his joystick and stands. As he does, the living room fades away, and the scene shifts again. Halliday now stands in a dim cavern, where light from unseen torches flickers off the damp walls. In the same instant, Halliday's appearance also changes once again, as he morphs into his famous OASIS avatar, Anorak—a tall, robed wizard with a slightly more handsome version of the adult Halliday's face (minus the eyeglasses). Anorak is dressed in his trademark black robes, with his avatar's emblem (a large calligraphic letter "A") embroidered on each sleeve.

"Before I died," Anorak says, speaking in a much deeper voice, "I created my own Easter egg, and hid it somewhere inside my most popular videogame—the OASIS. The first person to find my Easter egg will inherit my entire fortune."

Another dramatic pause.

"The egg is well hidden. I didn't just leave it lying under a rock somewhere. I suppose you could say that it's locked inside a safe that is bur-ied in a secret room that lies hidden at the center of a maze located somewhere"—he reaches up to tap his right temple—"up here.

"But don't worry. I've left a few clues lying around to get everyone started. And here's the first one." Anorak makes a grand gesture with his right hand, and three keys appear, spinning slowly in the air in front of him. They appear to be made of copper, jade, and clear crystal. As the keys continue to spin, Anorak recites a piece of verse, and as he speaks each line, it appears briefly in flaming subtitles across the bottom of screen:

Three hidden keys open three secret gates
Wherein the errant will be tested for worthy traits
And those with the skill to survive these straits
Will reach The End where the prize awaits

As he finishes, the jade and crystal keys vanish, leaving only the copper key, which now hangs on a chain around Anorak's neck.

The camera follows Anorak as he turns and continues farther into the dark cavern. A few seconds later, he arrives at a pair of massive wooden doors set into the cavern's rocky wall. These doors are banded with steel, and there are shields and dragons carved into their surfaces. "I couldn't playtest this particular game, so I worry that I may have hidden my Easter egg a little too well. Made it too difficult to reach. I'm not sure. If that's the case, it's too late to change anything now. So I guess we'll see."

Anorak throws open the double doors, revealing an immense treasure room filled with piles of glittering gold coins and jewel-encrusted gob-lets.[*] Then he steps into the open doorway and turns to face the viewer, stretching out his arms to hold open the giant double doors.[†]

---

[*] Analysis reveals dozens of curious items hidden among the mounds of treasure, most notably: several early home computers (an Apple IIe, a Commodore 64, an Atari 800XL, and a TRS-80 Color Computer 2), dozens of videogame controllers for a variety of game systems, and hundreds of polyhedral dice like those used in old tabletop role-playing games.

[†] A freeze-frame of this scene appears nearly identical to a painting by Jeff Easley that appeared on the cover of the *Dungeon Master's Guide,* a Dungeons & Dragons rulebook published in 1983.

"So without further ado," Anorak announces, "let the hunt for Halliday's Easter egg begin!" Then he vanishes in a flash of light, leaving the viewer to gaze through the open doorway at the glittering mounds of treasure that lay beyond.

Then the screen fades to black.

•   •   •

At the end of the video, Halliday included a link to his personal website, which had changed drastically on the morning of his death. For over a decade, the only thing posted there had been a short looping animation that showed his avatar, Anorak, sitting in a medieval library, hunched over a scarred worktable, mixing potions and poring over dusty spellbooks, with a large painting of a black dragon visible on the wall behind him.

But now that animation was gone, and in its place there was a high-score list like those that used to appear in old coin-operated videogames. The list had ten numbered spots, and each displayed the initials JDH—James Donovan Halliday—followed by a score of six zeros. This high-score list quickly came to be known as "the Scoreboard."

Just below the Scoreboard was an icon that looked like a small leather-bound book, which linked to a free downloadable copy of *Anorak's Almanac*, a collection of hundreds of Halliday's undated journal entries. The *Almanac* was over a thousand pages long, but it contained few details about Halliday's personal life or his day-to-day activities. Most of the entries were his stream-of-consciousness observations on various classic videogames, science-fiction and fantasy novels, movies, comic books, and '80s pop culture, mixed with humorous diatribes denouncing everything from organized religion to diet soda.

The Hunt, as the contest came to be known, quickly wove its way into global culture. Like winning the lottery, finding Halliday's Easter egg became a popular fantasy among adults and children alike. It was a game anyone could play, and at first, there seemed to be no right or wrong way to play it. The only thing *Anorak's Almanac* seemed to indicate was that a familiarity with Halliday's various obsessions would be essential to finding the egg. This led to a global fascination with 1980s pop culture. Fifty years after the decade had ended, the movies, music, games, and fashions of the 1980s were all the rage once again. By 2041, spiked hair and acid-washed jeans were back in style, and covers of hit '80s pop songs by contemporary bands dominated the music charts. People who had actually been teenagers in the 1980s, all now approaching old age, had the strange experience of seeing the fads and fashions of their youth embraced and studied by their grandchildren.

A new subculture was born, composed of the millions of people who now devoted every free moment of their lives to searching for Halliday's egg. At first, these individuals were known simply as "egg hunters," but this was quickly truncated to the nickname "gunters."

During the first year of the Hunt, being a gunter was highly fashionable, and nearly every OASIS user claimed to be one.

When the first anniversary of Halliday's death arrived, the fervor surrounding the contest began to die down. An entire year had passed and no one had found anything. Not a single key or gate. Part of the problem was the sheer size of the OASIS. It contained thousands of simulated worlds where the keys might be hidden, and it could take a gunter years to conduct a thorough search of any one of them.

Despite all of the "professional" gunters who boasted on their blogs that they were getting closer to a breakthrough every day, the truth gradually became apparent: No one really even knew exactly what it was they were looking for, or where to start looking for it.

Another year passed.

And another.

Still nothing.

The general public lost all interest in the contest. People began to assume it was all just an outlandish hoax perpetrated by a rich nut job. Others believed that even if the egg really did exist, no one was ever going to find it. Meanwhile, the OASIS continued to evolve and grow in popularity, protected from takeover attempts and legal challenges by the ironclad terms of Halliday's will and the army of rabid lawyers he had tasked with administering his estate.

Halliday's Easter egg gradually moved into the realm of urban legend, and the ever-dwindling tribe of gunters gradually became the object of ridicule. Each year, on the anniversary of Halliday's death, newscasters jokingly reported on their continued lack of progress. And each year, more gunters called it quits, concluding that Halliday had indeed made the egg impossible to find.

And another year went by.

And another.

Then, on the evening of February 11, 2045, an avatar's name appeared at the top of the Scoreboard, for the whole world to see. After five long years, the Copper Key had finally been found, by an eighteen-year-old kid living in a trailer park on the outskirts of Oklahoma City.

That kid was me.

Dozens of books, cartoons, movies, and miniseries have attempted to tell the story of everything that happened next, but every single one of them got it wrong. So I want to set the record straight, once and for all.

Level One

Being human totally sucks most of the time.
Videogames are the only thing that
make life bearable.

—Anorak's Almanac, Chapter 91, Verses 1–2

0001

I was jolted awake by the sound of gunfire in one of the neighboring stacks. The shots were followed by a few minutes of muffled shouting and screaming, then silence.

Gunfire wasn't uncommon in the stacks, but it still shook me up. I knew I probably wouldn't be able to fall back asleep, so I decided to kill the remaining hours until dawn by brushing up on a few coin-op classics. Galaga, Defender, Asteroids. These games were outdated digital dinosaurs that had become museum pieces long before I was born. But I was a gunter, so I didn't think of them as quaint low-res antiques. To me, they were hallowed artifacts. Pillars of the pantheon. When I played the classics, I did so with a determined sort of reverence.

I was curled up in an old sleeping bag in the corner of the trailer's tiny laundry room, wedged into the gap between the wall and the dryer. I wasn't welcome in my aunt's room across the hall, which was fine by me. I preferred to crash in the laundry room anyway. It was warm, it afforded me a limited amount of privacy, and the wireless reception wasn't too bad. And, as an added bonus, the room smelled like liquid detergent and fabric softener. The rest of the trailer reeked of cat piss and abject poverty.

Most of the time I slept in my hideout. But the temperature had dropped below zero the past few nights, and as much as I hated staying at my aunt's place, it still beat freezing to death.

A total of fifteen people lived in my aunt's trailer. She slept in the smallest of its three bedrooms. The Depperts lived in the bedroom adjacent to hers, and the Millers occupied the large master bedroom at the end of the hall. There were six of them, and they paid the largest share of the rent. Our trailer wasn't as crowded as some of the other units in the stacks. It was a double-wide. Plenty of room for everybody.

I pulled out my laptop and powered it on. It was a bulky, heavy beast, almost ten years old. I'd found it in a trash bin behind the abandoned strip mall across the highway. I'd been able to coax it back to life by replacing its system memory and reloading the stone-age operating system. The processor was slower than a sloth by current standards, but it was fine for my needs. The laptop served as my portable research library, video arcade, and home theater system. Its hard drive was filled with old books, movies, TV show episodes, song files, and nearly every videogame made in the twentieth century.

I booted up my emulator and selected Robotron: 2084, one of my all-time favorite games. I'd always loved its frenetic pace and brutal simplicity. Robotron was all about instinct and reflexes. Playing old videogames never failed to clear my mind and set me at ease. If I was feeling depressed or frustrated about my lot in life, all I had to do was tap the Player One button, and my worries would instantly slip away as my mind focused itself on the relentless pixelated onslaught on the screen in front of me. There, inside the game's two-dimensional universe, life was simple: *It's just you against the machine. Move with your left hand, shoot with your right, and try to stay alive as long as possible.*

I spent a few hours blasting through wave after wave of Brains, Spheroids, Quarks, and Hulks in my unending battle to *Save the Last Human Family!* But eventually my fingers started to cramp up and I began to lose my rhythm. When that happened at this level, things deteriorated quickly. I burned through all of my extra lives in a matter of minutes, and my two least-favorite words appeared on the screen: GAME OVER.

I shut down the emulator and began to browse through my video files. Over the past five years, I'd downloaded every single movie, TV show, and cartoon mentioned in *Anorak's Almanac.* I still hadn't watched all of them yet, of course. That would probably take decades.

I selected an episode of *Family Ties,* an '80s sitcom about a middle-class family living in central Ohio. I'd downloaded the show because it had been one of Halliday's favorites, and I figured there was a chance that some clue related to the Hunt might be hidden in one of the episodes. I'd become addicted to the show immediately, and had now watched all 180 episodes, multiple times. I never seemed to get tired of them.

Sitting alone in the dark, watching the show on my laptop, I always found myself imagining that *I* lived in that warm, well-lit house, and that those smiling, understanding people were *my* family. That there was nothing so wrong in the world that we couldn't sort it out by the end of a single half-hour episode (or maybe a two-parter, if it was something really serious).

My own home life had never even remotely resembled the one depicted in *Family Ties,* which was probably why I loved the show so much. I was the only child of two teenagers, both refugees who'd met in the stacks where I'd grown up. I don't remember my father. When I was just a few months old, he was shot dead while looting a grocery store during a power blackout. The only thing I really knew about him was that he loved comic books. I'd found several old flash drives in a box of his things, containing complete runs of *The Amazing Spider-Man, The X-Men,* and *Green Lantern.* My mom once told me that my dad had given me an alliterative name, Wade Watts, because he thought it sounded like the secret identity of a superhero. Like Peter Parker or Clark Kent. Knowing that made me think he must have been a cool guy, despite how he'd died.

My mother, Loretta, had raised me on her own. We'd lived in a small RV in another part of the stacks. She had two full-time OASIS jobs, one as a telemarketer, the other as an escort in an online brothel. She used to make me wear earplugs at night so I wouldn't hear her in the next room, talking dirty to tricks in other time zones. But the earplugs didn't work very well, so I would watch old movies instead, with the volume turned way up.

I was introduced to the OASIS at an early age, because my mother used it as a virtual babysitter. As soon as I was old enough to wear a visor and a pair of haptic gloves, my mom helped me create my first OASIS avatar. Then she stuck me in a corner and went back to work, leaving me to explore an entirely new world, very different from the one I'd known up until then.

From that moment on, I was more or less raised by the OASIS's interactive educational programs, which any kid could access for free. I spent a big chunk of my childhood hanging out in a virtual-reality simulation of Sesame Street, singing songs with friendly Muppets and playing interactive games that taught me how to walk, talk, add, subtract, read, write, and share. Once I'd mastered those skills, it didn't take me long to discover that the OASIS was also the world's biggest public library, where even a penniless kid like me had access to every book ever written, every song ever recorded, and every movie, television show, videogame, and piece of artwork ever created. The collected knowledge, art, and amusements of all human civilization were there, waiting for me. But gaining access to all of that information turned out to be something of a mixed blessing. Because that was when I found out the truth.

• • •

I don't know, maybe your experience differed from mine. For me, growing up as a human being on the planet Earth in the twenty-first century was a real kick in the teeth. Existentially speaking.

The worst thing about being a kid was that no one told me the truth about my situation. In fact, they did the exact opposite. And, of course, I believed them, because I was just a kid and I didn't know any better. I mean, Christ, my brain hadn't even grown to full size yet, so how could I be expected to know when the adults were bullshitting me?

So I swallowed all of the dark ages nonsense they fed me. Some time passed. I grew up a little, and I gradually began to figure out that pretty much *everyone* had been lying to me about pretty much *everything* since the moment I emerged from my mother's womb.

This was an alarming revelation.

It gave me trust issues later in life.

I started to figure out the ugly truth as soon as I began to explore the free OASIS libraries. The facts were right there waiting for me, hidden in old books written by people who weren't afraid to be honest. Artists and scientists and philosophers and poets, many of them long dead. As I read the words they'd left behind, I finally began to get a grip on the situation. My situation. *Our* situation. What most people referred to as "the human condition."

It was not good news.

I wish someone had just told me the truth right up front, as soon as I was old enough to understand it. I wish someone had just said:

"Here's the deal, Wade. You're something called a 'human being.' That's a really smart kind of animal. Like every other animal on this planet, we're descended from a single-celled organism that lived millions of years ago. This happened by a process called evolution, and you'll learn more about it later. But trust me, that's really how we all got here. There's proof of it everywhere, buried in the rocks. That story you heard? About how we were all created by a super-powerful dude named God who lives up in the sky? Total bullshit. The whole God thing is actually an ancient fairy tale that people have been telling one another for thousands of years. We made it all up. Like Santa Claus and the Easter Bunny.

"Oh, and by the way . . . there's no Santa Claus or Easter Bunny. Also bullshit. Sorry, kid. Deal with it.

"You're probably wondering what happened before you got here. An awful lot of stuff, actually. Once we evolved into humans, things got pretty interesting. We figured out how to grow food and domesticate animals so we didn't have to spend all of our time hunting. Our tribes got much bigger, and we spread across the entire planet like an unstoppable virus. Then, after fighting a bunch of wars with each other over land, resources, and our made-up gods, we eventually got all of our tribes organized into a 'global civilization.' But, honestly, it wasn't all that organized, or civilized, and we continued to fight a lot of wars with each other. But we also figured out how to do science, which helped us develop technology. For a bunch of hairless apes, we've actually managed to invent some pretty incredible things. Computers. Medicine. Lasers. Microwave ovens. Artificial hearts. Atomic bombs. We even sent a few guys to the moon and brought them back. We also created a global communications network that lets us all talk to each other, all around the world, all the time. Pretty impressive, right?

"But that's where the bad news comes in. Our global civilization came at a huge cost. We needed a whole bunch of energy to build it, and we got that energy by burning fossil fuels, which came from dead plants and animals buried deep in the ground. We used up most of this fuel before you got here, and now it's pretty much all gone. This means that we no longer have enough energy to keep our civilization running like it was before. So we've had to cut back. Big-time. We call this the Global Energy Crisis, and it's been going on for a while now.

"Also, it turns out that burning all of those fossil fuels had some nasty side effects, like raising the temperature of our planet and screwing up the environment. So now the polar ice caps are melting, sea levels are rising, and the weather is all messed up. Plants and animals are dying off in record numbers, and lots of people are starving and homeless. And we're still fighting wars with each other, mostly over the few resources we have left.

"Basically, kid, what this all means is that life is a lot tougher than it used to be, in the Good Old Days, back before you were born. Things used to be awesome, but now they're kinda terrifying. To be honest, the future doesn't look too bright. You were born at a pretty crappy time in history. And it looks like things are only gonna get worse from here on out. Human civilization is in 'decline.' Some people even say it's 'collapsing.'

"You're probably wondering what's going to happen to you. That's easy. The same thing is going to happen to you that has happened to every other human being who has ever lived. You're going to die. We all die. That's just how it is.

"What happens when you die? Well, we're not completely sure. But the evidence seems to suggest that *nothing* happens. You're just dead, your brain stops working, and then you're not around to ask annoying questions anymore. Those stories you heard? About going to a wonderful place called 'heaven' where there is no more pain or death and you live forever in a state of perpetual happiness? Also total bullshit. Just like all that God stuff. There's no evidence of a heaven and there never was. We made that up too. Wishful thinking. So now you have to live the rest of your life knowing you're going to die someday and disappear forever.

"Sorry."

— • • •

OK, on second thought, maybe honesty isn't the best policy after all. Maybe it isn't a good idea to tell a newly arrived human being that he's been born into a world of chaos, pain, and poverty just in time to watch everything fall to pieces. I discovered all of that gradually over several years, and it still made me feel like jumping off a bridge.

Luckily, I had access to the OASIS, which was like having an escape hatch into a better reality. The OASIS kept me sane. It was my playground and my preschool, a magical place where anything was possible.

The OASIS is the setting of all my happiest childhood memories. When my mom didn't have to work, we would log in at the same time and play games or go on interactive storybook adventures together. She used to have to force me to log out every night, because I never wanted to return to the real world. Because the real world sucked.

I never blamed my mom for the way things were. She was a victim of fate and cruel circumstance, like everyone else. Her generation had it the hardest. She'd been born into a world of plenty, then had to watch it all slowly vanish. More than anything, I remember feeling sorry for her. She was depressed all the time, and taking drugs seemed to be the only thing she truly enjoyed. Of course, they were what eventually killed her. When I was eleven years old, she shot a bad batch of something into her arm and died on our ratty fold-out sofa bed while listening to music on an old mp3 player I'd repaired and given to her the previous Christmas.

That was when I had to move in with my mom's sister, Alice. Aunt Alice didn't take me in out of kindness or familial responsibility. She did it to get the extra food vouchers from the government every month. Most of the time, I had to find food on my own. This usually wasn't a problem, because I had a talent for finding and fixing old computers and busted OASIS consoles, which I sold to pawnshops or traded for food vouchers. I earned enough to keep from going hungry, which was more than a lot of my neighbors could say.

The year after my mom died, I spent a lot of time wallowing in self-pity and despair. I tried to look on the bright side, to remind myself that, orphaned or not, I was still better off than most of the kids in Africa. And Asia. And North America, too. I'd always had a roof over my head and more than enough food to eat. And I had the OASIS. My life wasn't so bad. At least that's what I kept telling myself, in a vain attempt to stave off the epic loneliness I now felt.

Then the Hunt for Halliday's Easter egg began. That was what saved me, I think. Suddenly I'd found something worth doing. A dream worth chasing. For the last five years, the Hunt had given me a goal and purpose. A quest to fulfill. A reason to get up in the morning. Something to look forward to.

The moment I began searching for the egg, the future no longer seemed so bleak.

＊ ＊ ＊

I was halfway through the fourth episode of my *Family Ties* mini-marathon when the laundry room door creaked open and my aunt Alice walked in, a malnourished harpy in a housecoat, clutching a basket of dirty clothes. She looked more lucid than usual, which was bad news. She was much easier to deal with when she was high.

She glanced over at me with the usual look of disdain and started to load her clothes into the washer. Then her expression changed and she peeked around the dryer to get a better look at me. Her eyes went wide when she spotted my laptop. I quickly closed it and began to shove it into my backpack, but I knew it was already too late.

"Hand it over, Wade," she ordered, reaching for the laptop. "I can pawn it to help pay our rent."

"No!" I shouted, twisting away from her. "Come on, Aunt Alice. I need it for school."

"What you *need* is to show some *gratitude!*" she barked. "Everyone else around here has to pay rent. I'm tired of you leeching off of me!"

"You keep all of my food vouchers. That more than covers my share of the rent."

"The hell it does!" She tried again to grab the laptop out of my hands, but I refused to let go of it. So she turned and stomped back to her room. I knew what was coming next, so I quickly entered a command on my laptop that locked its keyboard and erased the hard drive.

Aunt Alice returned a few seconds later with her boyfriend, Rick, who was still half-asleep. Rick was perpetually shirtless, because he liked to show off his impressive collection of prison tattoos. Without saying a word, he walked over and raised a fist at me threateningly. I flinched and handed over the laptop. Then he and Aunt Alice walked out, already discussing how much the computer might fetch at a pawnshop.

Losing the laptop wasn't a big deal. I had two spares stowed in my hideout. But they weren't nearly as fast, and I would have to reload all of my media onto them from backup drives. A total pain in the ass. But it was my own fault. I knew the risk of bringing anything of value back here.

The dark blue light of dawn was starting to creep in through the laundry room window. I decided it might be a good idea to leave for school a little early today.

I dressed as quickly and quietly as possible, pulling on the worn corduroys, baggy sweater, and oversize coat that comprised my entire winter wardrobe. Then I put on my backpack and climbed up onto the washing machine. After pulling on my gloves, I slid open the frost-covered window. The arctic morning air stung my cheeks as I gazed out over the uneven sea of trailer rooftops.

My aunt's trailer was the top unit in a "stack" twenty-two mobile homes high, making it a level or two taller than the majority of the stacks immediately surrounding it. The trailers on the bottom level rested on the ground, or on their original concrete foundations, but the units stacked above them were suspended on a reinforced modular scaffold, a haphazard metal latticework that had been constructed piecemeal over the years.

We lived in the Portland Avenue Stacks, a sprawling hive of discolored tin shoeboxes rusting on the shores of I-40, just west of Oklahoma City's decaying skyscraper core. It was a collection of over five hundred individual stacks, all connected to each other by a makeshift network of recycled pipes, girders, support beams, and footbridges. The spires of a dozen ancient construction cranes (used to do the actual stacking) were positioned around the stacks' ever-expanding outer perimeter.

The top level or "roof" of the stacks was blanketed with a patchwork array of old solar panels that provided supplemental power to the units below. A bundle of hoses and corrugated tubing snaked up and down the side of each stack, supplying water to each trailer and carrying away sewage (luxuries not available in some of the other stacks scattered around the city). Very little sunlight made it to the bottom level (known as the "floor"). The dark, narrow strips of ground between the stacks were clogged with the skeletons of abandoned cars and trucks, their gas tanks emptied and their exit routes blocked off long ago.

One of our neighbors, Mr. Miller, once explained to me that trailer parks like ours had originally consisted of a few dozen mobile homes arranged in neat rows on the ground. But after the oil crash and the onset of the energy crisis, large cities had been flooded with refugees from surrounding suburban and rural areas, resulting in a massive urban housing shortage. Real estate within walking distance of a big city became far too valuable to waste on a flat plane of mobile homes, so someone had cooked up the brilliant idea of, as Mr. Miller put it, "stacking the sumbitches," to maximize the use of ground space. The idea caught on in a big way, and trailer parks across the country had quickly evolved into "stacks" like this one—strange hybrids of shantytowns, squatter settlements, and refugee camps. They were now scattered around the outskirts of most major cities, each one overflowing with uprooted rednecks like my parents, who—desperate for work, food, electricity, and reliable OASIS access—had fled their dying small towns and had used the last of their gasoline (or their beasts of burden) to haul their families, RVs, and trailer homes to the nearest metropolis.

Every stack in our park stood at least fifteen mobile homes high (with the occasional RV, shipping container, Airstream trailer, or VW microbus mixed in for variety). In recent years, many of the stacks had grown to a height of twenty units or more. This made a lot of people nervous. Stack collapses weren't that uncommon, and if the scaffold supports buckled at the wrong angle, the domino effect could bring down four or five of the neighboring stacks too.

Our trailer was near the northern edge of the stacks, which ran up to a crumbling highway overpass. From my vantage point at the laundry room window, I could see a thin stream of electric vehicles crawling along the cracked asphalt, carrying goods and workers into the city. As I stared out at the grim skyline, a bright sliver of the sun peeked over the horizon. Watching it rise, I performed a mental ritual: Whenever I saw the sun, I reminded myself that I was looking at a *star*. One of over a hundred billion stars in our galaxy. A galaxy that was just one of billions of other galaxies in the observable universe. This helped me keep things in perspective. I'd started doing it after watching a science program from the early '80s called *Cosmos*.

I slipped out the window as quietly as possible and, clutching the bottom of the window frame, slid down the cold surface of the trailer's metal siding. The steel platform on which the trailer rested was only slightly wider and longer than the trailer itself, leaving a ledge about a foot and a half wide all the way around. I carefully lowered myself until my feet rested on this ledge, then reached up to close the window behind me. I grabbed hold of a rope I'd strung there at waist level to serve as a handhold and began to sidestep along the ledge to the corner of the platform. From there I was able to descend the ladderlike frame of the scaffolding. I almost always took this route when leaving or returning to my aunt's trailer. A rickety metal staircase was bolted to the side of the stack, but it shook and knocked against the scaffolding, so I couldn't use it without announcing my presence. Bad news. In the stacks, it was best to avoid being heard or seen, whenever possible. There were often dangerous and desperate people about—the sort who would rob you, rape you, and then sell your organs on the black market.

Descending the network of metal girders had always reminded me of old platform videogames like Donkey Kong or BurgerTime. I'd seized upon this idea a few years earlier when I coded my first Atari 2600 game (a gunter rite of passage, like a Jedi building his first lightsaber). It was a Pitfall rip-off called The Stacks where you had to navigate through a vertical maze of trailers, collecting junk computers, snagging food-voucher power-ups, and avoiding meth addicts and pedophiles on your way to school. My game was a lot more fun than the real thing.

As I climbed down, I paused next to the Airstream trailer three units below ours, where my friend Mrs. Gilmore lived. She was a sweet old lady in her mid-seventies, and she always seemed to get up ridiculously early. I peeked in her window and saw her shuffling around in her kitchen, making breakfast. She spotted me after a few seconds, and her eyes lit up.

"Wade!" she said, cracking open her window. "Good morning, my dear boy."

"Good morning, Mrs. G," I said. "I hope I didn't startle you."

"Not at all," she said. She pulled her robe tight against the draft coming in the window. "It's freezing out there! Why don't you come in and have some breakfast? I've got some soy bacon. And these powdered eggs aren't too bad, if you put enough salt on them. . . ."

"Thanks, but I can't this morning, Mrs. G. I have to get to school."

"All right. Rain check, then." She blew me a kiss and started to close the window. "Try not to break your neck climbing around out there, OK, Spider-Man?"

"Will do. See ya later, Mrs. G." I waved good-bye to her and continued my descent.

Mrs. Gilmore was a total sweetheart. She let me crash on her couch when I needed to, although it was hard for me to sleep there because of all her cats. Mrs. G was super-religious and spent most of her time in the OASIS, sitting in the congregation of one of those big online megachurches, singing hymns, listening to sermons, and taking virtual tours of the Holy Land. I fixed her ancient OASIS console whenever it went on the fritz, and in return, she answered my endless questions about what it had been like for her to grow up during the 1980s. She knew the coolest bits of '80s trivia—stuff you couldn't learn from books or movies. She was always praying for me too. Trying her hardest to save my soul. I never had the heart to tell her that I thought organized religion was a total crock. It was a pleasant fantasy that gave her hope and kept her going—which was exactly what the Hunt was for me. To quote the *Almanac*: "People who live in glass houses should shut the fuck up."

When I reached the bottom level, I jumped off the scaffold and dropped the few remaining feet to the ground. My rubber boots crunched into the slush and frozen mud. It was still pretty dark down here, so I took out my flashlight and headed east, weaving my way through the dark maze, doing my best to remain unseen while being careful to avoid tripping over a shopping cart, engine block, or one of the other pieces of junk littering the narrow alleys between the stacks. I rarely saw anyone out at this time of the morning. The commuter shuttles ran only a few times a day, so the residents lucky enough to have a job would already be waiting at the bus stop by the highway. Most of them worked as day laborers in the giant factory farms that surrounded the city.

After walking about half a mile, I reached a giant mound of old cars and trucks piled haphazardly along the stacks' eastern perimeter. Decades ago, the cranes had cleared the park of as many abandoned vehicles as possible, to make room for even more stacks, and they'd dumped them in huge piles like this one all around the settlement's perimeter. Many of them were nearly as tall as the stacks themselves.

I walked to the edge of the pile, and after a quick glance around to make sure I wasn't being watched or followed, I turned sideways to squeeze through a gap between two crushed cars. From there, I ducked, clambered, and sidestepped my way farther and farther into the ramshackle mountain of twisted metal, until I reached a small open space at the rear of a buried cargo van. Only the rear third of the van was visible. The rest was concealed by the other vehicles stacked on and around it. Two overturned pickup trucks lay across the van's roof at different angles, but most of their weight was supported by the cars stacked on either side, creating a kind of protective arch that had prevented the van from being crushed by the mountain of vehicles piled above it.

I pulled out a chain I kept around my neck, on which there hung a single key. In a stroke of luck, this key had still been hanging from the van's ignition when I'd first discovered it. Many of these vehicles had been in working condition when they were abandoned. Their owners had simply no longer been able to afford fuel for them, so they'd just parked them and walked away.

I pocketed my flashlight and unlocked the van's rear right door. It opened about a foot and a half, giving me just enough room to squeeze inside. I pulled the door closed behind me and locked it again. The van's rear doors had no windows, so I was hunched over in total darkness for a second, until my fingers found the old power strip I'd duct-taped to the ceiling. I flipped it on, and an old desk lamp flooded the tiny space with light.

The crumpled green roof of a compact car covered the crushed opening where the windshield had been, but the damage to the van's front end didn't extend beyond the cab. The rest of the interior remained intact. Someone had removed all of the van's seats (probably to use as furniture), leaving a small "room" about four feet wide, four feet high, and nine feet long.

This was my hideout.

I'd discovered it four years earlier, while searching for discarded computer parts. When I first opened the door and gazed into the van's darkened interior, I knew right away that I'd found something of immeasurable value: privacy. This was a place no one else knew about, where I wouldn't have to worry about getting hassled or slapped around by my aunt or whatever loser she was currently dating. I could keep my things here without worrying they'd be stolen. And, most important, it was a place where I could access the OASIS in peace.

The van was my refuge. My Batcave. My Fortress of Solitude. It was where I attended school, did my homework, read books, watched movies, and played videogames. It was also where I conducted my ongoing quest to find Halliday's Easter egg.

I'd covered the walls, floor, and ceiling with Styrofoam egg cartons and pieces of carpeting in an effort to soundproof the van as much as possible. Several cardboard boxes of busted laptops and computer parts sat in the corner, next to a rack of old car batteries and a modified exercise bike I'd rigged up as a recharger. The only furniture was a folding lawn chair.

I dropped my backpack, shrugged off my coat, and hopped on the exercise bike. Charging the batteries was usually the only physical exercise I got each day. I pedaled until the meter said the batteries had a full charge, then sat down in my chair and switched on the small electric heater I kept beside it. I pulled off my gloves and rubbed my hands in front of the filaments as they began to glow bright orange. I couldn't leave the heater on for very long, or it would drain the batteries.

I opened the rat-proof metal box where I kept my food cache and took out some bottled water and a packet of powdered milk. I mixed these together in a bowl, then dumped in a generous serving of Fruit Rocks cereal. Once I'd wolfed it down, I retrieved an old plastic *Star Trek* lunch box I kept hidden under the van's crushed dashboard. Inside were my school-issued OASIS console, haptic gloves, and visor. These items were, by far, the most valuable things I owned. Far too valuable to carry around with me.

I pulled on my elastic haptic gloves and flexed my fingers to make sure none of the joints was sticking. Then I grabbed my OASIS console, a flat black rectangle about the size of a paperback book. It had a wireless network antenna built into it, but the reception inside the van was for shit, since it was buried under a huge mound of dense metal. So I'd rigged up an external antenna and mounted it on the hood of a car at the top of the junk pile. The antenna cable snaked up through a hole I'd punched in the van's ceiling. I plugged it into a port on the side of the console, then slipped on my visor. It fit snugly around my eyes like a pair of swimmer's goggles, blocking out all external light. Small earbuds extended from the visor's temples and automatically plugged themselves into my ears. The visor also housed two built-in stereo voice microphones to pick up everything I said.

I powered on the console and initiated the log-in sequence. I saw a brief flash of red as the visor scanned my retinas. Then I cleared my throat and said my log-in pass phrase, being careful to enunciate: "You have been recruited by the Star League to defend the Frontier against Xur and the Ko-Dan Armada."

My pass phrase was also verified, along with my voice pattern, and then I was logged in. The following text appeared, superimposed in the center of my virtual display:

Identity verification successful.
Welcome to the OASIS, Parzival!
Login Completed: 07:53:21 OST-2.10.2045

As the text faded away, it was replaced by a short message, just three words long. This message had been embedded in the log-in sequence by James Halliday himself, when he'd first programmed the OASIS, as an homage to the simulation's direct ancestors, the coin-operated video-games of his youth. These three words were always the last thing an OASIS user saw before leaving the real world and entering the virtual one:

READY PLAYER ONE

My avatar materialized in front of my locker on the second
floor of my high school—the exact spot where I'd been standing when I'd
logged out the night before.

I glanced up and down the hallway. My virtual surroundings looked
almost (but not quite) real. Everything inside the OASIS was beautifully
rendered in three dimensions. Unless you pulled focus and stopped to
examine your surroundings more closely, it was easy to forget that everything you were seeing was computer-generated. And that was with my
crappy school-issued OASIS console. I'd heard that if you accessed the
simulation with a new state-of-the-art immersion rig, it was almost impossible to tell the OASIS from reality.

I touched my locker door and it popped open with a soft metallic click.
The inside was sparsely decorated. A picture of Princess Leia posing with
a blaster pistol. A group photo of the members of Monty Python in their
Holy Grail costumes. James Halliday's *Time* magazine cover. I reached up
and tapped the stack of textbooks on the locker's top shelf and they vanished, then reappeared in my avatar's item inventory.

Aside from my textbooks, my avatar had only a few meager possessions: a flashlight, an iron shortsword, a small bronze shield, and a suit
of banded leather armor. These items were all nonmagical and of low
quality, but they were the best I could afford. Items in the OASIS had
just as much value as things in the real world (sometimes more), and you
couldn't pay for them with food vouchers. The OASIS credit was the coin

of the realm, and in these dark times, it was also one of the world's most stable currencies, valued higher than the dollar, pound, euro, or yen.

A small mirror was mounted inside my locker door, and I caught a glimpse of my virtual self as I closed it. I'd designed my avatar's face and body to look, more or less, like my own. My avatar had a slightly smaller nose than me, and he was taller. And thinner. And more muscular. And he didn't have any teenage acne. But aside from these minor details, we looked more or less identical. The school's strictly enforced dress code required that all student avatars be human, and of the same gender and age as the student. No giant two-headed hermaphrodite demon unicorn avatars were allowed. Not on school grounds, anyway.

You could give your OASIS avatar any name you liked, as long as it was unique. Meaning you had to pick a name that hadn't already been taken by someone else. Your avatar's name was also your e-mail address and chat ID, so you wanted it to be cool and easy to remember. Celebrities had been known to pay huge sums of money to buy an avatar name they wanted from a cyber-squatter who had already reserved it.

When I'd first created my OASIS account, I'd named my avatar Wade° the°Great. After that, I kept changing it every few months, usually to something equally ridiculous. But my avatar had now had the same name for over five years. On the day the Hunt began, the day I'd decided to become a gunter, I'd renamed my avatar Parzival, after the knight of Arthurian legend who had found the Holy Grail. The other more common spellings of that knight's name, Perceval and Percival, had already been taken by other users. But I preferred the name Parzival, anyway. I thought it had a nice ring to it.

People rarely used their real names online. Anonymity was one of the major perks of the OASIS. Inside the simulation, no one knew who you really were, unless you wanted them to. Much of the OASIS's popularity and culture were built around this fact. Your real name, fingerprints, and retinal patterns were stored in your OASIS account, but Gregarious Simulation Systems kept that information encrypted and confidential. Even GSS's own employees couldn't look up an avatar's true identity. Back when Halliday was still running the company, GSS had won the right to keep every OASIS user's identity private in a landmark Supreme Court ruling.

When I'd first enrolled in the OASIS public school system, I was re-

quired to give them my real name, avatar name, mailing address, and Social Security number. That information was stored in my student profile,
but only my principal had access to that. None of my teachers or fellow
students knew who I really was, and vice versa.

Students weren't allowed to use their avatar names while they were at
school. This was to prevent teachers from having to say ridiculous things
like "Pimp°Grease, please pay attention!" or "BigWang69, would you
stand up and give us your book report?" Instead, students were required
to use their real first names, followed by a number, to differentiate them
from other students with the same name. When I enrolled, there were
already two other students at my school with the first name Wade, so I'd
been assigned the student ID of Wade3. That name floated above my avatar's head whenever I was on school grounds.

The school bell rang and a warning flashed in the corner of my display,
informing me that I had forty minutes until the start of first period. I
began to walk my avatar down the hall, using a series of subtle hand motions to control its movements and actions. I could also use voice commands to move around, if my hands were otherwise occupied.

I strolled in the direction of my World History classroom, smiling and
waving to the familiar faces I passed. I was going to miss this place when
I graduated in a few months. I wasn't looking forward to leaving school.
I didn't have the money to attend college, not even one in the OASIS,
and my grades weren't good enough for a scholarship. My only plan after
graduation was to become a full-time gunter. I didn't have much choice.
Winning the contest was my one chance of escaping the stacks. Unless I
wanted to sign a five-year indenturement contract with some corporation,
and that was about as appealing to me as rolling around in broken glass
in my birthday suit.

As I continued down the hallway, other students began to materialize
in front of their lockers, ghostly apparitions that rapidly solidified. The
sound of chattering teenagers began to echo up and down the corridor.
Before long, I heard an insult hurled in my direction.

"Hey, hey! If it isn't Wade Three!" I heard a voice shout. I turned and
saw Todd13, an obnoxious avatar I recognized from my Algebra II class.
He was standing with several of his friends. "Great outfit, slick," he said.
"Where did you snag the sweet threads?"

My avatar was wearing a black T-shirt and blue jeans, one of the free default skins you could select when you created your account. Like his Cro-Magnon friends, Todd13 wore an expensive designer skin, probably purchased in some offworld mall.

"Your mom bought them for me," I retorted without breaking my stride. "Tell her I said thanks, the next time you stop at home to breast-feed and pick up your allowance." Childish, I know. But virtual or not, this was still high school—the more childish an insult, the more effective it was.

My jab elicited laughter from a few of his friends and the other students standing nearby. Todd13 scowled and his face actually turned red—a sign that he hadn't bothered to turn off his account's real-time emotion feature, which made your avatar mirror your facial expressions and body language. He was about to reply, but I muted him first, so I didn't hear what he said. I just smiled and continued on my way.

The ability to mute my peers was one of my favorite things about attending school online, and I took advantage of it almost daily. The best thing about it was that they could *see* that you'd muted them, and they couldn't do a damn thing about it. There was never any fighting on school grounds. The simulation simply didn't allow it. The entire planet of Ludus was a no-PvP zone, meaning that no player-versus-player combat was permitted. At this school, the only real weapons were words, so I'd become skilled at wielding them.

●　●　●

I'd attended school in the real world up until the sixth grade. It hadn't been a very pleasant experience. I was a painfully shy, awkward kid, with low self-esteem and almost no social skills—a side effect of spending most of my childhood inside the OASIS. Online, I didn't have a problem talking to people or making friends. But in the real world, interacting with other people—especially kids my own age—made me a nervous wreck. I never knew how to act or what to say, and when I did work up the courage to speak, I always seemed to say the wrong thing.

My appearance was part of the problem. I was overweight, and had been for as long as I could remember. My bankrupt diet of government-subsidized sugar-and-starch-laden food was a contributing factor, but I was also an OASIS addict, so the only exercise I usually got back then was running away from bullies before and after school. To make matters worse, my limited wardrobe consisted entirely of ill-fitting clothes from thrift stores and donation bins—the social equivalent of having a bull's-eye painted on my forehead.

Even so, I tried my best to fit in. Year after year, my eyes would scan the lunchroom like a T-1000, searching for a clique that might accept me. But even the other outcasts wanted nothing to do with me. I was too weird, even for the weirdos. And girls? Talking to girls was out of the question. To me, they were like some exotic alien species, both beautiful and terrifying. Whenever I got near one of them, I invariably broke out in a cold sweat and lost the ability to speak in complete sentences.

For me, school had been a Darwinian exercise. A daily gauntlet of ridicule, abuse, and isolation. By the time I entered sixth grade, I was beginning to wonder if I'd be able to maintain my sanity until graduation, still six long years away.

Then, one glorious day, our principal announced that any student with a passing grade-point average could apply for a transfer to the new OASIS public school system. The real public school system, the one run by the government, had been an underfunded, overcrowded train wreck for decades. And now the conditions at many schools had gotten so terrible that every kid with half a brain was being encouraged to stay at home and attend school online. I nearly broke my neck sprinting to the school office to submit my application. It was accepted, and I transferred to OASIS Public School #1873 the following semester.

Prior to my transfer, my OASIS avatar had never left Incipio, the planet at the center of Sector One where new avatars were spawned at the time of their creation. There wasn't much to do on Incipio except chat with other noobs or shop in one of the giant virtual malls that covered the planet. If you wanted to go somewhere more interesting, you had to pay a teleportation fare to get there, and that cost money, something I didn't have. So my avatar was stranded on Incipio. That is, until my new school e-mailed me a teleportation voucher to cover the cost of my avatar's transport to Ludus, the planet where all of the OASIS public schools were located.

There were hundreds of school campuses here on Ludus, spread out evenly across the planet's surface. The schools were all identical, because the same construction code was copied and pasted into a different location whenever a new school was needed. And since the buildings were just pieces of software, their design wasn't limited by monetary constraints, or even by the laws of physics. So every school was a grand palace of learning,

with polished marble hallways, cathedral-like classrooms, zero-g gymna-
siums, and virtual libraries containing every (school board–approved)
book ever written.

On my first day at OPS #1873, I thought I'd died and gone to heaven.
Now, instead of running a gauntlet of bullies and drug addicts on my walk
to school each morning, I went straight to my hideout and stayed there all
day. Best of all, in the OASIS, no one could tell that I was fat, that I had
acne, or that I wore the same shabby clothes every week. Bullies couldn't
pelt me with spitballs, give me atomic wedgies, or pummel me by the bike
rack after school. No one could even touch me. In here, I was safe.

• • •

When I arrived in my World History classroom, several students were
already seated at their desks. Their avatars all sat motionless, with their
eyes closed. This was a signal that they were "engaged," meaning they
were currently on phone calls, browsing the Web, or logged into chat
rooms. It was poor OASIS etiquette to try to talk to an engaged avatar.
They usually just ignored you, and you'd get an automated message telling you to piss off.

I took a seat at my desk and tapped the Engage icon at the edge of my
display. My own avatar's eyes slid shut, but I could still see my surroundings. I tapped another icon, and a large two-dimensional Web browser
window appeared, suspended in space directly in front of me. Windows
like this one were visible to only my avatar, so no one could read over my
shoulder (unless I selected the option to allow it).

My homepage was set to the Hatchery, one of the more popular gunter
message forums. The Hatchery's site interface was designed to look and
operate like an old pre-Internet dial-up bulletin board system, complete
with the screech of a 300-baud modem during the log-in sequence. Very
cool. I spent a few minutes scanning the most recent message threads,
taking in the latest gunter news and rumors. I rarely posted anything to
the boards, even though I made sure to check them every day. I didn't see
much of interest this morning. The usual gunter clan flame wars. Ongoing arguments about the "correct" interpretation of some cryptic passage
in *Anorak's Almanac*. High-level avatars bragging about some new magic
item or artifact they'd obtained. This crap had been going on for years
now. In the absence of any real progress, gunter subculture had become
mired in bravado, bullshit, and pointless infighting. It was sad, really.

My favorite message threads were those devoted to bashing the Sixers. "Sixers" was the derogatory nickname gunters had given to employees of Innovative Online Industries. IOI (pronounced *eye-oh-eye*) was a global communications conglomerate and the world's largest Internet service provider. A large portion of IOI's business centered around providing access to the OASIS and on selling goods and services inside it. For this reason, IOI had attempted several hostile takeovers of Gregarious Simulation Systems, all of which had failed. Now they were trying to seize control of GSS by exploiting a loophole in Halliday's will.

IOI had created a new department within the company that they called their "Oology Division." ("Oology" was originally defined as "the science of studying birds' eggs," but in recent years it had taken on a second meaning: the "science" of searching for Halliday's Easter egg.) IOI's Oology Division had but one purpose: to win Halliday's contest and seize control of his fortune, his company, and the OASIS itself.

Like most gunters, I was horrified at the thought of IOI taking control of the OASIS. The company's PR machine had made its intentions crystal clear. IOI believed that Halliday never properly monetized his creation, and they wanted to remedy that. They would start charging a monthly fee for access to the simulation. They would plaster advertisements on every visible surface. User anonymity and free speech would become things of the past. The moment IOI took it over, the OASIS would cease to be the open-source virtual utopia I'd grown up in. It would become a corporate-run dystopia, an overpriced theme park for wealthy elitists.

IOI required its egg hunters, which it referred to as "oologists," to use their employee numbers as their OASIS avatar names. These numbers were all six digits in length, and they also began with the numeral "6," so everyone began calling them the *Sixers*. These days, most gunters referred to them as "the Suxorz." (Because they sucked.)

To become a Sixer, you had to sign a contract stipulating, among other things, that if you found Halliday's egg, the prize would become the sole property of your employer. In return, IOI gave you a bimonthly paycheck, food, lodging, health-care benefits, and a retirement plan. The company also provided your avatar with high-end armor, vehicles, and weapons, and covered all of your teleportation fares. Joining the Sixers was a lot like joining the military.

Sixers weren't hard to spot, because they all looked identical. They were all required to use the same hulking male avatar (regardless of the operator's true gender), with close-cropped dark hair and facial features left at the system default settings. And they all wore the same navy blue uniform. The only way to tell these corporate drones apart was by checking the six-digit employee number stamped on their right breast, just beneath the IOI corporate logo.

Like most gunters, I loathed the Sixers and was disgusted by their very existence. By hiring an army of contract egg hunters, IOI was perverting the entire spirit of the contest. Of course, it could be argued that all the gunters who had joined clans were doing the same thing. There were now hundreds of gunter clans, some with thousands of members, all working together to find the egg. Each clan was bound by an ironclad legal agreement stating that if one clan member won the contest, all members would share the prize. Solos like me didn't care much for the clans, either, but we still respected them as fellow gunters—unlike the Sixers, whose goal was to hand the OASIS over to an evil multinational conglomerate intent on ruining it.

My generation had never known a world without the OASIS. To us, it was much more than a game or an entertainment platform. It had been an integral part of our lives for as far back as we could remember. We'd been born into an ugly world, and the OASIS was our one happy refuge. The thought of the simulation being privatized and homogenized by IOI horrified us in a way that those born before its introduction found difficult to understand. For us, it was like someone threatening to take away the sun, or charge a fee to look up at the sky.

The Sixers gave gunters a common enemy, and Sixer bashing was a favorite pastime in our forums and chat rooms. A lot of high-level gunters had a strict policy of killing (or trying to kill) every Sixer who crossed their path. Several websites were devoted to tracking Sixer activities and movements, and some gunters spent more time hunting the Sixers than they did searching for the egg. The bigger clans actually held a yearly competition called "Eighty-Six the Suxorz," with a prize for the clan who managed to kill the largest number of them.

After checking a few other gunter forums, I tapped a bookmark icon for one of my favorite websites, Arty's Missives, the blog of a female gunter named Art3mis (pronounced "Artemis"). I'd discovered it about three years ago and had been a loyal reader ever since. She posted these great rambling essays about her search for Halliday's egg, which she called a "maddening MacGuffin hunt." She wrote with an endearing, intelligent voice, and her entries were filled with self-deprecating humor and witty, sardonic asides. In addition to posting her (often hysterical) interpretations of passages in the *Almanac,* she also linked to the books, movies, TV shows, and music she was currently studying as part of her Halliday research. I assumed that all of these posts were filled with misdirection and misinformation, but they were still highly entertaining.

It probably goes without saying that I had a massive cyber-crush on Art3mis.

She occasionally posted screenshots of her raven-haired avatar, and I sometimes (always) saved them to a folder on my hard drive. Her avatar had a pretty face, but it wasn't unnaturally perfect. In the OASIS, you got used to seeing freakishly beautiful faces on everyone. But Art3mis's features didn't look as though they'd been selected from a beauty drop-down menu on some avatar creation template. Her face had the distinctive look of a real person's, as if her true features had been scanned in and mapped onto her avatar. Big hazel eyes, rounded cheekbones, a pointy chin, and a perpetual smirk. I found her unbearably attractive.

Art3mis's body was also somewhat unusual. In the OASIS, you usually saw one of two body shapes on female avatars: the absurdly thin yet wildly popular supermodel frame, or the top-heavy, wasp-waisted porn starlet physique (which looked even less natural in the OASIS than it did in the real world). But Art3mis's frame was short and Rubenesque. All curves.

I knew the crush I had on Art3mis was both silly and ill-advised. What did I really know about her? She'd never revealed her true identity, of course. Or her age or location in the real world. There was no telling what she really looked like. She could be fifteen or fifty. A lot of gunters even questioned whether she was really female, but I wasn't one of them. Probably because I couldn't bear the idea that the girl with whom I was virtually smitten might actually be some middle-aged dude named Chuck, with back hair and male-pattern baldness.

In the years since I'd first started reading Arty's Missives, it had become one of the most popular blogs on the Internet, now logging several million hits a day. And Art3mis was now something of a celebrity, at least in gunter circles. But fame hadn't gone to her head. Her writing was still as funny and self-deprecating as ever. Her newest blog post was titled "The John Hughes Blues," and it was an in-depth treatise on her six favorite John Hughes teen movies, which she divided into two separate trilogies: The "Dorky Girl Fantasies" trilogy (*Sixteen Candles, Pretty in Pink,* and *Some Kind of Wonderful*) and the "Dorky Boy Fantasies" trilogy (*The Breakfast Club, Weird Science,* and *Ferris Bueller's Day Off*).

Just as I'd finished reading it, an instant message window popped up on my display. It was my best friend, Aech. (OK, if you want to split hairs, he was my only friend, not counting Mrs. Gilmore.)

Aech: Top o' the morning, amigo.

Parzival: Hola, compadre.

Aech: What are you up to?

Parzival: Just surfing the turf. You?

Aech: Got the Basement online. Come and hang out before school, fool.

Parzival: Sweet! I'll be there in a sec.

I closed the IM window and checked the time. I still had about half an hour until class started. I grinned and tapped a small door icon at the edge of my display, then selected Aech's chat room from my list of favorites.

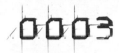

0003

The system verified that I was on the chat room's access list and allowed me to enter. My view of the classroom shrank from the limits of my peripheral vision to a small thumbnail window in the lower right of my display, allowing me to monitor what was in front of my avatar. The rest of my field of vision was now filled with the interior of Aech's chat room. My avatar appeared just inside the "entrance," a door at the top of a carpeted staircase. The door didn't lead anywhere. It didn't even open. This was because the Basement and its contents didn't exist as a part of the OASIS. Chat rooms were stand-alone simulations—temporary virtual spaces that avatars could access from anywhere in OASIS. My avatar wasn't actually "in" the chat room. It only appeared that way. Wade3/ Parzival was still sitting in my World History classroom with his eyes closed. Logging into a chat room was a little like being in two places at once.

Aech had named his chat room the Basement. He'd programmed it to look like a large suburban rec room, circa the late 1980s. Old movie and comic book posters covered the wood-paneled walls. A vintage RCA television stood in the center of the room, hooked up to a Betamax VCR, a LaserDisc player, and several vintage videogame consoles. Bookshelves lined the far wall, filled with role-playing game supplements and back issues of *Dragon* magazine.

Hosting a chat room this large wasn't cheap, but Aech could afford it. He made quite a bit of dough competing in televised PvP arena games after school and on the weekends. Aech was one of the highest-ranked combatants in the OASIS, in both the Deathmatch and Capture the Flag leagues. He was even more famous than Art3mis.

Over the past few years, the Basement had become a highly exclusive hangout for elite gunters. Aech granted access only to people he deemed worthy, so being invited to hang out in the Basement was a big honor, especially for a third-level nobody like me.

As I descended the staircase, I saw a few dozen other gunters milling around, with avatars that varied wildly in appearance. There were humans, cyborgs, demons, dark elves, Vulcans, and vampires. Most of them were gathered around the row of old arcade games against the wall. A few others stood by the ancient stereo (currently blasting "The Wild Boys" by Duran Duran), browsing through Aech's giant rack of vintage cassette tapes.

Aech himself was sprawled on one of the chat room's three couches, which were arrayed in a U-shape in front of the TV. Aech's avatar was a tall, broad-shouldered Caucasian male with dark hair and brown eyes. I'd asked him once if he looked anything like his avatar in real life, and he'd jokingly replied, "Yes. But in real life, I'm even *more* handsome."

As I walked over, he glanced up from the Intellivision game he was playing. His distinctive Cheshire grin stretched from ear to ear. "Z!" he shouted. "What is *up*, amigo?" He stretched out his right hand and gave me five as I dropped onto the couch opposite him. Aech had started calling me "Z" shortly after I met him. He liked to give people single-letter nicknames. Aech pronounced his own avatar's name just like the letter "H."

"What up, Humperdinck?" I said. This was a game we played. I always called him by some random H name, like Harry, Hubert, Henry, or Hogan. I was making guesses at his real first name, which, he'd once confided to me, began with the letter "H."

I'd known Aech for a little over three years. He was also a student on Ludus, a senior at OPS #1172, which was on the opposite side of the planet from my school. We'd met one weekend in a public gunter chat room and hit it off immediately, because we shared all of the same interests. Which is to say *one* interest: a total, all-consuming obsession with Halliday and his Easter egg. A few minutes into our first conversation, I knew Aech was the real deal, an elite gunter with some serious mental kung fu. He had his '80s trivia down cold, and not just the canon stuff, either. He was a true Halliday scholar. And he'd apparently seen the same qualities in me, because he'd given me his contact card and invited me to hang out in the Basement whenever I liked. He'd been my closest friend ever since.

Over the years, a friendly rivalry had gradually developed between us. We did a lot of trash-talking about which one of us would get his name up on the Scoreboard first. We were constantly trying to out-geek each other with our knowledge of obscure gunter trivia. Sometimes we even conducted our research together. This usually consisted of watching cheesy '80s movies and TV shows here in his chat room. We also played a lot of videogames, of course. Aech and I had wasted countless hours on two-player classics like Contra, Golden Axe, Heavy Barrel, Smash TV, and Ikari Warriors. Aside from yours truly, Aech was the best all-around gamer I'd ever encountered. We were evenly matched at most games, but he could trounce me at certain titles, especially anything in the first-person shooter genre. That was his area of expertise, after all.

I didn't know anything about who Aech was in the real world, but I got the sense his home life wasn't that great. Like me, he seemed to spend every waking moment logged into the OASIS. And even though we'd never actually met in person, he'd told me more than once that I was his best friend, so I assumed he was just as isolated and lonely as I was.

"So what did you do after you bailed last night?" he asked, tossing me the other Intellivision controller. We'd hung out here in his chat room for a few hours the previous evening, watching old Japanese monster movies.

"Nada," I said. "Went home and brushed up on a few classic coin-ops."

"Unnecessary."

"Yeah. But I was in the mood." I didn't ask him what he'd done the night before, and he didn't volunteer any details. I knew he'd probably gone to Gygax, or somewhere equally awesome, to speedrun through a few quests and rack up some XPs. He just didn't want to rub it in. Aech could afford to spend a fair amount of time off-world, following up leads and searching for the Copper Key. But he never lorded this over me, or ridiculed me for not having enough dough to teleport anywhere. And he never insulted me by offering to loan me a few credits. It was an unspoken rule among gunters: If you were a solo, you didn't want or need help, from anyone. Gunters who wanted help joined a clan, and Aech and I both agreed that clans were for suck-asses and poseurs. We'd both vowed to remain solos for life. We still occasionally had discussions about the egg, but these conversations were always guarded, and we were careful to avoid talking about specifics.

After I beat Aech at three rounds of Tron: Deadly Discs, he threw down his Intellivision controller in disgust and grabbed a magazine off the floor. It was an old issue of *Starlog*. I recognized Rutger Hauer on the cover, in a *Ladyhawke* promotional photo.

"*Starlog*, eh?" I said, nodding my approval.

"Yep. Downloaded every single issue from the Hatchery's archive. Still working my way through 'em. I was just reading this great piece on *Ewoks: The Battle for Endor*."

"Made for TV. Released in 1985," I recited. *Star Wars* trivia was one of my specialties. "Total garbage. A real low point in the history of the Wars."

"Says you, assface. It has some great moments."

"No," I said, shaking my head. "It doesn't. It's even worse than that first Ewok flick, *Caravan of Courage*. They shoulda called it *Caravan of Suck*."

Aech rolled his eyes and went back to reading. He wasn't going to take the bait. I eyed the magazine's cover. "Hey, can I have a look at that when you're done?"

He grinned. "Why? So you can read the article on *Ladyhawke*?"

"Maybe."

"Man, you just love that crapburger, don't you?"

"Blow me, Aech."

"How many times have you seen that sapfest? I know you've made me sit through it at least twice." He was baiting *me* now. He knew *Ladyhawke* was one of my guilty pleasures, and that I'd seen it over two dozen times.

"I was doing you a favor by making you watch it, noob," I said. I shoved a new cartridge into the Intellivision console and started up a single-player game of Astrosmash. "You'll thank me one day. Wait and see. *Ladyhawke* is canon."

"Canon" was the term we used to classify any movie, book, game, song, or TV show of which Halliday was known to have been a fan.

"Surely, you must be joking," Aech said.

"No, I am not joking. And don't call me Shirley."

He lowered the magazine and leaned forward. "There is no way Halliday was a fan of *Ladyhawke*. I guarantee it."

"Where's your proof, dipshit?" I asked.

"The man had taste. That's all the proof I need."

"Then please explain to me why he owned *Ladyhawke* on both VHS *and* LaserDisc?" A list of all the films in Halliday's collection at the time of his death was included in the appendices of *Anorak's Almanac*. We both had the list memorized.

"The guy was a billionaire! He owned millions of movies, most of which he probably never even watched! He had DVDs of *Howard the Duck* and *Krull*, too. That doesn't mean he *liked* them, asshat. And it sure as hell doesn't make them *canon*."

"It's not really up for debate, Homer," I said. "*Ladyhawke* is an eighties classic."

"It's fucking *lame*, is what it is! The swords look like they were made out of tinfoil. And that soundtrack is *epically lame*. Full of synthesizers and shit. By the motherfucking Alan Parsons Project! Lame-o-rama! *Beyond* lame. *Highlander II* lame."

"Hey!" I feigned hurling my Intellivision controller at him. "Now you're just being insulting! *Ladyhawke*'s cast alone makes the film canon! Roy Batty! Ferris Bueller! And the dude who played Professor Falken in *WarGames*!" I searched my memory for the actor's name. "John Wood! Reunited with Matthew Broderick!"

"A real low point in both of their careers," he said, laughing. He loved arguing about old movies, even more than I did. The other gunters in the chat room were now starting to form a small crowd around us to listen in. Our arguments were often high in entertainment value.

"You must be stoned!" I shouted. "*Ladyhawke* was directed by Richard fucking Donner! *The Goonies*? *Superman: The Movie*? You're saying *that guy* sucks?"

"I don't care if Spielberg directed it. It's a chick flick disguised as a sword-and-sorcery picture. The only genre film with less balls is probably . . . freakin' *Legend*. Anyone who actually enjoys *Ladyhawke* is a bona fide USDA-choice pussy!"

Laughter from the peanut gallery. I was actually getting a little pissed off now. I was a big fan of *Legend* too, and Aech knew it.

"Oh, so I'm a pussy? You're the one with the Ewok fetish!" I snatched the *Starlog* out of his hands and threw it against a *Revenge of the Jedi* poster on the wall. "I suppose you think your extensive knowledge of Ewok culture is gonna help you find the egg?"

"Don't start on the Endorians again, man," he said, holding up an index finger. "I've warned you. I will ban your ass. I swear." I knew this was a hollow threat, so I was about to push the Ewok thing even further, maybe give him some crap for referring to them as "Endorians." But just then, a new arrival materialized on the staircase. A total lamer by the name of I-rok. I let out a groan. I-rok and Aech attended the same school and had a few classes together, but I still couldn't figure out why Aech had granted him access to the Basement. I-rok fancied himself an elite gunter, but he was nothing but an obnoxious poseur. Sure, he did a lot of teleporting around the OASIS, completing quests and leveling up his avatar, but he didn't actually *know* anything. And he was always brandishing an over-size plasma rifle the size of a snowmobile. Even in chat rooms, where it was totally pointless. The guy had no sense of decorum.

"Are you cocks arguing about *Star Wars* again?" he said, descending the steps and walking over to join the crowd around us. "That shit is so played out, yo."

I turned to Aech. "If you want to ban someone, why don't you start with this clown?" I hit Reset on the Intellivision and started another game.

"Shut your hole, Penis-ville!" I-rok replied, using his favorite mispronunciation of my avatar's name. "He doesn't ban me 'cause he knows I'm *elite*! Ain't that right, Aech?"

"No," Aech said, rolling his eyes. "That *ain't right*. You're about as elite as my great-grandmother. And she's dead."

"Screw you, Aech! And your dead grandma!"

"Gee, I-rok," I muttered. "You always manage to elevate the intelligence level of the conversation. The whole room just lights up the moment you arrive."

"So sorry to upset you, Captain No-Credits," I-rok said. "Hey, shouldn't you be on Incipio panhandling for change right now?" He reached for the second Intellivision controller, but I snatched it up and tossed it to Aech.

He scowled at me. "Prick."

"Poseur."

"Poseur? Penis-ville is calling *me* a poseur?" He turned to address the small crowd. "This chump is so broke that he has to bum rides to Grey-hawk, just so he can kill kobolds for copper pieces! And he's calling *me* a poseur!"

This elicited a few snickers from the crowd, and I felt my face turn red under my visor. Once, about a year ago, I'd made the mistake of hitching a ride off-world with I-rok to try to gain a few experience points. After dropping me in a low-level quest area on Greyhawk, the jerk had followed me. I'd spent the next few hours slaying a small band of kobolds, waiting for them to respawn, and then slaying them again, over and over. My avatar was still only first level at the time, and it was one of the only safe ways for me to level up. I-rok had taken several screenshots of my avatar that night and labeled them "Penis-ville the Mighty Kobold Slayer." Then he'd posted them to the Hatchery. He still brought it up every chance he got. He was never going to let me live it down.

"That's right, I called you a poseur, poseur." I stood and got up in his grille. "You're an ignorant know-nothing twink. Just because you're fourteenth-level, it doesn't make you a gunter. You actually have to possess some *knowledge*."

"Word," Aech said, nodding his agreement. We bumped fists. More snickering from the crowd, now directed at I-rok.

I-rok glared at us a moment. "OK. Let's see who the real poseur is," he said. "Check this out, girls." Grinning, he produced an item from his inventory and held it up. It was an old Atari 2600 game, still in the box. He purposefully covered the game's title with his hand, but I recognized the cover artwork anyway. It was a painting of a young man and woman in ancient Greek attire, both brandishing swords. Lurking behind them were a minotaur and a bearded guy with an eye patch. "Know what this is, hotshot?" I-rok said, challenging me. "I'll even give you a clue. . . . It's an Atari game, released as part of a contest. It contained several puzzles, and if you solved them, you could win a prize. Sound familiar?"

I-rok was always trying to impress us with some clue or piece of Halliday lore he foolishly believed he'd been the first to uncover. Gunters loved to play the game of one-upmanship and were constantly trying to prove they had acquired more obscure knowledge than everyone else. But I-rok totally sucked at it.

"You're joking, right?" I said. "You just now discovered the Swordquest series?"

I-rok deflated.

"You're holding Swordquest: Earthworld," I continued. "The first game in the Swordquest series. Released in 1982." I smiled wide. "Can you name the next three games in the series?"

His eyes narrowed. He was, of course, stumped. Like I said, he was a total poseur.

"Anyone else?" I said, opening the question up to the floor. The gunters in the crowd eyed each other, but no one spoke up.

"Fireworld, Waterworld, and Airworld," Aech answered.

"Bingo!" I said, and we bumped fists again. "Although Airworld was never actually finished, because Atari fell on hard times and canceled the contest before it was completed."

I-rok quietly put the game box back in his inventory.

"You should join up with the Suxorz, I-rok," Aech said, laughing. "They could really use someone with your vast stores of knowledge."

I-rok flipped him the bird. "If you two fags already knew about the Swordquest contest, how come I've never once heard you mention it?"

"Come on, I-rok," Aech said, shaking his head. "Swordquest: Earthworld was Atari's unofficial sequel to Adventure. Every gunter worth their salt knows about that contest. How much more obvious can you get?"

I-rok tried to save some face. "OK, if you're both such experts, who programmed all of the Swordquest games?"

"Dan Hitchens and Tod Frye," I recited. "Try asking me something difficult."

"I got one for you," Aech interjected. "What were the prizes Atari gave out to the winner of each contest?"

"Ah," I said. "Good one. Let's see. . . . The prize for the Earthworld contest was the Talisman of Penultimate Truth. It was solid gold and encrusted with diamonds. The kid who won it melted it down to pay for college, as I recall."

"Yeah, yeah," Aech prodded. "Quit stalling. What about the other two?"

"I'm not stalling. The Fireworld prize was the Chalice of Light, and the Waterworld prize was supposed to be the Crown of Life, but it was never awarded, due to the cancellation of the contest. Same goes for the Airworld prize, which was supposed to be a Philosopher's Stone."

Aech grinned and gave me a double high five, then added, "And if the contest hadn't been canceled, the winners of the first four rounds would have competed for the grand prize, the Sword of Ultimate Sorcery."

I nodded. "The prizes were all mentioned in the *Swordquest* comic books that came with the games. Comic books which happen to be visible in the treasure room in the final scene of *Anorak's Invitation*, by the way."

The crowd burst into applause. I-rok lowered his head in shame.

Since I'd become a gunter, it had been obvious to me that Halliday had drawn inspiration for his contest from the Swordquest contest. I had no idea if he'd borrowed any of the puzzles from them too, but I'd studied the games and their solutions thoroughly, just to be safe.

"Fine. You win," I-rok said. "But you both obviously need to get a life."

"And you," I said, "obviously need to find a new hobby. Because you clearly lack the intelligence and commitment to be a gunter."

"No doubt," Aech said. "Try doing some *research* for a change, I-rok. I mean, did you ever hear of Wikipedia? It's free, douchebag."

I-rok turned and walked over to the long boxes of comic books stacked on the other side of the room, as if he'd lost interest in the discussion. "Whatever," he said over his shoulder. "If I didn't spend so much time *offline, getting laid*, I'd probably know just as much worthless shit as you two do."

Aech ignored him and turned back to me. "What were the names of the twins who appeared in the *Swordquest* comic books?"

"Tarra and Torr."

"Damn, Z! You are the *man*."

"Thanks, Aech."

A message flashed on my display, informing me that the three-minute-warning bell had just rung in my classroom. I knew Aech and I-rok were seeing the same warning, because our schools operated on the same schedule.

"Time for another day of higher learning," Aech said, standing up.

"Drag," I-rok said. "See you losers later." He gave me the finger; then his avatar disappeared as he logged out of the chat room. The other gunters began to log out and vanish too, until only Aech and I remained.

"Seriously, Aech," I said. "Why do you let that moron hang out here?"

"Because he's fun to beat at videogames. And his ignorance gives me hope."

"How so?"

"Because if most of the other gunters out there are as clueless as I-rok—and they are, Z, believe me—that means you and I really do have a shot at winning the contest."

I shrugged. "I guess that's one way to look at it."

"Wanna hang after school again tonight? Around seven or so? I've got a few errands to run, but then I'm gonna tackle some of the stuff on my need-to-watch list. A *Spaced* marathon, perhaps?"

"Oh, hell yes," I said. "Count me in."

We logged out simultaneously, just as the final bell began to ring.

0004

My avatar's eyes slid open, and I was back in my World History classroom. The seats around me were now filled with other students, and our teacher, Mr. Avenovich, was materializing at the front of the classroom. Mr. A's avatar looked like a portly, bearded college professor. He sported an infectious grin, wire-rimmed spectacles, and a tweed jacket with patches on the elbows. When he spoke, he somehow always managed to sound like he was reading a passage from Dickens. I liked him. He was a good teacher.

Of course, we didn't know who Mr. Avenovich really was or where he lived. We didn't know his real name, or even if "he" was really a man. For all we knew, he could have been a small Inuit woman living in Anchorage, Alaska, who had adopted this appearance and voice to make her students more receptive to her lessons. But for some reason, I suspected that Mr. Avenovich's avatar looked and sounded just like the person operating it.

All of my teachers were pretty great. Unlike their real-world counterparts, most of the OASIS public school teachers seemed to genuinely enjoy their job, probably because they didn't have to spend half their time acting as babysitters and disciplinarians. The OASIS software took care of that, ensuring that students remained quiet and in their seats. All the teachers had to do was teach.

It was also a lot easier for online teachers to hold their students' attention, because here in the OASIS, the classrooms were like holodecks. Teachers could take their students on a virtual field trip every day, without ever leaving the school grounds.

During our World History lesson that morning, Mr. Avenovich loaded up a stand-alone simulation so that our class could witness the discovery of King Tut's tomb by archaeologists in Egypt in AD 1922. (The day before, we'd visited the same spot in 1334 BC and had seen Tutankhamen's empire in all its glory.)

In my next class, Biology, we traveled through a human heart and watched it pumping from the inside, just like in that old movie *Fantastic Voyage.*

In Art class we toured the Louvre while all of our avatars wore silly berets.

In my Astronomy class we visited each of Jupiter's moons. We stood on the volcanic surface of Io while our teacher explained how the moon had originally formed. As our teacher spoke to us, Jupiter loomed behind her, filling half the sky, its Great Red Spot churning slowly just over her left shoulder. Then she snapped her fingers and we were standing on Europa, discussing the possibility of extraterrestrial life beneath the moon's icy crust.

I spent my lunch period sitting in one of the green fields bordering the school, staring at the simulated scenery while I munched on a protein bar with my visor on. It beat staring at the inside of my hideout. I was a senior, so I was allowed to go off-world during lunch if I wanted to, but I didn't have that kind of spare dough to blow.

Logging into the OASIS was free, but traveling around inside it wasn't. Most of the time, I didn't have enough credits to teleport off-world and get back to Ludus. When the last bell rang each day, the students who had things to do in the real world would log out of the OASIS and vanish. Everyone else would head off-world. A lot of kids owned their own interplanetary vehicles. School parking lots all over Ludus were filled with UFOs, TIE fighters, old NASA space shuttles, Vipers from *Battlestar Galactica,* and other spacecraft designs lifted from every sci-fi movie and TV show you can think of. Every afternoon I would stand on the school's front lawn and watch with envy as these ships filled the sky, zooming off to explore the simulation's endless possibilities. The kids who didn't own ships would either hitch a ride with a friend or stampede to the nearest transport terminal, headed for some offworld dance club, gaming arena, or rock concert. But not me. I wasn't going anywhere. I was stranded on Ludus, the most boring planet in the entire OASIS.

The Ontologically Anthropocentric Sensory Immersive Simulation was a big place.

When the OASIS had first been launched, it contained only a few hundred planets for users to explore, all created by GSS programmers and artists. Their environments ran the gamut, from sword-and-sorcery settings to cyberpunk-themed planetwide cities to irradiated postapocalyptic zombie-infested wastelands. Some planets were designed with painstaking detail. Others were randomly generated from a series of templates. Each one was populated with a variety of artificially intelligent NPCs (nonplayer characters)—computer-controlled humans, animals, monsters, aliens, and androids with which OASIS users could interact.

GSS had also licensed preexisting virtual worlds from their competitors, so content that had already been created for games like Everquest and World of Warcraft was ported over to the OASIS, and copies of Norrath and Azeroth were added to the growing catalog of OASIS planets. Other virtual worlds soon followed suit, from the Metaverse to the Matrix. The *Firefly* universe was anchored in a sector adjacent to the *Star Wars* galaxy, with a detailed re-creation of the *Star Trek* universe in the sector adjacent to that. Users could now teleport back and forth between their favorite fictional worlds. Middle Earth. Vulcan. Pern. Arrakis. Magrathea. Discworld, Mid-World, Riverworld, Ringworld. Worlds upon worlds.

For the sake of zoning and navigation, the OASIS had been divided equally into twenty-seven cube-shaped "sectors," each containing hundreds of different planets. (The three-dimensional map of all twenty-seven sectors distinctly resembled an '80s puzzle toy called a Rubik's Cube. Like most gunters, I knew this was no coincidence.) Each sector measured exactly ten light-hours across, or about 10.8 billion kilometers. So if you were traveling at the speed of light (the fastest speed attainable by any spacecraft inside the OASIS), you could get from one side of a sector to the other in exactly ten hours. That sort of long-distance travel wasn't cheap. Spacecraft that could travel at light speed were rare, and they required fuel to operate. Charging people for virtual fuel to power their virtual spaceships was one of the ways Gregarious Simulation Systems generated revenue, since accessing the OASIS was free. But GSS's primary source of income came from teleportation fares. Teleportation was the fastest way to travel, but it was also the most expensive.

Traveling around inside the OASIS wasn't just costly—it was also dangerous. Each sector was divided up into many different zones that varied in size and shape. Some zones were so large that they encompassed several planets, while others covered only a few kilometers on the surface of a single world. Each zone had a unique combination of rules and parameters. Magic would function in some zones and not in others. The same was true of technology. If you flew your technology-based starship into a zone where technology didn't function, your engines would fail the moment you crossed the zone border. Then you'd have to hire some silly gray-bearded sorcerer with a spell-powered space barge to tow your ass back into a technology zone.

Dual zones permitted the use of both magic and technology, and null zones didn't allow either. There were pacifist zones where no player-versus-player combat was allowed, and player-versus-player zones where it was every avatar for themselves.

You had to be careful whenever you entered a new zone or sector. You had to be prepared.

But like I said, I didn't have that problem. I was stuck at school.

Ludus had been designed as a place of learning, so the planet had been created without a single quest portal or gaming zone anywhere on its surface. The only thing to be found here were thousands of identical school campuses separated by rolling green fields, perfectly landscaped parks, rivers, meadows, and sprawling template-generated forests. There were no castles, dungeons, or orbiting space fortresses for my avatar to raid. And there were no NPC villains, monsters, or aliens for me to fight, so there was no treasure or magic items for me to plunder.

This totally sucked, for a lot of reasons.

Completing quests, fighting NPCs, and gathering treasure were the only ways a low-level avatar like mine could earn experience points (XPs). Earning XPs was how you increased your avatar's power level, strength, and abilities.

A lot of OASIS users didn't care about their avatar's power level or bother with the gaming aspects of the simulation at all. They only used the OASIS for entertainment, business, shopping, and hanging out with their friends. These users simply avoided entering any gaming or PvP zones where their defenseless first-level avatars could be attacked by NPCs or by other players. If you stayed in safe zones, like Ludus, you didn't have to worry about your avatar getting robbed, kidnapped, or killed.

I hated being stuck in a safe zone.

If I was going to find Halliday's egg, I knew I would eventually have to venture out in the dangerous sectors of the OASIS. And if I wasn't powerful or well-armed enough to defend myself, I wasn't going to stay alive for very long.

Over the past five years, I'd managed to slowly, gradually raise my avatar up to third level. This hadn't been easy. I'd done it by hitching rides off-world with other students (mostly Aech) who happened to be headed to a planet where my wuss avatar could survive. I'd have them drop me near a newbie-level gaming zone and spend the rest of the night or weekend slaying orcs, kobolds, or some other piddly class of monster that was too weak to kill me. For each NPC my avatar defeated, I would earn a few meager experience points and, usually, a handful of copper or silver coins dropped by my slain foes. These coins were instantly converted to credits, which I used to pay the teleportation fare back to Ludus, often just before the final school bell rang. Sometimes, but not often, one of the NPCs I killed would drop an item. That was how I'd obtained my avatar's sword, shield, and armor.

I'd stopped hitching rides with Aech at the end of the previous school year. His avatar was now above thirtieth level, and so he was almost always headed to a planet where it wasn't safe for my avatar. He was happy to drop me on some noob world along the way, but if I didn't earn enough credits to pay for my fare back to Ludus, I'd wind up missing school because I was stuck on some other planet. This was not an acceptable excuse. I'd now racked up so many unexcused absences that I was in danger of being expelled. If that happened, I would have to return my school-issued OASIS console and visor. Worse, I'd be transferred back to school in the real world to finish out my senior year there. I couldn't risk that.

So these days I rarely left Ludus at all. I was stuck here, and stuck at third level. Having a third-level avatar was a colossal embarrassment. None of the other gunters took you seriously unless you were at least tenth level. Even though I'd been a gunter since day one, everyone still considered me a noob. It was beyond frustrating.

In desperation, I'd tried to find a part-time after-school job, just to earn some walking-around money. I applied for dozens of tech support and programming jobs (mostly grunt construction work, coding parts of OASIS malls and office buildings), but it was completely hopeless. Millions of college-educated *adults* couldn't get one of those jobs. The Great Recession was now entering its third decade, and unemployment was still at a record high. Even the fast-food joints in my neighborhood had a two-year waiting list for job applicants.

So I remained stuck at school. I felt like a kid standing in the world's greatest video arcade without any quarters, unable to do anything but walk around and watch the other kids play.

After lunch, I headed to my favorite class, Advanced OASIS Studies. This was a senior-year elective where you learned about the history of the OASIS and its creators. Talk about an easy A.

For the past five years, I'd devoted all of my free time to learning as much as I possibly could about James Halliday. I'd exhaustively studied his life, accomplishments, and interests. Over a dozen different Halliday biographies had been published in the years since his death, and I'd read them all. Several documentary films had also been made about him, and I'd studied those, too. I'd studied every word Halliday had ever written, and I'd played every videogame he'd ever made. I took notes, writing down every detail I thought might be related to the Hunt. I kept everything in a notebook (which I'd started to call my "grail diary" after watching the third Indiana Jones film).

The more I'd learned about Halliday's life, the more I'd grown to idolize him. He was a god among geeks, a nerd über-deity on the level of Gygax, Garriott, and Gates. He'd left home after high school with nothing but his wits and his imagination, and he'd used them to attain worldwide fame and amass a vast fortune. He'd created an entirely new reality that now provided an escape for most of humanity. And to top it all off, he'd turned his last will and testament into the greatest videogame contest of all time.

I spent most of my time in Advanced OASIS Studies class annoying our teacher, Mr. Ciders, by pointing out errors in our textbook and raising my hand to interject some relevant bit of Halliday trivia that I (and I alone) thought was interesting. After the first few weeks of class, Mr. Ciders had stopped calling on me unless no one else knew the answer to his question.

Today, he was reading excerpts from *The Egg Man,* a bestselling Halliday biography that I'd already read four times. During his lecture, I kept having to resist the urge to interrupt him and point out all of the really important details the book left out. Instead, I just made a mental note of each omission, and as Mr. Ciders began to recount the circumstances of Halliday's childhood, I once again tried to glean whatever secrets I could from the strange way Halliday had lived his life, and from the odd clues about himself he'd chosen to leave behind.

• • •

James Donovan Halliday was born on June 12, 1972, in Middletown, Ohio. He was an only child. His father was an alcoholic machine operator and his mother was a bipolar waitress.

By all accounts, James was a bright boy, but socially inept. He had an extremely difficult time communicating with the people around him. Despite his obvious intelligence, he did poorly in school, because most of his attention was focused on computers, comic books, sci-fi and fantasy novels, movies, and above all else, videogames.

One day in junior high, Halliday was sitting alone in the cafeteria reading a *Dungeons & Dragons Player's Handbook.* The game fascinated him, but he'd never actually played it, because he'd never had any friends to play it with. A boy in his class named Ogden Morrow noticed what Halliday was reading and invited him to attend one of the weekly D&D gaming sessions held at his house. There, in Morrow's basement, Halliday was introduced to an entire group of "mega geeks" just like himself They immediately accepted him as one of their own, and for the first time in his life, James Halliday had a circle of friends.

Ogden Morrow eventually became Halliday's business partner, collaborator, and best friend. Many would later liken the pairing of Morrow and Halliday to that of Jobs and Wozniak or Lennon and McCartney. It was a partnership destined to alter the course of human history.

At age fifteen, Halliday created his first videogame, Anorak's Quest. He programmed it in BASIC on a TRS-80 Color Computer he'd received the previous Christmas (though he'd asked his parents for the slightly more expensive Commodore 64). Anorak's Quest was an adventure game set in Chthonia, the fantasy world Halliday had created for his high-school Dungeons & Dragons campaign. "Anorak" was a nickname Halliday had been given by a female British exchange student at his high school. He liked the name Anorak so much that he'd used it for his favorite D&D character, the powerful wizard who later appeared in many of his video-games.

Halliday created Anorak's Quest for fun, to share with the guys in his D&D gaming group. They all found the game addictive, and lost count-less hours attempting to solve its intricate riddles and puzzles. Ogden Morrow convinced Halliday that Anorak's Quest was better than most of the computer games currently on the market, and encouraged him to try selling it. He helped Halliday create some simple cover artwork for the game, and together, the two of them hand-copied Anorak's Quest onto dozens of 5¼-inch floppy disks and stuck them into Ziploc bags along with a single photocopied sheet of instructions. They began selling the game on the software rack at their local computer store. Before long, they couldn't make copies fast enough to meet the demand.

Morrow and Halliday decided to start their own videogame company, Gregarious Games, which initially operated out of Morrow's basement. Halliday programmed new versions of Anorak's Quest for the Atari 800XL, Apple II, and Commodore 64 computers, and Morrow began plac-ing ads for the game in the back of several computer magazines. Within six months, Anorak's Quest became a national bestseller.

Halliday and Morrow almost didn't graduate from high school because they spent most of their senior year working on Anorak's Quest II. And instead of going off to college, they both focused all of their energy on their new company, which had now grown too large for Morrow's base-ment. In 1990, Gregarious Games moved into its first real office, located in a run-down strip mall in Columbus, Ohio.

Over the next decade, the small company took the videogame industry by storm, releasing a series of bestselling action and adventure games, all using a groundbreaking first-person graphics engine created by Halliday. Gregarious Games set a new standard for immersive gaming, and every time they released a new title, it pushed the envelope of what seemed pos-sible on the computer hardware available at the time.

The rotund Ogden Morrow was naturally charismatic, and he handled all of the company's business affairs and public relations. At every Gregarious Games press conference, Morrow grinned infectiously from behind his unruly beard and wire-rimmed spectacles, using his natural gift for hype and hyperbole. Halliday seemed to be Morrow's polar opposite in every way. He was tall, gaunt, and painfully shy, and he preferred to stay out of the limelight.

People employed by Gregarious Games during this period say that Halliday frequently locked himself in his office, where he programmed incessantly, often going without food, sleep, or human contact for days or even weeks.

On the few occasions that Halliday agreed to do interviews, his behavior came off as bizarre, even by game-designer standards. He was hyperkinetic, aloof, and so socially inept that the interviewers often came away with the impression he was mentally ill. Halliday tended to speak so rapidly that his words were often unintelligible, and he had a disturbing high-pitched laugh, made even more so because he was usually the only one who knew what he was laughing *about*. When Halliday got bored during an interview (or conversation), he would usually get up and walk out without saying a word.

Halliday had many well-known obsessions. Chief among them were classic videogames, sci-fi and fantasy novels, and movies of all genres. He also had an extreme fixation on the 1980s, the decade during which he'd been a teenager. Halliday seemed to expect everyone around him to share his obsessions, and he often lashed out at those who didn't. He was known to fire longtime employees for not recognizing an obscure line of movie dialogue he quoted, or if he discovered they weren't familiar with one of his favorite cartoons, comic books, or videogames. (Ogden Morrow would always hire the employee back, usually without Halliday ever noticing.)

As the years went on, Halliday's already-stunted social skills seemed to deteriorate even further. (Several exhaustive psychological studies were done on Halliday following his death, and his obsessive adherence to routine and preoccupation with a few obscure areas of interest led many psychologists to conclude that Halliday had suffered from Asperger's syndrome, or from some other form of high-functioning autism.)

Despite his eccentricities, no one ever questioned Halliday's genius. The games he created were addictive and wildly popular. By the end of the twentieth century, Halliday was widely recognized as the greatest videogame designer of his generation—and, some would argue, of all time.

Ogden Morrow was a brilliant programmer in his own right, but his true talent was his knack for business. In addition to collaborating on the company's games, he masterminded all of their early marketing campaigns and shareware distribution schemes, with astounding results. When Gregarious Games finally went public, their stock immediately shot into the stratosphere.

By their thirtieth birthdays, Halliday and Morrow were both multimillionaires. They purchased mansions on the same street. Morrow bought a Lamborghini, took several long vacations, and traveled the world. Halliday bought and restored one of the original DeLoreans used in the *Back to the Future* films, continued to spend nearly all of his time welded to a computer keyboard, and used his newfound wealth to amass what would eventually become the world's largest private collection of classic videogames, *Star Wars* action figures, vintage lunch boxes, and comic books.

At the height of its success, Gregarious Games appeared to fall dormant. Several years elapsed during which they released no new games. Morrow made cryptic announcements, saying the company was working on an ambitious project that would move them in an entirely new direction. Rumors began to circulate that Gregarious Games was developing some sort of new computer gaming hardware and that this secret project was rapidly exhausting the company's considerable financial resources. There were also indications that both Halliday and Morrow had invested most of their own personal fortunes in the company's new endeavor. Word began to spread that Gregarious Games was in danger of going bankrupt.

Then, in December 2012, Gregarious Games rebranded itself as Gregarious Simulation Systems, and under this new banner they launched their flagship product, the only product GSS would ever release: the OASIS—the Ontologically Anthropocentric Sensory Immersive Simulation.

The OASIS would ultimately change the way people around the world lived, worked, and communicated. It would transform entertainment, social networking, and even global politics. Even though it was initially marketed as a new kind of massively multiplayer online game, the OASIS quickly evolved into a new way of life.

● ● ●

In the days before the OASIS, massively multiplayer online games (MMOs) were among the first shared synthetic environments. They allowed thousands of players to simultaneously coexist inside a simulated world, which they connected to via the Internet. The overall size of these environments was relatively small, usually just a single world, or a dozen or so small planets. MMO players could only see these online environments through a small two-dimensional window—their desktop computer monitor—and they could only interact with it by using keyboards, mice, and other crude input devices.

Gregarious Simulation Systems elevated the MMO concept to an entirely new level. The OASIS didn't limit its users to just one planet, or even a dozen. The OASIS contained hundreds (and eventually thousands) of high-resolution 3-D worlds for people to explore, and each one was beautifully rendered in meticulous graphical detail, right down to bugs and blades of grass, wind and weather patterns. Users could circumnavigate each of these planets and never see the same terrain twice. Even in its first primitive incarnation, the scope of the simulation was staggering.

Halliday and Morrow referred to the OASIS as an "open-source reality," a malleable online universe that anyone could access via the Internet, using their existing home computer or videogame console. You could log in and instantly escape the drudgery of your day-to-day life. You could create an entirely new persona for yourself, with complete control over how you looked and sounded to others. In the OASIS, the fat could become thin, the ugly could become beautiful, and the shy, extroverted. Or vice versa. You could change your name, age, sex, race, height, weight, voice, hair color, and bone structure. Or you could cease being human altogether, and become an elf, ogre, alien, or any other creature from literature, movies, or mythology.

In the OASIS, you could become whomever and whatever you wanted to be, without ever revealing your true identity, because your anonymity was guaranteed.

Users could also alter the content of the virtual worlds inside the OASIS, or create entirely new ones. A person's online presence was no longer limited to a website or a social-networking profile. In the OASIS, you could create your own private planet, build a virtual mansion on it, furnish and decorate it however you liked, and invite a few thousand friends over for a party. And those friends could be in a dozen different time zones, spread all over the globe.

The keys to the success of the OASIS were the two new pieces of interface hardware that GSS had created, both of which were required to access the simulation: the OASIS visor and haptic gloves.

The wireless one-size-fits-all OASIS visor was slightly larger than a pair of sunglasses. It used harmless low-powered lasers to draw the stunningly real environment of the OASIS right onto its wearer's retinas, completely immersing their entire field of vision in the online world. The visor was light-years ahead of the clunky virtual-reality goggles available prior to that time, and it represented a paradigm shift in virtual-reality technology—as did the lightweight OASIS haptic gloves, which allowed users to directly control the hands of their avatar and to interact with their simulated environment as if they were actually inside it. When you picked up objects, opened doors, or operated vehicles, the haptic gloves made you *feel* these nonexistent objects and surfaces as if they were really right there in front of you. The gloves let you, as the television ads put it, "reach in and touch the OASIS." Working together, the visor and the gloves made entering the OASIS an experience unlike anything else available, and once people got a taste of it, there was no going back.

The software that powered the simulation, Halliday's new OASIS Reality Engine, also represented a huge technological breakthrough. It managed to overcome limitations that had plagued previous simulated realities. In addition to restricting the overall size of their virtual environments, earlier MMOs had been forced to limit their virtual populations, usually to a few thousand users per server. If too many people were logged in at the same time, the simulation would slow to a crawl and avatars would freeze in midstride as the system struggled to keep up. But the OASIS utilized a new kind of fault-tolerant server array that could draw additional processing power from every computer connected to it. At the time of its initial launch, the OASIS could handle up to five million simultaneous users, with no discernible latency and no chance of a system crash.

A massive marketing campaign promoted the launch of the OASIS. The pervasive television, billboard, and Internet ads featured a lush green oasis, complete with palm trees and a pool of crystal blue water, surrounded on all sides by a vast barren desert.

GSS's new endeavor was a massive success from day one. The OASIS was what people had been dreaming of for decades. The "virtual reality" they had been promised for so long was finally here, and it was even better than they'd imagined. The OASIS was an online utopia, a holodeck for the home. And its biggest selling point? It was *free.*

Most online games of the day generated revenue by charging users a monthly subscription fee for access. GSS only charged a onetime sign-up fee of *twenty-five cents,* for which you received a lifetime OASIS account. The ads all used the same tagline: *The OASIS—it's the greatest videogame ever created, and it only costs a quarter.*

At a time of drastic social and cultural upheaval, when most of the world's population longed for an escape from reality, the OASIS provided it, in a form that was cheap, legal, safe, and not (medically proven to be) addictive. The ongoing energy crisis contributed greatly to the OASIS's runaway popularity. The skyrocketing cost of oil made airline and automobile travel too expensive for the average citizen, and the OASIS became the only getaway most people could afford. As the era of cheap, abundant energy drew to a close, poverty and unrest began to spread like a virus. Every day, more and more people had reason to seek solace inside Halliday and Morrow's virtual utopia.

Any business that wanted to set up shop inside the OASIS had to rent or purchase virtual real estate (which Morrow dubbed "surreal estate") from GSS. Anticipating this, the company had set aside Sector One as the simulation's designated business zone and began to sell and rent millions of blocks of surreal estate there. City-sized shopping malls were erected in the blink of an eye, and storefronts spread across planets like time-lapse footage of mold devouring an orange. Urban development had never been so easy.

In addition to the billions of dollars that GSS raked in selling land that didn't actually exist, they made a killing selling virtual objects and vehicles. The OASIS became such an integral part of people's day-to-day social lives that users were more than willing to shell out real money to buy accessories for their avatars: clothing, furniture, houses, flying cars, magic swords and machine guns. These items were nothing but ones and zeros stored on the OASIS servers, but they were also status symbols. Most items only cost a few credits, but since they cost nothing for GSS to manufacture, it was all profit. Even in the throes of an ongoing economic recession, the OASIS allowed Americans to continue engaging in their favorite pastime: shopping.

The OASIS quickly became the single most popular use for the Internet, so much so that the terms "OASIS" and "Internet" gradually became synonymous. And the incredibly easy-to-use three-dimensional OASIS OS, which GSS gave away for free, became the single most popular computer operating system in the world.

Before long, billions of people around the world were working and playing in the OASIS every day. Some of them met, fell in love, and got married without ever setting foot on the same continent. The lines of distinction between a person's real identity and that of their avatar began to blur.

It was the dawn of new era, one where most of the human race now spent all of their free time inside a videogame.

0006

The rest of my school day passed quickly until my final class, Latin.

Most students took a foreign language they might actually be able to use someday, like Mandarin, or Hindi, or Spanish. I'd decided to take Latin because James Halliday had taken Latin. He'd also occasionally used Latin words and phrases in his early adventure games. Unfortunately, even with the limitless possibilities of the OASIS at her disposal, my Latin teacher, Ms. Rank, still had a hard time making her lessons interesting. And today she was reviewing a bunch of verbs I'd already memorized, so I found my attention drifting almost immediately.

While a class was in session, the simulation prevented students from accessing any data or programs that weren't authorized by their teacher, to prevent kids from watching movies, playing games, or chatting with each other instead of paying attention to the lesson. Luckily, during my junior year, I'd discovered a bug in the school's online library software, and by exploiting it, I could access any book in the school's online library, including *Anorak's Almanac*. So whenever I got bored (like right now) I would pull it up in a window on my display and read over my favorite passages to pass the time.

Over the past five years, the *Almanac* had become my bible. Like most books nowadays, it was only available in electronic format. But I'd wanted to be able to read the *Almanac* night or day, even during one of the stacks' frequent power outages, so I'd fixed up an old discarded laser printer and used it to print out a hard copy. I put it in an old three-ring binder that I kept in my backpack and studied until I knew every word by heart.

The *Almanac* contained thousands of references to Halliday's favorite books, TV shows, movies, songs, graphic novels, and videogames. Most of these items were over forty years old, and so free digital copies of them could be downloaded from the OASIS. If there was something I needed that wasn't legally available for free, I could almost always get it by using Guntorrent, a file-sharing program used by gunters around the world.

When it came to my research, I never took any shortcuts. Over the past five years, I'd worked my way down the entire recommended gunter reading list. Douglas Adams. Kurt Vonnegut. Neal Stephenson. Richard K. Morgan. Stephen King. Orson Scott Card. Terry Pratchett. Terry Brooks. Bester, Bradbury, Haldeman, Heinlein, Tolkien, Vance, Gibson, Gaiman, Sterling, Moorcock, Scalzi, Zelazny. I read every novel by every single one of Halliday's favorite authors.

And I didn't stop there.

I also watched every single film he referenced in the *Almanac.* If it was one of Halliday's favorites, like *WarGames, Ghostbusters, Real Genius, Better Off Dead,* or *Revenge of the Nerds,* I rewatched it until I knew every scene by heart.

I devoured each of what Halliday referred to as "The Holy Trilogies": *Star Wars* (original and prequel trilogies, in that order), *Lord of the Rings, The Matrix, Mad Max, Back to the Future,* and *Indiana Jones.* (Halliday once said that he preferred to pretend the other *Indiana Jones* films, from *Kingdom of the Crystal Skull* onward, didn't exist. I tended to agree.)

I also absorbed the complete filmographies of each of his favorite directors. Cameron, Gilliam, Jackson, Fincher, Kubrick, Lucas, Spielberg, Del Toro, Tarantino. And, of course, Kevin Smith.

I spent three months studying every John Hughes teen movie and memorizing all the key lines of dialogue.

Only the meek get pinched. The bold survive.

You could say I covered all the bases.

I studied Monty Python. And not just *Holy Grail,* either. Every single one of their films, albums, and books, and every episode of the original BBC series. (Including those two "lost" episodes they did for German television.)

I wasn't going to cut any corners.

I wasn't going to miss something obvious.

Somewhere along the way, I started to go overboard.

I may, in fact, have started to go a little insane.

I watched every episode of *The Greatest American Hero, Airwolf, The A-Team, Knight Rider, Misfits of Science,* and *The Muppet Show.*

What about *The Simpsons,* you ask?

I knew more about Springfield than I knew about my own city.

Star Trek? Oh, I did my homework. *TOS, TNG, DS9.* Even *Voyager* and *Enterprise.* I watched them all in chronological order. The movies, too. *Phasers locked on target.*

I gave myself a crash course in '80s Saturday-morning cartoons.

I learned the name of every last goddamn Gobot and Transformer.

Land of the Lost, Thundarr the Barbarian, He-Man, Schoolhouse Rock!, G.I. Joe—I knew them all. *Because knowing is half the battle.*

Who was my friend, when things got rough? *H.R. Pufnstuf.*

Japan? Did I cover Japan?

Yes. Yes indeed. Anime and live-action. *Godzilla, Gamera, Star Blazers, The Space Giants,* and *G-Force. Go, Speed Racer, Go.*

I wasn't some dilettante.

I wasn't screwing around.

I memorized every last Bill Hicks stand-up routine.

Music? Well, covering all the music wasn't easy.

It took some time.

The '80s was a long decade (ten whole years), and Halliday didn't seem to have had very discerning taste. He listened to everything. So I did too. Pop, rock, new wave, punk, heavy metal. From the Police to Journey to R.E.M. to the Clash. I tackled it all.

I burned through the entire They Might Be Giants discography in under two weeks. Devo took a little longer.

I watched a lot of YouTube videos of cute geeky girls playing '80s cover tunes on ukuleles. Technically, this wasn't part of my research, but I had a serious cute-geeky-girls-playing-ukuleles fetish that I can neither explain nor defend.

I memorized lyrics. Silly lyrics, by bands with names like Van Halen, Bon Jovi, Def Leppard, and Pink Floyd.

I kept at it.

I burned the midnight oil.

Did you know that Midnight Oil was an Australian band, with a 1987 hit titled "Beds Are Burning"?

I was obsessed. I wouldn't quit. My grades suffered. I didn't care.

I read every issue of every comic book title Halliday had ever collected. I wasn't going to have anyone questioning my commitment.

Especially when it came to the videogames.

Videogames were my area of expertise.

My double-weapon specialization.

My dream *Jeopardy!* category.

I downloaded every game mentioned or referenced in the *Almanac*, from Akalabeth to Zaxxon. I played each title until I had mastered it, then moved on to the next one.

You'd be amazed how much research you can get done when you have no life whatsoever. Twelve hours a day, seven days a week, is a lot of study time.

I worked my way through every videogame genre and platform. Classic arcade coin-ops, home computer, console, and handheld. Text-based adventures, first-person shooters, third-person RPGs. Ancient 8-, 16-, and 32-bit classics written in the previous century. The harder a game was to beat, the more I enjoyed it. And as I played these ancient digital relics, night after night, year after year, I discovered I had a talent for them. I could master most action titles in a few hours, and there wasn't an adventure or role-playing game I couldn't solve. I never needed any walkthroughs or cheat codes. Everything just clicked. And I was even better at the old arcade games. When I was in the zone on a high-speed classic like Defender, I felt like a hawk in flight, or the way I thought a shark must feel as it cruises the ocean floor. For the first time, I knew what it was to be a natural at something. To have a gift.

But it wasn't my research into old movies, comics, or videogames that had yielded my first real clue. That had come while I was studying the history of old pen-and-paper role-playing games.

• • •

Reprinted on the first page of *Anorak's Almanac* were the four rhyming lines of verse Halliday had recited in the *Invitation* video.

Three hidden keys open three secret gates
Wherein the errant will be tested for worthy traits
And those with the skill to survive these straits
Will reach The End where the prize awaits

At first, this seemed to be the only direct reference to the contest in the entire almanac. But then, buried among all those rambling journal entries and essays on pop culture, I discovered a hidden message.

Scattered throughout the text of the *Almanac* were a series of marked letters. Each of these letters had a tiny, nearly invisible "notch" cut into its outline. I'd first noticed these notches the year after Halliday died. I was reading my hard copy of the *Almanac* at the time, and so at first I thought the notches were nothing but tiny printing imperfections, perhaps due to the paper or the ancient printer I'd used to print out the *Almanac*. But when I checked the electronic version of the book available on Halliday's website, I found the same notches on the exact same letters. And if you zoomed in on one of those letters, the notches stood out as plain as day.

Halliday had put them there. He'd marked these letters for a reason.

There turned out to be one hundred and twelve of these notched letters scattered throughout the book. By writing them down in the order they appeared, I discovered that they spelled something. I nearly died of excitement as I wrote it down in my grail diary:

> *The Copper Key awaits explorers*
> *In a tomb filled with horrors*
> *But you have much to learn*
> *If you hope to earn*
> *A place among the high scorers*

Other gunters had also discovered this hidden message, of course, but they were all wise enough to keep it to themselves. For a while, anyway. About six months after I discovered the hidden message, this loudmouth MIT freshman found it too. His name was Steven Pendergast, and he decided to get his fifteen minutes of fame by sharing his "discovery" with the media. The newsfeeds broadcast interviews with this moron for a month, even though he didn't have the first clue about the message's meaning. After that, going public with a clue became known as "pulling a Pendergast."

Once the message became public knowledge, gunters nicknamed it "the Limerick." The entire world had known about it for almost four years now, but no one seemed to understand its true meaning, and the Copper Key still had yet to be found.

I knew Halliday had frequently used similar riddles in many of his early adventure games, and each of those riddles had made sense in the context of its game. So I devoted an entire section of my grail diary to deciphering the Limerick, line by line.

The Copper Key awaits explorers

This line seemed pretty straightforward. No hidden meaning that I could detect.

In a tomb filled with horrors.

This line was trickier. Taken at face value, it seemed to say that the key was hidden in a tomb somewhere, one filled with horrifying stuff. But then, during the course of my research, I discovered an old Dungeons & Dragons supplement called *Tomb of Horrors,* which had been published in 1978. From the moment I saw the title, I was certain the second line of the Limerick was a reference to it. Halliday and Morrow had played Advanced Dungeons & Dragons all through high school, along with several other pen-and-paper role-playing games, like GURPS, Champions, Car Wars, and Rolemaster.

Tomb of Horrors was a thin booklet called a "module." It contained detailed maps and room-by-room descriptions of an underground labyrinth infested with undead monsters. D&D players could explore the labyrinth with their characters as the dungeon master read from the module and guided them through the story it contained, describing everything they saw and encountered along the way.

As I learned more about how these early role-playing games worked, I realized that a D&D module was the primitive equivalent of a quest in the OASIS. And D&D characters were just like avatars. In a way, these old role-playing games had been the first virtual-reality simulations, created long before computers were powerful enough to do the job. In those days, if you wanted to escape to another world, you had to create it yourself, using your brain, some paper, pencils, dice, and a few rule books. This realization kind of blew my mind. It changed my whole perspective on the Hunt for Halliday's Easter egg. From then on, I began to think of the Hunt as an elaborate D&D module. And Halliday was obviously the dungeon master, even if he was now controlling the game from beyond the grave.

I found a digital copy of the sixty-seven-year-old *Tomb of Horrors* module buried deep in an ancient FTP archive. As I studied it, I began to develop a theory: Somewhere in the OASIS, Halliday had re-created the Tomb of Horrors, and he'd hidden the Copper Key inside it.

I spent the next few months studying the module and memorizing all of its maps and room descriptions, in anticipation of the day I would finally figure out where it was located. But that was the rub: The Limerick didn't appear to give any hint as to *where* Halliday had hidden the damn thing. The only clue seemed to be "you have much to learn if you hope to earn a place among the high scorers."

I recited those words over and over in my head until I wanted to howl in frustration. *Much to learn.* Yeah, OK, fine. I have much to learn about *what*?

There were literally thousands of worlds in the OASIS, and Halliday could have hidden his re-creation of the Tomb of Horrors on any one of them. Searching every planet, one by one, would take forever. Even if I'd had the means to do so.

A planet named Gygax in Sector Two seemed like the obvious place to start looking. Halliday had coded the planet himself, and he'd named it after Gary Gygax, one of the creators of Dungeons & Dragons and the author of the original *Tomb of Horrors* module. According to Gunterpedia (a gunter wiki), the planet Gygax was covered with re-creations of old D&D modules, but *Tomb of Horrors* was not one of them. There didn't appear to be a re-creation of the tomb on any of the other D&D-themed worlds in the OASIS either. Gunters had turned all of those planets upside down and scoured every square inch of their surfaces. Had a re-creation of the Tomb of Horrors been hidden on one of them, it would have been found and logged long ago.

So the tomb had to be hidden somewhere else. And I didn't have the first clue where. But I told myself that if I just kept at it and continued doing research, I'd eventually learn what I needed to know to figure out the tomb's hiding place. In fact, that was probably what Halliday meant by "you have much to learn if you hope to earn a place among the high scorers."

If any other gunters out there shared my interpretation of the Limerick, so far they'd been smart enough to keep quiet about it. I'd never seen any posts about the Tomb of Horrors on any gunter message boards. I realized, of course, that this might be because my theory about the old D&D module was completely lame and totally off base.

So I'd continued to watch and read and listen and study, preparing for the day when I finally stumbled across the clue that would lead me to the Copper Key.

And then it finally happened. Right while I was sitting there daydreaming in Latin class.

Our teacher, Ms. Rank, was standing at the front of the class, slowly conjugating Latin verbs. She said them in English first, then in Latin, and each word automatically appeared on the board behind her as she spoke it. Whenever we were doing tedious verb conjugation, I always got the lyrics to an old *Schoolhouse Rock!* song stuck in my head: "To run, to go, to get, to give. Verb! You're what's happenin'!"

I was quietly humming this tune to myself when Ms. Rank began to conjugate the Latin for the verb "to learn." "To Learn. *Discere*," she said. "Now, this one should be easy to remember, because it's similar to the English word 'discern,' which also means 'to learn.'"

Hearing her repeat the phrase "to learn" was enough to make me think of the Limerick. *You have much to learn if you hope to earn a place among the high scorers.*

Ms. Rank continued, using the verb in a sentence. "We go to school to learn," she said. *"Petimus scholam ut litteras discamus."*

And that was when it hit me. Like an anvil falling out of the sky, directly onto my skull. I gazed around at my classmates. What group of people has "much to learn"?

Students. High-school students.

I was on a planet filled with students, all of whom had "much to learn."

What if the Limerick was saying that the tomb was hidden right here, on Ludus? The very planet where I'd been twiddling my thumbs for the past five years?

Then I remembered that *ludus* was also a Latin word, meaning "school." I pulled up my Latin dictionary to double-check the definition, and that was when I discovered the word had more than one meaning. Ludus could mean "school," but it could also mean "sport" or "game."

Game.

I fell out of my folding chair and landed with a thud on the floor of my hideout. My OASIS console tracked this movement and attempted to make my avatar drop to the floor of my Latin classroom, but the classroom conduct software prevented it from moving and a warning flashed on my display: PLEASE REMAIN SEATED DURING CLASS!

I told myself not to get too excited. I might be jumping to conclusions. There were hundreds of private schools and universities located on other planets inside the OASIS. The Limerick might refer to one of them. But I didn't think so. Ludus made more sense. James Halliday had donated billions to fund the creation of the OASIS public school system here, as a way to demonstrate the huge potential of the OASIS as an educational tool. And prior to his death, Halliday had set up a foundation to ensure that the OASIS public school system would always have the money it needed to operate. The Halliday Learning Foundation also provided impoverished children around the globe with free OASIS hardware and Internet access so that they could attend school inside the OASIS.

GSS's own programmers had designed and constructed Ludus and all of the schools on it. So it was entirely possible that Halliday was the one who'd given the planet its name. And he would also have had access to the planet's source code, if he'd wanted to hide something here.

The realizations continued to detonate in my brain like atomic bombs going off, one after another.

According to the original D&D module, the entrance to the Tomb of Horrors was hidden near "a low, flat-topped hill, about two hundred yards wide and three hundred yards long." The top of the hill was covered with large black stones that were arranged in such a way that, if you viewed them from a great height, they resembled the eye sockets, nose holes, and teeth of a human skull.

But if there was a hill like that hidden somewhere on Ludus, wouldn't someone have stumbled across it by now?

Maybe not. Ludus had hundreds of large forests scattered all over its surface, in the vast sections of empty land that stood between the thousands of school campuses. Some of these forests were enormous, covering dozens of square miles. Most students never even set foot inside them, because there was nothing of interest to do or see there. Like its fields and rivers and lakes, Ludus's forests were just computer-generated landscaping, placed there to fill up the empty space.

Of course, during my avatar's long stay on Ludus, I'd explored a few of the forests within walking distance of my school, out of boredom. But all they contained were thousands of randomly generated trees and the occasional bird, rabbit, or squirrel. (These tiny creatures weren't worth any experience points if you killed them. I'd checked.)

So it was entirely possible that somewhere, hidden in one of Ludus's large, unexplored patches of forestland, there was a small stone-covered hill that resembled a human skull.

I tried pulling up a map of Ludus on my display, but I couldn't. The system wouldn't let me, because class was still in session. The hack I used to access books in the school's online library didn't work for the OASIS atlas software.

"Shit!" I blurted out in frustration. The classroom conduct software filtered this out, so neither Ms. Rank nor my classmates heard it. But another warning flashed on my display: PROFANITY MUTED—MISCONDUCT WARNING!

I looked at the time on my display. Exactly seventeen minutes and twenty seconds left until the end of the school day. I sat there with clenched teeth and counted off each second, my mind still racing.

Ludus was an inconspicuous world in Sector One. There wasn't supposed to be anything but schools here, so this was the last place a gunter would think to look for the Copper Key. It was definitely the last place *I* had ever thought to look, and that alone proved it was a perfect hiding place. But why would Halliday have chosen to hide the Copper Key here? Unless . . .

He'd wanted a schoolkid to find it.

I was still reeling from the implications of that thought when the bell finally rang. Around me, the other students began to file out of the room or vanish in their seats. Ms. Rank's avatar also disappeared, and in moments I was all alone in the classroom.

I pulled up a map of Ludus on my display. It appeared as a three-dimensional globe floating in front of me, and I gave it a spin with my hand. Ludus was a relatively small planet by OASIS standards, about a third the size of Earth's moon, with a circumference of exactly one thousand kilometers. A single contiguous continent covered the surface. There were no oceans, just a few dozen large lakes placed here and there. Since OASIS planets weren't real, they didn't have to obey the laws of nature. On Ludus, it was perpetually daytime, regardless of where you stood on the surface, and the sky was always a perfect cloudless blue. The stationary sun that hung overheard was nothing but a virtual light source, programmed into the imaginary sky.

On the map, the school campuses appeared as thousands of identical numbered rectangles dotting the planet's surface. They were separated by rolling green fields, rivers, mountain ranges, and forests. The forests were of all shapes and sizes, and many of them bordered one of the schools. Next to the map, I pulled up the *Tomb of Horrors* module. Near the front, it contained a crude illustration of the hill concealing the tomb. I took a screenshot of this illustration and placed it in the corner of my display.

I frantically searched my favorite warez sites until I found a high-end image-recognition plug-in for the OASIS atlas. Once I downloaded the software via Guntorrent, it took me a few more minutes to figure out how to make it scan the entire surface of Ludus for a hill with large black stones arranged in a skull-like pattern. One with a size, shape, and appearance that matched the illustration from the *Tomb of Horrors* module.

After about ten minutes of searching, the software highlighted a possible match.

I held my breath as I placed the close-up image from the Ludus map beside the illustration from the D&D module. The shape of the hill and the skull pattern of the stones both matched the illustration perfectly.

I decreased the magnification on the map a bit, then pulled back far enough to confirm that the northern edge of the hill ended in a cliff of sand and crumbling gravel. Just like in the original Dungeons & Dragons module.

I let out a triumphant yell that echoed in the empty classroom and bounced off the walls of my tiny hideout. I'd done it. I'd actually found the Tomb of Horrors!

When I finally managed to calm down, I did some quick calculations. The hill was near the center of a large amoeba-shaped forest located on the opposite side of Ludus, over four hundred kilometers from my school.

My avatar could run at a maximum speed of five kilometers an hour, so it would take me over three days to get there on foot if I ran nonstop the entire time. If I could teleport, I could be there within minutes. The fare wouldn't be much for such a short distance, maybe a few hundred credits. Unfortunately, that was still more than my current OASIS account balance, which was a big fat zero.

I considered my options. Aech would lend me the money for the fare, but I didn't want to ask for his help. If I couldn't reach the tomb on my own, I didn't deserve to reach it at all. Besides, I'd have to lie to Aech about what the money was for, and since I'd never asked him for a loan before, any excuse I gave would make him suspicious.

Thinking about Aech, I couldn't help but smile. He was really going to freak when he found out about this. The tomb was hidden less than *seventy kilometers from his school!* Practically his backyard.

That thought triggered an idea, one that made me leap to my feet. I ran out of the classroom and down the hall.

Not only had I figured out a way to teleport to the other side of Ludus, I knew how to get my school to pay for it.

Each OASIS public school had a bunch of different athletic teams, including wrestling, soccer, football, baseball, volleyball, and a few other sports that couldn't be played in the real world, like Quidditch and zero-gravity Capture the Flag. Students went out for these teams just like they did at schools in the real world, and they played using elaborate sports-capable haptic rigs that required them to actually do all of their own running, jumping, kicking, tackling, and so on. The teams had nightly practice, held pep rallies, and traveled to other schools on Ludus to compete against them. Our school gave out free teleportation vouchers to any student who wanted to attend an away game, so we could sit up in the stands and root for old OPS #1873. I'd only taken advantage of this once, when our Capture the Flag team had played against Aech's school in the OPS championships.

When I arrived in the school office, I scanned the activities schedule and found what I was looking for right away. That evening, our football team was playing an away game against OPS #0571, which was located roughly an hour's run from the forest where the tomb was hidden.

I reached out and selected the game, and a teleportation voucher instantly appeared in my avatar's inventory, good for one free round-trip to OPS #0571.

I stopped at my locker long enough to drop off my textbooks and grab my flashlight, sword, shield, and armor. Then I sprinted out the front entrance and across the expansive green lawn in front of the school.

When I reached the red borderline that marked the edge of the school grounds, I glanced around to make sure no one was watching me, then stepped across the line. As I did, the WADE3 nametag floating above my head changed to read PARZIVAL. Now that I was off school grounds, I could use my avatar name once again. I could also turn off my nametag completely, which was what I did now, because I wanted to travel incognito.

The nearest transport terminal was a short walk from the school, at the end of a cobblestone path. It was a large domed pavilion supported by a dozen ivory pillars. Each pillar bore an OASIS teleportation icon, a capital "T" in the center of a blue hexagon. School had only been out for a few minutes now, so there was a steady stream of avatars filing into the terminal. Inside were long rows of blue teleportation booths. Their shape and color always reminded me of Doctor Who's TARDIS. I stepped into the first empty booth I saw, and the doors closed automatically. I didn't need to enter my destination on the touchscreen because it was already encoded on my voucher. I just slid the voucher into a slot and a world map of Ludus appeared on the screen, showing a line from my present location to my destination, a flashing green dot next to OPS #0571. The booth instantly calculated the distance I would be traveling (462 kilometers) and the amount my school would be invoiced for the fare (103 credits). The voucher was verified, the fare showed as PAID, and my avatar vanished.

I instantly reappeared in an identical booth, inside an identical transport terminal on the opposite side of the planet. As I ran outside, I spotted OPS #0571 off to the south. It looked exactly like my own school, except the surrounding landscape was different. I spotted some students from my school, walking toward the nearby football stadium, on their way to watch the game and root for our team. I wasn't sure why they bothered. They could just as easily have watched the game via vidfeed. And any empty seats in the stands would be filled with randomly generated NPC fans who would wolf down virtual sodas and hot dogs while cheering wildly. Occasionally, they would even do "the wave."

I was already running in the opposite direction, across a rolling green field that stretched out behind the school. A small mountain range loomed in the distance, and I could see the amoeba-shaped forest at its base.

I turned on my avatar's autorun feature, then opened my inventory and selected three of the items listed there. My armor appeared on my body, my shield appeared in a sling on my back, and my sword appeared in its scabbard, hanging at my side.

I was almost to the edge of the forest when my phone rang. The ID said it was Aech. Probably calling to see why I hadn't logged into the Basement yet. But if I answered the call, he would see a live video feed of my avatar, running across a field at top speed, with OPS #0571 shrinking in the distance behind me. I could conceal my current location by taking the call as audio only, but that might make him suspicious. So I let the call roll to my vidmail. Aech's face appeared in a small window on my display. He was calling from a PvP arena somewhere. Dozens of avatars were locked in fierce combat on a multitiered playing field behind him.

"Yo, Z! What are you up to? Jerking off to *Ladyhawke*?" He flashed his Cheshire grin. "Give me a shout. I'm still planning to pop some corn and have a *Spaced* marathon. You down?" He hung up and his image winked out.

I sent a text-only reply, saying I had a ton of homework and couldn't hang tonight. Then I pulled up the *Tomb of Horrors* module and began to read through it again, page by page. I did this slowly and carefully, because I was pretty sure it contained a detailed description of everything I was about to face.

"In the far reaches of the world, under a lost and lonely hill," read the module's introduction, "lies the sinister TOMB OF HORRORS. This labyrinthine crypt is filled with terrible traps, strange and ferocious monsters, rich and magical treasures, and somewhere within rests the evil Demi-Lich."

That last bit worried me. A lich was an undead creature, usually an incredibly powerful wizard or king who had employed dark magic to bind his intellect to his own reanimated corpse, thus achieving a perverted form of immortality. I'd encountered liches in countless videogames and fantasy novels. They were to be avoided at all costs.

I studied the map of the tomb and the descriptions of its many rooms. The tomb's entrance was buried in the side of a crumbling cliff. A tunnel led down into a labyrinth of thirty-three rooms and chambers, each filled with a variety of vicious monsters, deadly traps, and (mostly cursed) treasure. If you somehow managed to survive all of the traps and find your way through the labyrinth, you would eventually reach the crypt of

Acererak the Demi-Lich. The room was littered with treasure, but if you touched it, the undead King Acererak appeared and opened up a can of undead whup-ass on you. If, by some miracle, you managed to defeat the lich, you could take his treasure and leave the dungeon. Mission accomplished, quest completed.

If Halliday had re-created the Tomb of Horrors just as it was described in the module, I was in big trouble. My avatar was a third-level wimp, with nonmagical weapons and twenty-seven measly hit points. Nearly all of the traps and monsters described in the module could kill me easily. And if I somehow managed to make it past all of them and reach the crypt, the ultrapowerful lich could kill my avatar in seconds, just by looking at him.

But I had a few things going for me. First, I really didn't have much to lose. If my avatar was killed, I would lose my sword, shield, and leather armor, and the three levels I'd managed to gain over the past few years. I'd have to create a new first-level avatar, which would spawn at my last log-in location, in front of my school locker. But then I could just return to the tomb and try again. And again and again, every night, collecting XPs and increasing in levels until I finally figured out where the Copper Key was hidden. (There was no such thing as a backup avatar. OASIS users could have only one avatar at a time. It was possible for hackers to use modded visors to spoof their retinal patterns and thus create a second account for themselves. But if you got caught, you'd be banned from the OASIS for life, and you'd also be disqualified from participating in Halliday's contest. No gunter would ever take that risk.)

My other advantage (I hoped) was that I knew exactly what to expect once I entered the tomb, because the module provided me with a detailed map of the entire labyrinth. It also told me where all the traps were located, and how to disarm or avoid them. I also knew which rooms contained monsters, and where all of the weapons and treasure were hidden. Unless, of course, Halliday had changed things around. Then I was screwed. But at the moment, I was far too excited to be worried. After all, I'd just made the biggest, most important discovery of my life. I was just a few minutes away from the hiding place of the Copper Key!

I finally reached the edge of the forest and ran inside. It was filled with thousands of perfectly rendered maples, oaks, spruces, and tamaracks. The trees looked as though they had been generated and placed using standard OASIS landscape templates, but the detail put into them was stunning. I stopped to examine one of the trees closely and saw ants crawling along the intricate ridges in its bark. I took this as a sign I was on the right track.

There was no path through the forest, so I kept the map in the corner of my display and followed it to the skull-topped hill that marked the tomb entrance. It was right where the map said it would be, in a large glade at the center of the forest. As I stepped into the clearing, my heart felt like it was trying to beat its way out of my rib cage.

I climbed up onto the low hilltop, and it was like stepping into the illustration from the D&D module. Halliday had reproduced everything exactly. Twelve massive black stones were arranged on the hilltop in the same pattern, resembling the features of a human skull.

I walked to the northern edge of the hilltop and descended the crumbling cliff face I found there. By consulting the module map, I was able to locate the exact spot in the cliff where the entrance to the tomb was supposed to be buried. Then, using my shield as a shovel, I began to dig. Within a few minutes, I uncovered the mouth of a tunnel that led into a dark underground corridor. The floor of the corridor was a mosaic of colorful stones, with a winding path of red tiles set into it. Once again, just like in the D&D module.

I moved the Tomb of Horrors dungeon map to the top right corner of my display and made it slightly transparent. Then I strapped my shield to my back and took out my flashlight. I glanced around once more to make sure no one was watching me; then, clutching my sword in my other hand, I entered the Tomb of Horrors.

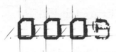

The walls of the corridor leading into the tomb were covered
with dozens of strange paintings depicting enslaved humans, orcs, elves,
and other creatures. Each fresco appeared in the exact location described
in the original D&D module. I knew that hidden in the tiled stone surface
of the floor were several spring-loaded trapdoors. If you stepped on one, it
snapped open and dropped you into a pit filled with poisoned iron spikes.
But because the location of each hidden trapdoor was clearly marked on
my map, I was able to avoid all of them.

So far, everything had followed the original module to the letter. If the
same was true for the rest of the tomb, I might be able to survive long
enough to locate the Copper Key. There were only a few monsters lurking
in this dungeon—a gargoyle, a skeleton, a zombie, some asps, a mummy,
and the evil demi-lich Acererak himself. Since the map told me where
each of them was hiding, I should be able to avoid fighting them. Unless,
of course, one of them was guarding the Copper Key. And I could already
guess who probably had that honor.

I tried to proceed carefully, as if I had no idea what to expect.

Avoiding the Sphere of Annihilation located at the end of the corridor, I
located a hidden door beside the last pit trap. It opened into a small sloping
passageway. My flashlight reached into the darkness ahead, flickering off
the damp stone walls. My surroundings made me feel like I was in a low-
budget sword-and-sorcery flick, like *Hawk the Slayer* or *The Beastmaster*.

I began to make my way through the dungeon, room by room. Even though I knew where all of the traps were located, I still had to proceed carefully to avoid them all. In a dark, forbidding chamber known as the Chapel of Evil, I found thousands of gold and silver coins hidden in the pews, right where they were supposed to be. It was more money than my avatar could carry, even with the Bag of Holding that I found. I gathered up as many of the gold coins as I could and they appeared in my inventory. The currency was automatically converted and my credit counter jumped to over twenty thousand, by far the largest amount of money I'd ever had. And in addition to the credits, my avatar received an equal number of experience points for obtaining the coins.

As I continued deeper into the tomb, I obtained several magic items along the way. A +1 Flaming Sword. A Gem of Seeing. A +1 Ring of Protection. I even found a suit of +3 Full Plate armor. These were the first magic items my avatar had ever possessed, and they made me feel unstoppable.

When I put on the suit of magical armor, it shrank to fit my avatar perfectly. Its gleaming chrome appearance reminded me of the bad-ass armor worn by the knights in *Excalibur*. I actually switched to a third-person view for a few seconds, just to admire how cool my avatar looked wearing it.

The farther I went, the more confident I became. The tomb's layout and contents continued to match the module description exactly, down to the last detail. That is, until I reached the Pillared Throne Room.

It was a large square chamber with a high ceiling, filled with dozens of massive stone columns. A huge raised dais stood at the far end of the room, atop which rested an obsidian throne inlaid with silver and ivory skulls.

All this matched the module description exactly, with one huge difference. The throne was supposed to be empty, but it wasn't. The demi-lich Acererak was sitting on it, glaring down at me silently. A dusty gold crown glinted on his withered head. He appeared exactly as he did on the cover of the original *Tomb of Horrors* module. But according to its text, Acererak wasn't supposed to be here. He was supposed to be waiting in a burial chamber much deeper in the dungeon.

I considered running but decided against it. If Halliday had placed the lich in this room, perhaps he'd placed the Copper Key here too. I had to find out.

I walked across the chamber to the foot of the dais. From here I could see the lich more clearly. His teeth were two rows of pointed cut diamonds arrayed in a lipless grin, and a large ruby was set in each of his eye sockets.

For the first time since entering the tomb, I wasn't sure what to do next.

My chances of surviving one-on-one combat with a demi-lich were nonexistent. My wimpy +1 Flaming Sword couldn't even affect him, and the two magic rubies in his eye sockets had the power to suck out my avatar's life force and kill me instantly. Even a party of six or seven high-level avatars would have had a difficult time defeating him.

I silently wished (not for the last time) that the OASIS was like an old adventure game and that I could save my place. But it wasn't, and I couldn't. If my avatar died here, it would mean starting over with nothing. But there was no point in hesitating now. If the lich killed me, I would come back tomorrow night and try again. The entire tomb should reset when the OASIS server clock struck midnight. If it did, all of the hidden traps I'd disarmed would reset themselves, and the treasure and magic items would reappear.

I tapped the Record icon at the edge of my display so that whatever happened next would be stored in a vidcap file I could play back and study later. But when I tapped the icon, I got a RECORDING NOT ALLOWED message. It seemed that Halliday had disabled recording inside the tomb.

I took a deep breath, raised my sword, and placed my right foot on the bottom step of the dais. As I did, there was a sound like cracking bones as Acererak slowly lifted his head. The rubies in his eye sockets began to glow with an intense red light. I took several steps backward, expecting him to leap down and attack me. But he didn't rise from his throne. Instead, he lowered his head and fixed me with his chilling gaze. "Greetings, Parzival," he said in a rasping voice. "What is it that you seek?"

This caught me off guard. According to the module, the lich wouldn't speak. He was just supposed to attack, leaving me with no choice but to kill him or run for my life.

"I seek the Copper Key," I replied. Then I remembered I was speaking to a king, so I quickly bowed my head, dropped to one knee, and added, "Your Majesty."

"Of course you do," Acererak said, motioning for me to rise. "And you've come to the right place." He stood, and his mummified skin cracked like old leather as he moved. I clutched my sword more tightly, still anticipating an attack.

"How can I know that you are worthy of possessing the Copper Key?" he asked.

Holy shit! How the hell was I supposed to answer *that*? And what if I gave the wrong answer? Would he suck out my soul and incinerate me?

I racked my brain for a suitable reply. The best I could come up with was, "Allow me to prove my worth, noble Acererak."

The lich let out a long, disturbing cackle that echoed off the chamber's stone walls. "Very well!" he said. "You shall prove your worth by facing me in a joust!"

I'd never heard of an undead lich king challenging someone to a joust. Especially not in a subterranean burial chamber. "All right," I said uncertainly. "But won't we be needing horses for that?"

"Not horses," he replied, stepping away from his throne. *"Birds."*

He waved a skeletal hand at his throne. There was a brief flash of light, accompanied by a transformation sound effect (which I was pretty sure had been lifted from the old *Super Friends* cartoon). The throne melted and morphed into an old coin-operated videogame cabinet. Two joysticks protruded from its control panel, one yellow and one blue. I couldn't help but grin as I read the name on the game's backlit marquee: JOUST. Williams Electronics, 1982.

"Best two out of three games," Acererak rasped. "If you win, I shall grant you what you seek."

"What if *you* win?" I asked, already knowing the answer.

"If I am victorious," the lich said, the rubies in his eye sockets blazing even brighter, "then you shall die!" A ball of swirling orange flame appeared in his right hand. He raised it threateningly.

"Of course," I said. "That was my first guess. Just wanted to double-check."

The fireball in Acererak's hand vanished. He stretched out his leathery palm, which now held two shiny quarters. "The games are on me," he said. He stepped up to the Joust machine and dropped both quarters into the left coin slot. The game emitted two low electronic chimes and the credit counter jumped from zero to two.

Acererak took hold of the yellow joystick on the left side of the control panel and closed his bony fingers around it. "Art thou ready?" he croaked.

"Yeah," I said, taking a deep breath. I cracked my knuckles and grabbed the Player Two joystick with my left hand, poising my right hand over the Flap button.

Acererak rocked his head from left to right, cracking his neck. It sounded like a snapping tree branch. Then he slapped the Two Player button and the joust began.

Joust was a classic '80s arcade game with a strange premise. Each player controls a knight armed with a lance. Player One is mounted on an ostrich, while Player Two is mounted on a stork. You flap your wings to fly around the screen and "joust" with the other player, and also against several computer-controlled enemy knights (who are all mounted on buzzards). When you crash into an opponent, whoever's lance is higher on the screen wins the joust. The loser is killed and loses a life. Whenever you kill one of the enemy knights, his buzzard craps out a green egg that quickly hatches into another enemy knight if you don't scoop it up in time. There's also a winged pterodactyl that appears once in a while to wreak havoc.

I hadn't played Joust in over a year. It was one of Aech's favorite games, and for a while he'd had a Joust cabinet in his chat room. He used to challenge me to a game whenever he wanted to settle an argument or some asinine pop-culture dispute. For a few months, we played almost every day. In the beginning, Aech was slightly better than I was, and he had a habit of gloating over his victories. This had really irked me, so I started practicing Joust on my own, playing a few games a night against an AI opponent. I honed my skills until I finally got good enough to beat Aech, repeatedly and consistently. Then *I* began to gloat over him, savoring my revenge. The last time we'd played, I'd rubbed his nose in defeat so mercilessly that he'd flipped out and vowed never to play me again. Since then, we'd used Street Fighter II to settle our disputes.

My Joust skills were a lot rustier than I thought. I spent the first five minutes just trying to relax and to reacquaint myself with the controls and the rhythm of the game. During this time, Acererak managed to kill me twice, mercilessly slamming his winged mount into mine at the perfect trajectory. He handled the game's controls with the calculated perfection of a machine. Which, of course, was exactly what he was—cutting-edge NPC artificial intelligence, programmed by Halliday himself.

By the end of our first game, the moves and tricks I'd picked up during all those marathon bouts with Aech were starting to come back to me. But Acererak didn't need a warm-up. He was in perfect form from the outset, and there was no way I could make up for my weak showing at the start of the game. He killed off my last man before I even cleared 30,000 points. Embarrassing.

"One game down, Parzival," he said, flashing a rictus grin. "One more to go."

He didn't waste time by making me stand there and watch him play out the rest of his game. He reached up and found the power switch at the rear of the game cabinet, then flipped it off and back on. After the screen cycled through its chromatic Williams Electronics boot-up sequence, he snatched two more quarters out of thin air and dropped them into the game.

"Art thou ready?" he inquired again, hunching over the control panel.

I hesitated a moment, then asked, "Actually, would you mind if we switched sides? I'm used to playing on the left."

It was true. When Aech and I played in the Basement, I always took the ostrich side. Being on the right side during the first game had screwed up my rhythm a bit.

Acererak appeared to consider my request for a moment. Then he nodded. "Certainly," he said. He stepped back from the cabinet and we switched sides. It suddenly occurred to me just how absurd this scene was: a guy wearing a suit of armor, standing next to an undead king, both hunched over the controls of a classic arcade game. It was the sort of surreal image you'd expect to see on the cover of an old issue of *Heavy Metal* or *Dragon* magazine.

Acererak slapped the Two Player button, and my eyes locked on the screen.

The next game started out badly for me too. My opponent's movements were relentless and precise, and I spent the first few waves just trying to evade him. I was also distracted by the incessant click of his skeletal index finger as he tapped his Flap button.

I unclenched my jaw and cleared my mind, forcing myself not to think about where I was, who I was playing against, or what was at stake. I tried to imagine that I was back in the Basement, playing against Aech.

It worked. I slipped into the zone, and the tide began to turn in my favor. I began to find the flaws in the lich's playing style, the holes in his programming. This was something I'd learned over the years, mastering hundreds of different videogames. There was always a trick to beating a computer-controlled opponent. At a game like this, a gifted human player could always triumph over the game's AI, because software couldn't improvise. It could either react randomly, or in a limited number of predetermined ways, based on a finite number of preprogrammed conditions. This was an axiom in videogames, and would be until humans invented true artificial intelligence.

Our second game came right down to the wire, but by the end of it, I'd spotted a pattern to the lich's playing technique. By changing my ostrich's direction at a certain moment, I could get him to slam his stork into one of the oncoming buzzards. By repeating this move, I was able to pick off his extra lives, one by one. I died several times myself in the process, but I finally took him down during the tenth wave, with no extra lives of my own to spare.

I stepped back from the machine and sighed with relief. I could feel rivulets of sweat running down my forehead and around the edge of my visor. I wiped at my face with the sleeve of my shirt, and my avatar mimicked this motion.

"Good game," Acererak said. Then, to my surprise, he offered me his withered claw of a hand. I shook it, chuckling nervously as I did so.

"Yeah," I replied. "Good game, man." It occurred to me that, in a weird way, I was actually playing against Halliday. I quickly pushed the thought out of my head, afraid I might psych myself out.

Acererak once again produced two quarters and dropped them into the Joust machine. "This one is for all the marbles," he said. "Art thou ready?"

I nodded. This time, I took the liberty of slapping the Two Player button myself.

Our final tie-breaking game lasted longer than the first two combined. During the final wave, so many buzzards filled the screen that it was hard to move without getting dusted by one of them. The lich and I faced off one final time, at the very top of the playing field, both of us incessantly hitting our Flap buttons while slamming our joysticks left and right. Acererak made a final, desperate move to avoid my charge and dropped a micrometer too low. His final mount died in a tiny pixelated explosion.

PLAYER TWO GAME OVER appeared on the screen, and the lich let out a long bloodcurdling howl of rage. He smashed an angry fist into the side of the Joust cabinet, shattering it into a million tiny pixels that scattered and bounced across the floor. Then he turned to face me. "Congratulations, Parzival," he said, bowing low. "You played well."

"Thank you, noble Acererak," I replied, resisting the urge to jump up and down and shake my ass victoriously in his general direction. Instead,

I solemnly returned his bow. As I did, the lich transformed into a tall human wizard dressed in flowing black robes. I recognized him immediately. It was Halliday's avatar, Anorak.

I stared at him, utterly speechless. For years gunters had speculated that Anorak still roamed the OASIS, now as an autonomous NPC. Halliday's ghost in the machine.

"Now," the wizard said, speaking with Halliday's familiar voice. "Your reward."

The chamber filled with the sound of a full orchestra. Triumphant horns were quickly joined by a stirring string section. I recognized the music. It was the last track from John Williams's original *Star Wars* score, used in the scene where Princess Leia gives Luke and Han their medals (and Chewbacca, as you may recall, gets the shaft).

As the music built to a crescendo, Anorak stretched out his right hand. There, resting in his open palm, was the Copper Key, the item for which millions of people had been searching for the past five years. As he handed it to me, the music faded out, and in the same instant, I heard a chime sound. I'd just gained fifty thousand experience points, enough to raise my avatar all the way up to tenth level.

"Farewell, Sir Parzival," Anorak said. "I bid you good luck on your quest." And before I could ask what I was supposed to do next, or where I could find the first gate, his avatar vanished in a flash of light, accompanied by a teleportation sound effect I knew was lifted from the old '80s *Dungeons & Dragons* cartoon.

I found myself standing alone on the empty dais. I looked down at the Copper Key in my hand and felt overcome with wonder and elation. It looked just as it had in *Anorak's Invitation*: a simple antique copper key, its oval-shaped bow embossed with the roman numeral "I." I turned it over in my avatar's hand, watching the torchlight play across the roman numeral, and that was when I spotted two small lines of text engraved into the metal. I tilted the key up to the light and read them aloud: *"What you seek lies hidden in the trash on the deepest level of Daggorath."*

I didn't even need to read it a second time. I instantly understood its meaning. I knew exactly where I needed to go and what I would have to do once I got there.

"Hidden in the trash" was a reference to the ancient TRS-80 line of computers made by Tandy and Radio Shack in the '70s and '80s. Computer users of that era had given the TRS-80 the derogatory nickname of "Trash 80."

What you seek lies hidden in the trash.

Halliday's first computer had been a TRS-80, with a whopping 16K of RAM. And I knew exactly where to find a replica of that computer in the OASIS. Every gunter did.

In the early days of the OASIS, Halliday had created a small planet named Middletown, named after his hometown in Ohio. The planet was the site of a meticulous re-creation of his hometown as it was in the late 1980s. That saying about how you can never go home again? Halliday had found a way. Middletown was one of his pet projects, and he'd spent years coding and refining it. And it was well known (to gunters, at least) that one of the most detailed and accurate parts of the Middletown simulation was the re-creation of Halliday's boyhood home.

I'd never been able to visit it, but I'd seen hundreds of screenshots and vidcaps of the place. Inside Halliday's bedroom was a replica of his first computer, a TRS-80 Color Computer 2. I was positive that was where he'd hidden the First Gate. And the second line of text inscribed on the Copper Key told me how to reach it:

On the deepest level of Daggorath.

Dagorath was a word in Sindarin, the Elvish language J. R. R. Tolkien had created for *The Lord of the Rings*. The word *dagorath* meant "battle," but Tolkien had spelled the word with just one "g," not two. "Daggorath" (with two "g"s) could refer only to one thing: an incredibly obscure computer game called Dungeons of Daggorath released in 1982. The game had been made for just one platform, the TRS-80 Color Computer.

Halliday had written in *Anorak's Almanac* that Dungeons of Daggorath was the game that made him decide he wanted to become a videogame designer.

And Dungeons of Daggorath was one of the games sitting in the shoebox next to the TRS-80 in the re-creation of Halliday's childhood bedroom.

So all I had to do was teleport to Middletown, go to Halliday's house, sit down at his TRS-80, play the game, reach the bottom level of the dungeon, and . . . that was where I'd find the First Gate.

At least, that was my interpretation.

Middletown was in Sector Seven, a long way from Ludus. But I'd collected more than enough gold and treasure to pay for the teleportation fare to get there. By my avatar's previous standards, I was now filthy rich.

I checked the time: 11:03 p.m., OST (OASIS Server Time, which also happened to be Eastern Standard Time). I had eight hours before I had to be at school. That might be enough time. I could go for it, right now. Sprint like hell, back up through the dungeon to the surface, then high-tail it back to the nearest transport terminal. From there, I could teleport directly to Middletown. If I left right now, I should be able to reach Halliday's TRS-80 in under an hour.

I knew I should get some sleep first. I'd been logged into the OASIS for almost fifteen solid hours. And tomorrow was Friday. I could teleport to Middletown right after school and then I'd have the whole weekend to tackle the First Gate.

But who was I kidding? There was no way I'd be able to sleep tonight, or sit through school tomorrow. I had to go *now*.

I began to sprint for the exit, but then stopped in the middle of the chamber. Through the open door, I saw a long shadow bouncing on the wall, accompanied by the echo of approaching footsteps.

A few seconds later, the silhouette of an avatar appeared in the doorway. I was about to reach for my sword when I realized I was still holding the Copper Key in my hand. I shoved it into a pouch on my belt and fumbled my sword out of its scabbard. As I raised my blade, the avatar spoke.

"Who the hell are you?" the silhouette demanded. The voice sounded like it belonged to a young woman. One who was itching for a fight.

When I failed to answer, a stocky female avatar stepped out of the shadows and into the chamber's flickering torchlight. She had raven hair, styled Joan-of-Arc short, and appeared to be in her late teens or early twenties. As she got closer, I realized that I knew her. We'd never actually met, but I recognized her face from the dozens of screenshots she'd posted to her blog over the years.

It was Art3mis.

She wore a suit of scaled gunmetal-blue armor that looked more sci-fi than fantasy. Twin blaster pistols were slung low on her hips in quick-draw holsters, and there was a long, curved elvish sword in a scabbard across her back. She wore fingerless *Road Warrior*–style racing gloves and a pair of classic Ray-Ban shades. Overall, she seemed to be going for a sort of mid-'80s postapocalyptic cyberpunk girl-next-door look. And it was working for me, in a big way. In a word: *hot*.

As she walked toward me, the heels of her studded combat boots clicked on the stone floor. She halted just out of my sword's reach but did not draw her own blade. Instead, she slid her shades up onto her avatar's forehead—a blatant affectation, since sunglasses didn't actually affect a player's vision—and looked me up and down, making a show of sizing me up.

For a moment I was too star-struck to speak. To break my paralysis, I reminded myself that the person operating the avatar in front of me might not be a woman at all. This "girl," whom I'd been cyber-crushing on for the past three years, might very well be an obese, hairy-knuckled guy named Chuck. Once I'd conjured up that sobering image, I was able to focus on my situation, and the question at hand: *What was she doing here?* After five years of searching, I thought it was highly improbable that we'd both discovered the Copper Key's hiding place on the same night. Too big of a coincidence.

"Cat got your tongue?" she asked. "I said: Who. The hell. Are you?"

Like her, I had my avatar's nametag switched off. Clearly, I wanted to remain anonymous, especially under the circumstances. Couldn't she take the hint?

"Greetings," I said, bowing slightly. "I am Juan Sánchez Villa-Lobos Ramírez."

She smirked. "Chief metallurgist to King Charles the Fifth of Spain?"

"At your service," I replied, grinning. She'd caught my obscure *Highlander* quote and thrown another right back at me. It was Art3mis, all right.

"Cute." She glanced over my shoulder, up at the empty dais, then back at me. "So, spill it. How did you do?"

"Do at what?"

"Jousting against Acererak?" she said, as if it were obvious.

Suddenly, I understood. This wasn't the first time she'd been here. I wasn't the first gunter to decipher the Limerick and find the Tomb of Horrors. Art3mis had beaten me to it. And since she knew about the Joust game, she'd obviously already faced the lich herself. But if she already had the Copper Key, there wouldn't be any reason for her to come back here. So she clearly didn't have the key yet. She'd faced the lich at Joust and he'd beaten her. So she'd come back to try again. For all I knew, this could be her eighth or ninth attempt. And she obviously assumed the lich had beaten me, too.

"Hello?" she said, tapping her right foot impatiently. "I'm waiting?"

I considered making a break for it. Just running right past her, back out through the labyrinth and up to the surface. But if I ran, she might suspect that I had the key and decide to try to kill me to get it. The surface of Ludus was clearly marked as a safe zone on the OASIS map, so no player-versus-player combat was allowed. But I had no way of knowing if the same was true of this tomb, because it was underground, and it didn't even appear on the planet map.

Art3mis looked like a formidable opponent. Body armor. Blaster pistols. And that elvish sword she was carrying might be vorpal. If even half of the exploits she'd mentioned on her blog were true, her avatar was probably at least fiftieth level. Or higher. If PvP combat *was* permitted down here, she'd kick my tenth-level ass.

So I had to play this cool. I decided to lie.

"I got creamed," I said. "Joust isn't really my game."

She relaxed her posture slightly. That seemed to be the answer she wanted to hear. "Yeah, same here," she said in a commiserating tone. "Halliday programmed old King Acererak with some pretty wicked AI, didn't he? He's insanely hard to beat." She glanced down at my sword, which I was still brandishing defensively. "You can put that away. I'm not gonna bite you."

I kept my sword raised. "Is this tomb in a PvP zone?"

"Dunno. You're the first avatar I've ever run into down here." She tilted her head slightly and smiled. "I suppose there's only one way to find out."

She drew her sword, lightning fast, and turned into a clockwise spin, bringing its glowing blade around and down at me, all in a single blur of motion. At the last second, I managed to tilt my own blade upward to awkwardly parry the attack. But both of our swords halted in midair, inches apart, as if held back by some invisible force. A message flashed on my display: PLAYER-VERSUS-PLAYER COMBAT NOT PERMITTED HERE!

I breathed a sigh of relief. (I wouldn't learn until later that the keys were nontransferable. You couldn't drop one of them, or give them to another avatar. And if you were killed while holding one, it vanished right along with your body.)

"Well, there you have it," she said, grinning. "This is a no-PvP zone after all." She whipped her sword around in a figure-eight pattern, then smoothly replaced it in the scabbard on her back. Very slick.

I sheathed my own sword too, but without any fancy moves. "Halliday must not have wanted anyone to duel for the right to joust the king," I said.

"Yeah," she said, grinning. "Lucky for you."

"Lucky for *me*?" I replied, folding my arms. "How do you figure?"

She motioned to the empty dais behind me. "You must really be hurting for hit points right now, after fighting Acererak."

So . . . if Acererak beat you at Joust, then you had to fight him. *Good thing I won,* I thought. *Or else I'd probably be creating a new avatar right about now.*

"I've got hit points galore," I fibbed. "That lich was a total wuss."

"Oh really?" she said suspiciously. "I'm fifty-second level, and he's nearly killed me every time I've had to fight him. I have to stock up on extra healing potions every time I come down here." She eyed me a moment, then said, "I also recognize your sword and the armor you're wearing. You got them both right here in this dungeon, which means they're better than whatever your avatar had before. You look like a low-level wimpazoid to me, Juan Ramírez. And I think you're hiding something."

Now that I knew she couldn't attack me, I considered telling her the truth. Why not just whip out the Copper Key and show it to her? But I thought better of it. The smart move now was to split and head straight for Middletown while I still had a head start. She still didn't have the key and might not get it for several more days. If I hadn't already had so many hours of Joust practice under my belt, God knows how many attempts it would have taken me to beat Acererak.

"Think what you want, She-Ra," I said, moving past her. "Maybe I'll run in to you off-world sometime. We can duke it out then." I gave her a small wave. "See ya 'round."

"Where do you think you're going?" she said, following me.

"Home," I said, still walking.

"But what about the lich? And the Copper Key?" She motioned to the empty dais. "He'll respawn in a few minutes. When the OASIS server clock hits midnight, the whole tomb resets. If you wait right here, you'll get another shot at beating him, without having to make your way through all of those traps again first. That's why I've been coming here just before midnight, every other day. So I can get in two attempts in a row, back-to-back."

Clever. If I hadn't succeeded on my first try, I wondered how long it would have taken me to figure that out. "I thought we could take turns playing against him," I said. "I just played him, so it'll be your turn at midnight, OK? Then I'll come back after midnight tomorrow. We can alternate days until one of us beats him. Sound fair?"

"I suppose," she said, studying me. "But you should stick around anyway. Something different might happen if there are two avatars here at midnight. Anorak probably prepared for that contingency. Maybe two instances of the lich will appear, one for each of us to play? Or maybe—"

"I prefer to play in private," I said. "Let's just take turns, OK?" I was almost to the exit when she stepped in front of me, blocking my path.

"Come on, hold up a second," she said, her voice softening. "Please?"

I could have kept walking, right through her avatar. But I didn't. I was desperate to get to Middletown and locate the First Gate, but I was also standing in front of the famous Art3mis, someone I'd fantasized about meeting for years. And she was even cooler in person than I'd imagined. I was dying to spend more time with her. I wanted, as the '80s poet Howard Jones would say, to get to know her well. If I left now, I might never run into her again.

"Listen," she said, glancing at her boots. "I apologize for calling you a low-level wimpazoid. That was not cool. I insulted you."

"It's OK. You were right, actually. I'm only tenth level."

"Regardless, you're a fellow gunter. And a clever one too, or you wouldn't be standing here. So, I want you to know that I respect you, and acknowledge your skills. And I apologize for the trash talk."

"Apology accepted. No worries."

"Cool." She looked relieved. Her avatar's facial expressions were extremely realistic, which usually meant they were synched to those of their operator instead of controlled by software. She must've been using an expensive rig. "I was just a little freaked to find you here," she said. "I mean, I *knew* someone else would find this place eventually. Just not this quickly. I've had this tomb all to myself for a while now."

"How long?" I asked, not really expecting her to say.

She hesitated, then began to ramble. "Three weeks!" she said, exasperated. "I've been coming here for three freakin' weeks, trying to beat that stupid lich at that asinine game! And his AI is ridiculous! I mean, you know. I'd never even played Joust before this, and now it's driving me out of my gourd! I swear I was *this close* to finally beating his ass a few days ago, but then . . ." She raked her fingers through her hair in frustration. "Argh! I can't sleep. I can't eat. My grades are going down the tubes, because I've been ditching to practice Joust—"

I was about to ask if she went to school here on Ludus, but she continued to talk, faster and faster, as if a floodgate had opened in her brain. The words just poured out of her. She was barely pausing to breathe.

"—and I came here tonight, thinking this would be the night I finally beat that bastard and get the Copper Key, but when I got here, I saw that someone had already uncovered the entrance. So I realized my worst fear had finally come true. Someone else had found the tomb. So I ran all the way down here, totally freaking out. I mean, I wasn't *too* worried, because I didn't think anyone could possibly beat Acererak on their first try, but still—" She paused to take a deep breath and stopped abruptly.

"Sorry," she said a second later. "I tend to ramble when I'm nervous. Or excited. And right now I'm sort of both, because I've been dying to talk to someone about all of this, but obviously I couldn't tell a soul, right? You can't just mention in casual conversation that you—" She cut herself off again. "Man, I'm such a motormouth! A jabberjaw. A flibbertigibbet." She mimed zipping her lips, locking them, and tossing away the imaginary key. Without thinking, I mimed grabbing the key out of the air and unlocking her lips. This made her laugh—an honest, genuine laugh that involved a fair amount of snorting, which made me laugh too.

She was so charming. Her geeky demeanor and hyperkinetic speech pattern reminded me of Jordan, my favorite character in *Real Genius*. I'd never felt such an instant connection with another person, in the real world or in the OASIS. Not even with Aech. I felt light-headed.

When she finally got her laughter under control, she said, "I really need to set up a filter to edit out that laugh of mine."

"No, you shouldn't," I said. "It's a pretty great laugh, actually." I was wincing at every word coming out of my mouth. "I have a dorky laugh too."

Great, Wade, I thought. *You just called her laugh "dorky." Real smooth.*

But she just gave me a shy smile and mouthed the words "thank you."

I felt a sudden urge to kiss her. Simulation or not, I didn't care. I was working up the courage to ask for her contact card when she stuck out her hand.

"I forgot to introduce myself," she said. "I'm Art3mis."

"I know," I said, shaking her hand. "I'm actually a huge fan of your blog. I've been a loyal reader for years."

"Seriously?" Her avatar actually seemed to blush.

I nodded. "It's an honor to meet you," I said. "I'm Parzival." I realized that I was still holding her hand and made myself let go.

"Parzival, eh?" She tilted her head slightly. "Named after the knight of the Round Table who found the grail, right? Very cool."

I nodded, now even more smitten. I almost always had to explain my name to people. "And Artemis was the Greek goddess of the hunt, right?"

"Right! But the normal spelling was already taken, so I had to use a leet spelling, with a number three in place of the 'e.'"

"I know," I said. "You mentioned that once on your blog. Two years ago." I almost cited the date of the actual blog entry before I realized it would make me sound like even *more* of a cyber-stalking super-creep. "You said that you still run into noobs who prounounce it 'Art-three-miss.'"

"That's right," she said, grinning at me. "I did."

She stretched out a racing-gloved hand and offered me one of her contact cards. You could design your card to look like just about anything. Art3mis had coded hers to look like a vintage Kenner Star Wars action figure (still in the blister pack). The figure was a crude plastic rendering of her avatar, with the same face, hair, and outfit. Tiny versions of her guns and sword were included. Her contact info was printed on the card, above the figure:

Art3mis

52nd Level Warrior/Mage

(Vehicle Sold Separately)

On the back of the card were links to her blog, e-mail, and phone line.

Not only was this the first time a girl had ever given me her card, it was also, by far, the coolest contact card I had ever seen.

"This is, by far, the coolest contact card I have ever seen," I said. "Thank you!"

I handed her one of my own cards, which I'd designed to look like an original Atari 2600 Adventure cartridge, with my contact info printed on the label:

Parzival

10th Level Warrior

(Use with Joystick Controller)

"This is awesome!" she said, looking it over. "What a wicked design!"

"Thanks," I said, blushing under my visor. I wanted to propose marriage.

I added her card to my inventory, and it appeared on my item list, right below the Copper Key. Seeing the key listed there snapped me back to reality. What the hell was I doing, standing here making small talk with this girl when the First Gate was waiting for me? I checked the time. Less than five minutes until midnight.

"Listen, Art3mis," I said. "It was truly awesome to meet you. But I gotta get going. The server is about to reset, and I want to clear out of here before all of those traps and undead respawn."

"Oh . . . OK." She actually sounded disappointed! "I should probably prepare for my Joust match anyway. But here, let me hit you with a Cure Serious Wounds spell before you go."

Before I could protest, she laid a hand on my avatar's chest and muttered a few arcane words. My hit-point counter was already at maximum, so the spell had no effect. But Art3mis didn't know that. She was still under the assumption that I'd had to fight the lich.

"There you go," she said, stepping back.

"Thanks," I said. "But you shouldn't have. We're competitors, you know."

"I know. But we can still be friends, right?"

"I hope so."

"Besides, the Third Gate is still a long way off. I mean, it took five years for the two of us to get this far. And if I know Halliday's game-design strategy, things are just going to get harder from here on out." She lowered her voice. "Listen, are you sure you don't want to stick around? I bet we can both play at once. We can give each other Jousting tips. I've started to spot some flaws in the king's technique—"

Now I was starting to feel like a jerk for lying to her. "That's a really kind offer. But I have to go." I searched for a plausible excuse. "I've got school in the morning."

She nodded, but her expression shifted back to one of suspicion. Then her eyes widened, as though an idea had just occurred to her. Her pupils began to dart around, focused on the space in front of her, and I realized she was looking something up in a browser window. A few seconds later, her face contorted in anger.

"You lying bastard!" she shouted. "You dishonest sack of crap!" She made her Web browser window visible to me and spun it around. It displayed the Scoreboard on Halliday's website. In all the excitement, I'd forgotten to check it.

It looked just as it had for the past five years, with one change. My avatar's name now appeared at the very top of the list, in first place, with a score of 10,000 points beside it. The other nine slots still contained Halliday's initials, JDH, followed by zeros.

"Holy shit," I muttered. When Anorak had handed me the Copper Key, I'd become the first gunter in history to score points in the contest. And, I realized, since the Scoreboard was viewable to the entire world, my avatar had just become famous.

I checked the newsfeed headlines just to be sure. Every single one of them contained my avatar's name. Stuff like: MYSTERIOUS AVATAR "PARZIVAL" MAKES HISTORY and PARZIVAL FINDS COPPER KEY.

I stood there in a daze, forcing myself to breathe. Then Art3mis gave me a shove, which, of course, I didn't feel. She did knock my avatar backward a few feet, though. *"You beat him on your first try?"* she shouted.

I nodded. "He won the first game, but I won the last two. Just barely, though."

"Shiiiiiit!" she screamed, clenching her fists. "How in the hell did you beat him on your *first try?*" I got the distinct impression she wanted to sock me in the face.

"It was pure luck," I said. "I used to play Joust all the time against a friend of mine. So I'd already had a ton of preparation. I'm sure if you'd had as much practice—"

"Please!" she growled, holding up a hand. "Do not patronize me, OK?" She let out what I can only describe as a howl of frustration. "I don't believe this! Do you realize I've been trying to beat him for *five goddamn weeks!*"

"But a minute ago you said it was three weeks—"

"Don't interrupt me!" She gave me another shove. "I've been practicing Joust nonstop for over a month now! I'm seeing flying ostriches in my goddamn sleep!"

"That can't be pleasant."

"And you just walk in here and nail it on the first try!" She started pounding her fist into the center of her forehead, and I realized she was pissed at herself, not me.

"Listen," I said. "It really was luck. I've got a knack for classic arcade games. That's my specialty." I shrugged. "Stop hitting yourself like Rain Man, OK?"

She stopped and stared me. After a few seconds, she let out a long sigh. "Why couldn't it be Centipede? Or Ms. Pac-Man? Or BurgerTime? Then I'd probably have already cleared the First Gate by now!"

"Well, I don't know about *that,*" I said.

She glared at me a second, then gave me a devilish smile. She turned to face the exit and began to execute a series of elaborate gestures in the air in front of her while whispering the words of some incantation.

"Hey," I said. "Hold on a sec. What are you doing?"

But I already knew. As she finished casting her spell, a giant stone wall appeared, completely covering the chamber's only exit. Shit! She'd cast a Barrier spell. I was trapped inside the room.

"Oh, come on!" I shouted. "Why did you do that?"

"You seemed to be in an awful big hurry to get out of here. My guess is that when Anorak gave you the Copper Key, he also gave you some sort of clue about the location of the First Gate. Right? That's where you're headed next, isn't it?"

"Yeah," I said. I thought about denying it, but what was the point now?

"So unless you can nullify my spell—and I'm betting you can't, Mr. Tenth-Level Warrior—that barrier will keep you in here until just after midnight, when the server resets. All of those traps you disarmed on your way down here will reset. That should slow down your exit considerably."

"Yes," I said. "It will."

"And while you're busy making your way back up to the surface, I'll have another shot at defeating Acererak. And this time I'm gonna destroy him. Then I'll be right behind you, mister."

I folded my arms. "If the king has been beating your ass for the past five weeks, what makes you think you're finally going to win tonight?"

"Competition brings out the best in me," she replied. "It always has. And now I've got some serious competition."

I glanced over at the magical barrier she'd created. She was over fiftieth level, so it would remain in existence for the spell's maximum duration: fifteen minutes. All I could do was stand there and wait for it to dissipate. "You're evil, you know that?" I said.

She grinned and shook her head. "Chaotic Neutral, sugar."

I grinned back at her. "I'm still going to beat you to the First Gate, you know."

"Probably," she said. "But this is just the beginning. You'll still have to clear it. And there are still two more keys to find, and two more gates to clear. Plenty of time for me to catch up with you, and then leave you in the dust, ace."

"We'll see about that, lady."

She motioned to the window displaying the Scoreboard. "You're famous now," she said. "You realize what that means, don't you?"

"I haven't had much time to think about it yet."

"Well, I have. I've been thinking about it for the past five weeks. Your avatar's name on that Scoreboard is going to change everything. The public will become obsessed with the contest again, just like when it first began. The media is already going berserk. By tomorrow, Parzival will be a household name."

That thought made me a little queasy.

"You could become famous in the real world too," she said. "If you reveal your true identity to the media."

"I'm not an idiot."

"Good. Because there are billions of dollars up for grabs, and now everyone is going to assume you know how and where to find the egg. There are a lot of people who would kill for that information."

"I know that," I said. "And I appreciate your concern. But I'll be fine."

But I didn't feel fine. I hadn't really considered any of this, maybe because I'd never really believed I would actually be in this position.

We stood there in silence, watching the clock and waiting. "What would you do if you won?" she suddenly asked. "How would you spend all that money?"

I had spent a lot of time thinking about *that*. I daydreamed about it all the time. Aech and I had made absurd lists of things we would do and buy if we won the prize.

"I don't know," I said. "The usual, I guess. Move into a mansion. Buy a bunch of cool shit. Not be poor."

"Wow. Big dreamer," she said. "And after you buy your mansion and your 'cool shit,' what will you do with the hundred and thirty billion you'll have left over?"

Not wanting her to think I was some shallow idiot, I impulsively blurted out what I'd always dreamed of doing if I won. It was something I'd never told anyone.

"I'd have a nuclear-powered interstellar spacecraft constructed in

Earth's orbit," I said. "I'd stock it with a lifetime supply of food and water, a self-sustaining biosphere, and a supercomputer loaded with every movie, book, song, videogame, and piece of artwork that human civilization has ever created, along with a stand-alone copy of the OASIS. Then I'd invite a few of my closest friends to come aboard, along with a team of doctors and scientists, and we'd all get the hell out of Dodge. Leave the solar system and start looking for an extrasolar Earthlike planet."

I hadn't thought this plan all the way through yet, of course. I still had a lot of details to work out.

She raised an eyebrow. "That's pretty ambitious," she said. "But you do realize that nearly half the people on this planet are starving, right?" I detected no malice in her voice. She sounded like she genuinely believed I might not be aware of this fact.

"Yes, I know," I said defensively. "The reason so many people are starving is because we've wrecked the planet. The Earth is dying, you know? It's time to leave."

"That's a pretty negative outlook," she said. "If I win that dough, I'm going to make sure everyone on this planet has enough to eat. Once we tackle world hunger, then we can figure out how to fix the environment and solve the energy crisis."

I rolled my eyes. "Right," I said. "And after you pull off that miracle, you can genetically engineer a bunch of Smurfs and unicorns to frolic around this new perfect world you've created."

"I'm being serious," she said.

"You really think it's that simple?" I said. "That you can just write a check for two hundred and forty billion dollars and fix all the world's problems?"

"I don't know. Maybe not. But I'm gonna give it a shot."

"If you win."

"Right. If I win."

Just then, the OASIS server clock struck midnight. We both knew the second it happened, because the throne reappeared atop the dais, along with Acererak. He sat there motionless, looking just like he did when I'd first entered the room.

Art3mis glanced up at him, then back at me. She smiled and gave me a small wave. "I'll see you around, Parzival."

"Yeah," I replied. "See ya." She turned and began to walk toward the dais. I called after her. "Hey, Art3mis?"

She turned back. For some reason I felt compelled to help her, even though I knew I shouldn't. "Try playing on the left side," I said. "That's how I won. I think he might be easier to beat if he's playing the stork."

She stared at me for a second, possibly trying to gauge whether I was messing with her. Then she nodded and ascended the dais. Acererak came to life as soon as she set foot on the first step.

"Greetings, Art3mis," his voice boomed. "What is it that you seek?"

I couldn't hear her reply, but a few seconds later the throne transformed into the Joust game, just as it had earlier. Art3mis said something to the lich and the two of them switched sides, so that she was on the left. Then they began to play.

I watched them play from a distance until a few minutes later, when her Barrier spell dissipated. I cast one last glance up at Art3mis, then threw open the door and ran out.

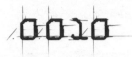

0010

It took me a little over an hour to make my way back through the tomb and up to the surface. The instant I crawled outside, a MESSAGES WAITING indicator began to flash on my display. I realized then that Halliday had placed the tomb inside a null-communication zone, so no one could receive calls, texts, or e-mail while they were inside. Probably to prevent gunters from calling for help or advice.

I checked my messages and saw that Aech had been trying to reach me since the moment my name appeared on the Scoreboard. He'd called over a dozen times and had also sent several text messages asking me what in the sweet name of Christ was going on and screaming at me in ALL CAPS to call him back right *now*. Just as I'd finished deleting these messages, I received another incoming call. It was Aech trying once again to reach me. I decided not to pick up. Instead, I sent him a short text message, promising to call as soon as I could.

As I ran out of the forest, I kept the Scoreboard up in the corner of my display so I'd know immediately if Art3mis won her Joust match and obtained the key. When I finally reached the transport terminal and jumped into the nearest booth, it was just after two o'clock in the morning.

I entered my destination on the booth's touchscreen, and a map of Middletown appeared on the display. I was prompted to select one of the planet's 256 transport terminals as my arrival point.

When Halliday had created Middletown, he hadn't placed just a single re-creation of his hometown there. He'd made 256 identical copies of it, spread out evenly across the planet's surface. I didn't think it would matter which copy of his hometown I went to, so I selected one at random, near the equator. Then I tapped CONFIRM to pay the fare, and my avatar vanished.

A millisecond later, I was standing inside a vintage 1980s phone booth located inside an old Greyhound bus station. I opened the door and stepped out. It was like stepping out of a time machine. Several NPCs milled around, all dressed in mid-1980s attire. A woman with a giant ozone-depleting hairdo bobbed her head to an oversize Walkman. A kid in a gray Members Only jacket leaned against the wall, working on a Rubik's Cube. A Mohawked punk rocker sat in a plastic chair, watching a *Riptide* rerun on a coin-operated television.

I located the exit and headed for it, drawing my sword as I went. The entire surface of Middletown was a PvP zone, so I had to proceed with caution.

Shortly after the Hunt began, this planet had turned into Grand Central Station, and all 256 copies of Halliday's hometown had been scoured and ransacked by an endless parade of gunters, all searching for keys and clues. The popular theory on the message boards was that Halliday had created multiple copies of his hometown so that several avatars could search it at the same time without fighting over a single location. Of course, all of this searching had yielded a big fat doughnut. No keys. No clues. No egg. Since then, interest in the planet had waned dramatically. But some gunters probably still came here on occasion.

If there was already another gunter inside Halliday's house when I got there, my plan was to make a run for it, then steal a car and drive twenty-five miles (in any direction) to the next identical copy of Middletown. And then the next, until I found an instance of Halliday's house that was unoccupied.

Outside the bus station, it was a beautiful Midwestern day. The reddish orange sun hovered low in the sky. Even though I'd never been to Middletown before, I'd done extensive research on it, so I knew Halliday had coded the planet so that no matter when you visited or where you were on the surface, it was always a perfect late-autumn afternoon, circa 1986.

I pulled up a map of the town and traced a route from my current location to Halliday's childhood home. It was about a mile to the north. I pointed my avatar in that direction and began to run. Looking around, I was astounded at the painstaking attention to detail. I'd read that Halliday had done all of the coding himself, drawing on his memories to recreate his hometown exactly as it was during his childhood. He'd used old street maps, phone books, photographs, and video footage for reference, to make everything as authentic and accurate as possible.

The place reminded me a lot of the town in the movie *Footloose*. Small, rural, and sparsely populated. The houses all seemed incredibly big and were placed ridiculously far apart. It astounded me that fifty years ago, even lower-income families had an entire house to themselves. The NPC citizens all looked like extras from a John Cougar Mellencamp video. I saw people out raking leaves, walking dogs, and sitting on porches. Out of curiosity, I waved at a few of them and got a friendly wave in return every time.

Clues as to the time period were everywhere. NPC-piloted cars and trucks cruised slowly up and down the shady streets, all of them gas-guzzling antiques: Trans-Ams, Dodge Omnis, IROC Z28s, and K-cars. I passed a service station, and the sign said gasoline was only ninety-three cents a gallon.

I was about to turn down Halliday's street when I heard a fanfare of trumpets. My eyes shot over to the Scoreboard window, still hovering in the corner of my display.

Art3mis had done it.

Her name now appeared directly below mine. Her score was 9,000 points—a thousand points less than mine. It appeared that I'd received a bonus for being the first avatar to obtain the Copper Key.

The full ramifications of the Scoreboard's existence occurred to me for the first time. From here on out, it would not only allow gunters to keep track of each other's progress, it would also show the entire world who the current frontrunners were, creating instant celebrities (and targets) in the process.

I knew, at that exact moment, Art3mis must be staring down at her own copy of the Copper Key, reading the clue engraved on its surface. I was sure she'd be able to decipher it just as quickly as I had. In fact, she was probably already on her way to Middletown right now.

That got me moving again. I now had only an hour's head start on her. Maybe less.

When I reached Cleveland Avenue, the street on which Halliday had grown up, I sprinted down the cracked sidewalk to the front steps of his childhood home. It looked just like the photographs I'd seen: a modest two-story colonial with red vinyl siding. Two late-'70s Ford sedans were parked in the driveway, one of them up on cinder blocks.

Looking at the replica Halliday had created of his old house, I tried to imagine what it had been like for him to grow up there. I'd read that in the real Middletown, Ohio, every house on this street had been demolished in the late '90s to make room for a strip mall. But Halliday had preserved his childhood forever, here in the OASIS.

I ran up the walkway and entered through the front door, which opened into the living room. I knew this room well, because it appeared in *Anorak's Invitation*. I recognized the simulated wood-grain paneling, the burnt orange carpet, and garish furniture that looked like it had been scavenged from several disco-era yard sales.

The house was empty. For whatever reason, Halliday had decided not to place NPC re-creations of himself or his deceased parents here. Perhaps that would have been too creepy, even for him. However, I did spot a familiar family photo on the living room wall. This portrait had been taken at the local Kmart in 1984, but Mr. and Mrs. Halliday were still dressed in late-'70s fashions. Twelve-year-old Jimmy stood between them, glowering at the camera from behind thick eyeglasses. The Hallidays looked like an ordinary American family. There was no hint that the stoic man in the brown leisure suit was an abusive alcoholic, that the smiling woman in the floral pantsuit was bipolar, or that the young boy in the faded Asteroids T-shirt would one day create an entirely new universe.

Looking around, I wondered why Halliday, who always claimed to have had a miserable childhood, had later become so nostalgic for it. I knew that if and when I finally escaped from the stacks, I'd never look back. And I definitely wouldn't create a detailed simulation of the place.

I glanced over at the bulky Zenith television and the Atari 2600 connected to it. The simulated wood grain on the Atari's plastic casing perfectly matched the simulated wood grain on the television cabinet and on the living room walls. Beside the Atari was a shoebox containing nine game cartridges: Combat, Space Invaders, Pitfall, Kaboom!, Star Raiders, The Empire Strikes Back, Starmaster, Yars' Revenge, and E.T. Gunters had attached a large amount of significance to the absence of Adventure, the game Halliday was seen playing on this very same Atari at the end of *Anorak's Invitation*. People had searched the entire Middletown simulation for a copy of it, but there didn't appear to be one anywhere on the whole planet. Gunters had brought copies of Adventure here from other planets, but when they tried to play them on Halliday's Atari, they never worked. So far, no one had been able to figure out why.

I did a quick search of the rest of the house and made sure no other avatars were present. Then I opened the door of James Halliday's room. It was empty, so I stepped inside and locked the door. Screenshots and simcaps of this room had been available for years, and I'd studied all of them closely. But this was my first time standing inside the "real thing." I got chills.

The carpet was a horrendous mustard color. So was the wallpaper. But the walls were almost entirely covered with movie and rock band posters: *Real Genius, WarGames, Tron,* Pink Floyd, Devo, Rush. A bookshelf stood just inside the door, overflowing with science-fiction and fantasy paperbacks (all titles I'd read, of course). A second bookshelf by the bed was crammed to capacity with old computer magazines and Dungeons & Dragons rule books. Several long boxes of comic books were stacked against the wall, each carefully labeled. And there on the battered wooden desk in the corner was James Halliday's first computer.

Like many home computers of its era, it was housed in the same case as its keyboard. TRS-80 COLOR COMPUTER 2, 16K RAM was printed on a label above the keys. Cables snaked out of the back of the machine, leading to an audiocassette recorder, a small color television, a dot-matrix printer, and a 300-baud modem. A long list of telephone numbers for dial-up bulletin board systems was taped to the desk beside the modem.

I sat down and located the power switch for the computer and the TV. I heard a crackle of static, followed by a low hum, as the TV warmed up. A moment later, the TRS-80's green start-up screen appeared, and I saw these words:

EXTENDED COLOR BASIC 1.1
COPYRIGHT (c) 1982 BY TANDY
OK

Below this was a flashing cursor, cycling through every color of the spectrum. I typed HELLO and hit the Enter key.

?SYNTAX ERROR appeared on the next line. "Hello" wasn't a valid command in BASIC, the only language the ancient computer understood.

I knew from my research that the cassette recorder functioned as the

TRS-80's "tape drive." It stored data as analog sound on magnetic audio-tapes. When Halliday had first started programming, the poor kid hadn't even had access to a floppy disk drive. He'd had to store his code on cassette tapes. A shoebox sat beside the tape drive, filled with dozens of these cassettes. Most of them were text adventure games: Raaka-tu, Bedlam, Pyramid, and Madness and the Minotaur. There were also a few ROM cartridges, which fit into a slot on the side of the computer. I dug around in the box until I found a cartridge with DUNGEONS OF DAGGORATH printed in crooked yellow text on its worn red label. The game's artwork depicted a first-person view of a long dungeon corridor blocked by a hulking blue giant with a large stone ax.

When a list of the games found in Halliday's bedroom had first appeared online, I'd made sure to download and master every single one of them, so I'd already solved Dungeons of Daggorath, about two years earlier. It had taken most of a weekend. The graphics were crude, but even so, the game was fun and incredibly addictive.

I knew from reading the message boards that during the past five years, several gunters had played and solved Dungeons of Daggorath right here on Halliday's TRS-80. Some had solved every single game in the shoebox, just to see if anything would happen. And nothing had. But none of those gunters had been in possession of the Copper Key.

My hands were trembling slightly as I powered off the TRS-80 and inserted the Dungeons of Daggorath cartridge. When I turned the computer back on, the screen flashed to black and a crude graphic of a wizard appeared, accompanied by some ominous sound effects. The wizard held a staff in one hand, and below him, printed in all capital letters, was the legend I DARE YE ENTER . . . THE DUNGEONS OF DAGGORATH!

I laid my fingers on the keyboard and began to play. As soon as I did, a jambox sitting on top of Halliday's dresser turned itself on, and familiar music began to blast out of it. It was Basil Poledouris's score for *Conan the Barbarian*.

That must be Anorak's way of letting me know I'm on the right track, I thought.

I quickly lost track of time. I forgot that my avatar was sitting in Halliday's bedroom and that, in reality, I was sitting in my hideout, huddled near the electric heater, tapping at the empty air in front of me, entering commands on an imaginary keyboard. All of the intervening layers slipped away, and I lost myself in the game within the game.

In Dungeons of Daggorath, you control your avatar by typing in commands, like TURN LEFT or GET TORCH, navigating your way through a maze of vector-graphic corridors while fighting off spiders, stone giants, blobs, and wraiths as you descend deeper and deeper, working your way down through the dungeon's five increasingly difficult levels. It took a while for the commands and quirks of the game to come back to me, but once they did, the game wasn't that difficult to solve. The ability to save my place at any time basically gave me infinite lives. (Although saving and reloading games from the tape drive proved to be a slow and tedious process. It often took several attempts and a lot of fiddling with the cassette deck's volume knob.) Saving my game also allowed me to log out for bathroom breaks, and to recharge my space heater.

While I was playing, the *Conan the Barbarian* score ended and the jambox clicked over and began to play the opposite side of the tape, treating me to the synthesizer-laden score for *Ladyhawke*. I couldn't wait to rub Aech's nose in that.

I reached the last level of the dungeon around four o'clock in the morning and faced off against the Evil Wizard of Daggorath. After dying and reloading twice, I finally defeated him, using an Elvish Sword and a Ring of Ice. I completed the game by picking up the wizard's magic ring, claiming it for myself. As I did, an image appeared on the screen, showing a wizard with a bright star on his staff and his robes. The text below read:
BEHOLD! DESTINY AWAITS THE HAND OF A NEW WIZARD!

I waited to see what would happen. For a moment, nothing did. Then Halliday's ancient dot-matrix printer came to life and noisily ground out a single line of text. The tractor feed spooled the page out of the top of the printer. I tore the sheet off and read what was there:
CONGRATULATIONS! YOU HAVE OPENED THE FIRST GATE!

I glanced around and saw that there was now a wrought-iron gate embedded in the bedroom wall, in the exact spot where the *WarGames* poster had been a second before. In the center of the gate was a copper-plated lock with a keyhole.

I climbed up on top of Halliday's desk so I could reach the lock, then slid the Copper Key into the keyhole and turned it. The entire gate began to glow, as if the metal had become superheated, and its double doors swung inward, revealing a field of stars. It appeared to be a portal into deep space.

"My God, it's full of stars," I heard a disembodied voice say. I recognized it as a sound bite from the film *2010*. Then I heard a low, ominous hum, followed by a piece of music from that film's score: "Also Sprach Zarathustra" by Richard Strauss.

I leaned forward and looked through the portal. Left and right, up and down. Nothing but an endless field of stars in all directions. Squinting, I could also make out a few tiny nebulae and galaxies in the distance.

I didn't hesitate. I jumped into the open gate. It seemed to pull me in, and I began to fall. But I fell forward instead of down, and the stars seemed to fall with me.

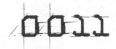

I found myself standing in an old video arcade, playing Galaga.

The game was already in progress. I had double ships and a score of 41,780 points. I glanced down and saw that my hands were on the controls. After a second or two of disorientation, I reflexively began to play, moving the joystick left just in time to avoid losing one of my ships.

Keeping one eye on the game, I tried to make sense of my surroundings. In my peripheral vision I was able to make out a Dig Dug game on my left and a Zaxxon machine to my right. Behind me, I could hear a cacophony of digital combat coming from dozens of other vintage arcade games. Then, as I finished clearing the wave on Galaga, I noticed my reflection in the game's screen. It wasn't my avatar's face I saw there. It was Matthew Broderick's face. A young pre–*Ferris Bueller* and pre-*Ladyhawke* Matthew Broderick.

Then I knew where I was. And *who* I was.

I was David Lightman, Matthew Broderick's character in the movie *WarGames*. And this was his first scene in the film.

I was *in the movie.*

I took a quick glance around and saw a detailed replica of 20 Grand Palace, the combination arcade/pizza joint featured in the film. Kids with feathered '80s hairstyles were clustered around each of the games. Others sat in booths, eating pizza and drinking sodas. "Video Fever" by the Beepers blasted out of a jukebox in the corner. Everything looked and sounded exactly as it did in the movie. Halliday had copied every last detail from the film and re-created it as an interactive simulation.

Holy shit.

I'd spent years wondering what challenges awaited me inside the First Gate. Never once had I imagined *this*. But I probably should have. *WarGames* had been one of Halliday's all-time favorite movies. Which was why I had watched it over three dozen times. Well, that, and also because it was completely awesome, with an old-school teenage computer hacker as the protagonist. And it looked like all of that research was about to pay off.

Now I heard a repetitive electronic beeping. It seemed to be coming from the right pocket of the jeans I was wearing. Keeping my left hand on the joystick, I reached in my pocket and pulled out a digital watch. The readout said 7:45 a.m. When I pushed one of the buttons to silence the alarm, a warning flashed in the center of my display: DAVID, YOU'RE GOING TO BE LATE FOR SCHOOL!

I used a voice command to pull up my OASIS map, hoping to learn where the gate had transported me. But it turned out that not only was I no longer on Middletown, I was no longer in the OASIS at all. My locator icon was in the middle of a blank screen, which meant I was OTM—off the map. When I'd stepped into the gate, it had transported my avatar into a stand-alone simulation, a virtual location separate from the OASIS. It seemed that the only way I could get back would be to clear the gate by completing the quest. But if this was a videogame, how was I supposed to play it? If this was a quest, what was my goal? I continued to play Galaga while pondering these questions. A second later, a young boy walked into the arcade and came over to me.

"Hi, David!" he said, his eyes on my game.

I recognized this kid from the movie. His name was Howie. In the film, Matthew Broderick's character hands his Galaga game off to Howie when he rushes off to school.

"Hi, David!" the boy repeated, in the same exact tone. As he spoke this time, his words also appeared as text, superimposed across the bottom of my display, like subtitles. Below this, flashing red, were the words FINAL DIALOGUE WARNING!

I began to understand. The simulation was warning me that this was my final chance to deliver the next line of dialogue from the movie. If I didn't say the line, I could guess what would probably happen next. GAME OVER.

But I didn't panic, because I *knew* the next line. I'd seen *WarGames* so many times that I knew the entire film by heart.

"Hi, Howie!" I said. But the voice I heard in my earphones was not my own. It was Matthew Broderick's voice. And as I spoke the line, the warning on my display vanished and a score of 100 points appeared, superimposed at the top of my display.

I racked my brain, trying to mentally replay the rest of the scene. The next line came to me. "How's it going?" I said, and my score jumped to 200 points.

"Pretty good," Howie replied.

I started to feel giddy. This was incredible. I was totally *inside the movie*. Halliday had transformed a fifty-year-old film into a real-time interactive videogame. I wondered how long it had taken him to program this thing.

Another warning flashed on my display: YOU'RE GOING TO BE LATE FOR SCHOOL, DAVID! HURRY!

I stepped away from the Galaga machine. "Hey, you wanna take this over?" I asked Howie.

"Sure," he replied, grabbing the controls. "Thanks!"

A green path appeared on the floor of the arcade, leading from where I stood to the exit. I started to follow it, then remembered to run back and grab my notebook off of the Dig Dug game, just like David had in the movie. As I did this, my score jumped another 100 points, and ACTION BONUS! appeared on my display.

"Bye, David!" Howie shouted.

"Bye!" I shouted back. Another 100 points. This was easy!

I followed the green path out of 20 Grand Palace and up the busy street a few blocks. I was now running along a tree-lined suburban street. I rounded a corner and saw that the path led directly to a large brick building. The sign over the door said Snohomish High School—David's school, and the setting of the next few scenes in the movie.

My mind was racing as I ran inside. If all I had to do was rattle off lines of dialogue from *WarGames* on cue for the next two hours, this was going to be a breeze. Without even knowing it, I'd totally overprepared. I probably knew *WarGames* even better than I knew *Real Genius* and *Better Off Dead*.

As I ran down the empty school hallway, another warning flashed in front of me: YOU'RE LATE FOR YOUR BIOLOGY CLASS!

I continued to sprint at top speed, following the green path, which was now pulsing brightly. It eventually led me to the door of a classroom on the second floor. Through the window, I could see that class was already in session. The teacher was up at the board. I saw my seat—the only empty one in the room.

It was right behind Ally Sheedy.

I opened the door and tiptoed inside, but the teacher spotted me right away.

"Ah, David! Nice of you to join us!"

. . .

Making it all the way to the end of the movie wound up being a lot harder than I anticipated. It only took me about fifteen minutes to figure out the "rules" of the game and to sort out how the scoring system worked. I was actually required to do a lot more than simply recite dialogue. I also had to perform all the actions that Broderick's character performed in the film, in the correct way and at the correct moment. It was like being forced to act the leading role in a play you'd watched many times but had never actually rehearsed.

For most of the movie's first hour, I was on edge, constantly trying to think ahead to have my next line of dialogue ready. Whenever I flubbed a line or didn't perform an action at the right moment, my score decreased and a warning flashed on my display. When I made two mistakes in a row, a FINAL WARNING message appeared. I wasn't sure what would happen if I got three strikes in a row, but my guess was that I'd either be expelled from the gate or that my avatar would simply be killed. I wasn't eager to find out which it would be.

Whenever I correctly performed seven actions or recited seven lines of dialogue in a row, the game would award me a "Cue Card Power-Up." The next time I blanked on what to do or say, I could select the Cue Card icon and the correct action or line of dialogue would appear on my display, sort of like a teleprompter.

During scenes that didn't involve my character, the simulation cut to a passive third-person perspective, and all I had to do was sit back and watch things play out, sort of like watching a cut scene in an old video-game. During these scenes, I could relax until my character came on-screen again. During one of these breaks, I tried to access a copy of the movie from my OASIS console's hard drive, with the intention of playing it in a window on my display so I could refer to it. But the system wouldn't let me. In fact, I found that I couldn't open any windows at all while inside the gate. When I tried, I got a warning: NO CHEATING. TRY TO CHEAT AGAIN AND IT'S *GAME OVER*!

Luckily, it turned out that I didn't need any help. Once I'd collected the maximum of five Cue Card Power-Ups I began to relax, and the game actually started to be fun. It wasn't hard to enjoy being *inside* one of my favorite flicks. After a while, I even discovered that I could earn bonus points by delivering a line in the exact tone and with the same inflection as in the film.

I didn't know it at the time, but I'd just become the first person to play an entirely new type of videogame. When GSS got wind of the *WarGames* simulation inside the First Gate (and they did a short time later), the company quickly patented the idea and began to buy up the rights to old movies and TV shows and convert them into immersive interactive games that they dubbed *Flicksyncs*. Flicksyncs became wildly popular. There turned out to be a huge market for games that allowed people to play a leading role in one of their favorite old movies or TV series.

By the time I reached the final scenes of the movie, I was starting to get twitchy from exhaustion. I'd now been up for over twenty-four hours straight, jacked in the entire time. The last action I had to perform was instructing the WOPR supercomputer to "play itself" at tic-tac-toe. Since every game the WOPR played ended in a tie, this had the improbable effect of teaching the artificially intelligent computer that global thermonuclear war, too, was a game in which "the only winning move is not to play." This prevented the WOPR from launching all of the United States' ICBMs at the Soviet Union.

I, David Lightman, a teenage computer geek from suburban Seattle, had single-handedly prevented the end of human civilization.

The NORAD command center erupted in celebration, and I waited for the movie's end credits to roll. But they didn't. Instead, all the characters around me vanished, leaving me alone in the giant war room. When I checked my avatar's reflection in a computer monitor, I saw that I no longer looked like Matthew Broderick. I'd changed back into Parzival.

I glanced around the empty NORAD command center, wondering what I was supposed to do next. Then all of the giant video display screens in front of me went blank, and four lines of glowing green text appeared on them. It was another riddle:

The captain conceals the Jade Key
in a dwelling long neglected
But you can only blow the whistle
once the trophies are all collected

I stood there for a second, staring at the words in stunned silence. Then I snapped out of my daze and quickly took several screenshots of the text. As I was doing this, the Copper Gate reappeared, embedded in a nearby wall. The gate was open, and through it I could see Halliday's bedroom. It was the exit. The way out.

I'd done it. I'd cleared the First Gate.

I glanced back up at the riddle on the viewscreens. It had taken me years to decipher the Limerick and locate the Copper Key. At first glance, this new riddle about the Jade Key looked like it might take just as long to figure out. I didn't understand a word of it. But I was also dead on my feet, and in no condition for further puzzle-solving. I could barely keep my eyes open.

I jumped through the exit and landed with a thud on the floor of Halliday's bedroom. When I turned around and looked at the wall, I saw that the gate was now gone and the *WarGames* poster had reappeared in its place.

I checked my avatar's stats and saw that I'd been awarded several hundred thousand experience points for clearing the gate, enough to raise my avatar from tenth level up to twentieth in one shot. Then I checked the Scoreboard:

HIGH SCORES:

1.	Parzival	**110000**	⛩
2.	Art3mis	**9000**	
3.	JDH	0000000	
4.	JDH	0000000	
5.	JDH	0000000	
6.	JDH	0000000	
7.	JDH	0000000	
8.	JDH	0000000	
9.	JDH	0000000	
10.	JDH	0000000	

My score had increased by 100,000 points, and a copper-colored gate icon now appeared beside it. The media (and everyone else) had probably been monitoring the Scoreboard since last night, so now the whole world would know that I'd cleared the First Gate.

I was too exhausted to consider the implications. All I could think about was sleep.

I ran downstairs and into the kitchen. The keys to the Halliday family car were on a pegboard next to the refrigerator. I grabbed them and rushed outside. The car (the one that wasn't up on blocks) was a 1982 Ford Thunderbird. The engine started on the second try. I backed out of the driveway and drove to the bus station.

From there, I teleported back to the transport terminal next to my school on Ludus. Then I went to my locker and dumped all of my avatar's newfound treasure, armor, and weapons inside before finally logging out of the OASIS.

When I pulled off my visor, it was 6:17 a.m. I rubbed my bloodshot eyes and gazed around the dark interior of my hideout, trying to wrap my head around everything that had just happened.

I suddenly realized how cold it was in the van. I'd been using the tiny space heater off and on all night and had drained the batteries. I was way too tired to get on the exercise bike and recharge them. And I didn't have the energy to make the trek back to my aunt's trailer, either. But the sun would be up soon, so I knew I could crash there in my hideout without worrying that I would freeze to death.

I slid off of my chair and onto the floor, then curled up in my sleeping bag. As I closed my eyes, I began to ponder the riddle of the Jade Key. But sleep swallowed me whole a few seconds later.

I had a dream. I was standing alone in the center of a scorched battlefield, with several different armies arrayed against me. An army of Sixers stood in front of me, and several different gunter clans surrounded me on all other flanks, brandishing swords and guns and weapons of powerful magic.

I looked down at my body. It wasn't Parzival's body; it was my own. And I was wearing armor made of paper. In my right hand was a toy plastic sword, and in my left was a large glass egg. It looked exactly like the glass egg that causes Tom Cruise's character so much grief in *Risky Business,* but somehow I knew that, in the context of my dream, it was supposed to be Halliday's Easter egg.

And I was standing there, out in the open, holding it for all the world to see.

In unison, the armies of my enemies let out a fierce battle cry and charged toward me. They converged on my position with bared teeth and blood in their eyes. They were coming to take the egg, and there was nothing I could do to stop them.

I knew I was dreaming, and so I expected to wake up before they reached me. But I didn't. The dream continued as the egg was ripped from my grasp, and I felt myself being torn to shreds.

I slept for over twelve hours and missed school entirely.

When I finally woke up, I rubbed my eyes and lay there in silence awhile, trying to convince myself that the events of the previous day had actually occurred. It all seemed like a dream to me now. Far too good to be real. Eventually, I grabbed my visor and got online to find out for sure.

Every single newsfeed seemed to be showing a screenshot of the Scoreboard. And my avatar's name was there at the top, in first place. Art3mis was still in second place, but the score beside her name had now increased to 109,000, just 1,000 points less than mine. And, like me, she had a copper-colored gate icon beside her score now too.

So she'd done it. While I'd slept, she'd deciphered the inscription on the Copper Key. Then she'd gone to Middletown, located the gate, and made it all the way through *WarGames*, just a few hours after I had.

I no longer felt quite so impressed with myself.

I flipped past a few more channels before stopping on one of the major newsfeed networks, where I saw two men sitting in front of a screenshot of the Scoreboard. The man on the left, some middle-aged intellectual type billed as "Edgar Nash, Gunter Expert" appeared to be explaining the scores to the newsfeed anchor beside him.

"—appears that the avatar named Parzival received slightly more points for being the first to find the Copper Key," Nash said, pointing to the Scoreboard. "Then, early this morning, Parzival's score increased another one hundred thousand points, and a Copper Gate icon appeared beside his score. The same change occurred to Art3mis's score a few hours later. This seems to indicate that both of them have now completed the first of the three gates."

"The famous Three Gates that James Halliday spoke of in the *Anorak's Invitation* video?" the anchor said.

"The very same."

"But Mr. Nash. After five years, how is it that two avatars accomplished this feat on the same day, within just a few hours of each other?"

"Well, I think there's only one plausible answer. These two people, Parzival and Art3mis, must be working together. They're probably both members of what is known as a 'gunter clan.' These are groups of egg hunters who—"

I frowned and changed the channel, surfing the feeds until I saw an overly enthusiastic reporter interviewing Ogden Morrow via satellite. *The* Ogden Morrow.

"—joining us live from his home in Oregon. Thanks for being with us today, Mr. Morrow!"

"No problem," Morrow replied. It had been almost six years since Morrow had last spoken to the media, but he didn't seem to have aged a day. His wild gray hair and long beard made him look like a cross between Albert Einstein and Santa Claus. That comparison was also a pretty good description of his personality.

The reporter cleared his throat, obviously a bit nervous. "Let me start off by asking what your reaction is to the events of the last twenty-four hours. Were you surprised to see those names appear on Halliday's Scoreboard?"

"Surprised? Yes, a little, I suppose. But 'excited' is probably a better word. Like everyone else, I've been watching and waiting for this to happen. Of course, I wasn't sure if I'd still be alive when it finally did! I'm glad that I am. It's all very exciting, isn't it?"

"Do you think these two gunters, Parzival and Art3mis, are working together?"

"I have no idea. I suppose it's possible."

"As you know, Gregarious Simulation Systems keeps all OASIS user records confidential, so we have no way of knowing their true identities. Do you think either of them will come forward and reveal themselves to the public?"

"Not if they're smart, they won't," Morrow said, adjusting his wire-rimmed spectacles. "If I were in their shoes, I'd do everything possible to remain anonymous."

"Why do you say that?"

"Because once the world discovers who they really are, they'll never have a moment's peace afterward. If people think you can help them find Halliday's egg, they'll never leave you alone. Trust me, I know from experience."

"Yes, I suppose you do." The reporter flashed a fake smile. "However, this network has contacted both Parzival and Art3mis via e-mail, and we've extended generous monetary offers to each of them in return for an exclusive interview, either in the OASIS or here in the real world."

"I'm sure they're receiving many such offers. But I doubt they'll accept," Morrow said. Then he looked straight into the camera, and I felt as if he was now speaking directly to me. "Anyone smart enough to accomplish what they have should know better than to risk everything by talking to the vultures in the media."

The reporter chuckled uncomfortably. "Ah, Mr. Morrow . . . I really don't think that's called for."

Morrow shrugged. "Too bad. I do."

The reporter cleared his throat again. "Well, moving on . . . Do you have any predictions about what changes we might see on the Scoreboard in the weeks to come?"

"I'm betting that those other eight empty slots will fill up pretty quickly."

"What makes you think so?"

"One person can keep a secret, but not two," he replied, staring directly into the camera again. "I don't know. Maybe I'm wrong. But I *am* sure of one thing. The Sixers are going to use every dirty trick at their disposal to learn the location of the Copper Key and the First Gate."

"You're referring to the employees of Innovative Online Industries?"

"Yes. IOI. The Sixers. Their sole purpose is to exploit loopholes in the contest rules and subvert the intention of Jim's will. The very soul of the OASIS is at stake here. The last thing Jim would have wanted is for his creation to fall into the hands of a fascist multinational conglomerate like IOI."

"Mr. Morrow, IOI owns this network. . . ."

"Of course they do!" Morrow shouted gleefully. "They own practically everything! Including you, pretty boy! I mean, did they tattoo a UPC code on your ass when they hired you to sit there and spout their corporate propaganda?"

The reporter began to stutter, glancing nervously at something off camera.

"Quick!" Morrow said. "You better cut me off before I say anything else!" He broke up into gales of laughter just as the network cut his satellite feed.

The reporter took a few seconds to regroup, then said, "Thank you again for joining us today, Mr. Morrow. Unfortunately that's all the time we have to speak with him. Now let's go back to Judy, who is standing by with a panel of renowned Halliday scholars—"

I smiled and closed the vidfeed window, pondering the old man's advice. I'd always suspected that Morrow knew more about the contest than he was letting on.

• • •

Morrow and Halliday had grown up together, founded a company together, and changed the world together. But Morrow had led a very different life from Halliday's—one involving a much greater connection to humanity. And a great deal more tragedy.

During the mid-'90s, back when Gregarious Simulation Systems was still just Gregarious Games, Morrow had moved in with his high-school sweetheart, Kira Underwood. Kira was born and raised in London. (Her birth name was Karen, but she'd insisted on being called Kira ever since her first viewing of *The Dark Crystal*.) Morrow met her when she spent her junior year as an exchange student at his high school. In his autobiography, Morrow wrote that she was the "quintessential geek girl," unabashedly obsessed with Monty Python, comic books, fantasy novels, and videogames. She and Morrow shared a few classes at school, and he was smitten with her almost immediately. He invited her to attend his weekly Dungeons & Dragons gaming sessions (just as he'd done with Halliday a few years earlier), and to his surprise, she accepted. "She became the lone female in our weekly gaming group," Morrow wrote. "And every single one of the guys developed a massive crush on her, including Jim. She was actually the one who gave him the nickname 'Anorak,' a British slang term for an obsessive geek. I think Jim adopted it as the name of his D and D character to impress her. Or maybe it was his way of trying to let her know he was in on the joke. The opposite sex made Jim extremely nervous, and Kira was the only girl I ever saw him speak to in a relaxed manner. But even then, it was only in character, as Anorak, during the course of our gaming sessions. And he would only address her as Leucosia, the name of her D and D character."

Ogden and Kira began dating. By the end of the school year, when it was time for her to return home to London, the two of them had openly declared their love for each other. They kept in touch during their remaining year of school by e-mailing every day, using an early pre-Internet computer bulletin board network called FidoNet. When they both graduated from high school, Kira returned to the States, moved in with Morrow, and became one of Gregarious Games' first employees. (For the first two years, she was their entire art department.) They got engaged a few years after the launch of the OASIS. They were married a year later, at which time Kira resigned from her position as an artistic director at GSS. (She was a millionaire now too, thanks to her company stock options.) Morrow stayed on at GSS for five more years. Then, in the summer of 2022, he announced he was leaving the company. At the time, he claimed it was for "personal reasons." But years later, Morrow wrote in his autobiography that he'd left GSS because "we were no longer in the videogame business," and because he felt that the OASIS had evolved into something horrible. "It had become a self-imposed prison for humanity," he wrote. "A pleasant place for the world to hide from its problems while human civilization slowly collapses, primarily due to neglect."

Rumors also surfaced that Morrow had chosen to leave because he'd had a huge falling-out with Halliday. Neither of them would confirm or deny these rumors, and no one seemed to know what sort of dispute had ended their long friendship. But sources within the company said that at the time of Morrow's resignation, he and Halliday had not spoken to each other directly in several years. Even so, when Morrow left GSS, he sold his entire share of the company directly to Halliday, for an undisclosed sum.

Ogden and Kira "retired" to their home in Oregon and started a nonprofit educational software company, Halcydonia Interactive, which created free interactive adventure games for kids. I'd grown up playing these games, all of which were set in the magical kingdom of Halcydonia. Morrow's games had transported me out of my grim surroundings as a lonely kid growing up in the stacks. They'd also taught me how to do math and solve puzzles while building my self-esteem. In a way, the Morrows were among my very first teachers.

For the next decade, Ogden and Kira enjoyed a peaceful, happy existence, living and working in relative seclusion. They tried to have children, but it wasn't in the cards for them. They'd begun to consider adoption when, in the winter of 2034, Kira was killed in a car accident on an icy mountain road just a few miles from their home.

After that, Ogden continued to run Halcydonia Interactive on his own. He managed to stay out of the limelight until the morning of Halliday's death, when his home was besieged by the media. As Halliday's former closest friend, everyone assumed he alone could explain why the deceased billionaire had put his entire fortune up for grabs. Morrow eventually held a press conference just to get everyone off his back. It was the last time he'd spoken to the media, until today. I'd watched the video of that press conference many, many times.

Morrow had begun it by reading a brief statement, saying that he hadn't seen or spoken to Halliday in over a decade. "We had a falling-out," he said, "and that is something I refuse to discuss, now or in the future. Suffice it to say, I have not communicated with James Halliday in over ten years."

"Then why did Halliday leave you his vast collection of classic coin-operated videogames?" a reporter asked. "All of his other material possessions are to be auctioned off. If you were no longer friends, why are you the only person he left anything to?"

"I have no idea," Morrow said simply.

Another reporter asked Morrow if he planned on looking for Halliday's Easter egg himself, since he'd known Halliday so well and would therefore probably have a better chance than anyone of finding it. Morrow reminded the reporter that the contest rules laid out in Halliday's will stated that no one who had ever worked for Gregarious Simulation Systems, or anyone in their immediate families, was eligible to take part in the contest.

"Did you have any idea what Halliday was working on all those years he was in seclusion?" another reporter asked.

"No. I suspected he might be working on some new game. Jim was always working on a new game. For him, making games was as necessary as breathing. But I never imagined he was planning something . . . of this magnitude."

"As the person who knew James Halliday the best, do you have any advice for the millions of people who are now searching for his Easter egg? Where do you think people should start looking for it?"

"I think Jim made that pretty obvious," Morrow replied, tapping a finger against his temple, just as Halliday had in the *Anorak's Invitation* video. "Jim always wanted everyone to share his obsessions, to love the same things he loved. I think this contest is his way of giving the entire world an incentive to do just that."

● ● ●

I closed my file on Morrow and checked my e-mail. The system informed me that I'd received over two million new unsolicited messages. These were automatically filed in a separate folder, so I could sort through them later. Only two new messages were left in my inbox, from people on my authorized contact list. One was from Aech. The other was from Art3mis.

I opened Aech's message first. It was vidmail, and his avatar's face appeared in a window. "Holy shit!" he shouted. "I don't believe this! Now you've cleared the motherfucking First Gate and you *still haven't phoned me*? Call my ass! Now! The second you get this!"

I considered waiting a few days to call Aech back but quickly abandoned that idea. I *needed* to talk to someone about all this, and Aech was my best friend. If there was anyone I could trust, it was him.

He picked up on the first ring, and his avatar appeared in a new window in front of me. "You dog!" he shouted. "You brilliant, sly, devious dog!"

"Hey, Aech," I said, trying to deadpan it. "What's new?"

"What's new? *What's new?* You mean, other than, you know, seeing my best friend's name appear *at the top of the Scoreboard*? Other than that, you mean?" He leaned forward so that his mouth completely filled the vidfeed window and shouted, "Other than that, not much! Not much new at all!"

I laughed. "Sorry it took me a while to call you. I had kind of a late night."

"No shit, you had a late night!" he said. "Look at you! How can you be so calm! Don't you realize what this means? This is huge! This is beyond epic! I mean . . . congratu-freakin'-lations, man!" He began to bow repeatedly. "I am not worthy!"

"Cut it out, OK? It's really not a big deal. I haven't actually *won* anything yet. . . ."

"Not a big deal!" he cried. "*Not. A. Big. Deal?* Are you kidding me? You're a legend now, man! You just became the first gunter in history to find the Copper Key! And clear the First Gate! You are a god, from this moment forth! Do you not realize this, fool?"

"Seriously. Stop it. I'm already freaked out enough as it is."

"Have you seen the news? The whole world is freaking out! And the gunter boards are going apeshit! And everyone is talking about *you*, amigo."

"I know. Listen, I hope you're not pissed at me for keeping you in the dark. I felt really weird about not returning your calls or telling you what I was up to. . . ."

"Oh, come on!" He rolled his eyes dismissively. "You know damn well that if I'd been in your shoes, I would have done the same thing. That's how the game is played. But"—his tone grew more serious—"I *am* curious to know how that Art3mis chick happened to find the Copper Key and clear the gate right after you did. Everyone seems to think you two were working together, but I know that's horseshit. So what happened? Was she following you or something?"

I shook my head. "No, she found the key's hiding place before I did. Last month, she said. She just wasn't able to obtain the key until now." I was silent for a second. "I can't really go into the details without, you know—"

Aech held up both hands. "No worries. I totally understand. I wouldn't want for you to accidentally drop any hints." He flashed his trademark Cheshire grin, and his gleaming white teeth seemed to take up half of the vidfeed window. "Actually, I should let you know where I am right now. . . ."

He adjusted his vidfeed's virtual camera so that it pulled back from a tight shot of his face to a much wider shot that revealed where he was—standing next to the flat-topped hill, just outside the entrance to the Tomb of Horrors.

My jaw dropped. "How in the hell—?"

"Well, when I saw your name all over the newsfeeds last night, it occurred to me that for as long as I've known you, you've never had the dough to do much traveling. Any traveling, really. So I figured that if you'd found the hiding place of the Copper Key, it probably had to be somewhere close to Ludus. Or maybe even *on* Ludus."

"Well done," I said, and I meant it.

"Not really. I spent hours racking my pea-sized brain before I finally thought to search the map of Ludus for the surface features described in the *Tomb of Horrors* module. But once I did, everything else clicked into place. And here I am."

"Congratulations."

"Yeah, well, it was pretty easy once you pointed me in the right direction." He glanced back over his shoulder at the tomb. "I've been searching for this place for years, and all this time it was within walking distance of my school! I feel like a total moron for not figuring it out on my own."

"You're not a moron," I said. "You deciphered the Limerick on your own, otherwise you wouldn't even know about the *Tomb of Horrors* module, right?"

"So, you're not pissed?" he said. "That I took advantage of my inside info?"

I shook my head. "No way. I would have done the same thing."

"Well, regardless, I owe you one. And I won't forget it."

I nodded toward the tomb behind him. "Have you been inside yet?"

"Yeah. I came back up here to call you, while I wait for the server to reset at midnight. The tomb is empty right now, because your friend, Art3mis, already blew through here earlier today."

"We're not friends," I said. "She just showed up, a few minutes after I got the key."

"Did you guys throw down?"

"No. The tomb is a no-PvP zone." I glanced at the time. "Looks like you've still got a few hours to kill before the reset."

"Yeah. I've been studying the original D and D module, trying to prepare myself," he said. "Wanna give me any tips?"

I grinned. "No. Not really."

"Didn't think so." He was silent for a few seconds. "Listen, I have to ask you something," he said. "Does anyone at your school know your avatar's name?"

"No. I've been careful to keep it a secret. No one there knows me as Parzival. Not even the teachers."

"Good," he said. "I took the same precaution. Unfortunately, several of the gunters who frequent the Basement know that we both attend school on Ludus, so they might be able to connect the dots. I'm worried about one in particular. . . ."

I felt a rush of panic. "I-rok?"

Aech nodded. "He's been calling me nonstop since your name appeared on the Scoreboard, asking what I know. I played dumb, and he seemed to buy it. But if my name shows up on the Scoreboard too, you can bet he'll start bragging that he knows us. And when he starts telling other gunters that you and I are both students on Ludus—"

"Shit!" I cursed. "Then every gunter in the sim will be headed here to search for the Copper Key."

"Right," Aech said. "And before long, the location of the tomb will be common knowledge."

I sighed. "Well, then you better get the key before that happens."

"I'll do my best." He held up a copy of the *Tomb of Horrors* module. "Now, if you'll excuse me, I'm going to reread this thing for the hundredth time today."

"Good luck, Aech," I said. "Give me a call once you've cleared the gate."

"*If* I clear the gate. . ."

"You will," I said. "And when you do, we should meet in the Basement to talk."

"You got it, amigo."

He waved good-bye and was about to end the call when I spoke up. "Hey, Aech?"

"Yeah?"

"You might want to brush up on your jousting skills," I said. "You know, between now and midnight."

He looked puzzled for a moment; then a smile of understanding spread across his face. "I got ya," he said. "Thanks, pal."

"Good luck."

As his vidfeed window winked out, I found myself wondering how Aech and I would remain friends through everything that lay ahead. Neither of us wanted to work as a team, so from here on out we would be in direct competition with each other. Would I eventually regret helping him today? Or come to resent that I'd unwittingly led him to the Copper Key's hiding place?

I pushed these thoughts aside and opened the e-mail from Art3mis. It was an old-fashioned text message.

> Dear Parzival,
>
> Congrats! See? You're famous now, just like I said. Although it looks like we've both been thrust into the limelight. Kinda scary, eh?
>
> Thanks for the tip about playing on the left side. You were right. Somehow, that did the trick. But don't go thinking I owe you any favors, mister. :-)
>
> The First Gate was pretty wild, wasn't it? Not at all what I expected. It would have been cool if Halliday had given me the option to play Ally Sheedy instead, but what can you do?
>
> This new riddle is a real head-scratcher, isn't it? I hope it doesn't take us another five years to decipher it.
>
> Anyhow, I just wanted to say that it was an honor to meet you. I hope our paths cross again soon.
>
> Sincerely,
>
> Art3mis
>
> ps—Enjoy being #1 while you can, pal. It won't last for long.

I reread her message several times, grinning like a dopey schoolboy. Then I typed out my reply:

> Dear Art3mis,
>
> Congratulations to you, too. You weren't kidding. Competition clearly brings out the best in you.
>
> You're welcome for the tip about playing on the left. You totally owe me a favor now. ;-)
>
> The new riddle is a cinch. I think I've already got it figured out, actually. What's the hold-up on your end?

It was an honor to meet you, too. If you ever feel like hanging out in a chat room, let me know.

MTFBWYA,

Parzival

ps—Are you challenging me? Bring the pain, woman.

After rewriting it a few dozen times, I tapped the Send button. Then I pulled up my screenshot of the Jade Key riddle and began to study it, syllable by syllable. But I couldn't seem to concentrate. No matter how hard I tried to focus, my mind kept drifting back to Art3mis.

0013

Rech cleared the First Gate early the next day.

His name appeared on the Scoreboard in third place, with a score of 108,000 points. The value of obtaining the Copper Key had dropped another 1,000 points for him, but the value of clearing the First Gate remained unchanged at 100,000.

I returned to school that same morning. I'd considered calling in sick, but was concerned that my absence might raise suspicions. When I got there, I realized I shouldn't have worried. Due to the sudden renewed interest in the Hunt, over half of the student body, and quite a few of the teachers, didn't bother showing up. Since everyone at school knew my avatar by the name Wade3, no one paid any attention to me. Roaming the halls unnoticed, I decided that I enjoyed having a secret identity. It made me feel like Clark Kent or Peter Parker. I thought my dad would probably have gotten a kick out of that.

That afternoon, I-rok sent e-mails to Aech and me, attempting to blackmail us. He said that if we didn't tell him how to find the Copper Key and the First Gate, he would post what he knew about us to every gunter message board he could find. When we refused, he made good on his threat and began telling anyone who would listen that Aech and I were both students on Ludus. Of course, he had no way of proving he really knew us, and by that time there were hundreds of other gunters claiming to be our close personal friends, so Aech and I were hoping his posts would go unnoticed. But they didn't, of course. At least two other gunters were sharp enough to connect the dots between Ludus, the Limerick, and the *Tomb of Horrors*. The day after I-rok let the cat out of the bag, the name "Daito" appeared in the fourth slot on the Scoreboard. Then, less than fifteen minutes later, the name "Shoto" appeared in the fifth slot. Somehow, they'd both obtained a copy of the Copper Key on the same day, without waiting for the server to reset at midnight. Then, a few hours later, both Daito and Shoto cleared the First Gate.

No one had ever heard of these avatars before, but their names seemed to indicate they were working together, either as a duo or as part of a clan. *Shoto* and *daito* were the Japanese names for the short and long swords worn by samurai. When worn as a set, the two swords were called *daisho*, and this quickly became the nickname by which the two of them were known.

Only four days had passed since my name had first appeared on the Scoreboard, and one new name had appeared below mine on each subsequent day. The secret was out now, and the hunt seemed to be shifting into high gear.

All week, I was unable to focus on anything my teachers were saying. Luckily, I only had two months of school left, and I'd already earned enough credits to graduate, even if I coasted from here on out. So I drifted from one class to the next in a daze, puzzling over the Jade Key riddle, reciting it again and again in my mind.

> *The captain conceals the Jade Key*
> *in a dwelling long neglected*
> *But you can only blow the whistle*
> *once the trophies are all collected*

According to my English Lit textbook, a poem with four lines of text and an alternate-line rhyme scheme was known as a quatrain, so that became my nickname for the riddle. Each night after school, I logged out of the OASIS and filled the blank pages of my grail diary with possible interpretations of the Quatrain.

What "captain" was Anorak talking about? Captain Kangaroo? Captain America? Captain Buck Rogers in the twenty-fifth century?

And where in the hell was this "dwelling long neglected"? That part of the clue seemed maddeningly nonspecific. Halliday's boyhood home on

Middletown couldn't really be classified as "neglected," but maybe he was talking about a different house in his hometown? That seemed too easy, and too close to the hiding place of the Copper Key.

At first, I thought the neglected dwelling might be a reference to *Revenge of the Nerds,* one of Halliday's favorite films. In that movie, the nerds of the title rent a dilapidated house and fix it up (during a classic '80s music montage). I visited a re-creation of the *Revenge of the Nerds* house on the planet Skolnick and spent a day searching it, but it proved to be a dead end.

The last two lines of the Quatrain were also a complete mystery. They seemed to say that once you found the neglected dwelling, you would have to collect a bunch of "trophies" and then blow some kind of whistle. Or did that line mean *blow the whistle* in the colloquial sense, as in "to reveal a secret or alert someone to a crime"? Either way, it didn't make any sense to me. But I continued to go over each line, word by word, until my brain began to feel like Aquafresh toothpaste.

＊　＊　＊

That Friday after school, the day Daito and Shoto cleared the First Gate, I was sitting in a secluded spot a few miles from my school, a steep hill with a solitary tree at the top. I liked to come here to read, to do my homework, or to simply enjoy the view of the surrounding green fields. I didn't have access to that kind of view in the real world.

As I sat under the tree, I sorted through the millions of messages still clogging my inbox. I'd been sifting through them all week. I'd received notes from people all over the globe. Letters of congratulation. Pleas for help. Death threats. Interview requests. Several long, incoherent diatribes from gunters whose quest for the egg had clearly driven them insane. I'd also received invitations to join four of the biggest gunter clans: the Oviraptors, Clan Destiny, the Key Masters, and Team Banzai. I told each of them thanks, but no thanks.

When I got tired of reading my "fan mail," I sorted out all the messages that were tagged as "business related" and began reading through those. I discovered that I'd received several offers from movie studios and book publishers, all interested in buying the rights to my life story. I deleted them all, because I'd decided never to reveal my true identity to the world. At least, not until after I found the egg.

I'd also received several endorsement-deal offers from companies who wanted to use Parzival's name and face to sell their services and products. An electronics retailer was interested in using my avatar to promote their line of OASIS immersion hardware so they could sell "Parzival-approved" haptic rigs, gloves, and visors. I also had offers from a pizza-delivery chain, a shoe manufacturer, and an online store that sold custom avatar skins. There was even a toy company that wanted to manufacture a line of Parzival lunch boxes and action figures. These companies were offering to pay me in OASIS credits, which would be transferred directly to my avatar's account.

I couldn't believe my luck.

I replied to every single one of the endorsement inquires, saying that I would accept their offers under the following conditions: I wouldn't have to reveal my true identity, and I would only do business through my OASIS avatar.

I started receiving replies within the hour, with contracts attached. I couldn't afford to have a lawyer look them over, but they all expired within a year's time, so I just went ahead and signed them electronically and e-mailed them back along with a three-dimensional model of my avatar, to be used for the commercials. I also received requests for an audio clip of my avatar's voice, so I sent them a synthesized clip of a deep baritone that made me sound like one of those guys who did voice-overs for movie trailers.

Once they received everything, my avatar's new sponsors informed me that they'd wire my first round of payments to my OASIS account within the next forty-eight hours. The amount of money I was going to receive wouldn't be enough to make me rich. Not by a long shot. But to a kid who'd grown up with nothing, it seemed like a fortune.

I did some quick calculations. If I lived frugally, I would have enough to move out of the stacks and rent a small efficiency apartment somewhere. For a year, at least. The very thought filled me with nervous excitement. I'd dreamed of escaping the stacks for as long as I could remember, and now it appeared that dream was about to come true.

With the endorsement deals taken care of, I continued to sort through my e-mail messages. When I sorted the remaining messages by sender, I discovered that I'd received over five thousand e-mails from Innovative Online Industries. Actually, they'd sent me five thousand copies of the same e-mail. They'd been resending the same message all week, since my name first appeared on the Scoreboard. And they were still resending it, once every minute.

The Sixers were mail-bombing me, to make sure they got my attention.

The e-mails were all marked *Maximum Priority,* with the subject line URGENT BUSINESS PROPOSITION—PLEASE READ IMMEDIATELY!

The second I opened one, a delivery confirmation was sent back to IOI, letting them know that I was finally reading their message. After that, they stopped resending it.

> Dear Parzival,
>
> First, allow me to congratulate you on your recent accomplishments, which we at Innovative Online Industries hold in the highest regard.
>
> On behalf of IOI, I wish to make you a highly lucrative business proposition, the exact details of which we can discuss in a private chatlink session. Please use the attached contact card to reach me at your earliest convenience, regardless of the day or hour.
>
> Given our reputation within the gunter community, I would understand if you were hesitant to speak with me. However, please be aware that if you choose not to accept our proposal, we intend to approach each of your competitors. At the very least, we hope you'll do us the honor of being the first to hear our generous offer. What have you got to lose?
>
> Thank you for your kind attention. I look forward to speaking with you.
>
> Sincerely,
>
> Nolan Sorrento
> Head of Operations
> Innovative Online Industries

Despite the message's reasonable tone, the threat behind it was crystal clear. The Sixers wanted to recruit me. Or they wanted to pay me to tell them how to find the Copper Key and clear the First Gate. And if I refused, they would go after Art3mis, then Aech, Daito, Shoto, and every other gunter who managed to get their name up on the Scoreboard. These shameless corporate sleazebags wouldn't stop until they found someone dumb enough or desperate enough to give in and sell them the information they needed.

My first impulse was to delete every single copy of the e-mail and pretend I'd never received it, but I changed my mind. I wanted to know exactly what IOI was going to offer. And I couldn't pass up the chance to meet Nolan Sorrento, the Sixers' infamous leader. There was no danger meeting with him via chatlink, as long as I was careful about what I said.

I considered teleporting to Incipio before my "interview," to buy a new skin for my avatar. Maybe a tailored suit. Something flashy and expensive. But then I thought better of it. I had nothing to prove to that corporate asshat. After all, I was famous now. I would roll into the meeting wearing my default skin and a fuck-off attitude. I would listen to their offer, then tell them to kiss my simulated ass. Maybe I'd record the whole thing and post it on YouTube.

I prepped for the meeting by pulling up a search engine and learning everything I could about Nolan Sorrento. He had a PhD in Computer Science. Prior to becoming head of operations at IOI, he'd been a high-profile game designer, overseeing the creation of several third-party RPGs that ran inside the OASIS. I'd played all of his games, and they were actually pretty good. He'd been a decent coder, back before he sold his soul. It was obvious why IOI had hired him to lead their lackeys. They figured a game designer would have the best chance of solving Halliday's grand videogame puzzle. But Sorrento and the Sixers had been at it for over five years and still had nothing to show for their efforts. And now that gunter avatar names were appearing on the Scoreboard left and right, the IOI brass had to be freaking out. Sorrento was probably catching all kinds of heat from his superiors. I wondered if it had been Sorrento's idea to try to recruit me, or if he'd been ordered to do it.

Once I'd done my homework on Sorrento, I felt like I was ready to sit down with the devil. I pulled up the contact card attached to Sorrento's e-mail and tapped the chatlink invitation icon at the bottom.

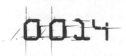

As I finished connecting to the chatlink session, my avatar materialized on a grand observation deck with a stunning view of over a dozen OASIS worlds suspended in black space beyond the curved window. I appeared to be on a space station or a very large transport ship; I couldn't tell which.

Chatlink sessions worked differently from chat rooms, and they were a lot more expensive to host. When you opened a chatlink, an insubstantial copy of your avatar was projected into another OASIS location. Your avatar wasn't actually there, and so it appeared to other avatars as a slightly transparent apparition. But you could still interact with the environment in a limited way—walking through doors, sitting in chairs, and so forth. Chatlinks were primarily used for business purposes, when a company wanted to host a meeting in a specific OASIS location without spending the time and money to transport everyone's avatars to it. This was the first time I'd ever used one.

I turned around and saw that my avatar was standing in front of a large C-shaped reception desk. The IOI corporate logo—giant, overlapping chrome letters twenty feet tall—floated above it. As I approached the desk, an impossibly beautiful blonde receptionist stood to greet me. "Mr. Parzival," she said, bowing slightly. "Welcome to Innovative Online Industries! Just a moment. Mr. Sorrento is already on his way to greet you."

I wasn't sure how that could be, since I hadn't warned them I was coming. While I waited, I tried to activate my avatar's vidfeed recorder, but

IOI had disabled recording in this chatlink session. They obviously didn't want me to have video evidence of what was about to go down. So much for my plan to post the interview on YouTube.

Less than a minute later, another avatar appeared, through a set of automatic doors on the opposite side of the observation deck. He headed right for me, boots clicking on the polished floor. It was Sorrento. I recognized him because he wasn't using a standard-issue Sixer avatar—one of the perks of his position. His avatar's face matched the photos of him I'd seen online. Blond hair and brown eyes, a hawkish nose. He did wear the standard Sixer uniform—a navy blue bodysuit with gold epaulettes at the shoulders and a silver IOI logo on his right breast, with his employee number printed beneath it: 655321.

"At last!" he said as he walked up, grinning like a jackal. "The famous Parzival has graced us with his presence!" He extended a gloved right hand. "Nolan Sorrento, chief of operations. It's an honor to meet you."

"Yeah," I said, doing my best to sound aloof. "Likewise, I guess." Even as a chatlink projection, my avatar could still mime shaking his outstretched hand. Instead I just stared down at it as if he were offering me a dead rat. He dropped it after a few seconds, but his smile didn't falter. It broadened.

"Please follow me." He led me across the deck and back through the automatic doors, which slid open to reveal a large launching bay. It contained a single interplanetary shuttlecraft emblazoned with the IOI logo. Sorrento began to board it, but I halted at the foot of the ramp.

"Why bother bringing me here via a chatlink?" I asked, motioning to the bay around us. "Why not just give me your sales pitch in a chat room?"

"Please, indulge me," he said. "This chatlink is *part* of our sales pitch. We want to give you the same experience you'd have if you came to visit our headquarters in person."

Right, I thought. *If I had come here in person, my avatar would be surrounded by thousands of Sixers and I'd be at your mercy.*

I joined him inside the shuttle. The ramp retracted and we launched out of the bay. Through the ship's wraparound windows I saw that we were leaving one of the Sixers' orbital space stations. Looming directly ahead of us was the planet IOI-1, a massive chrome globe. It reminded me of the killer floating spheres in the *Phantasm* films. Gunters referred to IOI-1 as "the Sixer homeworld." The company had constructed it shortly after the contest began, to serve as IOI's online base of operations.

Our shuttle, which seemed to be flying on automatic pilot, quickly reached the planet and began to skim its mirrored surface. I stared out the window as we did one complete orbit. As far as I knew, no gunter had ever been given this kind of tour.

From pole to pole, IOI-1 was covered with armories, bunkers, warehouses, and vehicle hangars. I also saw airfields dotting the surface, where rows of gleaming gunships, spacecraft, and mechanized battle tanks stood waiting for action. Sorrento said nothing as we surveyed the Sixer armada. He just let me take it all in.

I'd seen screenshots of IOI-1's surface before, but they'd been low-res and taken from high orbit, just beyond the planet's impressive defense grid. The larger clans had been openly plotting to nuke the Sixer Operations Complex for several years now, but they'd never managed to get past the defense grid or reach the planet's surface.

As we completed our orbit, the IOI Operations Complex swung into view ahead of us. It consisted of three mirror-surfaced towers—two rectangular skyscrapers on either side of a circular one. Seen from above, these three buildings formed the IOI logo.

The shuttle slowed and hovered above the O-shaped tower, then spiraled down to a small landing pad on the roof. "Impressive digs, wouldn't you agree?" Sorrento said, finally breaking his silence as we touched down and the ramp lowered.

"Not bad." I was proud of the calm in my voice. In truth, I was still reeling from everything I'd just seen. "This is an OASIS replica of the real IOI towers located in downtown Columbus, right?" I said.

Sorrento nodded. "Yes, the Columbus complex is our company headquarters. Most of my team works in this central tower. Our close proximity to GSS eliminates any possibility of system lag. And, of course, Columbus doesn't suffer from the rolling power blackouts that plague most major U.S. cities."

He was stating the obvious. Gregarious Simulation Systems was located in Columbus, and so was their main OASIS server vault. Redundant mirror servers were located all over the world, but they were all linked to the main node in Columbus. This was why, in the decades since the simulation's launch, the city had become a kind of high-tech Mecca. Columbus was where an OASIS user could get the fastest, most reliable connection to the simulation. Most gunters dreamed of moving there someday, me included.

I followed Sorrento off the shuttle and into an elevator adjacent to the landing pad. "You've become quite the celebrity these past few days," he said as we began to descend. "It must be very exciting for you. Probably a little scary, too, huh? Knowing you now possess information that millions of people would be willing to kill for?"

I'd been waiting for him to say something like this, so I had a reply prepared. "Do you mind skipping the scare tactics and the head games? Just tell me the details of your offer. I have other matters to attend to."

He grinned at me like I was a precocious child. "Yes, I'm sure you do," he said. "But please don't jump to any conclusions about our offer. I think you'll be quite surprised." Then, with a sudden touch of steel in his tone, he added, "In fact, I'm certain of it."

Doing my best to hide the intimidation I felt, I rolled my eyes and said, "Whatever, man."

A tone sounded as we reached the 106th floor, and the elevator doors swished open. I followed Sorrento past another receptionist and down a long, brightly lit corridor. The decor was something out of a utopian sci-fi flick. High-tech and immaculate. We passed several other Sixer avatars as we walked, and the moment they saw Sorrento, they each snapped to rigid attention and saluted him, as if he were some high-ranking general. Sorrento didn't return these salutes or acknowledge his underlings in any way.

Eventually, he led me into a huge open room that appeared to occupy most of the 106th floor. It contained a vast sea of high-walled cubicles, each containing a single person strapped into a high-end immersion rig.

"Welcome to IOI's Oology Division," Sorrento said with obvious pride.

"So, this is Suxorz Central, eh?" I said, glancing around.

"There's no need to be rude," Sorrento said. "This could be your team."

"Would I get my very own cubicle?"

"No. You'd have your own office, with a very nice view." He grinned. "Not that you'd spend much time looking at it."

I motioned to one of the new Habashaw immersion rigs. "Nice gear," I said. It really was, too. State-of-the-art.

"Yes, it *is* nice, isn't it?" he said. "Our immersion rigs are heavily modified, and they're all networked together. Our systems allow multiple operators to control any one of our oologist's avatars. So depending on the obstacles an avatar encounters during their quest, control can be instantly transferred to the team member with the skills best suited to deal with the situation."

"Yeah, but that's cheating," I said.

"Oh, come on now," he said, rolling his eyes. "There's no such thing. Halliday's contest doesn't have any rules. That's one of the many colossal mistakes the old fool made." Before I could reply, Sorrento started walking again, leading me on through the maze of cubicles. "All of our oologists are voice-linked to a support team," he continued. "Composed of Halliday scholars, videogame experts, pop-culture historians, and cryptologists. They all work together to help each of our avatars overcome any challenge and solve every puzzle they encounter." He turned and grinned at me. "As you can see, we've covered all the bases, Parzival. That's why we're going to win."

"Yeah," I said. "You guys have been doing a bang-up job so far. Bravo. Now, why is it that we're talking again? Oh, right. You guys have no clue where the Copper Key is, and you need my help to find it."

Sorrento narrowed his eyes; then he began to laugh. "I like you, kid," he said, grinning at me. "You're bright. And you've got cojones. Two qualities I greatly admire."

We continued walking. A few minutes later, we arrived in Sorrento's enormous office. Its windows afforded a stunning view of the surrounding "city." The sky was filled with aircars and spacecraft, and the planet's simulated sun was just beginning to set. Sorrento sat down behind his desk and offered me the chair directly across from him.

Here we go, I thought as I sat down. *Play it cool, Wade.*

"So I'll just cut to the chase," he said. "IOI wants to recruit you. As a consultant, to assist with our search for Halliday's Easter egg. You'll have all of our company's vast resources at your disposal. Money, weapons, magic items, ships, artifacts. You name it."

"What would my title be?"

"*Chief oologist,*" he replied. "You'd be in charge of the entire division, second-in-command only to me. I'm talking about five thousand highly trained combat-ready avatars, all taking orders directly from you."

"Sounds pretty sweet," I said, trying hard to sound nonchalant.

"Of course it does. But there's more. In exchange for your services, we're willing to pay you two million dollars a year, with a one-million-dollar signing bonus up front. And if and when you help us find the egg, you'll get a twenty-five-million-dollar bonus."

I pretended to add all of those numbers up on my fingers. "Wow," I said, trying to sound impressed. "Can I work from home, too?"

Sorrento couldn't seem to tell whether or not I was joking. "No," he said. "I'm afraid not. You'd have to relocate here to Columbus. But we'll provide you with excellent living quarters here on the premises. And a private office, of course. Your own state-of-the-art immersion rig—"

"Hold on," I said, holding up a hand. "You mean I'd have to live in the IOI skyscraper? With you? And all of the other Sux— *oologists*?"

He nodded. "Just until you help us find the egg."

I resisted the urge to gag. "What about benefits? Would I get health care? Dental? Vision? Keys to the executive washroom? Shit like that?"

"Of course." He was starting to sound impatient. "So? What do you say?"

"Can I think about it for a few days?"

"Afraid not," he said. "This could all be over in a few days. We need your answer now."

I leaned back and stared at the ceiling, pretending to consider the offer. Sorrento waited, watching me intently. I was about to give him my prepared answer when he raised a hand.

"Just listen to me a moment before you answer," Sorrento said. "I know most gunters cling to the absurd notion that IOI is evil. And that the Sixers are ruthless corporate drones with no honor and no respect for the 'true spirit' of the contest. That we're all sellouts. Right?"

I nodded, barely resisting the urge to say "That's putting it mildly."

"Well, that's ridiculous," he said, flashing an avuncular grin that I suspected was generated by whatever diplomacy software he was running. "The Sixers are really no different than a Gunter clan, albeit a well-funded one. We share all the same obsessions as gunters. And we have the same goal."

What goal is that? I wanted to shout. *To ruin the OASIS forever? To pervert and defile the only thing that has ever made our lives bearable?*

Sorrento seemed to take my silence as a cue that he should continue. "You know, contrary to popular belief, the OASIS really won't change that drastically when IOI takes control of it. Sure, we'll have to start charging everyone a monthly user fee. And increase the sim's advertising revenue. But we also plan to make a lot of improvements. Avatar content filters. Stricter construction guidelines. We're going to make the OASIS a better place."

No, I thought. *You're going to turn it into a fascist corporate theme park where the few people who can still afford the price of admission no longer have an ounce of freedom.*

I'd heard as much of this jerk's sales pitch as I could stand.

"OK," I said. "Count me in. Sign me up. Whatever you guys call it. I'm in."

Sorrento looked surprised. This clearly wasn't the answer he'd been expecting. He smiled wide and was about to offer me his hand again when I cut him off.

"But I have three minor conditions," I said. "First, I want a fifty-million-dollar bonus when I find the egg for you guys. Not twenty-five. Is that doable?"

He didn't even hesitate. "Done. What are your other conditions?"

"I don't want to be second-in-command," I said. "I want your job, Sorrento. I want to be in charge of the whole shebang. Chief of operations. *El Numero Uno*. Oh, and I want everyone to have to call me *El Numero Uno*, too. Is that possible?"

My mouth seemed to be operating independent of my brain. I couldn't help myself.

Sorrento's smile had vanished. "What else?"

"I don't want to work with you." I leveled a finger at him. "You give me the creeps. But if your superiors are willing to fire your ass and give me your position, I'm in. It's a done deal."

Silence. Sorrento's face was a stoic mask. He probably had certain emotions, like anger and rage, filtered out on his facial-recognition software.

"Could you check with your bosses and let me know if they'll agree to that?" I asked. "Or are they monitoring us right now? I'm betting they are." I waved to the invisible cameras. "Hi, guys! What do you say?"

There was a long silence, during which Sorrento simply glared at me. "Of course they're monitoring us," he said finally. "And they've just informed me that they're willing to agree to each of your demands." He didn't sound all that upset.

"Really?" I said. "Great! When can I start? And more importantly, when can you leave?"

"Immediately," he said. "The company will prepare your contract and send it to your lawyer for approval. Then we—*they* will fly you here to Columbus to sign the paperwork and close the deal." He stood. "That should conclude—"

"Actually—" I held up a hand, cutting him off again. "I've spent the last few seconds thinking this over a bit more, and I'm gonna have to pass on your offer. I think I'd rather find the egg on my own, thanks." I stood up. "You and the other Suxorz can all go fuck a duck."

Sorrento began to laugh. A long, hearty laugh that I found more than a little disturbing. "Oh, you're good! That was *so* good! You really had us going there, kid!" When his laughter tapered off, he said, "*That's* the answer I was expecting. So now, let me give you our second proposal."

"There's more?" I sat back down and put my feet up on his desk. "OK. Shoot."

"We'll wire five million dollars directly to your OASIS account, *right now,* in exchange for a walkthrough up to the First Gate. That's it. All you have to do is give us detailed step-by-step instructions on how to do what you've already done. We'll take it from there. You'll be free to continue searching for the egg on your own. And our transaction will remain a complete secret. No one ever need know of it."

I admit, I actually considered it for a second. Five million dollars would set me up for life. And even if I helped the Sixers clear the First Gate, there was no guarantee they'd be able to clear the other two. I still wasn't even sure if *I* would be able to do that.

"Trust me, son," Sorrento said. "You should take this offer. While you can."

His paternal tone irked me to no end, and that helped to steel my resolve. I couldn't sell out to the Sixers. If I did, and they did somehow manage to win the contest, I'd be the one responsible. There was no way I'd be able to live with that. I just hoped that Aech, Art3mis, and any other gunters they approached felt the same way.

"I'll pass," I said. I slid my feet off his desk and stood. "Thanks for your time."

Sorrento looked at me sadly, then motioned for me to sit back down. "Actually, we're not quite done here. We have one final proposal for you, Parzival. And I saved the best for last."

"Can't you take a hint? *You can't buy me.* So piss off. Adios. Good. Bye."

"Sit down, Wade."

I froze. Had he just used my real name?

"That's right," Sorrento barked. "We know who you are. Wade Owen Watts. Born August twelfth, 2024. Both parents deceased. And we also know *where* you are. You reside with your aunt, in a trailer park located at

700 Portland Avenue in Oklahoma City. Unit 56-K, to be exact. According to our surveillance team, you were last seen entering your aunt's trailer three days ago and you haven't left since. Which means you're still there right now."

A vidfeed window opened directly behind him, displaying a live video image of the stacks where I lived. It was an aerial view, maybe being shot from a plane or a satellite. From this angle, they could only monitor the trailer's two main exits. So they hadn't seen me leave through the laundry room window each morning, or return through it each night. They didn't know I was actually in my hideout right now.

"There you are," Sorrento said. His pleasant, condescending tone had returned. "You should really get out more, Wade. It's not healthy to spend all of your time indoors." The image magnified a few times, zooming in on my aunt's trailer. Then it switched over to thermal-imaging mode, and I could see the glowing outlines of over a dozen people, children and adults, sitting inside. Nearly all of them were motionless—probably logged into the OASIS.

I was too stunned to speak. How had they found me? It was supposed to be impossible for anyone to obtain your OASIS account information. And my address wasn't even *in* my OASIS account. You didn't have to provide it when you created your avatar. Just your name and retinal pattern. So how had they found out where I lived?

Somehow they must have gotten access to my school records.

"Your first instinct right now might be to log out and make a run for it," Sorrento said. "I urge you not to make that mistake. Your trailer is currently wired with a large quantity of high explosives." He pulled something that looked like a remote control out of his pocket and held it up. "And my finger is on the detonator. If you log out of this chatlink session, you will die within a few seconds. Do you understand what I'm saying to you, Mr. Watts?"

I nodded slowly, trying desperately to get a grip on the situation.

He was bluffing. He *had* to be bluffing. And even if he wasn't, he didn't know that I was actually half a mile away, in my hideout. Sorrento assumed that one of the glowing thermal outlines on the display was me.

If a bomb really did go off in my aunt's trailer, I'd be safe down here, under all these junk cars. Wouldn't I? Besides, they would never kill all those people just to get to me.

"How—?" That was all I could get out.

"How did we find out who you are? And where you live?" He grinned. "Easy. You screwed up, kid. When you enrolled in the OASIS public school system, you gave them your name and address. So they could mail you your report cards, I suppose."

He was right. My avatar's name, my real name, and my home address were all stored in my private student file, which only the principal could access. It was a stupid mistake, but I'd enrolled the year before the contest even began. Before I became a gunter. Before I learned to conceal my real-world identity.

"How did you find out I attend school online?" I asked. I already knew the answer, but I needed to stall for time.

"There's been a rumor circulating on the gunter message boards the past few days that you and your pal Aech both go to school on Ludus. When we heard that, we decided to contact a few OPS administrators and offer them a bribe. Do you know how little a school administrator makes a year, Wade? It's scandalous. One of your principals was kind enough to search the student database for the avatar name Parzival, and guess what?"

Another window appeared beside the live video feed of the stacks. It displayed my entire student profile. My full name, avatar name, student alias (Wade3), date of birth, Social Security number, and home address. My school transcripts. It was all there, along with an old yearbook photo, taken over five years ago—right before I'd transferred to school in the OASIS.

"We have your friend Aech's school records too. But he was smart enough to give a fake name and address when he enrolled. So finding him will take a bit longer."

He paused to let me reply, but I remained silent. My pulse was racing, and I had to keep reminding myself to breathe.

"So, that brings me to our final proposal." Sorrento rubbed his hands together excitedly, like a kid about to open a present. "Tell us how to reach the First Gate. Right now. Or we will kill you. Right now."

"You're bluffing," I heard myself say. But I didn't think he was. Not at all.

"No, Wade. I'm not. Think about it. With everything else that's going on in the world, do you think anyone will care about an explosion in some ghetto-trash rat warren in Oklahoma City? They'll assume it was a drug-lab accident. Or maybe a domestic terrorist cell trying to build a homemade bomb. Either way, it will just mean there are a few hundred less human cockroaches out there collecting food vouchers and using up precious oxygen. No one will care. And the authorities won't even blink."

He was right, and I knew it. I tried to stall for a few seconds so I could figure out what to do. "You'd kill me?" I said. "To win a videogame contest?"

"Don't pretend to be naïve, Wade," Sorrento said. "There are billions of dollars at stake here, along with control of one of the world's most profitable corporations, and of the OASIS itself. This is much more than a videogame contest. It always has been." He leaned forward. "But you can still come out a winner here, kid. If you help us, we'll still give you the five million. You can retire at age eighteen and spend the rest of your days living like royalty. Or you can die in the next few seconds. It's your call. But ask yourself this question—if your mother were still alive, what would she want you to do?"

That last question would really have pissed me off if I hadn't been so scared. "What's to stop you from killing me after I give you what you want?" I asked.

"Regardless of what you may think, we don't want to have to kill anyone unless it's absolutely necessary. Besides, there are two more gates, right?" He shrugged. "We might need your help to figure those out too. Personally, I doubt it. But my superiors feel differently. Regardless, you don't really have a choice at this point, do you?" He lowered his voice, as if he were about to share a secret. "So here's what's going to happen next. You're going to give me step-by-step instructions on how to obtain the Copper Key and clear the First Gate. And you're going to stay logged into this chatlink session while we verify everything you tell us. Log out before I say it's OK, and your whole world goes boom. Understand? Now start talking."

I considered giving them what they wanted. I really did. But I thought it through, and I couldn't come up with a single good reason why they would let me live, even if I helped them clear the First Gate. The only move that made sense was to kill me and take me out of the running. They sure as hell weren't going to give me five million dollars, or leave me alive to tell the media how IOI had blackmailed me. Especially if there really was a remote-controlled bomb planted in my trailer to serve as evidence.

No. The way I saw it, there were really only two possibilities: Either they were bluffing or they were going to kill me, whether I helped them or not.

I made my decision and summoned my courage.

"Sorrento," I said, trying to hide the fear in my voice, "I want you and your bosses to know something. You're never going to find Halliday's egg. You know why? Because he was smarter than all of you put together. It doesn't matter how much money you have or who you try to blackmail. *You're going to lose.*"

I tapped my Log-out icon, and my avatar began to dematerialize in front of him. He didn't seem surprised. He just looked at me sadly and shook his head. "Stupid move, kid," he said, just before my visor went black.

I sat there in the darkness of my hideout, wincing and waiting for the detonation. But a full minute passed and nothing happened.

I slid my visor up and pulled off my gloves with shaking hands. As my eyes began to adjust to the darkness, I let out a tentative sigh of relief. It had been a bluff after all. Sorrento had been playing an elaborate mind game with me. An effective one too.

As I was gulping down a bottle of water, I realized that I should log back in and warn Aech and Art3mis. The Sixers would go after them next.

I was pulling my gloves back on when I heard the explosion.

I felt the shock wave a split second after I heard the detonation and instinctively dropped to the floor of my hideout with my arms wrapped over my head. In the distance, I could hear the sound of rending metal as several trailer stacks began to collapse, ripping free of their scaffolding and crashing against one another like massive dominoes. These horrific sounds continued for what seemed like a very long time. Then it was silent again.

I eventually overcame my paralysis and opened the rear door of the van. In a nightmare-like daze, I made my way to the outskirts of the junk pile, and from there, I could see a giant pillar of smoke and flames rising from the opposite end of the stacks.

I followed the stream of people already running in that direction, along the northern perimeter of the stacks. The stack containing my aunt's trailer had collapsed into a fiery, smoking ruin, along with all of the stacks adjacent to it. There was nothing there now but a massive pile of twisted, flaming metal.

I kept my distance, but a large crowd of people had already gathered up ahead of me, standing as close to the blaze as they dared. No one bothered trying to enter the wreckage to look for survivors. It was obvious there weren't going to be any.

An ancient propane tank attached to one of the crushed trailers detonated in a small explosion, causing the crowd to scatter and dive for cover. Several more tanks detonated in rapid succession. After that, the onlookers moved much farther back and kept their distance.

The residents who lived in the nearby stacks knew that if the fire spread, they were in big trouble. So a lot of people were already scrambling to fight the blaze, using garden hoses, buckets, empty Big Gulp cups, and whatever else they could find. Before long, the flames were contained and the fire began to die out.

As I watched in silence, I could already hear the people around me murmuring, saying that it was probably another meth-lab accident, or that some idiot must have been trying to build a homemade bomb. Just as Sorrento had predicted.

That thought snapped me out of my daze. What was I thinking? The Sixers had just tried to kill me. They probably still had agents lurking here in the stacks, checking to make sure I was dead. And like a total idiot I was standing right out in the open.

I faded away from the crowd and hurried back to my hideout, being careful not to run, constantly glancing over my shoulder to make sure I wasn't being followed. Once I was back inside the van, I slammed and locked the door, then curled into a quivering ball in the corner. I stayed like that for a long time.

Eventually, the shock began to wear off, and the reality of what had just happened started to sink in. My aunt Alice and her boyfriend Rick were dead, along with everyone who had lived in our trailer, and in the trailers below and around it. Including sweet old Mrs. Gilmore. And if I had been at home, I would be dead now too.

I was jacked up on adrenaline, unsure of what to do next, overcome by a paralyzing mixture of fear and rage. I thought about logging into the OASIS to call the police, but then considered how they would react when I told them my story. They'd think I was a raving nut job. And if I called the media, they'd react the same way. There was no way anyone would believe my story. Not unless I revealed that I was Parzival, and maybe not even then. I didn't have a shred of proof against Sorrento and the Sixers. All traces of the bomb they'd planted were probably melting into slag right now.

Revealing my identity to the world so that I could accuse one of the world's most powerful corporations of blackmail and murder didn't seem like the smartest move. No one would believe me. I could barely believe it myself. IOI had actually tried to kill me. To prevent me from winning a videogame contest. It was insane.

I seemed to be safe in my hideout for the moment, but I knew I couldn't stay in the stacks much longer. When the Sixers found out I was still alive, they would come back here looking for me. I needed to get the hell out of Dodge. But I couldn't do that until I had some money, and my first endorsement checks wouldn't be deposited for another day or two. I would just have to lie low until then. But right now, I needed to talk to Aech, to warn him that he was next on the Sixers' hit list.

I was also desperate to see a friendly face.

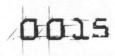

I grabbed my OASIS console and powered it on, then pulled on my visor and gloves. As I logged in, my avatar reappeared on Ludus, on the hilltop where I'd been sitting prior to my chat-room session with Sorrento. The moment my audio kicked in, I heard the earsplitting roar of engines coming from somewhere directly overheard. I stepped out from under the tree and looked up. I saw a squadron of Sixer gunships flying in formation, zooming south at low altitude, their sensors scanning the surface as they went.

I was about to duck back under the tree, out of sight, when I remembered that all of Ludus was a no-PvP zone. The Sixers couldn't harm me here. Even so, my nerves were still on edge. I continued to scan the sky and quickly spotted two more Sixer gunship squadrons off near the eastern horizon. A moment later, several more squadrons dropped in from orbit to the north and west. It looked like an alien invasion.

An icon flashed on my display, informing me that I had a new text message from Aech: *Where the hell are you? Call me ASAFP!*

I tapped his name on my contact list, and he answered on the first ring. His avatar's face appeared in my vidfeed window. He was wearing a grim expression.

"Did you hear the news?" he asked.

"What news?"

"The Sixers are on Ludus. Thousands of them. More arriving every minute. They're searching the planet, looking for the tomb."

"Yeah. I'm on Ludus right now. Sixer gunships everywhere. "

Aech scowled. "When I find I-rok, I'm going to kill him. Slowly. Then, when he creates a new avatar, I'm going to hunt him down and kill him again. If that moron had kept his mouth shut, the Sixers never would have thought to look here."

"Yeah. His forum posts were what tipped them off. Sorrento said so himself."

"Sorrento? As in *Nolan Sorrento*?"

I told him everything that had happened in the past few hours.

"They blew up your house?"

"Actually, it was a trailer," I said. "In a trailer park. They killed a lot of people here, Aech. It's probably already on the newsfeeds." I took a deep breath. "I'm freaking out. I'm scared."

"I don't blame you," he said. "Thank God you weren't home when it happened. . . ."

I nodded. "I almost never log in from home. Luckily, the Sixers didn't know that."

"What about your family?"

"It was my aunt's place. She's dead, I think. We . . . we weren't very close." This was a huge understatement, of course. My aunt Alice had never shown me much kindness, but she still hadn't deserved to die. But most of the wrenching guilt I now felt had to do with Mrs. Gilmore, and the knowledge that my actions had gotten her killed. She was one of the sweetest people I'd ever known.

I realized that I was sobbing. I muted my audio so Aech wouldn't hear, then took several deep breaths until I got myself under control again.

"I can't believe this!" Aech growled. "Those evil pricks. They're gonna pay, Z. Count on it. *We will make them pay for this.*"

I couldn't see how, but I didn't argue. I knew he was just trying to make me feel better.

"Where are you right now?" Aech asked. "Do you need help? Like, a place to stay or something? I can wire you some money if you need it."

"No, I'm OK," I said. "But thanks, man. I really appreciate the offer."

"De nada, amigo."

"Listen, did the Sixers send you the same e-mail they sent me?"

"Yeah. Thousands of them. But I decided it was best to ignore them."

I frowned. "I wish I'd been smart enough to do that."

"Dude, you had no way of knowing they were gonna try and kill you! Besides, they already had your home address. If you'd ignored their e-mails, they probably would have set off that bomb anyway."

"Listen, Aech . . . Sorrento said that your school records contained a fake home address, and that they don't know where to find you. But he might have been lying. You should leave home. Go somewhere safe. As soon as possible."

"Don't worry about me, Z. I stay mobile. Those bastards will never find me."

"If you say so," I replied, wondering what exactly he meant. "But I need to warn Art3mis, too. And Daito and Shoto, if I can reach them. The Sixers are probably doing everything they can to learn their identities too."

"That gives me an idea," he said. "We should invite all three of them to meet us in the Basement later tonight. Say around midnight? A private chat-room session. Just the five of us."

My mood brightened at the prospect of seeing Art3mis again. "Do you think they'll all agree to come?"

"Yeah, if we let them know their lives depend on it." He smirked. "And we're going to have the world's top five gunters together in one chat room. Who's gonna sit that out?"

•　•　•

I sent Art3mis a short message, asking her to meet us in Aech's private chat room at midnight. She replied just a few minutes later, promising to be there. Aech told me he'd managed to reach Daito and Shoto, and they had both also agreed to attend. The meeting was set.

I didn't feel like being alone, so I logged into the Basement about an hour early. Aech was already there, surfing the newsfeeds on the ancient RCA television. Without saying a word, he got up and gave me a hug. Even though I couldn't actually feel it, I found it surprisingly comforting. Then we both sat down and watched the news coverage together while we waited for the others to arrive.

Every channel was airing OASIS footage showing the hordes of Sixer spacecraft and troops that were currently arriving on Ludus. It was easy for everyone to guess why they were there, and so now every gunter in the simulation was also headed for Ludus. Transport terminals all over the planet were jammed with incoming avatars.

"So much for keeping the tomb's location a secret," I said, shaking my head.

"It was bound to leak out eventually," Aech said, shutting off the TV. "I just didn't think it would happen this fast."

We both heard an entrance alert chime as Art3mis materialized at the top of the staircase. She was wearing the same outfit she'd had on the night we met. She waved to me as she descended the steps. I waved back, then made introductions.

"Aech, meet Art3mis. Art3mis, this is my best friend, Aech."

"Pleasure to meet you," Art3mis said, extending her right hand.

Aech shook it. "Likewise." He flashed his Cheshire grin. "Thanks for coming."

"Are you kidding? How could I miss it? The very first meeting of the High Five."

"The High Five?" I said.

"Yeah," Aech said. "That's what they're calling us on all of the message boards now. We hold the top five high-score slots on the Scoreboard. So we're the High Five."

"Right," I said. "At least for the time being."

Art3mis grinned at that, then turned and began to wander around the Basement, admiring the '80s decor. "Aech, this is, by far, the coolest chat room I've ever seen."

"Thank you." He bowed his head. "Kind of you to say."

She stopped to browse through the shelf of role-playing game supplements. "You've re-created Morrow's basement perfectly. Every last detail. I want to *live* here."

"You've got a permanent spot on the guest list. Log in and hang out anytime."

"Really?" she said, clearly delighted. "Thank you! I will. You're the man, Aech."

"Yes," he said, smiling. "It's true. I am."

They really seemed to be hitting it off, and it was making me crazy jealous. I didn't want Art3mis to like Aech, or vice versa. I wanted her all to myself.

Daito and Shoto logged in a moment later, appearing simultaneously at the top of the basement staircase. Daito was the taller of the two, and appeared to be in his late teens. Shoto was a foot shorter and looked much younger. Maybe about thirteen. Both avatars looked Japanese, and they bore a striking resemblance to one another, like snapshots of the same young man taken five years apart. They wore matching suits of traditional samurai armor, and each had both a short wakizashi and a longer katana strapped to his belt.

"Greetings," the taller samurai said. "I am Daito. And this is my little brother, Shoto. Thank you for the invitation. We are honored to meet all three of you."

They bowed in unison. Aech and Art3mis returned the bow, and I quickly followed suit. As we each introduced ourselves, Daito and Shoto bowed to us once again, and once again we each returned the gesture.

"All right," Aech said, once all the bowing had ended. "Let's get this party started. I'm sure you've all seen the news. The Sixers are swarming all over Ludus. Thousands of them. They're conducting a systematic search of the entire surface of the planet. Even if they don't know exactly what they're looking for, it still won't be long before they find the entrance to the tomb—"

"Actually," Art3mis interrupted, "they already found it. Over thirty minutes ago."

We all turned to look at her.

"That hasn't been reported on the newsfeeds yet," Daito said. "Are you sure?"

She nodded. "Afraid so. When I heard about the Sixers this morning, I decided to hide an uplink camera in some trees near the tomb entrance, to keep an eye on the area." She opened a vidfeed window in the air in front of her and spun it around so the rest of us could see. It showed a wide shot of the flat-topped hill and the clearing around it, looking down from a spot in one of the trees high above. From this angle, it was easy to see that the large black stones on top of the hill were arranged to look like a human skull. We could also see that the entire area was crawling with Sixers, and more seemed to be arriving every second.

But the most disturbing thing we saw on the vidfeed was the large transparent dome of energy that now covered the entire hill.

"Son of a bitch," Aech said. "Is that what I think it is?"

Art3mis nodded. "A force field. The Sixers installed it just after the first of them arrived. So . . ."

"So from here on out," Daito said, "any gunter who finds the tomb won't be able to get inside. Not unless they can somehow get through that force field."

"Actually, they've put up *two* force fields," Art3mis said. "A small field with a larger field over it. They lower them in sequence, whenever they want to let more Sixers enter the tomb. Like an air lock." She pointed to the window. "Watch. They're doing it now."

A squadron of Sixers marched down the loading ramp of a gunship parked nearby. They were all lugging equipment containers. As they approached the outer force field, it vanished, revealing a smaller domed field inside the first. As soon as the squadron reached the wall of the inner force field, the outer field reappeared. A second later, the inner force field was dropped, allowing the Sixers to enter the tomb.

There was a long silence while we all contemplated this new development.

"I suppose it could be worse," Aech said finally. "If the tomb were in a PvP zone, those assholes would already have laser cannons and robot sentries mounted everywhere, to vaporize anyone who approached the area."

He was right. Since Ludus was a safe zone, the Sixers couldn't harm gunters who approached the tomb. But there was nothing to stop them from erecting a force field to keep them out. So that was exactly what they'd done.

"The Sixers have obviously been planning for this moment for some time now," Art3mis said, closing her vidfeed window.

"They won't be able to keep everyone out for very long," Aech said. "When the clans find out about this, it'll be all-out war. There will be thousands of gunters attacking that force field with everything they've got. RPGs. Fireballs. Cluster bombs. Nukes. It's gonna get ugly. They'll turn that forest into a wasteland."

"Yeah, but in the meantime, Sixer avatars will be farming the Copper Key and then filing their avatars through the First Gate, one after another, in a freakin' conga line."

"But how can they do this?" Shoto asked, his young voice brimming with rage. He looked to his brother. "It's not fair. They're not playing fair."

"They don't have to. There are no laws in the OASIS, little brother," Daito said. "The Sixers can do whatever they please. They won't stop until someone stops them."

"The Sixers have no honor," Shoto said, scowling.

"You guys don't know the half of it," Aech said. "That's why Parzival and I asked you all here." He turned to me. "Z, do you want to tell them what happened?"

I nodded and turned to the others. First, I told them about the e-mail I'd received from IOI. They'd all received the same invitation, but had wisely ignored it. Then I related the details of my chat-room session with Sorrento, doing my best not to leave anything out. Finally, I told them how our conversation had ended—with a bomb detonating at my home address. By the time I'd finished, their avatars all wore looks of stunned disbelief.

"Jesus," Art3mis whispered. "No joke? They tried to kill you?"

"Yeah. They would have succeeded, too, if I'd been at home. I was just lucky."

"Now you all know how far the Sixers are willing to go to stop us from beating them to the egg," Aech said. "If they're able to locate any one of us, we're dead meat."

I nodded. "So you should all take precautions to protect yourselves and your identities," I said. "If you haven't already."

They all nodded. There was another long silence.

"There's still one thing I don't understand," Art3mis said a moment later. "How did the Sixers know to look for the tomb on Ludus? Did someone tip them off?" She glanced around at each of us, but there was no hint of accusation in her voice.

"They must have seen the rumors about Parzival and Aech that were posted on all of the gunter message boards," Shoto said. "That's how we knew to look there."

Daito winced, then punched his little brother in the shoulder. "Didn't I tell you to keep quiet, blabbermouth?" he hissed. Shoto looked sheepish and clammed up.

"What rumors?" Art3mis asked. She looked at me. "What's he talking about? I haven't had time to check the boards in a few days."

"Several posts were made by gunters who claimed to know Parzival and Aech, saying they were both students on Ludus." He turned to Aech and me. "My brother and I have spent the past two years searching for the Tomb of Horrors. We've scoured dozens of worlds looking for it. But we never thought to look on Ludus. Not until we heard that you attended school there."

"It never occurred to me that attending school on Ludus was something I needed to keep a secret," I said. "So I didn't."

"Yeah, and it's lucky for us that you didn't," Aech said. He turned to the others. "Parzival unintentionally tipped me off about the tomb's location, too. I never thought to look for it on Ludus, either, until his name appeared on the Scoreboard."

Daito nudged his younger brother, and they both faced me and bowed. "You were the first to find the tomb's hiding place, so we owe you our gratitude for leading us to it."

I returned their bow. "Thanks, guys. But actually, Art3mis here found it first. Totally on her own. A month before I did."

"Yeah, for all the good it did me," Art3mis said. "I couldn't defeat the lich at Joust. I'd been at it for weeks when this punk showed up and did it on his first try." She explained how we met, and how she finally managed to beat the king the following day, right after the server reset at midnight.

"I have Aech here to thank for my jousting prowess," I said. "We used to play all the time, here in the Basement. That's the only reason I beat the king on my first attempt."

"Ditto," Aech said. He stretched out his hand and we bumped fists.

Daito and Shoto both smiled. "It was the same with us," Daito said. "My brother and I have been playing Joust against one another for years, because the game was mentioned in *Anorak's Almanac*."

"Great," Art3mis said, throwing up her hands. "Good for you guys. You were all prepared in advance. I'm so happy for you. Bravo." She gave us all a sarcastic golf clap, which made everyone laugh. "Now, can we adjourn the Mutual Admiration Society and get back to the topic at hand?"

"Sure," Aech said, smiling. "What *was* the topic at hand?"

"The Sixers?" Art3mis offered.

"Right! Of course!" Aech rubbed the back of his neck while biting his lower lip, something he always did when he was trying to gather his thoughts. "You said they found the tomb less than an hour ago, right? So any minute now, they'll reach the throne room and face off against the lich. But what do you think happens when multiple avatars enter the burial chamber at the same time?"

I turned to Daito and Shoto. "Your names appeared on the Scoreboard on the same day, just a few minutes apart. So you entered the throne room together, didn't you?"

Daito nodded. "Yes," he said. "And when we stepped on the dais, two copies of the king appeared, one for each of us to play."

"Great," Art3mis said. "So it might be possible for hundreds of Sixers to joust for the Copper Key at the same time. Or even thousands."

"Yeah," Shoto said. "But to get the key, each Sixer has to beat the lich at Joust, which we all know isn't easy."

"The Sixers are using hacked immersion rigs," I said. "Sorrento was boasting about it to me. They've got it set up so that different users can control the actions of every one of their avatars. So they can just have their best Joust players take control of each Sixer avatar during the match against Acererak. One after the other."

"Cheating bastards," Aech repeated.

"The Sixers have no honor," Daito said, shaking his head.

"Yeah," Art3mis said, rolling her eyes. "We've established that."

"It gets worse," I said. "Every Sixer has a support team made up of Halliday scholars, videogame experts, and cryptologists who are there to help them beat every challenge and solve every puzzle they encounter. Playing through the *WarGames* simulation will be a piece of cake for them. Someone will just feed them the dialogue."

"Unbelievable," Aech muttered. "How are we supposed to compete with that?"

"We can't," Art3mis said. "Once they have the Copper Key, they'll probably locate the First Gate just as quickly as we all did. It won't take them very long to catch up with us. And once they have the riddle about the Jade Key, they'll have their eggheads working around the clock to decipher it."

"If they find the Jade Key's hiding place before we do, they'll barricade it, too," I said. "And then the five of us will be in the same boat everyone else is in right now."

Art3mis nodded. Aech kicked the coffee table in frustration. "This isn't even remotely fair," he said. "The Sixers have a huge advantage over all of us. They've got an endless supply of money, weapons, vehicles, and avatars. There are thousands of them, all working together."

"Right," I said. "And each of us is on our own. Well, except for you two." I nodded at Daito and Shoto. "But you know what I mean. They've got us outnumbered and outgunned, and that isn't going to change anytime soon."

"What are you suggesting?" Daito asked. He suddenly sounded uneasy.

"I'm not suggesting anything," I said. "I'm just stating the facts, as I see them."

"Good," Daito replied. "Because it sounded like you were about to propose some sort of alliance between the five of us."

Aech studied him carefully. "So? Would that be such a terrible idea?"

"Yes, it would," Daito said curtly. "My brother and I hunt alone. We don't want or need your help."

"Oh really?" Aech said. "A second ago, you admitted needing Parzival's help to find the Tomb of Horrors."

Daito's eyes narrowed. "We would have found it on our own eventually."

"Right," Aech said. "It probably would have only taken you another *five years*."

"Come on, Aech," I said, stepping between them. "This isn't helping."

Aech and Daito glared at each other in silence, while Shoto stared up at his brother uncertainly. Art3mis just stood back and watched, looking somewhat amused.

"We didn't come here to be insulted," Daito said finally. "We're leaving."

"Hold on, Daito," I said. "Just wait a second, will you? Let's just talk this out. We shouldn't part as enemies. We're all on the same side here."

"No," Daito said. "We're not. You're all strangers to us. For all we know, any one of you could be a Sixer spy."

Art3mis laughed out loud at that, then covered her mouth. Daito ignored her. "This is pointless," he said. "Only one person can be the first to find the egg and win the prize," he said. "And that person will be either me or my brother."

And with that, Daito and Shoto both abruptly logged out.

"That went well," Art3mis said, once their avatars had vanished.

I nodded. "Yeah, real smooth, Aech. Way to build bridges."

"What did *I* do?" he said defensively. "Daito was being a complete asshole! Besides, it's not like we were asking him to team up, anyway. I'm an avowed solo. And so are you. And Art3mis here looks like the lone-wolf type too."

"Guilty as charged," she said, grinning. "But even so, there is an argument to be made for forming an alliance against the Sixers."

"Maybe," Aech said. "But think about it. If you find the Jade Key before either of us do, are you going to be generous and tell us where it is?"

Art3mis smirked. "Of course not."

"Me neither," Aech said. "So there's no point in discussing an alliance."

Art3mis shrugged. "Well, then it looks like the meeting is over. I should probably get going." She winked at me. "The clock is ticking. Right, boys?"

"Tick tock," I said.

"Good luck, fellas." She gave us both a wave. "See ya around."

"See ya," we both answered in unison.

I watched her avatar slowly disappear, then turned to find Aech smiling at me. "What are you grinning about?" I asked.

"You've got a crush on her, don't you?"

"What? On Art3mis? No—"

"Don't deny it, Z. You were making googly eyes at her the whole time she was here." He did his impression of this, clasping both hands to his chest and batting his eyelashes like a silent film star. "I recorded the whole chat session. Do you want me to play it back for you, so you can see how silly you looked?"

"Stop being a dick."

"It's understandable, man," Aech said. "That girl is super cute."

"So, have you had any luck with the new riddle?" I said, deliberately changing the subject. "That quatrain about the Jade Key?"

"Quatrain?"

"'A poem or stanza with four lines and an alternating rhyme scheme,'" I recited. "It's called a quatrain."

Aech rolled his eyes. "You're too much, man."

"What? That's the proper term for it, asshead!"

"It's just a riddle, dude. And no. I haven't had any luck figuring it out yet."

"Me neither," I said. "So we probably shouldn't be standing around jabbering at each other. Time to put our noses to the grindstone."

"I concur," he said. "But—"

Just then, a stack of comic books on the other side of the room slid off the end table where they were piled and crashed to the floor, as if something had knocked them over. Aech and I both jumped, then exchanged confused looks.

"What the hell was that?" I said.

"I don't know." Aech walked over and examined the scattered comics. "Maybe a software glitch or something?"

"I've never seen a chat-room glitch like that," I said, scanning the empty room. "Could someone else be in here? An invisible avatar, eavesdropping on us?"

Aech rolled his eyes. "No way, Z," he said. "You're getting way too paranoid. This is an encrypted private chat room. No one can enter without my permission. You know that."

"Right," I said, still freaked out.

"Relax. It was a glitch." He rested a hand on my shoulder. "Listen. Let me know if you change your mind about needing a loan. Or a place to crash. OK?"

"I'll be all right," I said. "But thanks, amigo."

We bumped fists again, like the Wonder Twins activating their powers.

"I'll catch you later. Good luck, Z."

"Same to you, Aech."

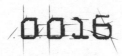

0016

A few hours later, the remaining slots on the Scoreboard began to fill up, one after another, in rapid succession. Not with avatar names, but with IOI employee numbers. Each would appear with a score of 5,000 points (which now appeared to be the fixed value for obtaining the Copper Key); then the score would jump by another 100,000 points a few hours later, once that Sixer had cleared the First Gate. By the end of the day, the Scoreboard looked like this:

HIGH SCORES:

1.	Parzival	**110,000**	⛩
2.	Art3mis	**109,000**	⛩
3.	Aech	**108,000**	⛩
4.	Daito	**107,000**	⛩
5.	Shoto	**106,000**	⛩
6.	IOI-655321	**105,000**	⛩
7.	IOI-643187	**105,000**	⛩
8.	IOI-621671	**105,000**	⛩
9.	IOI-678324	**105,000**	⛩
10.	IOI-637330	**105,000**	⛩

I recognized the first Sixer employee number to appear, because I'd seen it printed on Sorrento's uniform. He'd probably insisted that his avatar be the first to obtain the Copper Key and clear the gate. But I had a hard time believing he'd done it on his own. There was no way he was that good at Joust. Or that he knew *WarGames* by heart. But I now knew that he didn't have to be. When he reached a challenge he couldn't handle, like winning at Joust, he could just hand control of his avatar off to one of his underlings. And during the *WarGames* challenge he'd probably just had someone feeding him all of the dialogue via his hacked immersion rig.

Once the remaining empty slots were filled, the Scoreboard began to grow in length, to display rankings beyond tenth place. Before long, twenty avatars were listed on the Scoreboard. Then thirty. Over the next twenty-four hours, over sixty Sixer avatars cleared the First Gate.

Meanwhile, Ludus had become the most popular destination in the OASIS. Transport terminals all over the planet were spitting out a steady stream of gunters who then swarmed across the globe, creating chaos and disrupting classes on every school campus. The OASIS Public School Board saw the writing on the wall, and the decision was quickly made to evacuate Ludus and relocate all of its schools to a new location. An identical copy of the planet, Ludus II, was created in the same sector, a short distance away from the original. All students were given a day off from school while a backup copy of the planet's original source code was copied over to the new site (minus the Tomb of Horrors code Halliday had secretly added to it at some point). Classes resumed on Ludus II the following day, and Ludus was left for the Sixers and gunters to fight over.

News spread quickly that the Sixers were encamped around a small flat-topped hill at the center of a remote forest. The tomb's exact location appeared on the message boards that evening, along with screenshots showing the force field the Sixers had erected to keep everyone else out. These screenshots also clearly showed the skull pattern of the stones on the hilltop. In a matter of hours, the connection to the *Tomb of Horrors* D&D module was posted to every single gunter message board. Then it hit the newsfeeds.

All of the large gunter clans immediately banded together to launch a full-scale assault on the Sixers' force field, trying everything they could think of to bring it down or circumvent it. The Sixers had installed teleportation disruptors, which prevented anyone from transporting inside the force field via technological means. They had also stationed a team of high-level wizards around the tomb. These magic users cast spells around the clock, keeping the entire area encased in a temporary null-magic zone. This prevented the force fields from being bypassed by any magical means.

The clans began to bombard the outer force field with rockets, missiles, nukes, and harsh language. They laid siege to the tomb all night, but the following morning, both force fields remained intact.

In desperation, the clans decided to break out the heavy artillery. They pooled their resources and purchased two very expensive, very powerful antimatter bombs on eBay. They detonated both of them in sequence, just a few seconds apart. The first bomb took down the outer shield, and the second bomb finished the job. The moment the second force field went down, thousands of gunters (all unharmed by the bomb blasts, due to the no-PvP zone) swarmed into the tomb and clogged the corridors of the dungeon below. Soon, thousands of gunters (and Sixers) had crammed into the burial chamber, all ready to challenge the lich king to a game of Joust. Multiple copies of the king appeared, one for every avatar who set foot on the dais. Ninety-five percent of the gunters who challenged him lost and were then killed. But a few gunters were successful, and at the bottom of the Scoreboard, listed after the High Five and the dozens of IOI employee numbers, new avatar names began to appear. Within a few days, the list of avatars on the Scoreboard was over a hundred names long.

Now that the area was full of gunters, it became impossible for the Sixers to put their force field back in operation. Gunters were mobbing them and destroying their ships and equipment on sight. So the Sixers gave up on their barricade, but they continued to send avatars into the Tomb of Horrors to farm copies of the Copper Key. No one could do anything to stop them.

* * *

The day after the explosion in the stacks, there was a brief story about it on one of the local newsfeeds. They showed a video clip of volunteers sifting through the wreckage for human remains. What they did find couldn't be identified.

It seemed that the Sixers had also planted a large amount of drug-manufacturing equipment and chemicals at the scene, to make it look like a meth lab in one of the trailers had exploded. It worked like a charm. The cops didn't bother to investigate any further. The stacks were so dense around the pile of crushed and charred trailers that it was too dangerous to try to clear them out with one of the old construction cranes. They just left the wreckage where it was, to slowly rust into the earth.

As soon as the first endorsement payment arrived in my account, I bought a one-way bus ticket to Columbus, Ohio, set to depart at eight the following morning. I paid extra for a first-class seat, which came with a comfier chair and a high-bandwidth uplink jack. I planned to spend most of the long ride east logged into the OASIS.

Once my trip was booked, I inventoried everything in my hideout and packed the items I wanted to take with me into an old rucksack. My school-issued OASIS console, visor, and gloves. My dog-eared printout of *Anorak's Almanac*. My grail diary. Some clothes. My laptop. Everything else I left behind.

When it got dark, I climbed out of the van, locked it, and hurled the keys off into the junk pile. Then I hoisted the rucksack and walked out of the stacks for the last time. I didn't look back.

I kept to busy streets and managed to avoid getting mugged on the way to the bus terminal. A battered customer-service kiosk stood just inside the door, and after a quick retinal scan it spat out my ticket. I sat by the gate, reading my copy of the *Almanac*, until it was time to board the bus.

It was a double-decker, with armor plating, bulletproof windows, and solar panels on the roof. A rolling fortress. I had a window seat, two rows behind the driver, who was encased in a bulletproof Plexiglas box. A team of six heavily armed guards rode on the bus's upper deck, to protect the vehicle and its passengers in the event of a hijacking by road agents or scavengers—a distinct possibility once we ventured out into the lawless badlands that now existed outside of the safety of large cities.

Every single seat on the bus was occupied. Most of the passengers put on their visors the moment they sat down. I left mine off for a while, though. Long enough to watch the city of my birth recede from view on the road behind us as we rolled through the sea of wind turbines that surrounded it.

The bus's electric motor had a top speed of about forty miles an hour, but due to the deteriorating interstate highway system and the countless stops the bus had to make at charging stations along the way, it took several days for me to reach my destination. I spent nearly all of that time logged into the OASIS, preparing to start my new life.

The first order of business was to create a new identity. This wasn't that difficult, now that I had some money. In the OASIS, you could buy almost any kind of information if you knew where to look and who to ask, and if you didn't mind breaking the law. There were plenty of desperate and corrupt people working for the government (and for every major corporation), and these people often sold information on the OASIS black market.

My new status as a world-famous gunter gave me all kinds of underworld credibility, which helped me get access to a highly exclusive illegal data-auction site known as the L33t Haxorz Warezhaus, and for a shockingly small amount of money, I was able to purchase a series of access procedures and passwords for the USCR (United States Citizen Registry) database. Using these, I was able to log into the database and access my existing citizen profile, which had been created when I enrolled for school. I deleted my fingerprints and retinal patterns, then replaced them with those of someone deceased (my father). Then I copied my own fingerprints and retinal patterns into a completely new identity profile that I'd created, under the name Bryce Lynch. I made Bryce twenty-two years old and gave him a brand-new Social Security number, an immaculate credit rating, and a bachelor's degree in Computer Science. When I wanted to become my old self again, all I had to do was delete the Lynch identity and copy my prints and retinal patterns back over to my original file.

Once my new identity was set up, I began searching the Columbus classifieds for a suitable apartment and found a relatively inexpensive room in an old high-rise hotel, a relic from the days when people physically traveled for business and pleasure. The rooms had all been converted into one-room efficiency apartments, and each unit had been modified to meet the very specific needs of a full-time gunter. It had everything I wanted. Low rent, a high-end security system, and steady, reliable access to as much electricity as I could afford. Most important, it offered a direct fiber-optic connection to the main OASIS server vault, which was located just a few miles away. This was the fastest and most secure type of Internet connection available, and since it wasn't provided by IOI or one of its subsidiaries, I wouldn't have to be paranoid about them monitoring my connection or trying to trace my location. I would be safe.

I spoke with a rental agent in a chat room, and he showed me around a virtual mock-up of my new digs. The place looked perfect. I rented the room under my new name and paid six months' rent up front. That kept the agent from asking any questions.

• • •

Sometimes, during the late hours of the night, as the bus slowly hummed along the crumbling highway, I removed my visor and stared out the window. I'd never been outside of Oklahoma City before, and I was curious to see what the rest of the country looked like. But the view was perpetually bleak, and each decaying, overcrowded city we rolled through looked just like the last.

Finally, after it felt like we'd been crawling along the highway for months, the Columbus skyline appeared on the horizon, glittering like Oz at the end of the yellow brick road. We arrived around sunset, and already there were more electric lights burning in the city than I'd ever seen at one time. I'd read that giant solar arrays were positioned throughout the city, along with two heliostat power plants on its outskirts. They drank in the sun's power all day, stored it, and fed it back out each night.

As we pulled into the Columbus bus terminal, my OASIS connection cut out. As I pulled off my visor and filed off the bus with the other passengers, the reality of my situation finally began to hit home. I was now a fugitive, living under an assumed name. Powerful people were out looking for me. People who wanted me dead.

As I stepped off the bus, I suddenly felt as though a heavy weight were resting on my chest. I was having a hard time breathing. Maybe I was having a panic attack. I forced myself to take deep breaths and tried to calm down. All I had to do was to get to my new apartment, set up my rig, and log back into the OASIS. Then everything would be all right. I would be back in familiar surroundings. I would be safe.

I hailed an autocab and entered my new address on the touchscreen. The synthesized voice of the cab's computer told me the drive would take an estimated thirty-two minutes with the current traffic conditions. During the ride, I stared out the window at the dark city streets. I still felt light-headed and anxious. I kept glancing at the meter to see how much farther we had to go. Finally, the cab pulled up in front of my new apartment building, a slate-gray monolith on the banks of the Scioto, just at the edge of the Twin Rivers ghetto. I noticed a discolored outline on the building's façade where the Hilton logo used to be, back when the place had been a hotel.

I thumbed my fare and climbed out of the cab. Then I took one last look around, inhaled one final breath of fresh air, and carried my bag through the front door and into the lobby. When I stepped inside the security checkpoint cage, my fingerprints and retinal patterns were scanned, and my new name flashed on the monitor. A green light lit up and the cage door slid open, allowing me to continue on to the elevators.

My apartment was on the forty-second floor, number 4211. The security lock mounted outside required another retinal scan. Then the door slid open and the interior lights switched on. There was no furniture in the cube-shaped room, and only one window. I stepped inside, closed the door, and locked it behind me. Then I made a silent vow not to go outside again until I had completed my quest. I would abandon the real world altogether until I found the egg.

Level Two

I'm not crazy about reality, but it's
still the only place to get a decent meal.

—Groucho Marx

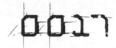

Art3mis: You there?

Parzival: Yes! Hey! I can't believe you finally responded to one of my chat requests.

Art3mis: Only to ask you to cut it out. It's a bad idea for us to start chatting.

Parzival: Why? I thought we were friends.

Art3mis: You seem like a great guy. But we're competitors. Rival gunters. Sworn enemies. You know the drill.

Parzival: We don't have to talk about anything related to the Hunt. . . .

Art3mis: Everything is related to the Hunt.

Parzival: Come on. At least give it at shot. Let's start over. Hi, Art3mis! How have you been?

Art3mis: Fine. Thanks for asking. You?

Parzival: Outstanding. Listen, why are we using this ancient text-only chat interface? I can host a virtual chat room for us.

Art3mis: I prefer this.

Parzival: Why?

Art3mis: As you may recall, I tend to ramble in real time. When I have to type out everything I want to say, I come off as less of a flibbertigibbet.

Parzival: I don't think you're a flibbertigibbet. You're enchanting.

Art3mis: Did you just use the word "enchanting"?

Parzival: What I typed is right there in front of you, isn't it?

Art3mis: That's very sweet. But you're full of crap.

Parzival: I am totally and completely serious.

Art3mis: So, how's life at the top of the Scoreboard, hotshot? Sick of being famous yet?

Parzival: I don't feel famous.

Art3mis: Are you kidding? The whole world is dying to find out who you really are. You're a rock star, man.

Parzival: You're just as famous as I am. And if I'm such a rock star, how come the media always portrays me as some unwashed geek who never goes outside?

Art3mis: I take it you saw that SNL skit they did about us?

Parzival: Yes. Why does everyone assume I'm an antisocial nut job?

Art3mis: You're not antisocial?

Parzival: No! Maybe. OK, yes. But I have excellent personal hygiene.

Art3mis: At least they got your gender correct. Everyone thinks I'm a man in real life.

Parzival: That's because most gunters are male, and they can't accept the idea that a woman has beaten and/or outsmarted them.

Art3mis: I know. Neanderthals.

Parzival: So you're telling me, definitively, that you are a female? IRL?

Art3mis: You should have already figured that out on your own, Clouseau.

Parzival: I did. I have.

Art3mis: Have you?

Parzival: Yes. After analyzing the available data, I've concluded that you must be a female.

Art3mis: Why must I?

Parzival: Because I don't want to find out that I've got a crush on some 300 lb. dude named Chuck who lives in his mother's basement in suburban Detroit.

Art3mis: You've got a crush on me?

Parzival: You should have already figured that out on your own, Clouseau.

Art3mis: What if I were a 300 lb. gal named Charlene, who lives in her mom's basement in suburban Detroit? Would you still have a crush on me then?

Parzival: I don't know. Do you live in your mother's basement?

Art3mis: No.

Parzival: Yeah. Then I probably still would.

Art3mis: So I'm supposed to believe you're one of those mythical guys who only cares about a woman's personality, and not about the package it comes in?

Parzival: Why is it that you assume I'm a man?

Art3mis: Please. It's obvious. I get nothing but boy-vibes coming from you.

Parzival: Boy-vibes? What, do I use masculine sentence structure or something?

Art3mis: Don't change the subject. You were saying you have a crush on me?

Parzival: I've had a crush on you since before we even met. From reading your blog and watching your POV. I've been cyber-stalking you for years.

Art3mis: But you still don't really know anything about me. Or my real personality.

Parzival: This is the OASIS. We exist as nothing but raw personality in here.

Art3mis: I beg to differ. Everything about our online personas is filtered through our avatars, which allows us to control how we look and sound to others. The OASIS lets you be whoever you want to be. That's why everyone is addicted to it.

Parzival: So, IRL, you're nothing like the person I met that night in the tomb?

Art3mis: That was just one side of me. The side I chose to show you.

Parzival: Well, I liked that side. And if you showed me your other sides, I'm sure I'd like those, too.

Art3mis: You say that now. But I know how these things work. Sooner or later, you'll demand to see a picture of the real me.

Parzival: I'm not the sort who makes demands. Besides, I'm definitely not going to show you a photo of me.

Art3mis: Why? Are you butt ugly?

Parzival: You're such a hypocrite!

Art3mis: So? Answer the question, Claire. Are you ugly?

Parzival: I must be.

Art3mis: Why?

Parzival: The female of the species has always found me repellent.

Art3mis: I don't find you repellent.

Parzival: Of course not. That's because you're an obese man named Chuck who likes to chat up ugly young boys online.

Art3mis: So you're a young man?

Parzival: Relatively young.

Art3mis: Relative to what?

Parzival: To a fifty-three-year-old guy like you, Chuck. Does your mom let you live in that basement rent-free or what?

Art3mis: Is that really what you're picturing?

Parzival: If it were, I wouldn't be chatting with you right now.

Art3mis: So what do you imagine I look like, then?

Parzival: Like your avatar, I suppose. Except, you know, without the armor, guns, or glowing sword.

Art3mis: You're kidding, right? That's the first rule of online romances, pal. No one ever looks anything like their avatar.

Parzival: Are we going to have an online romance? <crosses fingers>

Art3mis: No way, ace. Sorry.

Parzival: Why not?

Art3mis: No time for love, Dr. Jones. My cyber-porn addiction eats up most of my free time.

          And searching for the Jade Key takes up the rest. That's what I should be doing right now, in fact.

Parzival: Yeah. So should I. But talking to you is more fun.

Art3mis: How about you?

Parzival: How about me what?

Art3mis: Do you have time for an online romance?

Parzival: I've got time for you.

Art3mis: You're too much.

Parzival: I'm not even laying it on thick yet.

Art3mis: Do you have a job? Or are you still in high school?

Parzival: High school. I graduate next week.

Art3mis: You shouldn't reveal stuff like that! I could be a Sixer spy trying to profile you.

Parzival: The Sixers already profiled me, remember? They blew up my house. Well, it was a trailer. But they blew it up.

Art3mis: I know. I'm still freaked out about that. I can only imagine how you feel.

Parzival: Revenge is a dish best served cold.

Art3mis: Bon appetit. What do you do when you're not hunting?

Parzival: I refuse to answer any more questions until you start reciprocating.

Art3mis: Fine. Quid pro quo, Dr. Lecter. We'll take turns asking questions. Go ahead.

Parzival: Do you work, or go to school?

Art3mis: College.

Parzival: Studying what?

Art3mis: It's my turn. What do you do when you're not hunting?

Parzival: Nothing. Hunting is all I do. I'm hunting right now, in fact. Multitasking all over the goddamn place.

Art3mis: Same here.

Parzival: Really? I'll keep an eye on the Scoreboard then. Just in case.

Art3mis: You do that, ace.

Parzival: What are you studying? In college?

Art3mis: Poetry and Creative Writing.

Parzival: That makes sense. You're a fantastic writer.

Art3mis: Thanks for the compliment. How old are you?

Parzival: Just turned 18 last month. You?

Art3mis: Don't you think we're getting a little too personal now?

Parzival: Not even remotely.

Art3mis: 19.

Parzival: Ah. An older woman. Hot.

Art3mis: That is, if I *am* a woman . . .

Parzival: Are you a woman?

Art3mis: It's not your turn.

Parzival: Fine.

Art3mis: How well do you know Aech?

Parzival: He's been my best friend for five years. Now, spill it. Are you a woman? And by that I mean are you a human female who has never had a sex-change operation?

Art3mis: That's pretty specific.

Parzival: Answer the question, Claire.

Art3mis: I am, and always have been, a human female. Have you ever met Aech IRL?

Parzival: No. Do you have any siblings?

Art3mis: No. You?

Parzival: Nope. You got parents?

Art3mis: They died. The flu. So I was raised by my grandparents. You got parentage?

Parzival: No. Mine are dead too.

Art3mis: It kinda sucks, doesn't it? Not having your parents around.

Parzival: Yeah. But a lot of people are worse off than me.

Art3mis: I tell myself that all the time. So . . . are you and Aech working as a duo?

Parzival: Oh, here we go. . . .

Art3mis: Well? Are you?

Parzival: No. He asked me the same thing about you and me, you know. Because you cleared the First Gate a few hours after I did.

Art3mis: Which reminds me—why did you give me that tip? About changing sides on the Joust game?

Parzival: I felt like helping you.

Art3mis: Well, you shouldn't make that mistake again. Because I'm the one who's going to win. You do realize that, right?

Parzival: Yeah, yeah. We'll see.

Art3mis: You're not holding up your end of our Q & A, goof. You're, like, five questions behind.

Parzival: Fine. What color is your hair? IRL?

Art3mis: Brunette.

Parzival: Eyes?

Art3mis: Blue.

Parzival: Just like your avatar, eh? Do you have the same face and body, too?

Art3mis: As far as you know.

Parzival: OK. What's your favorite movie? Of all time?

Art3mis: It changes. Right now? Probably Highlander.

Parzival: You've got great taste, lady.

Art3mis: I know. I have a thing for evil bald bad guys. The Kurgan is too sexy.

Parzival: I'm going to shave my head right now. And start wearing leather.

Art3mis: Send photos. Listen, I gotta go in a few minutes, Romeo. You can ask me one last question. Then I need to get some sleep.

Parzival: When can we chat again?

Art3mis: After one of us finds the egg.

Parzival: That could take years.

Art3mis: So be it.

Parzival: Can I at least keep e-mailing you?

Art3mis: Not a good idea.

Parzival: You can't stop me from e-mailing you.

Art3mis: Actually, I can. I can block you on my contact list.

Parzival: You wouldn't do that, though. Would you?

Art3mis: Not if you don't force me to.

Parzival: Harsh. Unnecessarily harsh.

Art3mis: Good night, Parzival.

Parzival: Farewell, Art3mis. Sweet dreams.

chatlog ends. 2.27.2045–02:51:38 OST

• • •

I started e-mailing her. At first I showed restraint and only wrote her once a week. To my surprise, she never failed to respond. Usually it was with just a single sentence, saying she was too busy to reply. But her replies eventually got longer and we began to correspond. A few times a week at first. Then, as our e-mails grew longer and more personal, we started writing each other at least once a day. Sometimes more. Whenever an e-mail from her arrived in my inbox, I dropped everything to read it.

Before long, we were meeting in private chat-room sessions at least once a day. We played vintage board games, watched movies, and listened to music. We talked for hours. Long, rambling conversations about everything under the sun. Spending time with her was intoxicating. We seemed to have everything in common. We shared the same interests. We were driven by the same goal. She got all of my jokes. She made me laugh. She made me think. She changed the way I saw the world. I'd never had such a powerful, immediate connection with another human being before. Not even with Aech.

I no longer cared that we were supposed to be rivals, and she didn't seem to either. We began to share details about our research. We told each other what movies we were currently watching and what books we were reading. We even began to exchange theories and to discuss our interpretations of specific passages in the *Almanac*. I couldn't make myself be cautious around her. A little voice in my head kept trying to tell me that every word she said could be disinformation and that she might just be playing me for a fool. But I didn't believe it. I trusted her, even though I had every reason not to.

I graduated from high school in early June. I didn't attend the graduation ceremony. I'd stopped attending classes altogether when I fled the stacks. As far as I knew, the Sixers thought I was dead, and I didn't want to tip them off by showing up for my last few weeks of school. Missing finals week wasn't a big deal, since I already had more than enough credits to receive my diploma. The school e-mailed a copy of it to me. They snail-mailed the actual diploma to my address in the stacks, which no longer existed, so I don't know what became of it.

When I finished school, I'd intended to devote all of my time to the Hunt. But all I really wanted to do was spend time with Art3mis.

∙ ∙ ∙

When I wasn't hanging out with my new online pseudo-girlfriend, I devoted the rest of my time to leveling up my avatar. Gunters called this "making the climb to ninety-nine," because ninety-ninth level was the maximum power level an avatar could attain. Art3mis and Aech had both recently done it, and I felt compelled to catch up. It actually didn't take me very long. I now had nothing but free time, and I had the money and the means to fully explore the OASIS. So I began to complete every quest I could find, sometimes jumping five or six levels in one day. I became a split-class Warrior/Mage. As my stats continued to increase, I honed my avatar's combat and spell-casting abilities while collecting a wide array of powerful weapons, magic items, and vehicles.

Art3mis and I even teamed up for a few quests. We visited the planet Goondocks and finished the entire Goonies quest in just one day. Arty played through it as Martha Plimpton's character, Stef, while I played as Mikey, Sean Astin's character. It was entirely too much fun.

I didn't spend all of my time goofing off. I tried to keep my head in the game. Really I did. At least once a day, I would pull up the Quatrain and try once again to decipher its meaning.

The captain conceals the Jade Key
in a dwelling long neglected
But you can only blow the whistle
once the trophies are all collected

For a while, I thought that the whistle in the third line might be a reference to a late-'60s Japanese TV show called *The Space Giants,* which had been dubbed in English and rebroadcast in the United States in the '70s and '80s. *The Space Giants* (called *Maguma Taishi* in Japan) featured a family of transforming robots who lived in a volcano and battled an evil alien villain named Rodak. Halliday referred to this show several times in *Anorak's Almanac,* citing it as one of his childhood favorites. One of the show's main characters was a boy named Miko, who would blow a special whistle to summon the robots to his aid. I watched all fifty-two ultra-cheesy episodes of *The Space Giants,* back-to-back, while wolfing down corn chips and taking notes. But when the viewing marathon was over, I still wasn't any closer to understanding the Quatrain's meaning. I'd hit another dead end. I decided that Halliday must be referring to some other whistle.

Then, one Saturday morning, I finally made a small breakthrough. I was watching a collection of vintage '80s cereal commercials when I paused to wonder why cereal manufacturers no longer included toy prizes inside every box. It was a tragedy, in my opinion. Another sign that civilization was going straight down the tubes. I was still pondering this when an old Cap'n Crunch commercial came on, and that was when I made a connection between the first and third lines of the Quatrain: *The captain conceals the Jade Key . . . But you can only blow the whistle . . .*

Halliday was alluding to a famous '70s hacker named John Draper, better known by the alias Captain Crunch. Draper was one of the first phone phreaks, and he was famous for discovering that the toy plastic whistles found as prizes in boxes of Cap'n Crunch cereal could be used to make free long-distance phone calls, because they emitted a 2600-hertz tone that tricked the old analog phone system into giving you free access to the line.

The captain conceals the Jade Key

That had to be it. "The captain" was Cap'n Crunch, and "the whistle" was the famous toy plastic whistle of phone phreak lore.

Maybe the Jade Key was disguised as one of those toy plastic whistles, and it was hidden in a box of Cap'n Crunch cereal. . . . But where was that cereal box hidden?

In a dwelling long neglected

I still didn't know what long-neglected dwelling that line referred to, or where to look for it. I visited every neglected dwelling I could think of. Re-creations of the *Addams Family* house, the abandoned shack in the *Evil Dead* trilogy, Tyler Durden's flophouse in *Fight Club,* and the Lars Homestead on Tattooine. No luck finding the Jade Key inside any of them. Dead end after dead end.

> **But you can only blow the whistle**
> **Once the trophies are all collected**

I still hadn't deciphered the meaning of that last line, either. What trophies did I have to collect? Or was that some kind of half-assed metaphor? There had to be a simple connection I wasn't making, a sly reference that I still wasn't clever or knowledgeable enough to catch.

Since then, I'd failed to make any more progress. Every time I revisited the Quatrain, my ongoing infatuation with Art3mis would undermine my ability to focus, and before long I would close my grail diary and call her up to see if she wanted to hang out. She almost always did.

I convinced myself that it was all right to slack off a bit, because no one else seemed to be making any progress in their search for the Jade Key. The Scoreboard remained unchanged. Everyone else seemed to be just as stumped as I was.

• • •

As the weeks continued to pass, Art3mis and I spent more and more time together. Even when our avatars were doing other things, we were sending e-mails and instant messages to each other. A river of words flowed between us.

I wanted more than anything to meet her in the real world. Face-to-face. But I didn't tell her this. I was certain she had strong feelings for me, but she also kept me at a distance. No matter how much I revealed about myself to her—and I wound up revealing just about everything, including my real name—she always adamantly refused to reveal any details about her own life. All I knew was that she was nineteen and that she lived somewhere in the Pacific Northwest. That was all she would tell me.

The image of her that formed in my mind was the most obvious one. I pictured her as a physical manifestation of her avatar. I imagined her with the same face, eyes, hair, and body. Even though she told me repeatedly that in reality she looked almost nothing like her avatar and that she wasn't nearly as attractive in person.

When I began to spend most of my time with Art3mis, Aech and I began to grow apart. Instead of hanging out several times a week, we chatted a few times a month. Aech knew I was falling for Art3mis, but he never gave me too much grief about it, even when I would bail on him at the last minute to hang out with her instead. He would just shrug, tell me to be careful, and say, "I sure hope you know what you're doing, Z."

I didn't, of course. My whole relationship with Art3mis was in defiance of all common sense. But I couldn't help falling for her. Somehow, without my realizing it, my obsession with finding Halliday's Easter egg was gradually being supplanted by my obsession with Art3mis.

Eventually, she and I began to go out on "dates," taking day trips to exotic OASIS locales and exclusive night spots. At first, Art3mis protested. She thought I should keep a low profile, because as soon as my avatar was spotted in public, the Sixers would know that their attempt to kill me had failed, and I'd be back on their hit list. But I told her I no longer cared. I was already hiding from the Sixers in the real world, and I refused to continue hiding from them in the OASIS, too. Besides, I had a ninety-ninth-level avatar now. I felt nigh invincible.

Maybe I was just trying to impress Art3mis by acting fearless. If so, I think it worked.

We still disguised our avatars before we went out, because we knew there would be tabloid headlines galore if Parzival and Art3mis started showing up in public together on a regular basis. But there was one exception. One night, she took me to see the *Rocky Horror Picture Show* in a huge stadium-sized movie theater on the planet Transsexual, where they held the most highly attended and longest-running weekly screening of the movie in the OASIS. Thousands of avatars came to every show, to sit in the stands and revel in the audience participation. Normally, only long-standing members of the Rocky Horror Fan Club were permitted to get up onstage and help act out the film in front of the giant movie screen, and only after they'd passed a grueling audition process. But Art3mis used her fame to pull a few strings, and she and I were both allowed to join the cast for that night's show. The whole planet was in a no-PvP zone, so I wasn't worried about getting ambushed by the Sixers. But I did have a serious case of stage fright when the show began.

Art3mis played a note-perfect Columbia, and I had the honor of playing her undead love interest, Eddie. I altered my avatar's appearance so that I looked exactly like Meat Loaf did in the role, but my performance and lip-synching still kinda sucked. Luckily, the audience cut me a lot of slack, because I was the famous gunter Parzival, and I was clearly having a blast.

That night was easily the most fun I'd ever had in my life up to that point. I told Art3mis so afterward, and that was when she leaned over and kissed me for the first time. I couldn't feel it, of course. But it still set my heart racing.

I'd heard all the clichéd warnings about the perils of falling for someone you only knew online, but I ignored them. I decided that whoever Art3mis really was, I was in love with her. I could feel it, deep in the soft, chewy caramel center of my being.

And then one night, like a complete idiot, I told her how I felt.

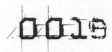

It was a Friday night, and I was spending another solitary eve-ning doing research, working my way through every episode of *Whiz Kids,* an early-'80s TV show about a teenage hacker who uses his computer skills to solve mysteries. I'd just finished watching the episode "Deadly Access" (a crossover with *Simon & Simon*) when an e-mail arrived in my inbox. It was from Ogden Morrow. The subject line read "We Can Dance If We Want To."

There was no text in the body of the e-mail. Just a file attachment—an invitation to one of the most exclusive gatherings in the OASIS: Ogden Morrow's birthday party. In the real world, Morrow almost never made public appearances, and in the OASIS, he came out of hiding only once a year, to host this event.

The invitation featured a photo of Morrow's world-famous avatar, the Great and Powerful Og. The gray-bearded wizard was hunched over an elaborate DJ mixing board, one headphone pressed to his ear, biting his lower lip in auditory ecstasy as his fingers scratched ancient vinyl on a set of silver turntables. His record crate bore a DON'T PANIC sticker and an anti-Sixer logo—a yellow number six with a red circle-and-slash over it. The text at the bottom read

Ogden Morrow's '80s Dance Party
in celebration of his 73rd birthday!
Tonight—10pm OST at the Distracted Globe
ADMIT ONE

I was flabbergasted. Ogden Morrow had actually taken the time to invite me to his birthday party. It felt like the greatest honor I'd ever received.

I called Art3mis, and she confirmed that she'd received the same e-mail. She said she couldn't pass up an invitation from Og himself, despite the obvious risks. So, naturally, I told her I would meet her there at the club. It was the only way I could avoid looking like a total wuss.

I knew that if Og had invited the two of us, he'd probably also invited the other members of the High Five. But Aech probably wouldn't show up, because he competed in a globally televised arena deathmatch every Friday night. And Shoto and Daito never entered a PvP zone unless it was absolutely necessary.

The Distracted Globe was a famous zero-gravity dance club on the planet Neonoir in Sector Sixteen. Ogden Morrow had coded the place himself decades ago and was still its sole owner. I'd never visited the Globe before. I wasn't much for dancing, or for socializing with the twinked-out wannabe-gunter überdorks who were known to frequent the place. But Og's birthday party was a special event, and so the usual clientele would be banished for the evening. Tonight, the club would be packed with celebrities—movie stars, musicians, and at least two members of the High Five.

I spent over an hour tweaking my avatar's hair and trying on different skins to wear to the club. I finally settled on some classic '80s-era attire: a light gray suit, exactly like the one Peter Weller wore in *Buckaroo Banzai*, complete with a red bow tie, along with a pair of vintage white Adidas high-tops. I also loaded my inventory with my best suit of body armor and a large amount of weaponry. One of the reasons the Globe was such a hip, exclusive club was because it was located in a PvP zone, one where both magic and technology functioned. So it was extremely dangerous to go there. Especially for a famous gunter like me.

There were hundreds of cyberpunk-themed worlds spread throughout the OASIS, but Neonoir was one of the largest and oldest. Seen from orbit, the planet was a shiny onyx marble covered in overlapping spiderwebs of pulsating light. It was always night on Neonoir, the world over, and its surface was an uninterrupted grid of interconnected cities packed with impossibly large skyscrapers. Its skies were filled with a continuous stream of flying vehicles whirring through the vertical cityscapes, and the streets below teemed with leather-clad NPCs and mirror-shaded avatars, all sporting high-tech weaponry and subcutaneous implants as they spouted city-speak straight out of *Neuromancer*.

The Distracted Globe was located at the western-hemisphere intersection of the Boulevard and the Avenue, two brightly lit streets that stretched completely around the planet along its equator and prime meridian. The club itself was a massive cobalt blue sphere, three kilometers in diameter, floating thirty meters off the ground. A floating crystal staircase led up to the club's only entrance, a circular opening at the bottom of the sphere.

I made a big entrance when I arrived in my flying DeLorean, which I'd obtained by completing a *Back to the Future* quest on the planet Zemeckis. The DeLorean came outfitted with a (nonfunctioning) flux capacitor, but I'd made several additions to its equipment and appearance. First, I'd installed an artificially intelligent onboard computer named KITT (purchased in an online auction) into the dashboard, along with a matching red *Knight Rider* scanner just above the DeLorean's grill. Then I'd outfitted the car with an oscillation overthruster, a device that allowed it to travel through solid matter. Finally, to complete my '80s super-vehicle theme, I'd slapped a Ghostbusters logo on each of the DeLorean's gullwing doors, then added personalized plates that read ECTO-88.

I'd had it only a few weeks now, but my time-traveling, Ghost Busting, Knight Riding, matter-penetrating DeLorean had already become my avatar's trademark.

I knew that leaving my sweet ride parked in a PvP zone was an open invitation for some moron to try to boost it. The DeLorean had several antitheft systems installed, and the ignition system was booby-trapped Max Rockatansky–style so that if any other avatar tried to start the car, the plutonium chamber would detonate in a small thermonuclear explosion. But keeping my car safe wouldn't be a problem here on Neonoir. As soon as I climbed out of the DeLorean I cast a Shrink spell on it, instantly reducing it to the size of a Matchbox car. Then I put the DeLorean in my pocket. Magic zones had their advantages.

Thousands of avatars were packed up against the velvet rope force fields that kept everyone without an invitation at bay. As I walked toward the entrance, the crowd bombarded me with a mix of insults, autograph requests, death threats, and tearful declarations of undying love. I had my body shield activated, but surprisingly, no one took a shot at me. I flashed the cyborg doorman my invitation, then mounted the long crystal staircase leading up into the club.

Entering the Distracted Globe was more than a little disorienting. The inside of the giant sphere was completely hollow, and its curved interior surface served as the club's bar and lounge area. The moment you passed through the entrance, the laws of gravity changed. No matter where you walked, your avatar's feet always adhered to the interior of the sphere, so you could walk in a straight line, up to the "top" of the club, then back down the other side, ending up right back where you started. The huge open space in the center of the sphere served as the club's zero-gravity "dance floor." You reached it simply by jumping off the ground, like Superman taking flight, and then swimming through the air, into the spherical zero-g "groove zone."

As I stepped through the entrance, I glanced up—or in the direction that was currently "up" to me at the moment—and took a long look around. The place was packed. Hundreds of avatars milled around like ants crawling around the inside of a giant balloon. Others were already out on the dance floor—spinning, flying, twisting, and tumbling in time with the music, which thumped out of floating spherical speakers that drifted throughout the club.

In the middle of all the dancers, a large clear bubble was suspended in space, at the absolute center of the club. This was the "booth" where the DJ stood, surrounded by turntables, mixers, decks, and dials. At the center of all that gear was the opening DJ, R2-D2, hard at work, using his various robotic arms to work the turntables. I recognized the tune he was playing: the '88 remix of New Order's "Blue Monday," with a lot of *Star Wars* droid sound samples mixed in.

As I made my way to the nearest bar, the avatars I passed all stopped to stare and point in my direction. I didn't pay them much notice, because I was busy scanning the club for Art3mis.

When I reached the bar, I ordered a Pan-Galactic Gargle Blaster from the female Klingon bartender and downed half of it. Then I grinned as R2 cued up another classic '80s tune. " 'Union of the Snake,' " I recited, mostly out of habit. "Duran Duran. Nineteen eighty-three."

"Not bad, ace," said a familiar voice, speaking just loud enough to be heard over the music. I turned to see Art3mis standing behind me. She was wearing evening attire: a gunmetal blue dress that looked like it was spray-painted on. Her avatar's dark hair was styled in a pageboy cut, perfectly framing her gorgeous face. She looked devastating.

She shouted at the barkeep. "Glenmorangie. On the rocks."

I smiled to myself. Connor MacLeod's favorite drink. Man, did I love this girl.

She winked at me as her drink appeared. Then she clinked her glass against mine and downed its contents in one swallow. The chattering of the avatars around us grew in volume. Word that Parzival and Art3mis were *here*, chatting each other up at the bar, was already spreading through the entire club.

Art3mis glanced up at the dance floor, then back at me. "So how about it, Percy?" she said. "Feel like cutting a rug?"

I scowled. "Not if you keep calling me 'Percy.'"

She laughed. Just then, the current song ended, and the club grew silent. All eyes turned upward, toward the DJ booth, where R2-D2 was currently dissolving in a shower of light, like someone "beaming out" in an original *Star Trek* episode. Then a huge cheer went up as a familiar gray-haired avatar beamed in, appearing behind the turntables. It was Og.

Hundreds of vidfeed windows materialized in the air, all over the club. Each displayed a live close-up image of Og in the booth, so that everyone could see his avatar clearly. The old wizard was wearing baggy jeans, sandals, and a faded *Star Trek: The Next Generation* T-shirt. He waved to the assembled, then cued up his first track, a dance remix of "Rebel Yell" by Billy Idol.

A cheer swept across the dance floor.

"I *love* this song!" Art3mis shouted. Her eyes darted up to the dance floor. I looked at her uncertainly. "What's wrong?" she said with mock sympathy. "Can't the boy dance?"

She abruptly locked into the beat, bobbing her head, gyrating her hips. Then she pushed off from the floor with both feet and began to float upward, drifting toward the groove zone. I stared up at her, temporarily frozen, mustering my courage.

"All right," I muttered to myself. "What the hell."

I bent my knees and pushed off hard from the floor. My avatar took flight, drifting upward and sliding alongside Art3mis. The avatars who were already on the dance floor moved aside to clear a path for us, a tunnel leading to the center of the dance floor. I could see Og hovering in his bubble, just a short distance above us. He was spinning around like a dervish, remixing the song on the fly while simultaneously adjusting the gravity vortex of the dance floor, so that he was actually spinning the club itself, like an ancient vinyl disc.

Art3mis winked at me, and then her legs melted together to form a mermaid's tail. She flapped her new tail fin once and shot ahead of me, her body undulating and thrusting in time with the machine-gun beat as she swam through the air. Then she spun back around to face me, suspended and floating, smiling and holding out her hand, beckoning me to join her. Her hair floated in a halo around her head, like she was underwater.

When I reached her, she took my hand. As she did, her mermaid tail vanished and her legs reappeared, whirling and scissoring to the beat.

Not trusting my instincts any further, I loaded up a piece of high-end avatar dance software called Travoltra, which I'd downloaded and tested earlier that evening. The program took control of Parzival's movements, synching them up with the music, and all four of my limbs were transformed into undulating cosine waves. Just like that, I became a dancing fool.

Art3mis's eyes lit up in surprise and delight, and she began to mirror my movements, the two of us orbiting each other like accelerated electrons. Then Art3mis began shape-shifting.

Her avatar lost its human form and dissolved into a pulsing amorphous blob that changed its size and color in synch with the music. I selected the *mirror partner* option on my dance software and began to do the same. My avatar's limbs and torso began to flow and spin like taffy, encircling Art3mis, while strange color patterns flowed and shifted across my skin. I looked like Plastic Man, if he were tripping out of his mind on LSD. Then everyone else on the dance floor also began to shape-shift, melting into prismatic blobs of light. Soon, the center of the club looked like some otherworldly lava lamp.

When the song ended, Og took a bow, then queued up a slow song. "Time After Time" by Cyndi Lauper. All around us, avatars began to pair up.

I gave Art3mis a courtly bow and stretched out my hand. She smiled and took it. I pulled her close and we began to drift together. Og set the dance floor's gravity on a counterclockwise spin, making all of our avatars slowly rotate around the club's invisible central axis, like motes of dust floating inside a snow globe.

And then, before I could stop myself, the words just came out.

"I'm in love with you, Arty."

She didn't respond at first. She just looked at me in shock as our avatars continued to drift in orbit around each other, moving on autopilot. Then she switched to a private voice channel, so no one could eavesdrop on our conversation.

"You aren't in love with me, Z," she said. "You don't even know me."

"Yes I do," I insisted. "I know you better than I've ever known anyone in my entire life."

"You only know what I want you to know. You only see what I want you to see." She placed a hand on her chest. "This isn't my real body, Wade. Or my real face."

"I don't care! I'm in love with your mind—with the person you are. I couldn't care less about the packaging."

"You're just saying that," she said. There was an unsteadiness in her voice. "Trust me. If I ever let you see me in person, you would be repulsed."

"Why do you always say that?"

"Because I'm hideously deformed. Or I'm a paraplegic. Or I'm actually sixty-three years old. Take your pick."

"I don't care if you're all three of those things. Tell me where to meet you and I'll prove it. I'll get on a plane right now and fly to wherever you are. You know I will."

She shook her head. "You don't live in the real world, Z. From what you've told me, I don't think you ever have. You're like me. You live inside this illusion." She motioned to our virtual surroundings. "You can't possibly know what real love is."

"Don't say that!" I was starting to cry and didn't bother hiding it from her. "Is it because I told you I've never had a real girlfriend? And that I'm a virgin? Because—"

"Of course not," she said. "That isn't what this is about. *At all.*"

"Then what *is* it about? Tell me. Please."

"The Hunt. You know that. We've both been neglecting our quests to hang out with each other. We should be focused on finding the Jade Key right now. You can bet that's what Sorrento and the Sixers are doing. And everyone else."

"To hell with our competition! And the egg!" I shouted. "Didn't you hear what I just said? *I'm in love with you! And I want to be with you. More than anything.*"

She just stared at me. Or rather, her avatar stared blankly back at my avatar. Then she said, "I'm sorry, Z. This is all my fault. I let this get way out of hand. It has to stop."

"What do you mean? What has to stop?"

"I think we should take a break. Stop spending so much time together."

I felt like I'd been punched in the throat. "Are you breaking up with me?"

"No, Z," she said firmly. "I am *not* breaking up with you. That would be impossible, because *we are not together.*" There was suddenly venom in her voice. *"We've never even met!"*

"So then . . . you're just going to . . . stop talking to me?"

"Yes. I think that would be for the best."

"For how long?"

"Until the Hunt is over."

"But, Arty . . . That could take years."

"I realize that. And I'm sorry. But this is how it has to be."

"So winning that money is more important to you than me?"

"It's not about the money. It's about what I could do with it."

"Right. Saving the world. You're so fucking noble."

"Don't be a jerk," she said. "I've been searching for the egg for over five years. So have you. Now we're closer than ever to finding it. I can't just throw my chance away."

"I'm not asking you to."

"Yes, you are. Even if you don't realize it."

The Cyndi Lauper song ended and Og queued up another dance track— "James Brown Is Dead" by L.A. Style. The club erupted in applause.

I felt like a large wooden stake had been driven into my chest.

Art3mis was about to say something more—good-bye, I think—when we heard a thunderous boom directly up above us. At first, I thought it was Og, train-wrecking into a new dance track. But then I looked up and saw the large chunks of rubble tumbling at high speed onto the dance floor as avatars scattered to get out of the way. A gaping hole had just been blasted in the roof of the club, near the top of the globe. And a small army of Sixers was now pouring through it, swooping into the club on jet packs, firing blaster pistols as they came.

Total chaos broke out. Half of the avatars in the club swarmed toward the exit, while the other half drew weapons or began to cast spells, firing laser bolts, bullets, and fireballs back at the invading Sixers. There were more than a hundred of them, all armed to the teeth.

I couldn't believe the Sixers' bravado. Why would they be dumb enough to attack a room full of high-level gunters, on their own turf? They might kill a few of us, but they were going to lose some or all of their own avatars in the process. And for what?

Then I realized that most of the Sixers' incoming fire seemed to be directed at me and Art3mis. They were here to kill the two of us.

The news that Art3mis and I were here must have already hit the newsfeeds. And when Sorrento had learned that the top two gunters on the Scoreboard were hanging out in an unshielded PvP zone, he must have decided that it was too juicy a target to pass up. This was the Sixers' chance to take out their two biggest competitors in one shot. It was worth wasting a hundred or so of their highest-level avatars.

I knew my own recklessness had brought them down on us. I cursed myself for being so foolish. Then I drew my blasters and began to unload them at the cluster of Sixers nearest to me while also doing my best to dodge their incoming fire. I glanced over at Art3mis just in time to see her incinerate a dozen Sixers in the space of five seconds, using balls of blue plasma that she hurled out of her palms, while ignoring the steady stream of laser bolts and magic missiles ricocheting off her transparent body shield. I was taking heavy fire too. So far my own body shield was holding up, but it wasn't going to last much longer. Failure warnings were already flashing on my display, and my hit-point counter was starting to plummet.

In seconds, the situation escalated into the largest confrontation I'd ever witnessed. And it already seemed clear that Art3mis and I were going to be on the losing side.

I noticed that the music still hadn't stopped.

I glanced up at the DJ booth just in time to see it crack open as the Great and Powerful Og emerged from within. He looked really, really annoyed.

"You jerks think you can crash *my* birthday party?" he shouted. His avatar was still wearing a mic, so his words blasted over the club's speaker array, reverberating like the voice of God. The melee seemed to halt for a split second as all eyes turned to look at Og, who was now floating at the center of the dance floor. He stretched out his arms as he turned to face the onslaught of Sixers.

A dozen tines of red lightning erupted from each of Og's fingertips, branching out in all directions. Each tine struck a different Sixer avatar in the chest while somehow arcing harmlessly around everyone else.

In a millisecond, every single Sixer in the club was completely vaporized. Their avatars froze and glowed bright red for a few seconds, then simply vanished.

I was awestruck. It was the most incredible display of power by an avatar I'd ever seen.

"Nobody busts into my joint uninvited!" Og shouted, his voice echoing through the now-silent club. The remaining avatars (the ones who hadn't fled the club in terror or been killed in the brief battle) let out a victorious cheer. Og flew back into the DJ booth, which closed up around him like a transparent cocoon. "Let's get this party going again, shall we?" he said, dropping a needle on a techno remix of "Atomic" by Blondie. It took a moment for the shock to wear off, but then everyone started to dance again.

I looked around for Art3mis, but she seemed to have vanished. Then I spotted her avatar flying out of the new exit the Sixer attack had created. She stopped and hovered outside a moment, just long enough to glance back at me.

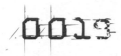

0013

My computer woke me up just before sundown, and I began my daily ritual.

"I'm up!" I shouted at the darkness. In the weeks since Art3mis had dumped me, I'd had a hard time getting out of bed in the morning. So I'd disabled my alarm's snooze feature and instructed the computer to blast "Wake Me Up Before You Go-Go" by Wham! I loathed that song with every fiber of my being, and getting up was the only way to silence it. It wasn't the most pleasant way to start my day, but it got me moving.

The song cut off, and my haptic chair reshaped and reoriented itself, transforming from a bed back into its chair configuration, lifting me into a sitting position as it did so. The computer began to bring the lights up slowly, allowing my eyes to adjust. No outside light ever penetrated my apartment. The single window had once provided a view of the Columbus skyline, but I'd spray-painted it completely black a few days after I moved in. I'd decided that everything outside the window was a distraction from my quest, so I didn't need to waste time staring at it. I didn't want to *hear* the outside world, either, but I hadn't been able to improve upon the apartment's existing soundproofing. So I had to live with the muffled sounds of wind and rain, and of street and air traffic. Even these could be a distraction. At times, I'd slip into a kind of trance, sitting with my eyes closed, oblivious to the passage of time, listening to the sounds of the world outside my room.

I'd made several other modifications to the apartment for the sake of security and convenience. First, I replaced the flimsy door with a new airtight armor-plated vacuum-sealed WarDoor. Whenever I needed something—food, toilet paper, new gear—I ordered it online, and someone brought it right to my door. Deliveries worked like this: First, the scanner mounted outside in the hallway would verify the delivery person's identity and my computer would confirm they were delivering something I'd actually ordered. Then the outer door would unlock itself and slide open, revealing a steel-reinforced air lock about the size of a shower stall. The delivery person would place the parcel, pizza, or whatever inside the air lock and step back. The outer door would hiss shut and relock itself; then the package would be scanned, X-rayed, and analyzed eight ways from Wednesday. Its contents would be verified and delivery confirmation would be sent. Then I would unlock and open the inner door and receive my goods. Capitalism would inch forward, without my actually having to interact face-to-face with another human being. Which was exactly how I preferred it, thank you.

The room itself wasn't much to look at, which was fine, because I spent as little time looking at it as possible. It was basically a cube, about ten meters long on each side. A modular shower and toilet unit were embedded in one wall, opposite the small ergonomic kitchen. I'd never actually used the kitchen to cook anything. My meals were all frozen or delivered. Microwave brownies were as close as I ever got to cooking.

The rest of the room was dominated by my OASIS immersion rig. I'd invested every spare cent I had in it. Newer, faster, or more versatile components were always being released, so I was constantly spending large chunks of my meager income on upgrades.

The crown jewel in my rig was, of course, my customized OASIS console. The computer that powered my world. I'd built it myself, piece by piece, inside a modded mirror-black Odinware sphere chassis. It had a new overclocked processor that was so fast its cycle-time bordered on precognition. And the internal hard drive had enough storage space to hold three digitized copies of Everything in Existence.

I spent the majority of my time in my Shaptic Technologies HC5000 fully adjustable haptic chair. It was suspended by two jointed robotic arms anchored to my apartment's walls and ceiling. These arms could rotate the chair on all four axes, so when I was strapped in to it, the unit could flip, spin, or shake my body to create the sensation that I was falling, flying, or sitting behind the wheel of a nuclear-powered rocket sled hurtling at Mach 2 through a canyon on the fourth moon of Altair VI.

The chair worked in conjunction with my Shaptic Bootsuit, a full-body haptic feedback suit. It covered every inch of my body from the neck down and had discreet openings so I could relieve myself without removing the entire thing. The outside of the suit was covered with an elaborate exoskeleton, a network of artificial tendons and joints that could both sense and inhibit my movements. Built into the inside of the suit was a weblike network of miniature actuators that made contact with my skin every few centimeters. These could be activated in small or large groups for the purpose of tactile simulation—to make my skin feel things that weren't really there. They could convincingly simulate the sensation of a tap on the shoulder, a kick to the shin, or a gunshot in the chest. (Built-in safety software prevented my rig from actually causing me any physical harm, so a simulated gunshot actually felt more like a weak punch.) I had an identical backup suit hanging in the MoshWash cleaning unit in the corner of the room. These two haptic suits made up my entire wardrobe. My old street clothes were buried somewhere in the closet, collecting dust.

On my hands, I wore a pair of state-of-the-art Okagami IdleHands haptic datagloves. Special tactile feedback pads covered both palms, allowing the gloves to create the illusion that I was touching objects and surfaces that didn't actually exist.

My visor was a brand-new pair of Dinatro RLR-7800 WreckSpex, featuring a top-of-the-line virtual retinal display. The visor drew the OASIS directly onto my retinas, at the highest frame rate and resolution perceptible to the human eye. The real world looked washed-out and blurry by comparison. The RLR-7800 was a not-yet-available-to-the-plebian-masses prototype, but I had an endorsement deal with Dinatro, so they sent me free gear (shipped to me through a series of remailing services, which I used to maintain my anonymity).

My AboundSound audio system consisted of an array of ultrathin speakers mounted on the apartment's walls, floor, and ceiling, providing 360 degrees of perfect spatial pin-drop sound reproduction. And the Mjolnur subwoofer was powerful enough to make my back teeth vibrate.

The Olfatrix smell tower in the corner was capable of generating over two thousand discernible odors. A rose garden, salty ocean wind, burning cordite—the tower could convincingly re-create them all. It also doubled as an industrial-strength air conditioner/purifier, which was primarily what I used it for. A lot of jokers liked to code really horrific smells into their simulations, just to mess with people who owned smell towers, so I usually left the odor generator disabled, unless I was in a part of the OASIS where I thought being able to smell my surroundings might prove useful.

On the floor, directly underneath my suspended haptic chair, was my Okagami Runaround omnidirectional treadmill. ("No matter where you go, there you are" was the manufacturer's slogan.) The treadmill was about two meters square and six centimeters thick. When it was activated, I could run at top speed in any direction and never reach the edge of the platform. If I changed direction, the treadmill would sense it, and its rolling surface would change direction to match me, always keeping my body near the center of its platform. This model was also equipped with built-in lifts and an amorphous surface, so that it could simulate walking up inclines and staircases.

You could also purchase an ACHD (anatomically correct haptic doll), if you wanted to have more "intimate" encounters inside the OASIS. ACHDs came in male, female, and dual-sex models, and were available with a wide array of options. Realistic latex skin. Servomotor-driven endoskeletons. Simulated musculature. And all of the attendant appendages and orifices one would imagine.

Driven by loneliness, curiosity, and raging teen hormones, I'd purchased a midrange ACHD, the Shaptic ÜberBetty, a few weeks after Art3mis stopped speaking to me. After spending several highly unproductive days inside a stand-alone brothel simulation called the Pleasuredome, I'd gotten rid of the doll, out of a combination of shame and self-preservation. I'd wasted thousands of credits, missed a whole week of work, and was on the verge of completely abandoning my quest for the egg when I confronted the grim realization that virtual sex, no matter how realistic, was really nothing but glorified, computer-assisted masturbation. At the end of the day, I was still a virgin, all alone in a dark room, humping a lubed-up robot. So I got rid of the ACHD and went back to spanking the monkey the old-fashioned way.

I felt no shame about masturbating. Thanks to *Anorak's Almanac*, I now thought of it as a normal bodily function, as necessary and natural as sleeping or eating.

AA 241:87—I would argue that masturbation is the human animal's most important adaptation. The very cornerstone of our technological civilization. Our hands evolved to grip tools, all right—including our own. You see, thinkers, inventors, and scientists are usually geeks, and geeks have a harder time getting laid than anyone. Without the built-in sexual release valve provided by masturbation, it's doubtful that early humans would have ever mastered the secrets of fire or discovered the wheel. And you can bet that Galileo, Newton, and Einstein never would have made their discoveries if they hadn't first been able to clear their heads by slapping the salami (or "knocking a few protons off the old hydrogen atom"). The same goes for Marie Curie. Before she discovered radium, you can be certain she first discovered the little man in the canoe.

It wasn't one of Halliday's more popular theories, but I liked it.

As I shuffled over to the toilet, a large flat-screen monitor mounted on the wall switched on, and the smiling face of Max, my system agent software, appeared on the screen. I'd programmed Max to start up a few minutes after I turned on the lights, so I could wake up a little bit before he started jabbering to me.

"G-g-good morning, Wade!" Max stuttered cheerily. "Rise and sh-sh-shine!"

Running system agent software was a little like having a virtual personal assistant—one that also functioned as a voice-activated interface with your computer. System agent software was highly configurable, with hundreds of preprogrammed personalities to choose from. I'd programmed mine to look, sound, and behave like Max Headroom, the (ostensibly) computer-generated star of a late-'80s talk show, a groundbreaking cyberpunk TV series, and a slew of Coke commercials.

"Good morning, Max," I replied groggily.

"I think you mean *good evening*, Rumpelstiltskin. It's 7:18 p.m., OASIS Sta-sta-standard Time, Wednesday, December thirtieth." Max was programmed to speak with a slight electronic stutter. In the mid-'80s, when the character of Max Headroom was created, computers weren't actually powerful enough to generate a photorealistic human figure, so Max had been portrayed by an actor (the brilliant Matt Frewer) who wore a lot of rubber makeup to make him *look* computer-generated. But the version of

Max now smiling at me on the monitor was pure software, with the best simulated AI and voice-recognition subroutines money could buy.

I'd been running a highly customized version of MaxHeadroom v3.4.1 for a few weeks now. Before that, my system agent software had been modeled after the actress Erin Gray (of *Buck Rogers* and *Silver Spoons* fame). But she'd proved to be way too distracting, so I'd switched to Max. He was annoying at times, but he also cracked me up. He did a pretty decent job of keeping me from feeling lonesome, too.

As I stumbled into the bathroom module and emptied my bladder, Max continued to address me from a small monitor mounted above the mirror. "Uh-oh! It appears you've sp-sp-sprung a leak!" he said.

"Get a new joke," I said. "Any news I should know about?"

"Just the usual. Wars, rioting, famine. Nothing that would interest you."

"Any messages?"

He rolled his eyes. "A few. But to answer your *real* question, no. Art3mis still hasn't called or written you back, lover boy."

"I've warned you. Don't call me that, Max. You're begging to be deleted."

"Touchy, touchy. Honestly, Wade. When did you get so s-s-sensitive?"

"I'll erase you, Max. I mean it. Keep it up and I'll switch back to Wilma Deering. Or I'll try out the disembodied voice of Majel Barrett."

Max made a pouty face and spun around to face the shifting digital wallpaper behind him—currently a pattern of multicolored vector lines. Max was always like this. Giving me grief was part of his preprogrammed personality. I actually sort of enjoyed it, because it reminded me of hanging out with Aech. And I really missed hanging out with Aech. A lot.

My gaze dropped to the bathroom mirror, but I didn't much like what I saw there, so I closed my eyes until I finished urinating. I wondered (not for the first time) why I hadn't painted the mirror black too, when I'd done the window.

The hour or so after I woke up was my least favorite part of each day, because I spent it in the real world. This was when I dealt with the tedious business of cleaning and exercising my physical body. I hated this part of the day because everything about it contradicted my other life. My real life, inside the OASIS. The sight of my tiny one-room apartment, my immersion rig, or my reflection in the mirror—they all served as a harsh reminder that the world I spent my days in was not, in fact, the real one.

"Retract chair," I said as I stepped out of the bathroom. The haptic chair instantly flattened itself again, then retracted so that it was flush against the wall, clearing a large empty space in the center of the room. I pulled on my visor and loaded up the Gym, a stand-alone simulation.

Now I was standing in a large modern fitness center lined with exercise equipment and weight machines, all of which could be perfectly simulated by my haptic suit. I began my daily workout. Sit-ups, stomach crunches, push-ups, aerobics, weight training. Occasionally, Max would shout words of encouragement. "Get those legs up, you s-s-sissy! Feel the burn!"

I usually got a little exercise while logged into the OASIS, by engaging in physical combat or running around the virtual landscape on my treadmill. But I spent the vast majority of my time sitting in my haptic chair, getting almost no exercise at all. I also had a habit of overeating when I was depressed or frustrated, which was most of the time. As a result, I'd gradually started to put on some extra pounds. I wasn't in the best shape to begin with, so I quickly reached a point where I could no longer fit comfortably in my haptic chair or squeeze in to my XL haptic suit. Soon, I would need to buy a new rig, with components from the Husky line.

I knew that if I didn't get my weight under control, I would probably die of sloth before I found the egg. I couldn't let that happen. So I made a snap decision and enabled the voluntary OASIS fitness lockout software on my rig. I'd regretted it almost immediately.

From then on, my computer monitored my vital signs and kept track of exactly how many calories I burned during the course of each day. If I didn't meet my daily exercise requirements, the system prevented me from logging into my OASIS account. This meant that I couldn't go to work, continue my quest, or, in effect, live my life. Once the lockout was engaged, you couldn't disable it for two months. And the software was bound to my OASIS account, so I couldn't just buy a new computer or go rent a booth in some public OASIS café. If I wanted to log in, I had no choice but to exercise first. This proved to be the only motivation I needed.

The lockout software also monitored my dietary intake. Each day I was allowed to select meals from a preset menu of healthy, low-calorie foods. The software would order the food for me online and it would be delivered to my door. Since I never left my apartment, it was easy for the program to keep track of everything I ate. If I ordered additional food on my own, it would increase the amount of exercise I had to do each day, to offset my additional calorie intake. This was some sadistic software.

But it worked. The pounds began to melt off, and after a few months, I was in near-perfect health. For the first time in my life I had a flat stomach, and muscles. I also had twice the energy, and I got sick a lot less frequently. When the two months ended and I was finally given the option to disable the fitness lockout, I decided to keep it in place. Now, exercising was a part of my daily ritual.

Once I finished with my weight training, I stepped onto my treadmill. "Begin morning run," I said to Max. "Bifrost track."

The virtual gym vanished. Now I was standing on a semitransparent running track, a curved looping ribbon suspended in a starry nebula. Giant ringed planets and multicolored moons were suspended in space all around me. The running track stretched out ahead of me, rising, falling, and occasionally spiraling into a helix. An invisible barrier prevented me from accidentally running off the edge of the track and plummeting into the starry abyss. The Bifrost track was another stand-alone simulation, one of several hundred track designs stored on my console's hard drive.

As I began to run, Max fired up my '80s music playlist. As the first song began, I quickly rattled off its title, artist, album, and year of release from memory: "'A Million Miles Away,' the Plimsouls, *Everywhere at Once*, 1983." Then I began to sing along, reciting the lyrics. Having the right '80s song lyric memorized might save my avatar's life someday.

When I finished my run, I pulled off my visor and began removing my haptic suit. This had to be done slowly to prevent damaging the suit's components. As I carefully peeled it off, the contact patches made tiny popping sounds as they pulled free of my skin, leaving tiny circular marks all over my body. Once I had the suit off, I placed it inside the cleaning unit and laid my clean spare suit out on the floor.

Max had already turned on the shower for me, setting the water temperature right where I liked it. As I jumped into the steam-filled stall, Max switched the music over to my shower tunes playlist. I recognized the opening riffs of "Change," by John Waite. From the *Vision Quest* soundtrack. Geffen Records, 1985.

The shower worked a lot like an old car wash. I just stood there while it did most of the work, blasting me from all angles with jets of soapy water, then rinsing me off. I had no hair to wash, because the shower also dispensed a nontoxic hair-removing solution that I rubbed all over my face and body. This eliminated the need for me to shave or cut my hair, both hassles I didn't need. Having smooth skin also helped make sure my haptic suit fit snugly. I looked a little freaky without any eyebrows, but I got used to it.

When the rinse jets cut off, the blow-dryers kicked on, blasting the moisture off of my skin in a matter of seconds. I stepped into the kitchen and took out a can of Sludge, a high-protein, vitamin D–infused breakfast drink (to help counteract my sunlight deprivation). As I gulped it down, my computer's sensors silently took note, scanning the barcode and adding the calories to my total for the day. With breakfast out of the way, I pulled on my clean haptic suit. This was less tricky than taking the suit off, but it still took time to do properly.

Once I had the suit on, I ordered the haptic chair to extend. Then I paused and spent a moment staring at my immersion rig. I'd been so proud of all this high-tech hardware when I'd first purchased it. But over the past few months, I'd come to see my rig for what it was: an elaborate contraption for deceiving my senses, to allow me to live in a world that didn't exist. Each component of my rig was a bar in the cell where I had willingly imprisoned myself.

Standing there, under the bleak fluorescents of my tiny one-room apartment, there was no escaping the truth. In real life, I was nothing but an antisocial hermit. A recluse. A pale-skinned pop culture–obsessed geek. An agoraphobic shut-in, with no real friends, family, or genuine human contact. I was just another sad, lost, lonely soul, wasting his life on a glorified videogame.

But not in the OASIS. In there, I was the great Parzival. World-famous gunter and international celebrity. People asked for my autograph. I had a fan club. Several, actually. I was recognized everywhere I went (but only when I wanted to be). I was paid to endorse products. People admired and looked up to me. I got invited to the most exclusive parties. I went to all the hippest clubs and never had to wait in line. I was a pop-culture icon, a VR rock star. And, in gunter circles, I was a legend. Nay, a god.

I sat down and pulled on my gloves and visor. Once my identity was verified, the Gregarious Simulation Systems logo appeared in front of me, followed by the log-in prompt.

Greetings, Parzival.
Please speak your pass phrase.

I cleared my throat and recited my pass phrase. Each word appeared on my display as I said it. "No one in the world ever gets what they want and that is beautiful."

There was a brief pause, and then I let out an involuntary sigh of relief as the OASIS faded into existence all around me.

My avatar slowly materialized in front of the control panel in my stronghold's command center, the same spot where I'd been sitting the night before, engaged in my evening ritual of staring blankly at the Quatrain until I drifted off to sleep and the system logged me out. I'd been staring at the damn thing for almost six months now, and I still hadn't been able to decipher it. No one had. Everyone had theories, of course, but the Jade Key still remained unfound, and top rankings on the Scoreboard remained static.

My command center was located under an armored dome embedded in the rocky surface of my own private asteroid. From here I had a sweeping 360-degree view of the surrounding cratered landscape, stretching to the horizon in all directions. The rest of my stronghold was belowground, in a vast subterranean complex that stretched all the way to the asteroid's core. I'd coded the entire thing myself, shortly after moving to Columbus. My avatar needed a stronghold, and I didn't want any neighbors, so I'd bought the cheapest planetoid I could find—this tiny barren asteroid in Sector Fourteen. Its designation was S14A316, but I'd renamed it Falco, after the Austrian rap star. (I wasn't a huge Falco fan or anything. I just thought it sounded like a cool name.)

Falco had only a few square kilometers of surface area, but it had still cost me a pretty penny. It had been worth it, though. When you owned your own world, you could build whatever you wanted there. And no one could visit it unless I granted them access, something I never gave to anyone. My stronghold was my home inside the OASIS. My avatar's sanctuary. It was the one place in the entire simulation where I was truly safe.

As soon as my log-in sequence completed, a window popped up on my display, informing me that today was an election day. Now that I was eighteen, I could vote, in both the OASIS elections and the elections for U.S. government officials. I didn't bother with the latter, because I didn't see the point. The once-great country into which I'd been born now resembled its former self in name only. It didn't matter who was in charge. Those people were rearranging deck chairs on the *Titanic* and everyone knew it. Besides, now that everyone could vote from home, via the OASIS, the only people who could get elected were movie stars, reality TV personalities, or radical televangelists.

I did take the time to vote in the OASIS elections, however, because their outcomes actually affected me. The voting process only took me a few minutes, because I was already familiar with all of the major issues GSS had put on the ballot. It was also time to elect the president and VP of the OASIS User Council, but that was a no-brainer. Like most gunters, I voted to reelect Cory Doctorow and Wil Wheaton (again). There were no term limits, and those two geezers had been doing a kick-ass job of protecting user rights for over a decade.

When I finished voting, I adjusted my haptic chair slightly and studied the command console in front of me. It was crammed with switches, buttons, keyboards, joysticks, and display screens. A bank of security monitors on my left were linked to virtual cameras placed throughout the interior and exterior of my stronghold. To my right, another bank of monitors displayed all of my favorite news and entertainment vidfeeds. Among these was my own channel: *Parzival-TV—Broadcasting obscure eclectic crap, 24-7-365.*

Earlier that year, GSS had added a new feature to every OASIS user's account: the POV (personal OASIS vidfeed) channel. It allowed anyone who paid a monthly fee to run their own streaming television network. Anyone logged into the simulation could tune in and watch your POV channel, from anywhere in the world. What you aired on your channel and who you allowed to view it were entirely up to you. Most users chose to run a "voyeur channel," which was like being the star of your own twenty-four-hour reality show. Hovering virtual cameras would follow your avatar around the OASIS as you went about your day-to-day activities. You could limit access to your channel so that only your friends could watch, or you could charge viewers by the hour to access your POV. A lot of second-tier celebrities and pornographers did this, selling their virtual lives at a per-minute premium.

Some people used their POV to broadcast live video of their real-world selves, or their dog, or their kids. Some people programmed nothing but old cartoons. The possibilities were endless, and the variety of stuff available seemed to grow more twisted every day. Nonstop foot fetish videos broadcast out of Eastern Europe. Amateur porn featuring deviant soccer moms in Minnesota. You name it. Every flavor of weirdness the human psyche could cook up was being filmed and broadcast online. The vast wasteland of television programming had finally reached its zenith, and the average person was no longer limited to fifteen minutes of fame. Now everyone could be on TV, every second of every day, whether or not anyone was watching.

Parzival-TV wasn't a voyeur channel. In fact, I never showed my avatar's face on my vidfeed. Instead, I programmed a selection of classic '80s TV shows, retro commercials, cartoons, music videos, and movies. Lots of movies. On the weekends, I showed old Japanese monster flicks, along with some vintage anime. Whatever struck my fancy. It didn't really matter what I programmed. My avatar was still one of the High Five, so my vidfeed drew millions of viewers every day, regardless of what I aired, and this allowed me to sell commercial time to my various sponsors.

Most of Parzival-TV's regular viewers were gunters who monitored my vidfeed with the hope that I'd inadvertently reveal some key piece of information about the Jade Key or the egg itself. I never did, of course. At the moment, Parzival-TV was wrapping up a nonstop two-day *Kikaider* marathon. *Kikaider* was a late-'70s Japanese action show about a red-and-blue android who beat the crap out of rubber-suited monsters in each episode. I had a weakness for vintage *kaiju* and *tokusatsu*, shows like *Spectreman*, *The Space Giants*, and *Supaidaman*.

I pulled up my programming grid and made a few changes to my evening lineup. I cleared away the episodes of *Riptide* and *Misfits of Science* I'd programmed and dropped in a few back-to-back flicks starring Gamera, my favorite giant flying turtle. I thought they should be real crowd pleasers. Then, to finish off the broadcast day, I added a few episodes of *Silver Spoons*.

Art3mis also ran her own vidfeed channel, Art3mivision, and I always kept one of my monitors tuned to it. Right now, she was airing her usual Monday evening fare: an episode of *Square Pegs*. After that would be *ElectraWoman and DynaGirl*, followed by back-to-back episodes of *Isis* and *Wonder Woman*. Her programming lineup hadn't changed in ages. But it didn't matter. She still got killer ratings. Recently, she'd also launched her own wildly successful clothing line for full-figured female avatars, under the label Art3Miss. She was doing really well for herself.

After that night in the Distracted Globe, Art3mis had cut off all contact with me. She blocked all of my e-mails, phone calls, and chat requests. She also stopped making posts to her blog.

I tried everything I could think of to reach her. I sent her avatar flowers. I made multiple trips to her avatar's stronghold, an armored palace on Benatar, the small moon she owned. I dropped mix tapes and notes on her palace from the air, like lovesick bombs. Once, in a supreme act of desperation, I stood outside her palace gates for two solid hours, with a boom box over my head, blasting "In Your Eyes" by Peter Gabriel at full volume.

She didn't come out. I don't even know if she was home.

I'd been living in Columbus for over five months now, and it had been eight long, torturous weeks since I'd last spoken to Art3mis. But I hadn't spent that time moping around and feeling sorry for myself. Well, not *all* of it, anyway. I'd tried to enjoy my "new life" as a world-famous sector-hopping gunter. Even though I'd maxxed out my avatar's power level, I continued to complete as many quests as possible, to add to my already impressive collection of weapons, magic items, and vehicles, which I kept in a vault deep within my stronghold. Questing kept me busy and served as a welcome distraction from the growing loneliness and isolation I felt.

I'd tried to reconnect with Aech after Art3mis had dumped me, but things weren't the same. We'd grown apart, and I knew it was my fault. Our conversations were now stilted and reserved, as if we were both afraid of revealing some key piece of information the other might be able to use. I could tell he no longer trusted me. And while I'd been off obsessing over Art3mis, it seemed Aech had become obsessed with being the first gunter to find the Jade Key. But it had been almost half a year since we'd cleared the First Gate, and the Jade Key's location still remained a mystery.

I hadn't spoken to Aech in almost a month. My last conversation with him had devolved into a shouting match, which had ended when I reminded Aech that he "never even would have found the Copper Key" if I hadn't led him straight to it. He'd glared at me in silence for a second, then logged out of the chat room. Stubborn pride kept me from calling him back right away to apologize, and now it seemed like too much time had passed.

Yeah. I was on a roll. In less than six months, I'd managed to wreck both of my closest friendships.

I flipped over to Aech's channel, which he called the H-Feed. He was currently showing a WWF match from the late '80s, featuring Hulk Hogan and Andre the Giant. I didn't even bother checking Daito and Shoto's channel, the Daishow, because I knew they'd be showing some old samurai movie. That's all those guys ever aired.

A few months after our confrontational first meeting in Aech's basement, I'd managed to form a tenuous friendship with Daito and Shoto when the three of us teamed up to complete an extended quest in Sector Twenty-two. It was my idea. I felt bad about how our first encounter had ended, and I waited for an opportunity to extend some sort of olive branch to the two samurai. It came when I discovered a hidden high-level quest called Shodai Urutoraman on the planet Tokusatsu. The creation date in the quest's colophon said it had been launched several years after Halliday's death, which meant it couldn't have any relation to the contest. It was also a Japanese-language quest, created by GSS's Hokkaido division. I could have tried to complete it on my own, using the Mandarax real-time translator software installed in all OASIS accounts, but it would have been risky. Mandarax had been known to garble or misinterpret quest instructions and cues, which could easily lead to fatal mistakes.

Daito and Shoto lived in Japan (they'd become national heroes there), and I knew that they both spoke Japanese and English fluently. So I'd contacted them to ask if they were interested in teaming up with me, just for this one quest. They were skeptical at first, but after I described the unique nature of the quest, and what I believed the payoff for solving it might be, they finally agreed. The three of us met outside the quest gate on Tokusatsu and entered it together.

The quest was a re-creation of all thirty-nine episodes of the original *Ultraman* TV series, which had aired on Japanese television from 1966 to 1967. The show's storyline centered around a human named Hayata who was a member of the Science Patrol, an organization devoted to fighting the hordes of giant Godzilla-like monsters that were constantly attacking Earth and threatening human civilization. When the Science Patrol encountered a threat they couldn't handle on their own, Hayata would use an alien device called a Beta Capsule to transform into an alien superbeing known as Ultraman. Then he would proceed to kick the monster-of-the-week's ass, using all sorts of kung-fu moves and energy attacks.

If I'd entered the quest gate by myself, I would have automatically played through the entire series storyline as Hayata. But because Shoto, Daito, and I had all entered at once, we were each allowed to select a different Science Patrol team member to play. We could then change or swap characters at the start of the next level or "episode." The three of us took turns playing Hayata and his Science Patrol teammates Hoshino and Arashi. As with most quests in the OASIS, playing as a team made it easier to defeat the various enemies and complete each of the levels.

It took us an entire week, often playing over sixteen hours a day, before we were finally able to clear all thirty-nine levels and complete the quest. As we stepped out of the quest gate, our avatars were each awarded a huge amount of experience points and several thousand credits. But the real prize for completing the quest was an incredibly rare artifact: Hayata's Beta Capsule. The small metal cylinder allowed the avatar who possessed it to transform into Ultraman once a day, for up to three minutes.

Since there were three of us, there was a debate over who should be allowed to keep the artifact. "Parzival should have it," Shoto had said, turning to his older brother. "He found this quest. We wouldn't even have known about it, were it not for him."

Of course, Daito had disagreed. "And he would not have been able to complete the quest without our help!" He said the only fair thing to do would be to auction off the Beta Capsule and split the proceeds. But there was no way I could allow that. The artifact was far too valuable to sell, and I knew it would end up in the hands of the Sixers, because they purchased nearly every major artifact that went up for auction. I also saw this as an opportunity to get on Daisho's good side.

"You two should keep the Beta Capsule," I said. "*Urutoraman* is Japan's greatest superhero. His powers belong in Japanese hands."

They were both surprised and humbled by my generosity. Especially Daito. "Thank you, Parzival-san," he said, bowing low. "You are a man of honor."

After that, the three of us had parted as friends, if not necessarily allies, and I considered that an ample reward for my efforts.

A chime sounded in my ears and I checked the time. It was almost eight o'clock. Time to make the doughnuts.

* * *

I was always hard-up for cash, no matter how frugal I tried to be. I had several large bills to pay each month, both in the real world and in the OASIS. My real-world expenses were pretty standard. Rent, electricity, food, water. Hardware repairs and upgrades. My avatar's expenses were far more exotic. Spacecraft repairs. Teleportation fees. Power cells. Ammunition. I purchased my ammo in bulk, but it still wasn't cheap. And my monthly teleportation expenses were often astronomical. My search for the egg required constant travel, and GSS kept raising their teleportation fares.

I'd already spent all of my remaining product endorsement dough. Most of it went toward the cost of my rig and buying my own asteroid. I earned a decent amount of money each month by selling commercial time on my POV channel and by auctioning off any unneeded magic items, armor, or weapons I acquired during my travels. But my primary source of income was my full-time job doing OASIS technical support.

When I'd created my new Bryce Lynch identity, I'd given myself a college degree, along with multiple technical certifications and a long, sterling work record as an OASIS programmer and app developer. However, despite my sterling bogus résumé, the only job I'd been able to get was as a tier-one technical support representative at Helpful Helpdesk Inc., one of the contract firms GSS used to handle OASIS customer service and support. Now I worked forty hours a week, helping morons reboot their OASIS consoles and update the drivers for their haptic gloves. It was grueling work, but it paid the rent.

I logged out of my own OASIS account and then used my rig to log into a separate OASIS account I'd been issued for work. The log-in process completed and I took control of a Happy Helpdesk avatar, a cookie-cutter Ken doll that I used to take tech-support calls. This avatar appeared inside a huge virtual call center, inside a virtual cubicle, sitting at a virtual desk, in front of a virtual computer, wearing a virtual phone headset.

I thought of this place as my own private virtual hell.

Helpful Helpdesk Inc. took millions of calls a day, from all over the world. Twenty-four seven, three sixty-five. One angry, befuddled cretin after another. There was no downtime between calls, because there were always several hundred morons in the call queue, all of them willing to wait on hold for hours to have a tech rep hold their hand and fix their problem. Why bother looking up the solution online? Why try to figure the problem out on your own when you could have someone else do your thinking for you?

As usual, my ten-hour shift passed slowly. It was impossible for help-desk avatars to leave their cubicles, but I found other ways to pass the time. My work account was rigged so that I couldn't browse outside websites, but I'd hacked my visor to allow me to listen to music or stream movies off my hard drive while I took calls.

When my shift finally ended and I logged out of work, I immediately logged back into my own OASIS account. I had thousands of new e-mail messages waiting, and I could tell just by their subject lines what had happened while I'd been at work.

Art3mis had found the Jade Key.

Like other gunters around the globe, I'd been dreading the next
change on the Scoreboard, because I knew it was going to give the Sixers
an unfair advantage.

A few months after we'd all cleared the First Gate, an anonymous
avatar had placed an ultrapowerful artifact up for auction. It was called
Fyndoro's Tablet of Finding, and it had unique powers that could give its
owner a huge advantage in the hunt for Halliday's Easter egg.

Most of the virtual items in the OASIS were created by the system at
random, and they would "drop" when you killed an NPC or completed
a quest. The rarest such items were artifacts, superpowerful magic items
that gave their owners incredible abilities. Only a few hundred of these
artifacts existed, and most of them dated back to the earliest days of the
OASIS, when it was still primarily an MMO game. Every artifact was
unique, meaning that only one copy of it existed in the entire simulation.
Usually, the way to obtain an artifact was to defeat some godlike villain at
the end of a high-level quest. If you got lucky, the bad guy would drop an
artifact when you killed him. You could also obtain an artifact by killing
an avatar who had one in its inventory, or by purchasing one in an online
auction.

Since artifacts were so rare, it was always big news when one went up
for auction. Some had been known to sell for hundreds of thousands of
credits, depending on their powers. The record had been set three years
ago when an artifact called the Cataclyst was auctioned off. According to

its auction listing, the Cataclyst was a sort of magical bomb, and it could be used only once. When it was detonated, it would kill every single avatar and NPC in the sector, including its owner. There was no defense against it. If you were unlucky enough to be in the same sector when it went off, you were a goner, regardless of how powerful or well protected you were.

The Cataclyst had sold to an anonymous bidder for just over a million credits. The artifact still hadn't been detonated, so its new owner still had it sitting around somewhere, waiting for the right time to use it. It was something of a running joke now. When a gunter was surrounded by avatars she didn't like, she would claim to have the Cataclyst in her inventory and threaten to detonate it. But most people suspected that the item had actually fallen into the Sixers' hands, along with countless other powerful artifacts.

Fyndoro's Tablet of Finding wound up selling for even more than the Cataclyst. According to the auction description, the tablet was a flat circle of polished black stone, and it had one very simple power. Once a day, its owner could write any avatar's name on its surface, and the tablet would display that avatar's location at that exact moment. However, this power had range limitations. If you were in a different OASIS sector than the avatar you were trying to find, the tablet would tell you only which sector your target was currently in. If you were already in the same sector, the tablet would tell you what planet your target was currently on (or closest to, if they were out in space). If you were already on the same planet as your target when you used the tablet, it would show you their exact coordinates on a map.

As the artifact's seller made sure to point out in his auction listing, if you used the tablet's power in conjunction with the Scoreboard, it arguably became the most valuable artifact in the entire OASIS. All you had to do was watch the top rankings on the Scoreboard and wait until someone's score increased. The second that happened, you could write that avatar's name on the tablet and it would tell you where they were at that exact moment, thus revealing the location of the key they'd just found, or the gate they'd just exited. Due to the artifact's range limitations, it might take two or three attempts to narrow down the exact location of a key or a gate, but even so, that was still information a lot of people would be willing to kill for.

When Fyndoro's Tablet of Finding went up for auction, a huge bidding war broke out between several of the large gunter clans. But when the auction finally ended, the tablet wound up selling to the Sixers for almost two million credits. Sorrento himself used his own IOI account to bid on the tablet. He waited until the last few seconds of the auction and then outbid everyone. He could have bid anonymously, but he obviously wanted the world to know who now possessed the artifact. It was also his way of letting those of us in the High Five know that from that moment forward, whenever one of us found a key or cleared a gate, the Sixers would be tracking us. And there was nothing we could do about it.

At first, I was worried the Sixers would also try to use the tablet to hunt down each of our avatars and kill us one at a time. But locating our avatars wouldn't do them any good unless we happened to be in a PvP zone at the time and were stupid enough to stay put until the Sixers could reach us. And since the tablet could be used only once a day, they would also run the risk of missing their window of opportunity if the Scoreboard changed on the same day they tried to use the tablet to locate one of us. They didn't take the chance. They kept the artifact in reserve and waited for their moment.

•　•　•

Less than a half hour after Art3mis's score increase, the entire Sixer fleet was spotted converging on Sector Seven. The moment the Scoreboard changed, the Sixers had obviously used Fyndoro's Tablet of Finding to try to ascertain Art3mis's exact location. Luckily, the Sixer avatar using the tablet (probably Sorrento himself) happened to be in a different sector from Art3mis, so the tablet didn't reveal what planet she was on. It only told the Sixers which sector she was currently in. And so the entire Sixer fleet had immediately hightailed it to Sector Seven.

Thanks to their complete lack of subtlety, the whole world now knew the Jade Key must be hidden somewhere in that sector. Naturally, thousands of gunters began to converge on it too. The Sixers had narrowed the search area for everyone. Luckily, Sector Seven contained hundreds of planets, moons, and other worlds, and the Jade Key could have been hidden on any one of them.

I spent the rest of the day in shock, reeling at the news that I'd been dethroned. That was exactly how the newsfeed headlines put it: PARZIVAL DETHRONED! ART3MIS NEW #1 GUNTER! SIXERS CLOSING IN!

Once I finally got a grip, I pulled up the Scoreboard and made myself stare at it for thirty solid minutes while I mentally berated myself.

HIGH SCORES:

1.	Art3mis	129,000	冊
2.	Parzival	110,000	冊
3.	Aech	108,000	冊冊
4.	Daito	107,000	冊
5.	Shoto	106,000	冊
6.	IOI-655321	105,000	冊
7.	IOI-643187	105,000	冊
8.	IOI-621671	105,000	冊
9.	IOI-678324	105,000	冊
10.	IOI-637330	105,000	冊

You've got no one but yourself to blame, I told myself. *You let success go to your head. You slacked off on your research. What, did you think lightning would strike twice? That eventually you'd just stumble across the clue you needed to find the Jade Key? Sitting in first place all that time gave you a false sense of security. But you don't have that problem now, do you, asshead? No, because instead of buckling down and focusing on your quest like you should have, you pissed away your lead. You wasted almost half a year screwing around and pining over some girl you've never even met in person. The girl who dumped you. The same girl who is going to end up beating you.*

Now . . . get your head back in the game, moron. Find that key.

Suddenly, I wanted to win the contest more than ever. Not just for the money. I wanted to prove myself to Art3mis. And I wanted the Hunt to be over, so that she would talk to me again. So that I could finally meet her in person, see her true face, and try to make sense of how I felt about her.

I cleared the Scoreboard off my display and opened up my grail diary, which had now grown into a vast mountain of data containing every scrap of information I'd collected since the contest began. It appeared as a jumble of cascading windows floating in front of me, displaying text, maps, photos, and audio and video files, all indexed, cross-referenced, and pulsing with life.

I kept the Quatrain open in a window that was always on top. Four lines of text. Twenty-four words. Thirty-four syllables. I'd stared at them so often and for so long that they'd nearly lost all meaning. Looking at them again now, I had to resist the urge to scream in rage and frustration.

> *The captain conceals the Jade Key*
> *in a dwelling long neglected*
> *But you can only blow the whistle*
> *once the trophies are all collected*

I knew the answer was right there in front of me. Art3mis had already figured it out.

I read over my notes about John Draper, aka Captain Crunch, and the toy plastic whistle that had made him famous in the annals of hacker lore. I still believed that these were the "captain" and "whistle" Halliday was referring to. But the rest of the Quatrain's meaning remained a mystery.

But now I possessed a new piece of information—the key was somewhere in Sector Seven. So I pulled up my OASIS atlas and began to search for planets with names I thought might somehow be related to the Quatrain. I found a few worlds named after famous hackers, like Woz and Mitnick, but none named after John Draper. Sector Seven also contained hundreds of worlds named after old Usenet newsgroups, and on one of these, the planet alt.phreaking, there was a statue of Draper posing with an ancient rotary phone in one hand and a Cap'n Crunch whistle in the other. But the statue had been erected three years after Halliday's death, so I knew it was a dead end.

I read through the Quatrain yet again, and this time the last two lines jumped out at me:

> *But you can only blow the whistle*
> *once the trophies are all collected*

Trophies. Somewhere in Sector Seven. I needed to find a collection of trophies in Sector Seven.

I did a quick search of my files on Halliday. From what I could tell, the only trophies he'd ever owned were the five Game Designer of the Year awards he'd won back around the turn of the century. These trophies were still on display in the GSS Museum in Columbus, but there were replicas of them on display inside the OASIS, on a planet called Archaide.

And Archaide was located in Sector Seven.

The connection seemed thin, but I still wanted to check it out. At the very least, it would make me feel like I was doing something productive for the next few hours.

I glanced over at Max, who was currently doing the samba on one of my command center's monitors. "Max, prep the *Vonnegut* for takeoff. If you're not too busy."

Max stopped dancing and smirked at me. "You got it, *El Comanchero!*"

I got up and walked over to my stronghold's elevator, which I'd modeled after the turbolift on the original *Star Trek* series. I rode down four levels to my armory, a massive vault filled with storage shelves, display cases, and weapon racks. I pulled up my avatar's inventory display, which appeared as a classic "paper doll" diagram of my avatar, onto which I could drag and drop various items and pieces of equipment.

Archaide was located in a PvP zone, so I decided to upgrade my gear and wear my Sunday best. I put on my gleaming +10 Hale Mail powered armor, then strapped on my favorite set of blaster pistols and slung a pump-action pistol-grip shotgun across my back, along with a +5 Vorpal Bastard Sword. I also grabbed a few other essential items. An extra pair of antigrav boots. A Ring of Magic Resistance. An Amulet of Protection. Some Gauntlets of Giant Strength. I hated the idea of needing something and not having it with me, so I usually ended up carrying enough equipment for three gunters. When I ran out of room on my avatar's body, I stored the additional gear in my Backpack of Holding.

Once I was properly outfitted, I hopped back on the elevator, and a few seconds later I arrived at the entrance of my hangar, located on the bottom level of my stronghold. Pulsing blue lights lined the runway, which ran up the center of the hangar to a massive pair of armored doors at the far end. These doors opened into the launch tunnel, which led up to a matching set of armored doors set into the asteroid's surface.

Standing on the left side of the runway was my battle-worn X-wing fighter. Parked on the right side was my DeLorean. Sitting on the runway itself was my most frequently used spacecraft, the *Vonnegut*. Max had already powered up the engines, and they emitted a low, steady roar that filled the hangar. The *Vonnegut* was a heavily modified Firefly-class transport vessel, modeled after the *Serenity* in the classic *Firefly* TV series. The ship had been named the *Kaylee* when I'd first obtained it, but I'd immediately rechristened it after one of my favorite twentieth-century novelists. Its new name was stenciled on the side of its battered gray hull.

I'd looted the *Vonnegut* from a cadre of Oviraptor clansmen who had foolishly attempted to hijack my X-wing while I was cruising through a large group of worlds in Sector Eleven known as the Whedonverse. The Oviraptors were cocky bastards with no clue who it was they were messing with. I was in a foul mood even before they'd opened fire on me. Otherwise, I probably would have just evaded them by jumping to light speed. But that day I decided to take their attack personally.

Ships were like most other items in the OASIS. Each one had specific attributes, weapons, and speed capabilities. My X-wing was far more maneuverable than the Oviraptors' large transport ship, so it was no trouble for me to avoid the barrage from their aftermarket guns, while I bombarded them with laser bolts and proton torpedoes. After I disabled their engines, I boarded the ship and proceeded to kill every avatar there. The captain tried to apologize when he saw who I was, but I wasn't in a forgiving mood. After I'd dispatched the crew, I parked my X-wing in the cargo hold and then cruised home in my new ship.

As I approached the *Vonnegut,* the loading ramp extended to the hangar floor. By the time I reached the cockpit, the ship was already lifting off. I heard the landing gear retract with a thud just as I seated myself at the controls.

"Max, lock up the house, and set a course for Archaide."

"Aye, C-c-captain," Max stuttered from one of the cockpit monitors. The hangar doors slid open, and the *Vonnegut* rocketed out the launch tunnel and up into the starry sky. As the ship cleared the surface, the armored tunnel doors slammed closed behind it.

I spotted several ships camped out in a high orbit above Falco. The usual suspects: crazed fans, wannabe disciples, and aspiring bounty hunters. A few of them, the ones currently turning to follow me, were tagalongs—people who spent most of their time trying to tail prominent gunters and gather intel on their movements so they could sell the information later. I was always able to lose these idiots by jumping to light speed. A lucky thing for them. If I couldn't lose someone who was trying to tail me, I usually had no choice but to stop and kill them.

As the *Vonnegut* made the jump to light speed, each of the planets on my viewscreen became a long streak of light. "Li-li-light speed engaged,

Captain," Max reported. "ETA to Archaide is estimated at fifty-three minutes. Fifteen if you want to use the nearest stargate."

Stargates were strategically located throughout each sector. They were really just giant spaceship-sized teleporters, but since they charged by the mass of your ship and the distance you wanted to travel, they were normally used only by corporations or extremely wealthy avatars with credits to burn. I was neither, but under the circumstances, I was willing to splurge a little.

"Let's take the stargate, Max. We're in kind of a hurry."

The *Vonnegut* dropped out of light speed, and Archaide sud-
denly filled the cockpit viewscreen. It stood out from the other planets
in the area because it wasn't coded to look real. All of the neighboring
planets were perfectly rendered, with clouds, continents, or impact craters
covering their curved surfaces. But Archaide had none of these features,
because it was home to the OASIS's largest classic videogame museum,
and its appearance had been designed as a tribute to the vector-graphic
games of the late '70s and early '80s. The planet's only surface feature was
a web of glowing green dots similar to the ground lights on an airport
runway. They were spaced evenly across the globe in a perfect grid, so
that, from orbit, Archaide resembled the vector-graphic Death Star from
Atari's 1983 Star Wars arcade game.

As Max piloted the *Vonnegut* down to the surface, I prepared for the
possibility of combat by charging up my armor and buffing my avatar
with several potions and nano packs. Archaide was both a PvP zone and
a chaos zone, which meant that both magic and technology functioned
here. So I made sure to load up all of my combat contingency macros.

The *Vonnegut*'s perfectly rendered steel loading ramp lowered to the
ground, standing out in sharp contrast against the digital blackness of
Archaide's surface. As I stepped off the ramp, I tapped a keypad on my
right wrist. The ramp retracted, and there was a sharp hum as the ship's
security system activated. A transparent blue shield appeared around the
Vonnegut's hull.

I gazed around at the horizon, which was just a jagged green vector line, denoting mountainous terrain. Here on the surface, Archaide looked exactly like the environment of the 1981 game Battlezone, another vector-graphic classic from Atari. In the distance, a triangular volcano spewed green pixels of lava. You could run toward that volcano for days and never reach it. It always remained at the horizon. Just like in an old videogame, the scenery never changed on Archaide, even if you circumnavigated the globe.

Following my instructions, Max had set the *Vonnegut* down in a landing lot near the equator in the eastern hemisphere. The lot was empty, and the surrounding area appeared deserted. I headed toward the nearest green dot. As I approached, I could see that it was actually the mouth of an entrance tunnel, a neon green circle ten meters in diameter leading belowground. Archaide was a hollow planet, and the museum exhibits were all located beneath the surface.

As I approached the nearest tunnel entrance, I heard loud music emanating from below. I recognized the song as "Pour Some Sugar on Me" by Def Leppard, off their *Hysteria* album (Epic Records, 1987). I reached the edge of the glowing green ring and jumped in. As my avatar plummeted down into the museum, the green vector-graphic theme disappeared and I found myself in high-resolution full-color surroundings. Everything around me looked completely real once again.

Below its surface, Archaide housed thousands of classic video arcades, each one a loving re-creation of an actual arcade that had once existed somewhere in the real world. Since the dawn of the OASIS, thousands of elderly users had come here and painstakingly coded virtual replicas of local arcades they remembered from their childhood, thus making them a permanent part of the museum. And each of these simulated game rooms, bowling alleys, and pizza joints was lined with classic arcade games. There was at least one copy of every coin-operated videogame ever made down here. The original game ROMs were all stored in the planet's OASIS code, and their wooden game cabinets were each coded to look like the antique originals. Hundreds of shrines and exhibits devoted to various game designers and publishers were also scattered throughout the museum.

The museum's various levels were comprised of vast caverns linked by a network of subterranean streets, tunnels, staircases, elevators, escalators, ladders, slides, trapdoors, and secret passageways. It was like a massive underground multilevel labyrinth. The layout made it extremely easy to get lost, so I kept a three-dimensional holographic map on my display. My avatar's present location was indicated by a flashing blue dot. I'd entered the museum next to an old arcade called Aladdin's Castle, close to the surface. I touched a point on the map near the core of the planet, indicating my destination, and the software mapped the quickest route for me to get there. I ran forward, following it.

The museum was divided into layers. Here, near the planet's mantle, you could find the last coin-operated videogames ever made, from the first few decades of the twenty-first century. These were mostly dedicated simulator cabinets with first-generation haptics—vibrating chairs and tilting hydraulic platforms. Lots of networked stock car simulators that allowed people to race each other. These games were the last of their kind. By that era, home videogame consoles had already made most coin-op games obsolete. After the OASIS went online, they stopped making them altogether.

As you ventured deeper into the museum, the games grew older and more archaic. Turn-of-the-century coin-ops. Lots of head-to-head fighting games with blocky polygon-rendered figures beating the crap out of each other on large flat-screen monitors. Shooting games played with crude haptic light guns. Dancing games. Once you reached the level below that, the games all began to look identical. Each was housed in a large rectangular wooden box containing a cathode picture tube with a set of crude game controls mounted in front of it. You used your hands and your eyes (and occasionally your feet) to play these games. There were no haptics. These games didn't make you feel anything. And the deeper I descended, the cruder the game graphics got.

The museum's bottom level, located in the planet core, was a spherical room containing a shrine to the very first videogame, Tennis for Two, invented by William Higinbotham in 1958. The game ran on an ancient analog computer and was played on a tiny oscilloscope screen about five inches in diameter. Next to it was a replica of an ancient PDP-1 computer running a copy of Spacewar!, the second videogame ever made, created by a bunch of students at MIT in 1962.

Like most gunters, I'd already visited Archaide a few times. I'd been to the core and had played both Tennis for Two and Spacewar! until I'd mastered them. Then I'd wandered around the museums' many levels, playing games and looking for clues Halliday might have left behind. But I'd never found anything.

I kept running, farther and farther down, until I reached the Gregarious Simulation Systems Museum, which was located just a few levels above the planet core. I'd been here once before too, so I knew my way around. There were exhibits devoted to all of GSS's most popular games, including several arcade ports of titles they'd originally released for home computers and consoles. It didn't take me long to find the exhibit where Halliday's five Game Designer of the Year trophies were displayed, next to a bronze statue of the man himself.

Within a few minutes, I knew I was wasting my time here. The GSS Museum exhibit was coded so that it was impossible to remove any of the items on display, so the trophies could not be "collected." I spent a few minutes trying in vain to cut one of them free of its pedestal with a laser welding torch before calling it quits.

Another dead end. This whole trip had been a waste of time. I took one last look around and headed for the exit, trying not to let my frustration get the best of me.

I decided to take a different route on my way back up to the surface, through a section of the museum I'd never fully explored on my previous visits. I wandered through a series of tunnels that led me into a giant, cavernous chamber. It contained a kind of underground city comprised entirely of pizza joints, bowling alleys, convenience stores, and, of course, video arcades. I wandered through the maze of empty streets, then down a winding back alley that dead-ended by the entrance of a small pizza shop.

I froze in my tracks when I saw the name of the place.

It was called Happytime Pizza, and it was a replica of a small family-run pizza joint that had existed in Halliday's hometown in the mid-1980s. Halliday appeared to have copied the code for Happytime Pizza from his Middletown simulation and hidden a duplicate of it here in the Archaide museum.

What the hell was it doing here? I'd never seen its existence mentioned on any of the gunter message boards or strategy guides. Was it possible no one had ever spotted it before now?

Halliday mentioned Happytime Pizza several times in the *Almanac,* so I knew he had fond memories of this place. He'd often come here after school, to avoid going home.

The interior re-created the atmosphere of a classic '80s pizza parlor and video arcade in loving detail. Several NPC employees stood behind the counter, tossing dough and slicing pies. (I turned on my Olfatrix tower and discovered that I could actually smell the tomato sauce.) The shop was divided into two halves, the game room and the dining room. The dining room had videogames in it as well—all of the glass-top tables were actually sit-down arcade games known as "cocktail cabinets." You could sit and play Donkey Kong on the table while you ate your pizza.

If I'd been hungry, I could have ordered a real slice of pizza at the counter. The order would have been forwarded to a pizza vendor near my apartment complex, the one I'd specified in my OASIS account's food service preference settings. Then a slice would have been delivered to my door in a matter of minutes, and the cost (including tip) would have been deducted from my OASIS account balance.

As I walked into the game room, I heard a Bryan Adams song blasting out of the speakers mounted on the carpeted walls. Bryan was singing about how, everywhere he went, the kids wanted to rock. I pressed my thumb to a plate on the change machine and bought a single quarter. I scooped it out of the stainless-steel tray and headed to the back of the game room, taking in all of the simulation's little details. I spotted a hand-written note taped to the marquee of a Defender game. It read BEAT THE OWNER'S HIGH SCORE AND WIN A FREE LARGE PIZZA!

A Robotron game was currently displaying its high-score list. Robotron allowed its all-time best player to enter an entire sentence of text beside their score instead of just their initials, and this machine's top dog had used his precious victory space to announce that *Vice-Principal Rundberg is a total douchebag!*

I continued farther into the dark electronic cave and walked up to a Pac-Man machine at the very back of the room, wedged between a Galaga and a Dig Dug. The black-and-yellow cabinet was covered with chips and scratches, and the garish side-art was peeling.

The Pac-Man game's monitor was dark, and there was an OUT OF ORDER sign taped to it. Why would Halliday include a broken game in this simu-lation? Was this just another atmospheric detail? Intrigued, I decided to investigate further.

I pulled the game cabinet out from the wall and saw that the power cord was unplugged. I plugged it back into the wall socket and waited for the game to boot up. It seemed to work fine.

As I was shoving the cabinet back into place, I spotted something. At the top of the game, resting on the metal brace that held the glass marquee in place, was a single quarter. The date on the coin was 1981—the year Pac-Man had been released.

I knew that back in the '80s, placing your quarter on a game's marquee was how you reserved the next turn on the machine. But when I tried to remove the quarter, it wouldn't budge. Like it was welded in place.

Weird.

I slapped the OUT OF ORDER sign on the neighboring Galaga cabinet and looked at the start-up screen, which was listing off the game's villainous ghosts: Inky, Blinky, Pinky, and Clyde. The high score at the top of the screen was 3,333,350 points.

Several things were strange about this. In the real world, Pac-Man machines didn't save their high score if they were unplugged. And the high-score counter was supposed to flip over at 1,000,000 points. But this machine displayed a high score of 3,333,350 points—just 10 points shy of the highest Pac-Man score possible.

The only way to beat that score would be to play a perfect game.

I felt my pulse quicken. I'd uncovered something here. Some sort of Easter egg, hidden inside this old coin-op videogame. It wasn't *the* Easter egg. Just *an* Easter egg. Some sort of challenge or puzzle, one I was almost certain had been created and placed here by Halliday. I didn't know if it had anything to do with the Jade Key. It might not be related to the egg at all. But there was only one way to find out.

I would have to play a perfect game of Pac-Man.

This was no easy feat. You had to play all 256 levels perfectly, all the way up to the final split-screen. And you had to eat every single dot, energizer, fruit, and ghost possible along the way, without ever losing a single life. Less than twenty perfect games had been documented in the game's sixty-year history. One of them, the fastest perfect game ever played, had been accomplished by James Halliday in just under four hours. He'd done it on an original Pac-Man machine located in the Gregarious Games break room.

Because I knew Halliday loved the game, I'd already done a fair amount of research on Pac-Man. But I'd never managed to play a perfect game. Of course, I'd never really made a serious attempt. Up until now, I'd never had a reason to.

I opened my grail diary and pulled up all of the Pac-Man–related data I'd ever collected. The original game code. The unabridged biography of the designer, Toru Iwatani. Every Pac-Man strategy guide ever written.

Every episode of the *Pac-Man* cartoon series. The ingredients for Pac-Man cereal. And, of course, patterns. I had Pac-Man pattern diagrams out the wazoo, along with hundreds of hours of archived video of the best Pac-Man players in history. I'd already studied a lot of this stuff, but I skimmed over it again now to refresh my memory. Then I closed my grail diary and studied the Pac-Man machine in front of me, like a gunfighter sizing up an opponent.

I stretched my arms, rolled my head and neck around on my shoulders, and cracked my knuckles.

When I dropped a quarter into the left coin slot, the game emitted a familiar electronic *bea-wup!* sound. I tapped the Player One button, and the first maze appeared on the screen.

I wrapped my right hand around the joystick and began to play, guiding my pizza-shaped protagonist through one maze after another. *Wakka-wakka-wakka-wakka*.

My synthetic surroundings faded away as I focused on the game and lost myself in its ancient two-dimensional reality. Just as with Dungeons of Daggorath, I was now playing a simulation within a simulation. A game within a game.

•　•　•

I had several false starts. I would play for an hour, or even two; then I'd make one tiny mistake and I'd have to reboot the machine and start all over. But I was now on my eighth attempt, and I'd been playing for six hours straight. I was rockin' like Dokken. This game had been Iceman-perfect so far. Two-hundred and fifty-five screens in and I still hadn't made a single mistake. I'd managed to nail all four ghosts with every single power pill (until the eighteenth maze, when they stop turning blue altogether), and I'd snagged every bonus fruit, bird, bell, and key that had appeared, without dying once.

I was having the best game of my life. This was it. I could feel it. Everything was finally falling in to place. I had *the glow*.

There was a spot in each maze, just above the starting position, where it was possible to "hide" Pac-Man for up to fifteen minutes. In that location, the ghosts couldn't find him. Using this trick, I'd been able to take two quick food and bathroom breaks during the past six hours.

As I chomped my way through the 255th screen, the song "Pac-Man

Fever" began to blast out of the game room stereo. A smile crept onto my face. I knew this had to be a small tip-of-the-hat from Halliday.

Sticking to my tried-and-true pattern one last time, I whipped the joystick right, slid into the secret door, then out the opposite side and straight down to snag the last few remaining dots, clearing the board. I took a deep breath as the outline of the blue maze began to pulse white. And then I saw it, staring me in the face. The fabled split-screen. The end of the game.

Then, in the worst case of bad timing imaginable, a Scoreboard alert flashed on my display, just a few seconds after I began to play through the final screen.

The top ten rankings appeared, superimposed over my view of the Pac-Man screen, and I glanced at them just long enough to see that Aech had now become the second person to find the Jade Key. His score had just jumped 19,000 points, putting him in second place and knocking me into third.

By some miracle, I managed not to flip out. I stayed focused on my Pac-Man game.

I gripped the joystick tighter, refusing to let this wreck my concentration. I was nearly finished! I only had to milk the final 6,760 possible points from this last garbled maze and then I would finally have the high score.

My heart pounded in time with the music as I cleared the unblcmished left half of the maze. Then I ventured into the twisted terrain of the right half, guiding Pac-Man through the pixelated on-screen refuse of the game's depleted memory. Hidden underneath all of those junk sprites and garbled graphics were nine more dots, worth ten points each. I couldn't see them, but I had their locations memorized. I quickly found and ate all nine, gaining 90 more points. Then I turned and ran into the nearest ghost—Clyde—and committed Pacicide, dying for the first time in the game. Pac-Man froze and withered into nothingness with an extended *beeewup*.

Each time Pac-Man died on this final maze, the nine hidden dots reappeared on the deformed right half of the screen. So to achieve the game's maximum possible score, I had to find and eat each of those dots five more times, once with each of my five remaining lives.

I did my best not to think about Aech, who I knew must be holding the Jade Key at that very moment. Right now, he was probably reading whatever clue was etched into its surface.

I pulled the joystick to the right, weaving through the digital debris one final time. I could have done it blindfolded by now. I fish-hooked around

Pinky to grab the two dots near the bottom, then another three in the center, and then the last four near the top.

I'd done it. I had the new high score: 3,333,360 points. A perfect game.

I took my hands off the controls and watched as all four ghosts converged on Pac-Man. GAME OVER flashed in the center of the maze.

I waited. Nothing happened. After a few seconds, the game's attract screen came back up, showing the four ghosts, their names, and their nicknames.

My gaze shot to the quarter sitting on the edge of the marquee brace. Earlier it had been welded in place, unmovable. But now it tumbled forward and fell end-over-end, landing directly in the palm of my avatar's hand. Then it vanished, and a message flashed on my display informing me that the quarter had automatically been added to my inventory. When I tried to take it back out and examine it, I found that I couldn't. The quarter icon remained in my inventory. I couldn't take it out or drop it.

If the quarter had any magical properties, they weren't revealed in its item description, which was completely empty. To learn anything more about the quarter, I would have to cast a series of high-level divination spells on it. That would take days and require a lot of expensive spell components, and even then there was no guarantee the spells would tell me anything.

But at the moment, I was having a hard time caring all that much about the mystery of the undroppable quarter. All I could think about was that Aech and Art3mis had now both beaten me to the Jade Key. And getting the high score on this Pac-Man game on Archaide obviously hadn't gotten me any closer to finding it myself. I really had been wasting my time here.

I headed back up to the planet's surface. Just as I was sitting down in the *Vonnegut*'s cockpit, an e-mail from Aech arrived in my inbox. I felt my pulse quicken when I saw its subject line: *Payback Time.*

Holding my breath, I opened the message and read it:

Dear Parzival,

You and I are officially even now, got that? I consider my debt to you hereby paid in full.

Better hurry. The Sixers must already be on their way there.

Good luck,
Aech

Below his signature was an image file he'd attached to the message. It was a high-resolution scan of the instruction manual cover for the text adventure game Zork—the version released in 1980 by Personal Software for the TRS-80 Model III.

I'd played and solved Zork once, a long time ago, back during the first year of the Hunt. But I'd also played hundreds of other classic text adventure games that year, including all of Zork's sequels, and so most of the details of the game had now faded in my memory. Most old text adventure games were pretty self-explanatory, so I'd never actually bothered to read the Zork instruction manual. I now knew that this had a been a colossal mistake.

On the manual's cover was a painting depicting a scene from the game. A swashbuckling adventurer wearing armor and a winged helmet stood with a glowing blue sword raised over his head, preparing to strike a troll cowering before him. The adventurer clutched several treasures in his other hand, and more treasures lay at his feet, scattered among human bones. A dark, fanged creature lurked just behind the hero, glowering malevolently.

All of this was in the painting's foreground, but my eyes had instantly locked on what was in the background: a large white house, with its front door and windows all boarded up.

A dwelling long neglected.

I stared at the image a few more seconds, just long enough to curse myself for not making the connection on my own, months ago. Then I fired the *Vonnegut*'s engines and set a course for another planet in Sector Seven, not far from Archaide. It was small world called Frobozz that was home to a detailed re-creation of the game Zork.

It was also, I now knew, the hiding place of the Jade Key.

Frobozz was located in a group of several hundred rarely vis-ited worlds known as the XYZZY Cluster. These planets all dated back to the early days of the OASIS, and each one re-created the environment of some classic text adventure game or MUD (multi-user dungeon). Each of these worlds was a kind of shrine—an interactive tribute to the OASIS's earliest ancestors.

Text adventure games (often referred to as "interactive fiction" by modern scholars) used text to create the virtual environment the player inhabited. The game program provided you with a simple written description of your surroundings, then asked what you wanted to do next. To move around or interact with your virtual surroundings, you keyed in text commands telling the game what you wanted your avatar to do. These instructions had to be very simple, usually composed of just two or three words, such as "go south" or "get sword." If a command was too complex, the game's simple parsing engine wouldn't be able to understand it. By reading and typing text, you made your way through the virtual world, collecting treasure, fighting monsters, avoiding traps, and solving puzzles until you finally reached the end of the game.

The first text adventure game I'd ever played was called Colossal Cave, and initially the text-only interface had seemed incredibly simple and crude to me. But after playing for a few minutes, I quickly became immersed in the reality created by the words on the screen. Somehow, the game's simple two-sentence room descriptions were able to conjure up vivid images in my mind's eye.

Zork was one of the earliest and most famous text adventure games. According to my grail diary, I'd played the game through to the end just once, all in one day, over four years ago. Since then, in a shocking display of unforgivable ignorance, I'd somehow forgotten two very important details about the game:

1. Zork began with your character standing outside a shuttered white house.

2. Inside the living room of that white house there was a trophy case.

To complete the game, every treasure you collected had to be returned to the living room and placed inside the trophy case.

Finally, the rest of the Quatrain made sense.

> *The captain conceals the Jade Key*
> *in a dwelling long neglected*
> *But you can only blow the whistle*
> *once the trophies are all collected*

Decades ago, Zork and its sequels had all been licensed and re-created inside the OASIS as stunning three-dimensional immersive simulations all located on the planet Frobozz, which was named after a character in the Zork universe. So the *dwelling long neglected*—the one I'd been trying to locate for the past six months—had been sitting right out in the open on Frobozz this entire time. Hiding in plain sight.

* * *

I checked the ship's navigational computer. Traveling at light speed, it would take me just over fifteen minutes to reach Frobozz. There was a good chance the Sixers would beat me there. If they did, there would probably already be a small armada of Sixer gunships waiting in orbit around the planet when I dropped out of light speed. I would have to fight my way through them to reach the surface, and then either lose them, or try to find the Jade Key with them still breathing down my neck. Not a good scenario.

Luckily, I had a backup plan. My Ring of Teleportation. It was one of the most valuable magic items in my inventory, looted from the hoard of a red dragon I'd slain on Gygax. The ring allowed my avatar to teleport once a month, to any location in the OASIS. I only used it in dire emergencies as a last-ditch means of escape, or when I needed to get somewhere in a big hurry. Like right now.

I quickly programmed the *Vonnegut*'s onboard computer to autopilot the ship to Frobozz. I instructed it to activate its cloaking device as soon as it dropped out of hyperspace, then locate me on the planet's surface and land somewhere nearby. If I was lucky, the Sixers wouldn't detect my ship and blast it out of the sky before it could reach me. If they did, I'd be stuck on Frobozz with no way to leave, while the entire Sixer army closed in on me.

I engaged the *Vonnegut*'s autopilot, then activated my Ring of Teleportation by speaking the command word, "Brundell." When the ring began to glow, I said the name of the planet where I wished to teleport. A world map of Frobozz appeared on my display. It was a large world, and like the planet Middletown, its surface was covered with hundreds of identical copies of the same simulation—in this case, re-creations of the Zork playing field. There were 512 copies of it, to be exact, which meant there were 512 white houses, spaced out evenly across the planet's surface. I should be able to obtain the Jade Key at any one of them, so I selected one of the copies at random on the map. My ring emitted a blinding flash of light, and a split second later my avatar was there, standing on the surface of Frobozz.

I opened my grail diary and located my original notes on how to solve Zork. Then I pulled up a map of the game's playing field and placed it in the corner of my display.

Surveying the skies, I didn't see any sign of the Sixers, but that didn't mean they hadn't already arrived. Sorrento and his underlings had probably just teleported to one of the other playing fields. Everybody knew that the Sixers had already been camped out in Sector Seven, waiting for this moment. As soon as they saw Aech's score increase, they would have used Fyndoro's Tablet of Finding and learned that he was currently on Frobozz. Which meant the entire Sixer armada would already be on its way here. So I needed to get to the key as quickly as possible, then get the hell of out Dodge.

I took a look around. My surroundings were eerily familiar.

The opening text description in the game Zork read as follows:

WEST OF HOUSE
You are standing in an open field west of a white house, with a boarded front door. There is
a small mailbox here.

>

My avatar now stood in that open field, just west of the white house. The front door of the old Victorian mansion was boarded up, and there was a mailbox just a few yards away from me, at the end of the walkway leading to the house. The house was surrounded by a dense forest, and beyond it I saw a range of jagged mountain peaks. Glancing off to my left, I spotted a path leading to the north, right where I knew it should be.

I ran around to the back of the house. I found a small window there, slightly ajar, and I forced it open and climbed inside. As expected, I found myself in the kitchen. A wooden table sat in the center of the room, and on it rested a long brown sack and a bottle of water. A chimney stood nearby, and a staircase led up to the attic. A hallway off to my left led to the living room. Just like the game.

But the kitchen also contained things that weren't mentioned in the game's text description of this room. A stove, a refrigerator, several wooden chairs, a sink, and a few rows of kitchen cabinets. I opened the fridge. It was full of junk food. Fossilized pizza, snack puddings, lunch meat, and a wide array of condiment packets. I checked the cupboards. They were filled with canned and dry goods. Rice, pasta, soup.

And cereal.

One entire cupboard was crammed with boxes of vintage breakfast cereals, most of which had been discontinued before I'd been born. Fruit Loops, Honeycombs, Lucky Charms, Count Chocula, Quisp, Frosted Flakes. And hidden way at the back was a lone box of Cap'n Crunch. Printed clearly on the front of it were the words FREE TOY WHISTLE INSIDE!

The captain conceals the Jade Key.

I dumped the contents of the box out on the counter, scattering golden cereal nuggets everywhere. Then I spotted it—a small plastic whistle encased in a clear cellophane envelope. I tore off the cellophane and held the whistle in my hand. It was yellow in color, with the cartoon face of Cap'n Crunch molded on one side and a small dog on the other. The words CAP'N CRUNCH BO'SUN WHISTLE were embossed on either side.

I raised the whistle to my avatar's lips and blew into it. But the whistle emitted no sound, and nothing happened.

You can only blow the whistle once the trophies are all collected.

I pocketed the whistle and opened the sack on the kitchen table. I saw a clove of garlic inside, and I added it to my inventory. Then I ran west, into the living room. The floor was covered with a large Oriental rug. Antique furniture, the kind I'd seen in films from the 1940s, was positioned around the room. A wooden door with odd characters carved into its surface was set into the west wall. And against the opposite wall there was a beautiful glass trophy case. It was empty. A battery-powered lantern sat on top of the case, and a shining sword was mounted on the wall directly above it.

I took the sword and the lantern, then rolled up the Oriental rug, uncovering the trapdoor I already knew was hidden underneath. I opened it, revealing a staircase that led down into a darkened cellar.

I turned on the lamp. As I descended the staircase, my sword began to glow.

• • •

I continued to refer to the Zork notes in my grail diary, which reminded me exactly how to make my way through the game's labyrinth of rooms, passageways, and puzzles. I collected all nineteen of the game's treasures as I went, returning repeatedly to the living room in the white house to place them in the trophy case, a few at a time. Along the way, I had to do battle with several NPCs: a troll, a Cyclops, and a really annoying thief. As for the legendary grue, lurking in the dark, waiting to dine on my flesh—I simply avoided him.

Aside from the Cap'n Crunch whistle hidden in the kitchen, I found no surprises or deviations from the original game. To solve this immersive three-dimensional version of Zork, I simply had to perform the exact same actions required to solve the original text-based game. By running at top speed and by never stopping to sightsee or second-guess myself, I managed to complete the game in twenty-two minutes.

Shortly after I collected the last of the game's nineteen treasures, a tiny brass bauble, a notice flashed in my display informing me that the *Vonnegut* had arrived outside. The autopilot had just landed the ship in the field to the west of the white house. Its cloaking device was still engaged and its shields were up. If the Sixers were already here, in orbit around the planet, I was hoping they hadn't spotted my ship.

I ran back to the living room of the white house one last time and placed the final treasure inside the trophy case. Just as in the original game, a map appeared inside the case, directing me to a hidden barrow that marked the end of the game. But I wasn't concerned with the map or with finishing the game. All of the "trophies" were now "collected" in the case, so I took out the Cap'n Crunch whistle. It had three holes across the top, and I covered the third one to generate the 2600-hertz tone that had made this whistle famous in the annals of hacker history. Then I blew one clear, shrill note.

The whistle transformed into a small key, and my score on the scoreboard increased by 18,000 points.

I was back in second place, a mere 1,000 points ahead of Aech.

A second later, the entire Zork simulation reset itself. The nineteen items in the trophy case vanished, returning to their original locations, and the rest of the house and the game's playing field returned to the same state in which I'd found them.

As I stared at the key in the palm of my hand, I felt a brief jolt of panic. The key was silver, not the milky green color of jade. But when I turned the key over and examined it more closely, I saw that it actually appeared to be wrapped in silver foil, like a stick of gum or a bar of chocolate. I carefully peeled the wrapper away, and a key made of polished green stone was revealed inside.

The Jade Key.

And just like the Copper Key, I saw that it had a clue etched into its surface:

Continue your quest by taking the test

I reread it several times, but had no immediate revelations as to its meaning, so I placed the key in my inventory, then examined the wrapper. It was silver foil on one side and white paper on the other. I didn't see any markings on either side.

Just then, I heard the muffled roar of approaching spacecraft and knew it must be the Sixers. It sounded like they were here in force.

I pocketed the wrapper and ran out of the house. Overhead, thousands of Sixer gunships filled the sky like an angry swarm of metal wasps. The ships were separating into small groups as they descended, heading off in different directions, as if to blanket the entire surface of the planet.

I didn't think the Sixers would be foolish enough to try to barricade all 512 instances of the white house. That strategy had worked for them on Ludus, but only for a few hours, and they'd only had one location to barricade. The entire planet of Frobozz was in a PvP zone, and both magic and technology functioned here, which meant that all bets were off. There would be hordes of gunters arriving here soon, armed to the teeth, and if the Sixers tried to keep all of them at bay, it would mean war on a scale never before seen in the history of the OASIS.

As I continued running across the field and up the ramp of my ship, I spotted a large squadron of gunships, about a hundred or so, descending from the sky directly above my location. They appeared to be headed straight for me.

Max had already powered up the *Vonnegut*'s engines, so I shouted for him to lift off as soon as I was aboard. When I reached the cockpit controls, I threw the throttle wide open, and the descending swarm of Sixer gunships banked hard to follow me. As my ship blasted its way skyward, I began to take heavy fire from several directions. But I was lucky. My ship was fast, and my shields were top-of-the-line, so they managed to hold up long enough for me to reach orbit. But they failed a few seconds later, and the *Vonnegut*'s hull suffered an alarming amount of damage in the handful of seconds it took me to make the jump to light speed.

It was a close call. The bastards almost got me.

• • •

My ship was in bad shape, so instead of returning directly to my stronghold, I headed to Joe's Garage, an orbital starship repair shop over in Sector Ten. Joe's was an honest NPC-operated establishment, with reasonable rates and lightning-fast service. I used them whenever the *Vonnegut* needed repairs or upgrades.

While Joe and his boys worked on my ship, I sent Aech a brief e-mail to say thanks. I told him that whatever debt he felt he owed me was now most definitely paid in full. I also copped to being a colossally insensitive, self-centered asshole and begged him to forgive me.

As soon as the repairs to my ship were finished, I headed back to my stronghold. Then I spent the rest of the day glued to the newsfeeds. The word about Frobozz was out, and every gunter with the means had already teleported there. Thousands of others were arriving by spacecraft every minute, to do battle with the Sixers and secure their own copy of the Jade Key.

The newsfeeds were airing live coverage of the hundreds of large-scale battles breaking out on Frobozz, around nearly every instance of the "dwelling long neglected." The big gunter clans had once again banded together to launch a coordinated attack on the Sixers' forces. It was the beginning of what would come to be known as the Battle of Frobozz, and casualties were already mounting on both sides.

I also kept a close eye on the Scoreboard, waiting to see evidence that the Sixers had begun to collect copies of the Jade Key while their forces held the opposition at bay. As I feared, the next score to increase was the one beside Sorrento's IOI employee number. It jumped 17,000 points, moving him into fourth place.

Now that the Sixers knew exactly where and how to obtain the Jade Key, I expected to see their other avatars' scores begin to jump as Sorrento's underlings followed his lead. But to my surprise, the next avatar to snag the Jade Key was none other than Shoto. He did it less than twenty minutes after Sorrento.

Somehow, Shoto had managed to evade the hordes of Sixers currently swarming all over the planet, enter an instance of the white house, collect all nineteen of the required treasures, and obtain his copy of the key.

I continued to watch the Scoreboard, expecting to see his brother Daito's score increase as well. But that never happened.

Instead, a few minutes after Shoto obtained his copy of the key, Daito's name disappeared from the Scoreboard entirely. There was only one possible explanation: Daito had just been killed.

Over the next twelve hours, chaos continued to reign on Frobozz as every gunter in the OASIS scrambled to reach the planet and join the fray.

The Sixers had dispersed their grand army across the globe in a bold attempt to blockade all 512 copies of the Zork playing field. But their forces, as vast and well-equipped as they were, were spread far too thin this time. Only seven more of their avatars managed to obtain the Jade Key that day. And when the gunter clans began their coordinated attack on the Sixers' forces, the "boobs in blue" began to suffer heavy casualties and were forced to pull back.

Within a matter of hours, the Sixer high command decided to deploy a new strategy. It had quickly become obvious that they wouldn't be able to maintain over five hundred different blockades or fend off the massive influx of gunters. So they regrouped all of their forces around ten adjacent instances of the Zork playing field near the planet's south pole. They installed powerful force shields over each of them and stationed armored battalions outside the shield walls.

This scaled-down strategy worked, and the Sixers' forces proved sufficient to hold those ten locations and prevent any other gunters from getting inside (and there wasn't much reason for other gunters to try, since over five hundred other instances of Zork now stood wide open and unprotected). Now that the Sixers could operate undisturbed, they basically formed ten lines of avatars outside each white house and began to run them through the process of obtaining the Jade Key, one after another. Everyone could plainly see what they were doing, because the digits beside each IOI employee number on the Scoreboard began to increase by 15,000 points.

At the same time, hundreds of gunter scores were increasing as well. Now that the location of the Jade Key was public knowledge, deciphering the Quatrain and figuring out how to obtain the key was relatively easy. It was there for the taking to anyone who had already cleared the First Gate.

As the Battle of Frobozz drew to a close, the rankings on the Scoreboard stood like this:

HIGH SCORES:

1.	Art3mis	129,000	卅
2.	Parzival	128,000	卅
3.	Aech	127,000	卅
4.	IOI-655321	122,000	卅
5.	Shoto	122,000	卅
6.	IOI-643187	120,000	卅
7.	IOI-621671	120,000	卅
8.	IOI-678324	120,000	卅
9.	IOI-637330	120,000	卅
10.	IOI-699423	120,000	卅

Even though Shoto had matched Sorrento's score of 122,000 points, Sorrento had achieved that score first, which must be the reason he'd remained in the higher slot. The relatively small point bonuses Art3mis, Aech, Shoto, and I had received for being the first to reach the Copper and Jade keys were what kept our names in the hallowed "High Five" slots. Sorrento had now earned one of these bonuses too. Seeing his IOI employee number above Shoto's name made me cringe.

Scrolling down, I saw that the Scoreboard was now over five thousand names long, with more being added every hour as new avatars finally managed to defeat Acererak at Joust and collect their own instance of the Copper Key.

No one on the message boards seemed to know what had happened to Daito, but the common assumption was that he'd been killed by the Sixers during the first few minutes of the Battle of Frobozz. Rumors about

exactly how he had died were running rampant, but no one had actually
been witness to his demise. Except for maybe Shoto, and he'd vanished. I
sent him a few chat requests, but got no reply. Like me, I assumed he was
focusing all of his energy on finding the Second Gate before the Sixers did.

•   •   •

I sat in my stronghold, staring at the Jade Key and reciting the words
etched into its spine, over and over, like a maddening mantra:

> *Continue your quest by taking the test*
> *Continue your quest by taking the test*
> *Continue your quest by taking the test*

Yes, but what test? What test was I supposed to take? The Kobayashi
Maru? The Pepsi Challenge? Could the clue have been any *more* vague?

I reached under my visor and rubbed my eyes in frustration. I decided
I needed to take a break and get some sleep. I pulled up my avatar's inventory and placed the Jade Key back inside. As I did, I noticed the silver foil
wrapper in the inventory slot beside it—the wrapper that had covered the
Jade Key when it first appeared in my hand.

I knew the secret to deciphering the riddle must involve the wrapper in
some way, but I still couldn't sort out how. I wondered if it might be a reference to *Willy Wonka and the Chocolate Factory,* but then decided against
it. There hadn't been any golden ticket inside the wrapper. It must have
some other purpose or meaning.

I stared at the wrapper and pondered this until I could no longer keep
my eyes open. Then I logged out and went to sleep.

A few hours later, at 6:12 a.m. OST, I was jolted awake by the gut-
wrenching sound of my Scoreboard alarm alerting me that one of the top
rankings had changed again.

Filled with a growing sense of dread, I logged in and pulled up the
Scoreboard, unsure of what to expect. Maybe Art3mis had finally cleared
Gate Two? Or perhaps Aech or Shoto had achieved that honor.

But all of their scores remained unchanged. To my horror, I saw that it
was Sorrento's score that had increased, by 200,000 points. And two gate
icons now appeared beside it.

Sorrento had just become the first person to find and clear the Second Gate. As a result, his avatar now stood in first place, at the top of the Scoreboard.

I sat there frozen, staring at Sorrento's employee number, silently weighing the repercussions of what had just happened.

Upon exiting the gate, Sorrento would have been given a clue as to the location of the Crystal Key. The key that would open the third and final gate. So now the Sixers were the only ones who possessed that clue. Which meant they were now closer to finding Halliday's Easter egg than anyone had ever been.

I suddenly felt ill, and I was also having a difficult time breathing. I realized I must be having some sort of panic attack. A total and complete freak-out. A massive mental meltdown. Whatever you want to call it. I went a little nuts.

I tried calling Aech, but he didn't pick up. Either he was still pissed off at me, or he had other, more pressing matters to attend to. I was about to call Shoto, but then I remembered that his brother's avatar had just been killed. He probably wasn't in a very receptive mood.

I considered flying to Benatar to try to get Art3mis to talk to me, but then I came to my senses. She'd had the Jade Key in her possession for several days, and she still hadn't been able to clear the Second Gate. Learning that the Sixers had done it in less than twenty-four hours had probably driven her into a psychotic rage. Or maybe a catatonic stupor. She probably didn't feel like talking to anyone right now, least of all me.

I tried calling her anyway. As usual, she didn't answer.

I was so desperate to hear a familiar voice that I resorted to talking to Max. In my current state, even his glib computer-generated voice was somehow comforting. Of course, it didn't take long for Max to run out of preprogrammed replies; and when he started to repeat himself the illusion that I was talking to another person was shattered, and I felt even more alone. You know you've totally screwed up your life when your whole world turns to shit and the only person you have to talk to is your system agent software.

I couldn't go back to sleep, so I stayed up watching the newsfeeds and scanning the gunter message boards. The Sixer armada remained on Frobozz, and their avatars were still farming copies of the Jade Key.

Sorrento had obviously learned from his previous mistake. Now that the Sixers alone knew the location of the Second Gate, they weren't going to be stupid enough to reveal its location to the world by trying to barricade it with their armada. But they were still taking full advantage of the situation. As the day progressed, the Sixers continued to walk additional avatars through the Second Gate. After Sorrento made it through, another ten Sixers cleared it during the following twenty-four hours. As each Sixer score increased by 200,000 points, Art3mis, Aech, Shoto, and I were all pushed farther and farther down the Scoreboard until we'd been knocked out of the top ten entirely, and the Scoreboard's main page displayed nothing but IOI employee numbers.

The Sixers now ruled the roost.

Then, when I was sure things couldn't possibly get any worse, they did. They got much, much worse. Two days after he cleared the Second Gate, Sorrento's score jumped another 30,000 points, indicating that he had just acquired the Crystal Key.

I sat there in my stronghold, staring at the monitors, watching all of this unfold in stunned horror. There was no denying it. The end of the contest was at hand. And it wasn't going to end like I'd always thought it would, with some noble, worthy gunter finding the egg and winning the prize. I'd been kidding myself for the past five and a half years. We all had. This story was not going to have a happy ending. The bad guys were going to win.

I spent the next twenty-four hours in a frantic funk, obsessively checking the Scoreboard every five seconds, expecting the end to come at any moment.

Sorrento, or one of his many "Halliday experts," had obviously been able to decipher the riddle and locate the Second Gate. But even though the proof was right there on the Scoreboard, I still had a hard time believing it. Up until now, the Sixers had only made progress by tracking Art3mis, Aech, or me. How had those same clueless asshats found the Second Gate on their own? Maybe they'd just gotten lucky. Or perhaps they'd discovered some new and innovative way to cheat. How else could they have solved the riddle so quickly, when Art3mis hadn't been able to do it with several days' head start?

My brain felt like hammered Play-Doh. I couldn't make any sense of the clue printed on the Jade Key. I was completely out of ideas. Even lame ones. I didn't know what to do or where to look next.

As the night went on, the Sixers continued to acquire copies of the

Crystal Key. Each time one of their scores increased it was like a knife in my heart. But I couldn't make myself stop checking the Scoreboard. I was utterly transfixed.

I felt myself inching toward complete hopelessness. My efforts over the past five years had been for nothing. I'd foolishly underestimated Sorrento and the Sixers. And I was about to pay the ultimate price for my hubris. Those soulless corporate lackeys were closing in on the egg at this very moment. I could sense it, with every fiber of my being.

I'd already lost Art3mis, and now I was going to lose the contest, too.

I'd already decided what I was going to do when it happened. First, I would choose one of the kids in my official fan club, someone with no money and a first-level newbie avatar, and give her every item I owned. Then I would activate the self-destruct sequence on my stronghold and sit in my command center while the whole place went up in a massive thermonuclear explosion. My avatar would die and GAME OVER would appear in the center of my display. Then I would rip off my visor and leave my apartment for the first time in six months. I would ride the elevator up to the roof. Or maybe I would even take the stairs. Get a little exercise.

There was an arboretum on the roof of my apartment building. I had never visited it, but I'd seen photos and admired the view via webcam. A transparent Plexiglas barrier had been installed around the ledge to keep people from jumping, but it was a joke. At least three determined individuals had managed to climb over it since I'd moved in.

I would sit up there and breathe the unfiltered city air for a while, feeling the wind on my skin. Then I would scale the barrier and hurl myself over the side.

This was my current plan.

I was trying to decide what tune I should whistle as I plummeted to my death when my phone rang. It was Shoto. I wasn't in the mood to talk, so I let his call roll to vidmail, then watched as Shoto recorded his message. It was brief. He said he needed to come to my stronghold to give me something. Something Daito had left to me in his will.

When I returned his call to arrange a meeting, I could tell Shoto was an emotional wreck. His quiet voice was filled with pain, and the depth of his despair was apparent on the features of his avatar's face. He seemed utterly despondent. In even worse shape than I was.

I asked Shoto why his brother had bothered to make out a "will" for his avatar, instead of just leaving his possessions in Shoto's care. Then Daito could simply create a new avatar and reclaim the items his brother was holding for him. But Shoto told me that his brother would not be creating a new avatar. Not now, or ever. When I asked why, he promised to explain when he saw me in person.

Max alerted me when Shoto arrived an hour or so later. I granted his ship clearance to enter Falco's airspace and told him to park in my hangar.

Shoto's vessel was a large interplanetary trawler named the *Kurosawa,* modeled after a ship called the *Bebop* in the classic anime series *Cowboy Bebop.* Daito and Shoto had used it as their mobile base of operations for as long as I'd known them. The ship was so big that it barely fit through my hangar doors.

I was standing on the runway to greet Shoto as he emerged from the *Kurosawa.* He was dressed in black mourning robes, and his face bore the same inconsolable expression I'd seen when we spoke on the phone.

"Parzival-san," he said, bowing low.

"Shoto-san." I returned the bow respectfully, then stretched out my palm, a gesture he recognized from the time we'd spent questing together. Grinning, he reached out and slipped me some skin. But then his dark expression immediately resurfaced. This was the first time I'd seen Shoto since the quest we'd shared on Tokusatsu (not counting those "Daisho Energy Drink" commercials he and his brother appeared in), and his avatar seemed to be a few inches taller than I remembered.

I led him up to one of my stronghold's rarely used "sitting rooms," a re-creation of the living room set from *Family Ties.* Shoto recognized the decor and nodded his silent approval. Then, ignoring the furniture, he seated himself in the center of the floor. He sat *seiza*-style, folding his legs under his thighs. I did the same, positioning myself so that our avatars faced each other. We sat in silence for a while. When Shoto was finally ready to speak, he kept his eyes on the floor.

"The Sixers killed my brother last night," he said, almost whispering.

At first, I was too stunned to reply. "You mean they killed his avatar?" I asked, even though I could already tell that wasn't what he meant.

Shoto shook his head. "No. They broke into his apartment, pulled him out of his haptic chair, and threw him off his balcony. He lived on the forty-third floor."

Shoto opened a browser window in the air beside us. It displayed a Japanese newsfeed article. I tapped it with my index finger, and the Mandarax software translated the text to English. The headline was ANOTHER OTAKU SUICIDE. The brief article below said that a young man, Toshiro Yoshiaki, age twenty-two, had jumped to his death from his apartment, located on the forty-third floor of a converted hotel in Shinjuku, Tokyo, where he lived alone. I saw a school photo of Toshiro beside the article. He was a young Japanese man with long, unkempt hair and bad skin. He didn't look anything like his OASIS avatar.

When Shoto saw that I'd finished reading, he closed the window. I hesitated a moment before asking, "Are you sure he didn't really commit suicide? Because his avatar had been killed?"

"No," Shoto said. "Daito did not commit seppuku. I'm sure of it. The Sixers broke into his apartment while we were engaged in combat with them on Frobozz. That's how they were able to defeat his avatar. By killing him, in the real world."

"I'm sorry, Shoto." I didn't know what else to say. I knew he was telling the truth.

"My real name is Akihide," he said. "I want you to know my true name."

I smiled, then bowed, briefly pressing my forehead to the floor. "I appreciate your trusting me with your true name," I said. "My true name is Wade." I could no longer see the point in keeping secrets.

"Thank you, Wade," Shoto said, returning the bow.

"You're welcome, Akihide."

He was silent for a moment; then he cleared his throat and began to talk about Daito. The words poured out of him. It was obvious he needed to talk to someone about what had happened. About what he'd lost.

"Daito's real name was Toshiro Yoshiaki. I didn't even know that until last night, until I saw the news article."

"But . . . I thought you were his brother?" I'd always assumed that Daito and Shoto lived together. That they shared an apartment or something.

"My relationship with Daito is difficult to explain." He stopped to clear his throat. "We were not brothers. Not in real life. Just in the OASIS. Do you understand? We only knew each other online. I never actually met him." He slowly raised his eyes to meet my gaze, to see if I was judging him.

I reached out and rested a hand on his shoulder. "Believe me, Shoto. I understand. Aech and Art3mis are my two best friends, and I've never met either of them in real life either. In fact, *you* are one of my closest friends too."

He bowed his head. "Thank you." I could tell by his voice that he was crying now.

"We're gunters," I said, trying to fill the awkward silence. "We live here, in the OASIS. For us, this is the only reality that has any meaning."

Akihide nodded. A few moments later he continued to talk.

He told me how he and Toshiro had met, six years ago, when they were both enrolled in an OASIS support group for *hikikomori*, young people who had withdrawn from society and chosen to live in total isolation. *Hikikomori* locked themselves in a room, read manga, and cruised the OASIS all day, relying on their families to bring them food. There had been *hikikomori* in Japan since back before the turn of the century, but their number had skyrocketed after the hunt for Halliday's Easter egg began. Millions of young men and women all over the country had locked themselves away from the world. They sometimes called these children the "missing millions."

Akihide and Toshiro became best friends and spent almost every day hanging out together in the OASIS. When the hunt for Halliday's Easter egg began, they'd immediately decided to join forces and search for it together. They made a perfect team, because Toshiro was a prodigy at videogames, while the much younger Akihide was well versed in American pop culture. Akihide's grandmother had attended school in the United States, and both of his parents had been born there, so Akihide had been raised on American movies and television, and he'd grown up learning to speak English and Japanese equally well.

Akihide and Toshiro's mutual love of samurai movies served as the inspiration for their avatars' names and appearances. Shoto and Daito had grown so close that they were now like brothers, so when they created their new gunter identities, they decided that in the OASIS they *were* brothers, from that moment on.

After Shoto and Daito cleared the First Gate and became famous, they gave several interviews with the media. They kept their identities a secret, but they did reveal that they were both Japanese, which made them instant celebrities in Japan. They began to endorse Japanese products and had a cartoon and a live-action TV series based on their exploits. At the height of their fame, Shoto had suggested to Daito that perhaps it was time for them to meet in person. Daito had flown into a rage and stopped speaking to Shoto for several days. After that, Shoto had never suggested it again.

Eventually, Shoto worked his way up to telling me how Daito's avatar had died. The two of them had been aboard the *Kurosawa*, cruising between planets in Sector Seven, when the Scoreboard informed them that Aech had obtained the Jade Key. When that happened, they knew the Sixers would use Fyndoro's Tablet of Finding to pinpoint Aech's exact location and that their ships would soon be converging on it.

In preparation for this, Daito and Shoto had spent the past few weeks planting microscopic tracking devices on the hulls of every Sixer gunship they could find. Using these devices, they were able to follow the gunships when they all abruptly changed course and headed for Frobozz.

As soon as Shoto and Daito learned that Frobozz was the Sixers' destination, they'd easily deciphered the meaning of the Quatrain. And by the time they reached Frobozz, just a few minutes later, they'd already figured out what they needed to do to obtain the Jade Key.

They landed the *Kurosawa* next to an instance of the white house that was still deserted. Shoto ran inside to collect the nineteen treasures and get the key, while Daito remained outside to stand guard. Shoto worked quickly, and he only had two treasures left to collect when Daito informed him by comlink that ten Sixer gunships were closing in on their location. He told his brother to hurry and promised to hold off the enemy until Shoto had the Jade Key. Neither of them knew if they'd have another chance to reach it.

As Shoto scrambled to get the last two treasures and place them in the trophy case, he remotely activated one of the *Kurosawa*'s external cameras and used it to record a short video of Daito's confrontation with the approaching Sixers. Shoto opened a window and played this video clip for me. But he averted his eyes until it was over. He obviously had no desire to watch it again.

On the vidfeed, I saw Daito standing alone in the field beside the white house. A small fleet of Sixer gunships was descending out of the sky, and they began to fire their laser cannons as soon as they were within range. A hailstorm of fiery red bolts began to rain down all around Daito. Behind him, in the distance, I could see more Sixer gunships setting down, and each one was off-loading squadrons of power-armored ground troops. Daito was surrounded.

The Sixers had obviously spotted the *Kurosawa* during its descent to the planet's surface, and they'd made killing the two samurai a priority.

Daito didn't hesitate to use the ace up his sleeve. He pulled out the Beta Capsule, held it aloft in his right hand, and activated it. His avatar instantly changed into Ultraman, a glowing-eyed red-and-silver alien superhero. As his avatar transformed, he also grew to a height of 156 feet.

The Sixer ground forces closing in on him froze in their tracks, staring up in frightened awe as Ultraman Daito snatched two gunships out of the sky and smashed them together, like a giant child playing with two tiny metal toys. He dropped the flaming wreckage to the ground and began to swat other Sixer gunships out of the sky like bothersome flies. The ships that escaped his deadly grasp banked around and sprayed him with laser bolts and machine-gun fire, but both deflected harmlessly off his armored alien skin. Daito let out a booming laugh that echoed across the landscape. Then he made a cross with his arms, intersecting at the wrists. A glowing energy beam blasted forth from his hands, vaporizing half a dozen gunships unlucky enough to fly through its path. Daito turned and swept the beam over the Sixer ground forces around him, frying them like terrified ants under a magnifying glass.

Daito appeared to be enjoying himself immensely. So much so that he paid little attention to the warning light embedded in the center of his chest, which had now begun to flash bright red. This was a signal that his three minutes as Ultraman had nearly elapsed and that his power was almost depleted. This time limit was Ultraman's primary weakness. If Daito failed to deactivate the Beta Capsule and return to human form before his three minutes were up, his avatar would die. But it was obvious that if he changed back into his human form right now, in the middle of the massive Sixer onslaught, he'd be killed instantly too. And Shoto would never be able to reach the ship.

I could see the Sixer troops around Daito screaming into their comlinks for backup, and additional Sixer gunships were still arriving in droves. Daito was blasting them out of the sky one at a time, with perfectly aimed bursts of his specium ray. And with each blast he fired, the warning light on his chest pulsed faster.

Then Shoto emerged from the white house and told his brother via comlink that he'd acquired the Jade Key. In that same instant, the Sixer ground forces spotted Shoto, and sensing a much easier target, they began to redirect their fire at his avatar.

Shoto made a mad dash for the *Kurosawa*. When he activated the Boots of Speed he was wearing, his avatar became a barely visible blur racing across the open field. As Shoto ran, Daito repositioned his giant form to provide him with as much cover as possible. Still firing energy blasts, he was able to keep the Sixers at bay.

Then Daito's voice broke in on the comlink. *"Shoto!"* he shouted. *"I think someone is here! Someone is inside—"*

His voice cut off. At the same moment, his avatar froze, as if he'd been turned to stone, and a log-out icon appeared directly over his head.

Logging out of your OASIS account while you were engaged in combat was the same thing as committing suicide. During the log-out sequence, your avatar froze in place for sixty seconds, during which time you were totally defenseless and susceptible to attack. The log-out sequence was designed this way to prevent avatars from using it as an easy way to escape a fight. You had to stand your ground or retreat to a safe location before you could log out.

Daito's log-out sequence had been engaged at the worst possible moment. As soon as his avatar froze, he began to take heavy laser and gunfire from all directions. The red warning light on his chest began to flash faster and faster until it finally went solid red. When that happened, Daito's giant form fell over and collapsed. As he fell, he barely missed crushing Shoto and the *Kurosawa*. As he hit the ground, his avatar's body transformed and shrank back to its normal size and appearance. Then it began to disappear altogether, slowly fading out of existence. When Daito's avatar vanished completely, it left behind a small pile of spinning items on the ground—everything he'd been carrying in his inventory, including the Beta Capsule. He was dead.

I saw another blur of motion on the vidfeed as Shoto ran back to collect Daito's items. Then he looped around and ran back aboard the *Kurosawa*. The ship lifted off and blasted into orbit, taking heavy fire the entire way.

I was reminded of my own desperate escape from Frobozz. Luckily for Shoto, his brother had wiped out most of the Sixer gunships in the vicinity, and reinforcements had yet to arrive.

Shoto was able to reach orbit and escape by making the jump to light speed. But just barely.

• • •

The video ended and Shoto closed the window.

"How do you think the Sixers found out where he lived?" I asked.

"I don't know," Shoto said. "Daito was careful. He covered his tracks."

"If they found him, they might be able to find you, too," I said.

"I know. I've taken precautions."

"Good."

Shoto removed the Beta Capsule from his inventory and held it out to me. "Daito would have wanted you to have this."

I held up a hand. "No, I think you should keep it. You might need it."

Shoto shook his head. "I have all of his other items," he said. "I don't need this. And I don't want it." He held the capsule out to me, insistent.

I took the artifact and examined it. It was a small metal cylinder, silver and black in color, with a red activation button on its side. Its size and shape reminded me of the lightsabers I owned. But lightsabers were a dime a dozen. I had over fifty in my collection. There was only one Beta Capsule, and it was a far more powerful weapon.

I raised the capsule with both hands and bowed. "Thank you, Shoto-san."

"Thank you, Parzival," he said, returning the bow. "Thank you for listening." He stood up slowly. Everything about his body language seemed to signal defeat.

"You haven't given up yet, have you?" I asked.

"Of course not." He straightened his body and gave me a dark smile. "But finding the egg is no longer my goal. Now, I have a new quest. A far more important one."

"And that is?"

"Revenge."

I nodded. Then I walked over and took down one of the samurai swords mounted on the wall and presented it to Shoto. "Please," I said. "Accept this gift. To aid you in your new quest."

Shoto took the sword and drew its ornate blade a few inches from the scabbard. "A Masamune?" he asked, staring at the blade in wonder.

I nodded. "Yes. And it's a plus-five Vorpal Blade, too."

Shoto bowed again to show his gratitude. *"Arigato."*

We rode the elevator back down to my hangar in silence. Just before he boarded his ship, Shoto turned to me. "How long do you think it will take the Sixers to clear the Third Gate?" he asked.

"I don't know," I said. "Hopefully, long enough for us to catch up with them."

"It's not over until the fat lady is singing, right?"

I nodded. "It's not over until it's over. And it's not over yet."

0026

I figured it out later that night, a few hours after Shoto left my stronghold.

I was sitting in my command center, holding the Jade Key and end-lessly reciting the clue printed on its surface: "'Continue your quest by taking the test.'"

In my other hand, I held the silver foil wrapper. My eyes darted from the key to the wrapper and back to the key again as I tried desperately to make the connection between them. I'd been doing this for hours, and it wasn't getting me anywhere.

I sighed and put the key away, then laid the wrapper flat on the control panel in front of me. I carefully smoothed out all of its folds and wrinkles. The wrapper was square in shape, six inches long on each edge. Silver foil on one side, dull white paper on the other.

I pulled up some image-analysis software and made a high-resolution scan of both sides of the wrapper. Then I magnified both images on my display and studied every micrometer. I couldn't find any markings or writing anywhere, on either side of the wrapper's surface.

I was eating some corn chips at the time, so I was using voice com-mands to operate the image-analysis software. I instructed it to demag-nify the scan of the wrapper and center the image on my display. As I did this, it reminded me of a scene in *Blade Runner,* where Harrison Ford's character, Deckard, uses a similar voice-controlled scanner to analyze a photograph.

I held up the wrapper and took another look at it. As the virtual light reflected off its foil surface, I thought about folding the wrapper into a paper airplane and sailing it across the room. That made me think of origami, which reminded me of another moment from *Blade Runner*. One of the final scenes in the film.

And that was when it hit me.

"*The unicorn,*" I whispered.

The moment I said the word "unicorn" aloud, the wrapper began to fold on its own, there in the palm of my hand. The square piece of foil bent itself in half diagonally, creating a silver triangle. It continued to bend and fold itself into smaller triangles and even smaller diamond shapes until at last it formed a four-legged figure that then sprouted a tail, a head, and finally, a horn.

The wrapper had folded itself into a silver origami unicorn. One of the most iconic images from *Blade Runner*.

I was already riding the elevator down to my hangar and shouting at Max to prep the *Vonnegut* for takeoff.

Continue your quest by taking the test.

Now I knew exactly what "test" that line referred to, and where I needed to go to take it. The origami unicorn had revealed everything to me.

• • •

Blade Runner was referenced in the text of *Anorak's Almanac* no less than fourteen times. It had been one of Halliday's top ten all-time favorite films. And the film was based on a novel by Philip K. Dick, one of Halliday's favorite authors. For these reasons, I'd seen *Blade Runner* over four dozen times and had memorized every frame of the film and every line of dialogue.

As the *Vonnegut* streaked through hyperspace, I pulled the Director's Cut of *Blade Runner* up in a window on my display, then jumped ahead to review two scenes in particular.

The movie, released in 1982, is set in Los Angeles in the year 2019, in a sprawling, hyper-technological future that had never come to pass. The story follows a guy named Rick Deckard, played by Harrison Ford. Deckard works as a "blade runner," a special type of cop who hunts down and kills replicants—genetically engineered beings that are almost indistinguishable from real humans. In fact, replicants look and act so much like real humans that the only way a blade runner can spot one is by using a polygraph-like device called a Voight-Kampff machine to test them.

Continue your quest by taking the test.

Voight-Kampff machines appear in only two scenes in the movie. Both of those take place inside the Tyrell Building, an enormous double-pyramid structure that houses the Tyrell Corporation, the company that manufactures the replicants.

Re-creations of the Tyrell Building were among the most common structures in the OASIS. Copies of it existed on hundreds of different planets, spread throughout all twenty-seven sectors. This was because the code for the building was included as a free built-in template in the OASIS WorldBuilder construction software (along with hundreds of other structures borrowed from various science-fiction films and television series). So for the past twenty-five years, whenever someone used the World-Builder software to create a new planet inside the OASIS, they could just select the Tyrell Building from a drop-down menu and insert a copy of it into their simulation to help fill out the skyline of whatever futuristic city or landscape they were coding. As a result, some worlds had over a dozen copies of the Tyrell Building scattered across their surfaces. I was currently hauling ass at light speed to the closest such world, a cyberpunk-themed planet in Sector Twenty-two called Axrenox.

If my suspicion was correct, every copy of the Tyrell Building on Axrenox contained a hidden entrance into the Second Gate, through the Voight-Kampff machines located inside. I wasn't worried about running into the Sixers, because there was no way they could have barricaded the Second Gate. Not with thousands of copies of the Tyrell Building on hundreds of different worlds.

Once I reached Axrenox, finding a copy of the Tyrell Building took only a few minutes. It was pretty hard to miss. A massive pyramid-shaped structure covering several square kilometers at its base, it towered above most of the structures adjacent to it.

I zeroed in on the first instance of the building I saw and headed straight for it. My ship's cloaking device was already engaged, and I left it activated when I set the *Vonnegut* down on one of the Tyrell Building's landing pads. Then I locked the ship and activated all of its security systems, hoping they'd be enough to keep it from getting stolen until I returned. Magic didn't function here, so I couldn't just shrink the ship and put it in my pocket, and leaving your vessel parked out in the open on a cyberpunk-themed world like Axrenox was like asking for it to get ripped off. The *Vonnegut* would be a target for the first leather-clad booster gang that spotted it.

I pulled up a map of the Tyrell Building template's layout and used it to locate a roof-access elevator a short distance from the platform where I'd landed. When I reached the elevator, I punched in the default security code on the code pad and crossed my fingers. I got lucky. The elevator doors hissed open. Whoever had created this section of the Axrenox cityscape hadn't bothered to reset the security codes in the template. I took this as a good sign. It meant they'd probably left everything else in the template at the default setting too.

As I rode the elevator down to the 440th floor, I powered on my armor and drew my guns. Five security checkpoints stood between the elevator and the room I needed to reach. Unless the template had been altered, fifty NPC Tyrell security guard replicants would be standing between me and my destination.

The shooting started as soon as the elevator doors slid open. I had to kill seven skin jobs before I could even make it out of the elevator car and into the hallway.

The next ten minutes played out like the climax of a John Woo movie. One of the ones starring Chow Yun Fat, like *Hard Boiled* or *The Killer*. I switched both of my guns to autofire and held down the triggers as I moved from one room to the next, mowing down every NPC in my path. The guards returned fire, but their bullets pinged harmlessly off my armor. I never ran out of ammo, because each time I fired a round, a new round was teleported into the bottom of the clip.

My bullet bill this month was going to be huge.

When I finally reached my destination, I punched in another code and locked the door behind me. I knew I didn't have much time. Klaxons were blaring throughout the building, and the thousands of NPC guards stationed on the floors below were probably already on their way up here to find me.

My footsteps echoed as I entered the room. It was deserted except for a large owl sitting on a golden perch. It blinked at me silently as I crossed the enormous cathedral-like room, which was a perfect re-creation of the office of the Tyrell Corporation's founder, Eldon Tyrell. Every detail from the film had been duplicated exactly. Polished stone floors. Giant marble pillars. The entire west wall was a massive floor-to-ceiling window offering a breathtaking view of the vast cityscape outside.

A long conference table stood beside the window. Sitting on top of it was a Voight-Kampff machine. It was about the size of a briefcase, with a row of unlabeled buttons on the front, next to three small data monitors.

When I walked up and sat down in front of the machine, it turned itself on. A thin robotic arm extended a circular device that looked like a retinal scanner, which locked into place directly level with the pupil of my right eye. A small bellows was built into the side of the machine, and it began to rise and fall, giving the impression that the device was breathing.

I glanced around, wondering if an NPC of Harrison Ford would appear, to ask me the same questions he asked Sean Young in the movie. I'd memorized all of her answers, just in case. But I waited a few seconds and nothing happened. The machine's bellows continued to rise and fall. In the distance, the security klaxons continued to wail.

I took out the Jade Key. The instant I did, a panel slid open in the surface of the Voight-Kampff machine, revealing a keyhole. I quickly inserted the Jade Key and turned it. The machine and the key both vanished, and in their place, the Second Gate appeared. It was a doorlike portal resting on top of the polished conference table. Its edges glowed with the same milky jade color as the key, and just like the First Gate, it appeared to lead into a vast field of stars.

I leapt up on the table and jumped inside.

• • •

I found myself standing just inside the entrance of a seedy-looking bowling alley with disco-era decor. The carpet was a garish pattern of green and brown swirls, and the molded plastic chairs were a faded orange color. The bowling lanes were all empty and unlit. The place was deserted. There weren't even any NPCs behind the front counter or the snack bar. I wasn't sure where I was supposed to be until I saw MIDDLETOWN LANES printed in huge letters on the wall above the bowling lanes.

At first, the only sound I heard was the low hum of the fluorescent lights overhead. But then I noticed a series of faint electronic chirps emanating from off to my left. I glanced in that direction and saw a darkened alcove just beyond the snack bar. Over this cavelike entrance was a sign. Eight bright red neon letters spelled out the words GAME ROOM.

There was a violent rush of wind, and the roar of what sounded like a hurricane tearing through the bowling alley. My feet began to slide across the carpet, and I realized that my avatar was being pulled toward the game room, as if a black hole had opened up somewhere in there.

As the vacuum yanked me through the game room entrance, I spotted a dozen videogames inside, all from the mid- to late '80s. Crime Fighters, Heavy Barrel, Vigilante, Smash TV. But I could now see that my avatar was being drawn toward one game in particular, a game that stood alone at the very back of the game room.

Black Tiger. Capcom, 1987.

A swirling vortex had opened in the center of the game's monitor, and it was sucking in bits of trash, paper cups, bowling shoes—everything that wasn't nailed down. Including me. As my avatar neared it, I reflexively reached out and grabbed the joystick of a Time Pilot machine. My feet were instantly lifted off the floor as the vortex continued to pull my avatar inexorably toward it.

At this point, I was actually grinning in anticipation. I was all prepared to pat myself on the back, because I'd mastered Black Tiger long ago, during the first year of the Hunt.

In the years prior to his death, when Halliday had been living in seclusion, the only thing he'd posted on his website was a brief looping animation. It showed his avatar, Anorak, sitting in his castle's library, mixing potions and poring over dusty spellbooks. This animation had run on a continuous loop for over a decade, until it was finally replaced by the Scoreboard on the morning Halliday died. In that animation, hanging on the wall behind Anorak, you could see a large painting of a black dragon.

Gunters had filled countless message board threads arguing about the meaning of the painting, about what the black dragon signified or whether it signified anything at all. But I'd been sure of its meaning from the start.

In one of the earliest journal entries in *Anorak's Almanac,* Halliday wrote that whenever his parents would start screaming at each other, he would sneak out of the house and ride his bike to the local bowling alley to play Black Tiger, because it was a game he could beat on just one quarter. *AA* 23:234: "For one quarter, Black Tiger lets me escape from my rotten existence for three glorious hours. Pretty good deal."

Black Tiger had first been released in Japan under its original title *Burakku Doragon.* Black Dragon. The game had been renamed for its

American release. I'd deduced that the black dragon painting on the wall of Anorak's study had been a subtle hint that *Burakku Doragon* would play a key role in the Hunt. So I'd studied the game until, like Halliday, I could reach the end on just one credit. After that, I continued to play it every few months, just to keep from getting rusty.

Now, it looked as if my foresight and diligence were about to pay off.

I was only able to hold on to the Time Pilot joystick for a few seconds. Then I lost my grip and my avatar was sucked directly into the Black Tiger game's monitor.

Everything went black for a moment. Then I found myself in surreal surroundings.

I was now standing inside a narrow dungeon corridor. On my left was a high gray cobblestone wall with a mammoth dragon skull mounted on it. The wall stretched up and up, vanishing into the shadows above. I couldn't make out any ceiling. The dungeon floor was composed of floating circular platforms arranged end to end in a long line that stretched out into the darkness ahead. To my right, beyond the platforms' edge, there was nothing—just an endless, empty black void.

I turned around, but there was no exit behind me. Just another high cobblestone wall, stretching up into the infinite blackness overhead.

I looked down at my avatar's body. I now looked exactly like the hero of Black Tiger—a muscular, half-naked barbarian warrior dressed in an armored thong and a horned helmet. My right arm disappeared in a strange metal gauntlet, from which hung a long retractable chain with a spiked metal ball on the end. My right hand deftly held three throwing daggers. When I hurled them off in the black void at my right, three more identical daggers instantly appeared in my hand. When I tried jumping, I discovered that I could leap thirty feet straight up and land back on my feet with catlike grace.

Now I understood. I was about to play Black Tiger, all right. But not the fifty-year-old, 2-D, side-scrolling platform game that I had mastered. I was now standing inside a new, immersive, three-dimensional version of the game that Halliday had created.

My knowledge of the original game's mechanics, levels, and enemies would definitely come in handy, but the game play was going to be completely different, and it would require an entirely different set of skills.

The First Gate had placed me inside one of Halliday's favorite movies, and now the Second Gate had put me inside one of his favorite video-games. While I was pondering the implication of this pattern, a message began to flash on my display: GO!

I looked around. An arrow etched into the stone wall on my left pointed the way forward. I stretched my arms and legs, cracked my knuckles, and took a deep breath. Then, readying my weapons, I ran forward, leaping from platform to platform, to confront the first of my adversaries.

. . .

Halliday had faithfully re-created every detail of Black Tiger's eight-level dungeon.

I got off to a rough start and lost a life before I even cleared the first boss. But then I began to acclimate to playing the game in three dimensions (and from a first-person perspective). Eventually, I found my groove.

I pressed onward, leaping from platform to platform, attacking in mid-air, dodging the relentless onslaught of blobs, skeletons, snakes, mummies, minotaurs, and yes, ninjas. Each enemy I vanquished dropped a pile of "Zenny coins" that I could later use to purchase armor, weapons, and potions from one of the bearded wise men scattered throughout each level. (These "wise men" apparently thought setting up a small shop in the middle of a monster-infested dungeon was a fine idea.)

There were no time-outs, and no way for me to pause the game. Once you entered a gate, you couldn't just stop and log out. The system wouldn't allow it. Even if you removed your visor, you would remain logged in. The only way out of a gate was to go through it. Or die.

I managed to clear all eight levels of the game in just under three hours. The closest I came to death was during my battle with the final boss, the Black Dragon, who, of course, looked exactly like the beast depicted in the painting in Anorak's study. I'd used up all of my extra lives, and my vitality bar was almost at zero, but I managed to keep moving and stay clear of the dragon's fiery breath while I slowly knocked down his life meter with a steady barrage of throwing daggers. When I struck the final killing blow, the dragon crumbled into digital dust in front of me.

I let out a long, exhausted sigh of relief.

Then, with no transition whatsoever, I found myself back in the bowling alley game room, standing in front of the Black Tiger game. In front of me, on the game's monitor, my armored barbarian was striking a heroic pose. The following text appeared below him:

YOU HAVE RETURNED PEACE AND PROSPERITY TO OUR NATION.
THANK YOU, BLACK TIGER!
CONGRATULATIONS ON YOUR STRENGTH AND WISDOM!

Then something strange happened—something that had never happened when I'd beaten the original game. One of the "wise men" from the
dungeon appeared on the screen, with a speech balloon that said, "Thank
you. I am indebted to you. Please accept a giant robot as your reward."

A long row of robot icons appeared below the wise man, stretching
across the screen horizontally. By moving the joystick left or right, I found
that I was able to scroll through a selection of over a hundred different
"giant robots." When one of these robots was highlighted, a detailed list
of its stats and weaponry appeared on the screen beside it.

There were several robots I didn't recognize, but most were familiar. I
spotted Gigantor, Tranzor Z, the Iron Giant, Jet Jaguar, the sphinx-headed
Giant Robo from *Johnny Sokko and His Flying Robot,* the entire Shogun
Warriors toy line, and many of the mechs featured in both the *Macross*
and *Gundam* anime series. Eleven of these icons were grayed out and had
a red "X" over them, and these robots could not be identified or selected.
I knew they must be the ones taken by Sorrento and the other Sixers who
had cleared this gate before me.

It seemed possible that I was about to be awarded a real, working re-
creation of whichever robot I selected, so I studied my options carefully,
searching for the one I thought would be the most powerful and well
armed. But I stopped cold when I saw Leopardon, the giant transforming
robot used by *Supaidaman,* the incarnation of Spider-Man who appeared
on Japanese TV in the late 1970s. I'd discovered *Supaidaman* during the
course of my research and had become somewhat obsessed with the show.
So I didn't care if Leopardon was the most powerful robot available. I had
to have him, regardless.

I highlighted that icon and tapped the Fire button. A twelve-inch-tall
replica of Leopardon appeared on top of the Black Tiger cabinet. I grabbed
it and placed it in my inventory. There were no instructions, and the item
description field was blank. I made a mental note to examine it later, when
I got back to my stronghold.

Meanwhile, on the Black Tiger monitor, the end credits had begun to
scroll over an image of the game's barbarian hero sitting on a throne with
a slender princess at his side. I respectfully read each of the programmers'

names. They were all Japanese, except for the very last credit, which read OASIS PORT BY J. D. HALLIDAY.

When the credits ended, the monitor went dark for a moment. Then a symbol slowly appeared in the center of the screen: a glowing red circle with a five-pointed star inside it. The points of the star extended just beyond the outer edge of the circle. A second later, an image of the Crystal Key appeared, spinning slowly in the center of the glowing red star.

I felt a rush of adrenaline, because I recognized the red star symbol, and I knew where it was meant to lead me.

I snapped several screenshots, just to be safe. A moment later, the monitor went dark, and the Black Tiger game cabinet melted and morphed into a door-shaped portal with glowing jade edges. The exit.

I let out a triumphant cheer and jumped through it.

When I emerged from the gate, my avatar reappeared back inside Tyrell's office. The Voight-Kampff machine had reappeared in its original location, resting on the table beside me. I checked the time. Over three hours had passed since I'd first entered the gate. The room was deserted, save for the owl, and the security klaxons were no longer wailing. The NPC guards must have busted in and searched this area while I was still inside the gate, because they no longer appeared to be looking for me. The coast was clear.

I made my way back to the elevator and up to the landing platform without incident. And thanks be to Crom, the *Vonnegut* was still parked right where I'd left it, its cloaking device still engaged. I ran on board and left Axrenox, jumping to light speed as soon as I reached orbit.

As the *Vonnegut* streaked through hyperspace, headed for the nearest stargate, I pulled up one of the screenshots I'd taken of the red star symbol. Then I opened my grail diary and accessed the subfolder devoted to the legendary Canadian rock band Rush.

Rush had been Halliday's favorite band, from his teens onward. He'd once revealed in an interview that he'd coded every single one of his videogames (including the OASIS) while listening exclusively to Rush albums. He often referred to Rush's three members—Neil Peart, Alex Lifeson, and Geddy Lee—as "the Holy Trinity" or "the Gods of the North."

In my grail diary, I had every single Rush song, album, bootleg, and music video ever made. I had high-res scans of all their liner notes and album artwork. Every frame of Rush concert footage in existence. Every radio and television interview the band had ever done. Unabridged biographies on each band member, along with copies of their side projects and solo work. I pulled up the band's discography and selected the album I was looking for: *2112*, Rush's classic sci-fi–themed concept album.

A high-resolution scan of the album's cover appeared on my display. The band's name and the album's title were printed over a field of stars, and below that, appearing as if reflected in the surface of a rippling lake, was the symbol I'd seen on the Black Tiger game's monitor: a red five-pointed star enclosed in a circle.

When I placed the album cover side by side with the screenshot of the game screen, the two symbols matched exactly.

2112's title track is an epic seven-part song, over twenty minutes in length. The song tells the story of an anonymous rebel living in the year 2112, a time when creativity and self-expression have been outlawed. The red star on the album's cover was the symbol of the Solar Federation, the oppressive interstellar society in the story. The Solar Federation was controlled by a group of "priests," who are described in Part II of the song, titled "The Temples of Syrinx." Its lyrics told me exactly where the Crystal Key was hidden:

> *We are the Priests of the Temples of Syrinx*
> *Our great computers fill the hallowed halls.*
> *We are the Priests of the Temples of Syrinx*
> *All the gifts of life are held within our walls.*

There was a planet in Sector Twenty-one named Syrinx. That was where I was headed now.

The OASIS atlas described Syrinx as "a desolate world with rocky terrain and no NPC inhabitants." When I accessed the planet's colophon, I saw that Syrinx's author was listed as "Anonymous." But I knew the planet must have been coded by Halliday, because its design matched the world described in *2112*'s liner notes.

2112 was originally released in 1976, back when most music was sold on twelve-inch vinyl records. The records came in cardboard sleeves with artwork and a track listing printed on them. Some album sleeves opened up like a book and included more artwork and liner notes inside, along with lyrics and information about the band. As I pulled up a scan of *2112*'s original fold-out album sleeve, I saw that there was a second image of the red star symbol on the inside. This one depicted a naked man cowering in front of the star, both his hands raised in fear.

On the opposite side of the record sleeve were the printed lyrics to all seven parts of the *2112* suite. The lyrics for each section were preceded by a paragraph of prose that augmented the narrative laid out in the lyrics. These brief vignettes were told from the point of view of *2112*'s anonymous protagonist.

The following text preceded the lyrics to Part I:

I lie awake, staring out at the bleakness of Megadon. City and sky become one, merging into a single plane, a vast sea of unbroken grey. The Twin Moons, just two pale orbs as they trace their way across the steely sky.

When my ship reached Syrinx, I saw the twin moons, By-Tor and Snow Dog, that orbited the planet. Their names were taken from another classic Rush song. And down below, on the planet's bleak gray surface, there were exactly 1,024 copies of Megadon, the domed city described in the liner notes. That was twice the number of Zork instances there'd been on Frobozz, so I knew the Sixers couldn't barricade them all.

With my cloaking device engaged, I selected the nearest instance of the city and landed the *Vonnegut* just outside the wall of its dome, watching my scopes for other ships.

Megadon was anchored atop a rocky plateau, on the edge of an immense cliff. The city appeared to be in ruins. Its massive transparent dome was riddled with cracks and looked as though it might collapse at any moment. I was able to enter the city by squeezing through one of the largest of these cracks, at the base of the dome.

The city of Megadon reminded me of an old 1950s sci-fi paperback cover painting depicting the crumbling ruins of a once-great technologically advanced civilization. In the absolute center of the city I found a towering obelisk-shaped temple with wind-blasted gray walls. A giant red star of the Solar Federation was emblazoned above the entrance.

I was standing before the Temple of Syrinx.

It wasn't covered by a force field, or surrounded by a detachment of Sixers. There wasn't a soul in sight.

I drew my guns and walked through the entrance of the temple.

Inside, mammoth obelisk-shaped supercomputers stood in long rows, filling the giant, cathedral-like temple. I wandered along these rows, listening to the deep hum of the machines, until I finally reached the center of the temple.

There, I found a raised stone altar with the five-pointed red star etched into its surface. As I stepped up to the altar, the humming of the computers ceased, and the chamber grew silent.

It appeared I was supposed to place something on the altar, an offering to the Temple of Syrinx. But what kind of offering?

The twelve-inch Leopardon robot I'd acquired after completing the Second Gate didn't seem to fit. I tried placing it on the altar anyway and nothing happened. I placed the robot back in my inventory and stood there for a moment, thinking. Then I remembered something else from the 2112 liner notes. I pulled them up and scanned over them again. There was my answer, in the text that preceded Part III—"Discovery":

Behind my beloved waterfall, in the little room that was hidden beneath the cave, I found it. I brushed away the dust of the years, and picked it up, holding it reverently in my hands. I had no idea what it might be, but it was beautiful. I learned to lay my fingers across the wires, and to turn the keys to make them sound differently. As I struck the wires with my other hand, I produced my first harmonious sounds, and soon my own music!

I found the waterfall near the southern edge of the city, just inside the curved wall of the atmospheric dome. As soon as I found it, I activated my jet boots and flew over the foaming river below the falls, then passed through the waterfall itself. My haptic suit did its best to simulate the sensation of torrents of falling water striking my body, but it felt more like someone pounding on my head, shoulders, and back with a bundle of sticks. Once I'd passed through the falls to the other side, I found the opening of a cave and went inside. The cave narrowed into a long tunnel, which terminated in a small, cavernous room.

I searched the room and discovered that one of the stalagmites protruding from the floor was slightly worn around the tip. I grabbed the stalagmite and pulled it toward me, but it didn't budge. I tried pushing, and it gave, bending as if on some hidden hinge, like a lever. I heard a rumble of grinding stone behind me, and I turned to see a trapdoor opening in the floor. A hole had also opened in the roof of the cave, casting a brilliant shaft of light down through the open trapdoor, into a tiny hidden chamber below.

I took an item out of my inventory, a wand that could detect hidden traps, magical or otherwise. I used it to make sure the area was clear, then jumped down through the trapdoor and landed on the dusty floor of the hidden chamber. It was a tiny cube-shaped room with a large rough-hewn stone standing against the north wall. Embedded in the stone, neck first, was an electric guitar. I recognized its design from the *2112* concert footage I'd watched during the trip here. It was a 1974 Gibson Les Paul, the exact guitar used by Alex Lifeson during the *2112* tour.

I grinned at the absurd Arthurian image of the guitar in the stone. Like every gunter, I'd seen John Boorman's film *Excalibur* many times, so it seemed obvious what I should do next. I reached out with my right hand, grasped the neck of the guitar, and pulled. The guitar came free of the stone with a prolonged metallic *shhingggg!*

As I held the guitar over my head, the metallic ringing segued into a guitar power chord that echoed throughout the cave. I stared down at the guitar, about to activate my jet boots again, to fly back up through the trapdoor and out of the cave. But then an idea occurred to me and I froze.

James Halliday had taken guitar lessons for a few years in high school. That was what had first inspired me to learn to play. I'd never held an actual guitar, but on a virtual axe, I could totally shred.

I searched my inventory and found a guitar pick. Then I opened my grail diary and pulled up the sheet music for *2112*, along with the guitar tablature for the song "Discovery," which describes the hero's discovery of the guitar in a room hidden behind a waterfall. As I began to play the song, the sound of the guitar blasted off the chamber walls and back out through the cave, despite the absence of any electricity or amplifiers.

When I finished playing the first measure of "Discovery," a message briefly appeared, carved into the stone from which I'd pulled the guitar.

> *The first was ringed in red metal*
> *The second, in green stone*
> *The third is clearest crystal*
> *and cannot be unlocked alone*

In seconds, the words began to vanish, fading from the stone along with the strains of the last note I'd played on the guitar. I quickly snapped a screenshot of the riddle, already trying to sort out its meaning. It was about the Third Gate, of course. And how it could not "be unlocked alone."

Had the Sixers played the song and discovered this message? I seriously doubted it. They would have pulled the guitar from the stone and immediately returned it to the temple.

If so, they probably didn't know there was some sort of trick to unlocking the Third Gate. And that would explain why they still hadn't reached the egg.

● ● ●

I returned to the temple and placed the guitar on the altar. As I did, the towering computers around me began to emit a cacophony of sound, like a grand orchestra tuning up. The noise built to a deafening crescendo before ceasing abruptly. Then there was a flash of light on the altar, and the guitar transformed into the Crystal Key.

When I reached out and picked up the key, a chime sounded, and my score on the Scoreboard increased by 25,000 points. When added to the 200,000 I'd received for clearing the Second Gate, that brought my total score up to 353,000 points, one thousand points more than Sorrento. I was back in first place.

But I knew this was no time to celebrate. I quickly examined the Crystal Key, tilting it up to study its glittering, faceted surface. I didn't see any words etched there, but I did find a small monogram etched in the center of the key's crystal handle, a single calligraphic letter "A" that I recognized immediately.

That same letter "A" appeared in the Character Symbol box on James Halliday's first Dungeons & Dragons character sheet. The very same monogram also appeared on the dark robes of his famous OASIS avatar, Anorak. And, I knew, that same emblematic letter adorned the front gates of Castle Anorak, his avatar's impregnable stronghold.

In the first few years of the Hunt, gunters had swarmed like hungry insects to any OASIS location that seemed like a possible hiding place for the three keys, specifically planets originally coded by Halliday himself. Chief among these was the planet Chthonia, a painstaking re-creation of the fantasy world Halliday had created for his high-school Dungeons & Dragons campaign, and also the setting of many of his early videogames. Chthonia had become the gunters' Mecca. Like everyone else, I'd felt obligated to make a pilgrimage there, to visit Castle Anorak. But the castle was impregnable and always had been. No avatar but Anorak himself had ever been able to pass through its entrance.

But now I knew there must be a way to enter Castle Anorak. Because the Third Gate was hidden somewhere inside.

• • •

When I got back to my ship, I blasted off and set a course for Chthonia in Sector Ten. Then I began to scan the newsfeeds, intending to check out the media frenzy my return to first place was generating. But my score wasn't the top story. No, the big news that afternoon was that the hiding place of Halliday's Easter egg had, at long last, finally been revealed to the world. It was, the news anchors said, located somewhere on the planet Chthonia, inside Castle Anorak. They knew this because the entire Sixer army was now encamped around the castle.

They'd arrived earlier that day, shortly after I'd cleared the Second Gate.

I knew the timing couldn't be a coincidence. My progress must have prompted the Sixers to end their covert attempts to clear the Third Gate and make its location public by barricading it before I or anyone else could reach it.

When I arrived at Chthonia a few minutes later, I did a cloaked flyby of the castle, just to gauge the lay of the land for myself. It was even worse than I'd imagined.

The Sixers had installed some type of magical shield over Castle An-orak, a semitransparent dome that completely covered the castle and the area around it. Encamped inside the shield wall was the entire Sixer army. A vast collection of troops, tanks, weapons, and vehicles surrounded the castle on all sides.

Several gunter clans were already on the scene, and they were making their first attempts to bring down the shield by launching high-yield nukes at it. Each detonation was followed by a brief atomic light show, and then the blast would dissipate harmlessly against the shield.

The attacks on the shield continued for the next few hours as the news spread and more and more gunters arrived on Chthonia. The clans launched every type of weapon they could think of at the shield, but nothing affected it. Not nukes, not fireballs, and not magic missiles. Eventually, a team of gunters tried to dig a tunnel under the dome wall, and that was when it was discovered that the shield was actually a complete sphere surrounding the castle, above- and belowground.

Later that night, several high-level gunter wizards finished casting a series of divination spells on the castle and announced on the message boards that the shield around the castle was generated by a powerful artifact called the Orb of Osuvox, which could only be operated by a wizard who was ninety-ninth level. According to the artifact's item description, it could create a spherical shield around itself, with a circumference of up to half a kilometer. This shield was impenetrable and indestructible and could vaporize just about anything that touched it. It could also be kept up indefinitely, as long as the wizard operating the orb remained immobile and kept both hands on the artifact.

In the days that followed, gunters tried everything they could think of to penetrate the shield. Magic. Technology. Teleportation. Counterspells. Other artifacts. Nothing worked. There was no way to get inside.

An air of hopelessness quickly swept through the gunter community. Solos and clansmen alike were ready to throw in the towel. The Sixers had the Crystal Key and exclusive access to the Third Gate. Everyone agreed that The End was near, that the Hunt was "all over but the crying."

During all of these developments, I somehow managed to keep my cool. There was a chance the Sixers hadn't even figured out how to open the Third Gate yet. Of course, they had plenty of time now. They could be slow and methodical. Sooner or later, they would stumble on the solution.

But I refused to give up. Until an avatar reached Halliday's Easter egg, anything was still possible.

Like any classic videogame, the Hunt had simply reached a new, more difficult level. A new level often required an entirely new strategy.

I began to formulate a plan. A bold, outrageous plan that would require epic amounts of luck to pull off. I set this plan in motion by e-mailing Art3mis, Aech, and Shoto. My message told them exactly where to find the Second Gate and how to obtain the Crystal Key. Once I was sure all three of them had received my message, I initiated the next phase of my plan. This was the part that terrified me, because I knew there was a good chance it was going to end up getting me killed. But at this point, I no longer cared.

I was going to reach the Third Gate, or die trying.

Level Three

Going outside is highly overrated.

—*Anorak's Almanac*, Chapter 17, Verse 32

When the IOI corporate police came to arrest me, I was right in the middle of the movie *Explorers* (1985, directed by Joe Dante). It's about three kids who build a spaceship in their backyard and then fly off to meet aliens. Easily one of the greatest kid flicks ever made. I'd gotten into the habit of watching it at least once a month. It kept me centered.

I had a thumbnail of my apartment building's external security camera feed at the edge of my display, so I saw the IOI Indentured Servant Retrieval Transport pull up out front, siren wailing and lights flashing. Then four jackbooted, riot-helmeted dropcops jumped out and ran into the building, followed by a guy in a suit. I continued to watch them on the lobby camera as they waved their IOI badges, blew past the security station, and filed onto the elevator.

Now they were on their way up to my floor.

"Max," I muttered, noting the fear in my own voice. "Execute security macro number one: *Crom, strong in his mountain*." This voice command instructed my computer to execute a long series of preprogrammed actions, both online and in the real world.

"You g-g-got it, Chief!" Max replied cheerfully, and a split second later, my apartment's security system switched into lockdown mode. My reinforced plate-titanium WarDoor swung down from the ceiling, slamming and locking into place over my apartment's built-in security door.

On the security camera mounted in the hallway outside my apartment, I watched the four dropcops get off the elevator and sprint down the hallway to my door. The two guys in front were carrying plasma welders. The other two held industrial-strength VoltJolt stun guns. The suit, who brought up the rear, was carrying a digital clipboard.

I wasn't surprised to see them. I knew why they were here. They were here to cut open my apartment and pull me out of it, like a chunk of Spam being removed from a can.

When they reached my door, my scanner gave them the once-over, and their ID data flashed on my display, informing me that all five of these men were IOI credit officers with a valid indenturement arrest warrant for one Bryce Lynch, the occupant of this apartment. So, in keeping with local, state, and federal law, my apartment building's security system immediately opened both of my security doors to grant them entrance. But the WarDoor that had just slammed into place kept them outside.

Of course, the dropcops expected me to have redundant security, which is why they'd brought plasma welders.

The IOI drone in the suit squeezed past the dropcops and gingerly pressed his thumb to my door intercom. His name and corporate title appeared on my display: *Michael Wilson, IOI Credit and Collections Division, Employee # IOI-481231.*

Wilson looked up into the lens of my hallway camera and smiled pleasantly. "Mr. Lynch," he said. "My name is Michael Wilson, and I'm with the Credit and Collections division of Innovative Online Industries." He consulted his clipboard. "I'm here because you have failed to make the last three payments on your IOI Visa card, which has an outstanding balance in excess of twenty thousand dollars. Our records also show that you are currently unemployed and have therefore been classified as impecunious. Under current federal law, you are now eligible for mandatory indenturement. You will remain indentured until you have paid your debt to our company in full, along with all applicable interest, processing and late fees, and any other charges or penalties that you incur henceforth." Wilson motioned toward the dropcops. "These gentlemen are here to assist me in apprehending you and escorting you to your new place of employment. We request that you open your door and grant us access to your residence. Please be aware that we are authorized to seize any personal belongings you have inside. The sale value of these items will, of course, be deducted from your outstanding credit balance."

As far as I could tell, Wilson recited all of this without taking a single breath, speaking in the flat monotone of someone who repeats the same sentences all day long.

After a brief pause, I replied through the intercom. "Sure thing, guys. Just give me a minute to get my pants on. Then I'll be right out."

Wilson frowned. "Mr. Lynch, if you do not grant us access to your residence within ten seconds, we are authorized to enter by force. The cost of any damage resulting from our forced entry, including all property damage and repair labor, will be added to your outstanding balance. Thank you."

Wilson stepped away from the intercom and nodded to the others. One of the dropcops immediately powered up his welder, and when the tip began to glow molten orange, he began cutting through my War-Door's titanium plating. The other welder moved a few feet farther down and began to cut a hole right through the wall of my apartment. These guys had access to the building's security specs, so they knew the walls of each apartment were lined with steel plating and a layer of concrete, which they could cut through much more quickly than the titanium WarDoor.

Of course, I'd taken the precaution of reinforcing my apartment's walls, floor, and ceiling, with a titanium alloy SageCage, which I'd assembled piece by piece. Once they cut through my wall, they would have to cut through the cage, too. But this would buy me only five or six extra minutes, at the most. Then they would be inside.

I'd heard that dropcops had a nickname for this procedure—cutting an indent out of a fortified residence so they could arrest him. They called it *doing a C-section*.

I dry-swallowed two of the antianxiety pills I'd ordered in preparation for this day. I'd already taken two earlier that morning, but they didn't seem to be working.

Inside the OASIS, I closed all the windows on my display and set my account's security level to maximum. Then I pulled up the Scoreboard, just to check it one last time and reassure myself that nothing had changed and that the Sixers still hadn't won. The top ten rankings had been static for several days now.

HIGH SCORES:

1.	Art3mis	354,000	卄卄
2.	Parzival	353,000	卄卄
3.	IOI-655321	352,000	卄卄
4.	Aech	352,000	卄卄
5.	IOI-643187	349,000	卄卄
6.	IOI-621671	348,000	卄卄
7.	IOI-678324	347,000	卄卄
8.	Shoto	347,000	卄卄
9.	IOI-637330	346,000	卄卄
10.	IOI-699423	346,000	卄卄

Art3mis, Aech, and Shoto had all cleared the Second Gate and obtained the Crystal Key within forty-eight hours of receiving my e-mail. When Art3mis received the 25,000 points for reaching the Crystal Key, it had put her back in first place, due to the point bonuses she'd already received for finding the Jade Key first, and the Copper Key second.

Art3mis, Aech, and Shoto had all tried to contact me since receiving my e-mail, but I hadn't answered any of their phone calls, e-mails, or chat requests. I saw no reason to tell them what I intended to do. They couldn't do anything to help me and would probably just try to talk me out of it.

There was no turning back now, anyway.

I closed the Scoreboard and took a long look around my stronghold, wondering if it was for the last time. Then I took several quick deep breaths, like a deep-sea diver preparing to submerge, and tapped the log-out icon on my display. The OASIS vanished, and my avatar reappeared inside my virtual office, a standalone simulation stored on my console's hard drive. I opened a console window and keyed in the command word to activate my computer's self-destruct sequence: SHITSTORM.

A progress meter appeared on my display, showing that my hard drive was now being zeroed out and wiped clean.

"Good-bye, Max," I whispered.

"Adios, Wade," Max said, just a few seconds before he was deleted.

Sitting in my haptic chair, I could already feel the heat coming from the other side of the room. When I pulled off my visor, I saw smoke pouring in through the holes being cut in the door and the wall. It was starting to get too thick for my apartment's air purifiers to handle. I began to cough.

The dropcop working on my door finished cutting his hole. The smoking circle of metal fell to the floor with a heavy metallic boom that made me jump in my chair.

As the welder stepped back, another dropcop stepped forward and used a small canister to spray some sort of freezing foam around the edge of the hole, cooling off the metal so they wouldn't burn themselves when they crawled inside. Which was what they were about to do.

"Clear!" one of them shouted from out in the hallway. "No visible weapons!"

One of the stun-gun wielding dropcops climbed through the hole first. Suddenly, he was standing right in front of me, his weapon leveled at my face.

"Don't move!" he shouted. "Or you get the juice, understand?"

I nodded that yes, I understood. It occurred to me then that this cop was the first visitor I'd ever had in my apartment in all the time I'd lived there.

The second dropcop to crawl inside wasn't nearly as polite. Without a word, he walked over and jammed a ball gag in my mouth. This was standard procedure, because they didn't want me to issue any more voice commands to my computer. They needn't have bothered. The moment the first dropcop had entered my apartment, an incendiary device had detonated inside my computer. It was already melting to slag.

When the dropcop finished strapping on the ball gag, he grabbed me by the exoskeleton of my haptic suit, yanked me out of my haptic chair like a rag doll, and threw me on the floor. The other dropcop hit the kill switch that opened my WarDoor, and the last two dropcops rushed in, followed by Wilson the suit.

I curled into a ball on the floor and closed my eyes. I started to shake involuntarily. I tried to prepare myself for what I knew was about to happen next.

They were going to take me outside.

"Mr. Lynch," Wilson said, smiling. "I hereby place you under corporate arrest." He turned to the dropcops. "Tell the repo team to come on up and clear this place out." He glanced around the room and noticed the thin line of smoke now pouring out of my computer. He looked at me and shook his head. "That was stupid. We could have sold that computer to help pay down your debt."

I couldn't reply around the ball gag, so I just shrugged and gave him the finger.

They tore off my haptic suit and left it for the repo team. I was totally naked underneath. They gave me a disposable slate-gray jumpsuit to put on, with matching plastic shoes. The suit felt like sandpaper, and it began to make me itch as soon as I put it on. They'd cuffed my hands, so it wasn't easy to scratch.

They dragged me out into the hall. The harsh fluorescents sucked the color out of everything and made it look like an old black-and-white film. As we rode the elevator down to the lobby, I hummed along with the Muzak as loudly as I could, to show them I wasn't afraid. When one of the dropcops waved his stun gun at me, I stopped.

They put a hooded winter coat on me in the lobby. They didn't want me catching pneumonia now that I was company property. A human resource. Then they led me outside, and sunlight hit my face for the first time in over half a year.

It was snowing, and everything was covered in a thin layer of gray ice and slush. I didn't know what the temperature was, but I couldn't remember ever feeling so cold. The wind cut right to my bones.

They herded me over to their transport truck. Two new indents already sat in the back, strapped into plastic seats, both wearing visors. People they'd arrested earlier that morning. The dropcops were like garbage collectors, making their daily rounds.

The indent on my right was a tall, thin guy, probably a few years older than me. He looked like he might be suffering from malnutrition. The other indent was morbidly obese, and I couldn't be sure of the person's gender. I decided to think of him as male. His face was obscured by a mop of dirty blond hair, and something that looked like a gas mask covered his nose and mouth. A thick black tube ran from the mask down to a nozzle on the floor. I wasn't sure of its purpose until he lurched forward, drawing his restraints tight, and vomited into the mask. I heard a vacuum activate, sucking the indent's regurgitated Oreos down the tube and into the floor. I wondered if they stored it in an external tank or just dumped it on the street. Probably a tank. IOI would probably have his vomit analyzed and put the results in his file.

"You feel sick?" one of the dropcops asked as he removed my ball gag. "Tell me now and I'll put a mask on you."

"I feel great," I said, not very convincingly.

"OK. But if I have to clean up your puke, I'll make sure you regret it."

They shoved me inside and strapped me down directly across from the skinny guy. Two of the dropcops climbed into the back with us, stowing their plasma welders in a locker. The other two slammed the rear doors and climbed into the cab up front.

As we pulled away from my apartment complex, I craned my neck to look through the transport's tinted rear windows, up at the building where I'd lived for the past year. I was able to spot my window up on the forty-second floor, because of its spray-painted black glass. The repo team was probably already up there by now. All of my gear was being disassembled, inventoried, tagged, boxed, and prepared for auction. Once they finished emptying out my apartment, custodial bots would scour and disinfect it. A repair crew would patch the outer wall and replace the door. IOI would be billed, and the cost of the repairs would be added to my outstanding debt to the company.

By midafternoon, the lucky gunter who was next on the apartment building's waiting list would get a message informing him that a unit had opened up, and by this evening, the new tenant would probably already be moved in. By the time the sun went down, all evidence that I'd ever lived there would be totally erased.

As the transport swung out onto High Street, I heard the tires crunch the salt crystals covering the frozen asphalt. One of the dropcops reached over and slapped a visor on my face. I found myself sitting on a sandy white beach, watching the sunset while waves crashed in front of me. This must be the simulation they used to keep indents calm during the ride downtown.

Using my cuffed hand, I pushed the visor up onto my forehead. The dropcops didn't seem to care or pay me any notice at all. So I craned my head again to stare out the window. I hadn't been out here in the real world for a long time, and I wanted to see how it had changed.

A thick film of neglect still covered everything in sight. The streets, the buildings, the people. Even the snow seemed dirty. It drifted down in gray flakes, like ash after a volcanic eruption.

The number of homeless people seemed to have increased drastically. Tents and cardboard shelters lined the streets, and the public parks I saw seemed to have been converted into refugee camps. As the transport rolled deeper into the city's skyscraper core, I saw people clustered on every street corner and in every vacant lot, huddled around burning barrels and portable fuel-cell heaters. Others waited in line at the free solar charging stations, wearing bulky, outdated visors and haptic gloves. Their hands made small, ghostly gestures as they interacted with the far more pleasant reality of the OASIS via one of GSS's free wireless access points.

Finally, we reached 101 IOI Plaza, in the heart of downtown.

I stared out the window in silent apprehension as the corporate headquarters of Innovative Online Industries Inc. came into view: two rectangular skyscrapers flanking a circular one, forming the IOI corporate logo. The IOI skyscrapers were the three tallest buildings in the city, mighty towers of steel and mirrored glass joined by dozens of connective walkways and elevator trams. The top of each tower disappeared into the sodium-vapor-drenched cloud layer above. The buildings looked identical to their headquarters in the OASIS on IOI-1, but here in the real world they seemed much more impressive.

The transport rolled into a parking garage at the base of the circular tower and descended a series of concrete ramps until we arrived in a large open area resembling a loading dock. A sign over a row of wide bay doors read IOI INDENTURED EMPLOYEE INDUCTION CENTER.

The other indents and I were herded off the transport, where a squad of stun gun–armed security guards was waiting to take custody of us. Our handcuffs were removed; then another guard began to swipe each of us with a handheld retina scanner. I held my breath as he held the scanner up to my eyes. A second later, the unit beeped and he read off the information on its display. "Lynch, Bryce. Age twenty-two. Full citizenship. No criminal record. Credit Default Indenturement." He nodded to himself and tapped a series of icons on his clipboard. Then I was led into a warm, brightly lit room filled with hundreds of other new indents. They were all shuffling through a maze of guide ropes, like weary overgrown children at some nightmarish amusement park. There seemed to be an equal number of men and women, but it was hard to tell, because nearly everyone shared my pale complexion and total lack of body hair, and we all wore the same gray jumpsuits and gray plastic shoes. We looked like extras from *THX 1138*.

The line fed into a series of security checkpoints. At the first checkpoint, each indent was given a thorough scan with a brand-new Meta-detector to make sure they weren't hiding any electronic devices on or in their persons. While I waited for my turn, I saw several people pulled out of line when the scanner found a subcutaneous minicomputer or a voice-controlled phone installed as a tooth replacement. They were led into another room to have the devices removed. A dude just ahead of me in line actually had a top-of-the-line miniature Sinatro OASIS console concealed inside a prosthetic testicle. Talk about balls.

Once I'd cleared a few more checkpoints, I was ushered into the testing area, a giant room filled with hundreds of small, soundproofed cubicles. I was seated in one of them and given a cheap visor and an even cheaper pair of haptic gloves. The gear didn't give me access to the OASIS, but I still found it comforting to put it on.

I was then given a battery of increasingly difficult aptitude tests intended to measure my knowledge and abilities in every area that might conceivably be of use to my new employer. These tests were, of course, cross-referenced with the fake educational background and work history that I'd given to my bogus Bryce Lynch identity.

I made sure to ace all of the tests on OASIS software, hardware, and networking, but I intentionally failed the tests designed to gauge my knowledge of James Halliday and the Easter egg. I definitely didn't want to get placed in IOI's Oology Division. There was a chance I might run into Sorrento there. I didn't think he'd recognize me—we'd never actually met in person, and I now barely resembled my old school ID photo—but I didn't want to risk it. I was already tempting fate more than anyone in their right mind ever would.

Hours later, when I finally finished the last exam, I was logged into a virtual chat room to meet with an indenturement counselor. Her name was Nancy, and in a hypnotic monotone, she informed me that, due to my exemplary test scores and impressive employment record, I had been "awarded" the position of OASIS Technical Support Representative II. I would be paid $28,500 a year, minus the cost of my housing, meals, taxes, medical, dental, optical, and recreation services, all of which would be deducted automatically from my pay. My remaining income (if there was any) would be applied to my outstanding debt to the company. Once my debt was paid in full, I would be released from indenturement. At that time, based on my job performance, it was possible I would be offered a permanent position with IOI.

This was a complete joke, of course. Indents were never able to pay off their debt and earn their release. Once they got finished slapping you with pay deductions, late fees, and interest penalties, you wound up owing them more each month, instead of less. Once you made the mistake of getting yourself indentured, you would probably remain indentured for life. A lot of people didn't seem to mind this, though. They thought of it as job security. It also meant they weren't going to starve or freeze to death in the street.

My "Indenturement Contract" appeared in a window on my display. It contained a long list of disclaimers and warnings about my rights (or lack thereof) as an indentured employee. Nancy told me to read it, sign it, and proceed to Indent Processing. Then she logged out of the chat room. I scrolled to the bottom of the contract without bothering to read it. It was over six hundred pages long. I signed the name Bryce Lynch, then verified my signature with a retinal scan.

Even though I was using a fake name, I wondered if the contract might still be legally binding. I wasn't sure, and I didn't really care. I had a plan, and this was part of it.

They led me down another corridor, into the Indenturement Process-ing Area. I was placed on a conveyor belt that carried me through a long series of stations. First, they took my jumpsuit and shoes and incinerated them. Then they ran me through a kind of human car wash—a series of machines that soaped, scrubbed, disinfected, rinsed, dried, and deloused me. Afterward, I was given a new gray jumpsuit and another pair of plas-tic slippers.

At the next station, a bank of machines gave me a complete physical, including a battery of blood tests. (Luckily, the Genetic Privacy Act made it illegal for IOI to sample my DNA.) Then I was given a series of inocula-tions with an array of automated needle guns that shot me in both shoul-ders and both ass cheeks simultaneously.

As I inched forward along the conveyor, flat-screen monitors mounted overhead showed the same ten-minute training film over and over, on an endless loop: "Indentured Servitude: Your Fast Track from Debt to Success!" The cast was made up of D-list television stars who cheerfully spouted corporate propaganda while relating the minutiae of IOI's inden-turement policy. After five viewings, I had every line of the damn thing memorized. By the tenth viewing, I was mouthing the words along with the actors.

"What can I expect after I complete my initial processing and get placed in my permanent position?" asked Johnny, the training film's main character.

You can expect to spend the rest of your life as a corporate slave, Johnny, I thought. But I kept watching as, once again, the helpful IOI Human Resources rep pleasantly told Johnny all about the day-to-day life of an indent.

Finally, I reached the last station, where a machine fitted me with a security anklet—a padded metal band that locked around my ankle, just above the joint. According to the training film, this device monitored my physical location and also granted or denied me access to different areas of the IOI office complex. If I tried to escape, remove the anklet, or cause trouble of any kind, the device was capable of delivering a paralyzing elec-trical shock. If necessary, it could also administer a heavy-duty tranquil-izer directly into my bloodstream.

After the anklet was on, another machine clamped a small electronic device onto my right earlobe, piercing it in two locations. I winced in pain and shouted a stream of profanity. I knew from the training film that I'd just been fitted with an OCT. OCT stood for "observation and communication tag." But most indents just referred to it as "eargear." It reminded me of the tags environmentalists used to put on endangered animals, to track their movements in the wild. The eargear contained a tiny comlink that allowed the main IOI Human Resources computer to make announcements and issue commands directly into my ear. It also contained a tiny forward-looking camera that let IOI supervisors see whatever was directly in front of me. Surveillance cameras were mounted in every room in the IOI complex, but that apparently wasn't enough. They also had to mount a camera to the side of every indent's head.

A few seconds after my eargear was attached and activated, I began to hear the placid monotone of the HR mainframe, droning instructions and other information. The voice drove me nuts at first, but I gradually got used to it. I didn't have much choice.

As I stepped off the conveyor, the HR computer directed me to a nearby cafeteria that looked like something out of an old prison movie. I was given a lime green tray of food. A tasteless soyburger, a lump of runny mashed potatoes, and some unrecognizable form of cobbler for dessert. I devoured all of it in a few minutes. The HR computer complimented me on my healthy appetite. Then it informed me that I was now permitted to make a five-minute visit to the bathroom. When I came out, I was directed onto an elevator with no buttons or floor indicator. When the doors slid open, I saw the following stenciled on the wall: INDENT HAB—BLOCK 05—TECHSUP REPS.

I shuffled off the elevator and down the carpeted hallway. It was quiet and dark. The only illumination came from small path lighting embedded in the floor. I'd lost track of the time. It seemed like days had passed since I'd been pulled out of my apartment. I was dead on my feet.

"Your first technical support shift begins in seven hours," the HR computer droned softly in my ear. "You have until then to sleep. Turn left at the intersection in front of you and proceed to your assigned hab-unit, number 42G."

I continued to do as I was told. I thought I was already getting pretty good at it.

The Hab Block reminded me of a mausoleum. It was a network of vaulted hallways, each lined with coffin-shaped sleeping capsules, row after row of them, stacked to the ceiling, ten high. Each column of hab-units was numbered, and the door of each capsule was lettered, A through J, with unit A at the bottom.

I eventually reached my unit, near the top of column number forty-two. As I approached it, the hatch irised open with a hiss, and a soft blue light winked on inside. I ascended the narrow access ladder mounted between the adjacent rows of capsules, then stepped onto the short platform beneath the hatch to my unit. When I climbed inside the capsule, the platform retracted and the hatch irised shut at my feet.

The inside of my hab-unit was an eggshell white injection-molded plastic coffin, a meter high, a meter wide, and two meters long. The floor of the capsule was covered with a gel-foam mattress pad and pillow. They both smelled like burned rubber, so I assumed they must be new.

In addition to the camera attached to the side of my head, there was a camera mounted above the door of my hab-unit. The company didn't bother hiding it. They wanted their indents to know they were being watched.

The unit's only amenity was the entertainment console—a large, flat touchscreen built into the wall. A wireless visor was snapped into a holder beside it. I tapped the touchscreen, activating the unit. My new employee number and position appeared at the top of the display: *Lynch, Bryce T.— OASIS TECH REP II—IOI Employee #338645*.

A menu appeared below, listing the entertainment programming to which I presently had access. It took only a few seconds to peruse my limited options. I could view only one channel: IOI-N—the company's twenty-four-hour news network. It provided a nonstop stream of company-related news and propaganda. I also had access to a library of training films and simulations, most of which were geared toward my new position as an OASIS technical support representative.

When I tried to access one of the other entertainment libraries, Vintage Movies, the system informed me that I wouldn't be granted access to a wider selection of entertainment options until I had received an above-average rating in three consecutive employee performance reviews. Then the system asked me if I wanted more information on the Indentured Employee Entertainment Reward Program. I didn't.

The only TV show I had access to was a company-produced sitcom called *Tommy Queue*. The synopsis said it was a "wacky situation comedy chronicling the misadventures of Tommy, a newly indentured OASIS tech rep struggling to achieve his goals of financial independence and on-the-job excellence!"

I selected the first episode of *Tommy Queue,* then unsnapped the visor and put it on. As I expected, the show was really just a training film with a laugh track. I had absolutely no interest in it. I just wanted to go to sleep. But I knew I was being watched, and that every move I made was being scrutinized and logged. So I stayed awake as long as I could, ignoring one episode of *Tommy Queue* after another.

Despite my best efforts, my thoughts drifted to Art3mis. Regardless of what I'd been telling myself, I knew she was the real reason I'd gone through with this lunatic plan. What the hell was wrong with me? There was a good chance I might never escape from this place. I felt buried under an avalanche of self-doubt. Had my dual obsessions with the egg and Art3mis finally driven me completely insane? Why would I take such an idiotic risk to win over someone I'd never actually met? Someone who appeared to have no interest in ever talking to me again?

Where was she right now? Did she miss me?

I continued to mentally torture myself like that until I finally drifted off to sleep.

IOI's Technical Support call center occupied three entire floors
of the headquarters' eastern I-shaped tower. Each of these floors contained
a maze of numbered cubicles. Mine was stuck back in a remote corner, far
from any windows. My cubicle was completely empty except for an adjustable office chair bolted to the floor. Several of the cubicles around me
were unoccupied, awaiting the arrival of other new indents.

I wasn't permitted to have any decorations in my cubicle, because I
hadn't earned that privilege yet. If I obtained a sufficient number of "perk
points" by getting high productivity and customer approval ratings, I
could "spend" some of them to purchase the privilege of decorating my
cube, perhaps with a potted plant or an inspirational poster of a kitten
hanging from a clothesline.

When I arrived in my cubicle, I grabbed my company-issued visor
and gloves from the rack on the bare cube wall and put them on. Then
I collapsed into my chair. My work computer was built into the chair's
circular base, and it activated itself automatically when I sat down. My
employee ID was verified and I was automatically logged into my work
account on the IOI intranet. I wasn't allowed to have any outbound access
to the OASIS. All I could really do was read work-related e-mails, view
support documentation and procedural manuals, and check my call time
statistics. That was it. And every move I made on the intranet was closely
monitored, controlled, and logged.

I put myself in the call queue and began my twelve-hour shift. I'd been an indent for only eight days now, but it already felt like I'd been imprisoned here for years.

The first caller's avatar appeared in front of me in my support chat room. His name and stats also appeared, floating in the air above him. He had the astoundingly clever name of "HotCock007."

I could see that it was going to be another fabulous day.

HotCock007 was a hulking bald barbarian with studded black leather armor and lots of demon tattoos covering his arms and face. He was holding a gigantic bastard sword nearly twice as long as his avatar's body.

"Good morning, Mr. HotCock007," I droned. "Thank you for calling technical support. I'm tech rep number 338645. How may I help you this evening?" The customer courtesy software filtered my voice, altering its tone and inflection to ensure that I always sounded cheerful and upbeat.

"Uh, yeah . . ." HotCock007 began. "I just bought this bad-ass sword, and now I can't even use it! I can't even attack nothing with it. What the hell is wrong with this piece of shit? Is it broke?"

"Sir, the only problem is that you're a complete fucking moron," I said.

I heard a familiar warning buzzer and a message flashed on my display:

COURTESY VIOLATION—FLAGS: *FUCKING, MORON*
LAST RESPONSE MUTED—VIOLATION LOGGED

IOI's patented customer courtesy software had detected the inappropriate nature of my response and muted it, so the customer didn't hear what I'd said. The software also logged my "courtesy violation" and forwarded it to Trevor, my section supervisor, so that he could bring it up during my next biweekly performance review.

"Sir, did you purchase this sword in an online auction?"

"Yeah," HotCock007 replied. "Paid out the ass for it too."

"Just a moment, sir, while I examine the item." I already knew what his problem was, but I needed to make sure before telling him or I'd get hit with a fine.

I tapped the sword with my index finger, selecting it. A small window opened and displayed the item's properties. The answer was right there, on the first line. This particular magic sword could only be used by an avatar who was tenth level or higher. Mr. HotCock007 was only seventh level. I quickly explained this to him.

"What?! That ain't fair! The guy who sold it to me didn't say nothing about that!"

"Sir, it's always advisable to make sure your avatar can actually use an item before you purchase it."

"Goddammit!" he shouted. "Well, what am I supposed to do with it now?"

"You could shove it up your ass and pretend you're a corn dog."

COURTESY VIOLATION—RESPONSE MUTED—VIOLATION LOGGED.

I tried again. "Sir, you might want to keep the item stored in your inventory until your avatar has attained tenth level. Or you may wish to put the item back up for auction yourself and use the proceeds to purchase a similar weapon. One with a power level commensurate to that of your avatar."

"Huh?" HotCock007 responded. "Whaddya mean?"

"Save it or sell it."

"Oh."

"Can I help you with anything else today, sir?"

"No, I don't guess—"

"Great. Thank you for calling technical support. Have an outstanding day."

I tapped the disconnect icon on my display, and HotCock007 vanished. Call Time: 2:07. As the next customer's avatar appeared—a red-skinned, large-breasted alien female named Vartaxxx—the customer satisfaction rating that HotCock007 had just given me appeared on my display. It was a 6, out of a possible score of 10. The system then helpfully reminded me that I needed to keep my average above 8.5 if I wanted to get a raise after my next review.

Doing tech support here was nothing like working from home. Here, I couldn't watch movies, play games, or listen to music while I answered the endless stream of inane calls. The only distraction was staring at the clock. (Or the IOI stock ticker, which was always at the top of every indent's display. You couldn't get rid of it.)

During each shift, I was given three five-minute restroom breaks. Lunch was thirty minutes. I usually ate in my cubicle instead of the cafeteria, so I wouldn't have to listen to the other tech reps bitch about their calls or boast about how many perk points they'd earned. I'd grown to despise the other indents almost as much as the customers.

I fell asleep five separate times during my shift. Each time, when the system saw that I'd drifted off, it sounded a warning klaxon in my ears, jolting me back awake. Then it noted the infraction in my employee data file. My narcolepsy had become such a consistent problem during my first week that I was now being issued two little red pills each day to help me stay awake. I took them too. But not until after I got off work.

When my shift finally ended, I ripped off my headset and visor and walked back to my hab-unit as quickly as I could. This was the only time each day I ever hurried anywhere. When I reached my tiny plastic coffin, I crawled inside and collapsed on the mattress, facedown, in the same exact position as the night before. And the night before that. I lay there for a few minutes, staring at the time readout on my entertainment console out of the corner of my eye. When it reached 7:07 p.m., I rolled over and sat up.

"Lights," I said softly. This had become my favorite word over the past week. In my mind, it had become synonymous with freedom.

The lights embedded in the shell of my hab-unit shut off, plunging the tiny compartment into darkness. If someone had been watching either of my live security vidfeeds, they would have seen a brief flash as the cameras switched to night-vision mode. Then I would have been clearly visible on their monitors once again. But, thanks to some sabotage I'd performed earlier in the week, the security cameras in my hab-unit and my eargear were now no longer performing their assigned tasks. So for the first time that day, I wasn't being watched.

That meant it was time to rock.

I tapped the entertainment center console's touchscreen. It lit up, presenting me with the same choices I'd had on my first night here: a handful of training films and simulations, including the complete run of *Tommy Queue* episodes.

If anyone checked the usage logs for my entertainment center, they would show that I watched *Tommy Queue* every night until I fell asleep, and that once I'd worked my way through all sixteen episodes, I'd started over at the beginning. The logs would also show that I fell asleep at roughly the same time every night (but not at *exactly* the same time), and that I slept like the dead until the following morning, when my alarm sounded.

Of course, I hadn't really been watching their inane corporate shitcom every night. And I wasn't sleeping, either. I'd actually been operating on about two hours of sleep a night for the past week, and it was beginning to take its toll on me.

But the moment the lights in my hab-unit went out, I felt energized and wide awake. My exhaustion seemed to vanish as I began to navigate through the entertainment center operation menus from memory, the fingers of my right hand dancing rapidly across the touchscreen.

About seven months earlier, I'd obtained a set of IOI intranet passwords from the L33t Haxorz Warezhaus, the same black-market data auction site where I'd purchased the information needed to create a new identity. I kept an eye on all of the black-market data sites, because you never knew what might be up for sale on them. OASIS server exploits. ATM hacks. Celebrity sex tapes. You name it. I'd been browsing through the L33t Haxorz Warezhaus auction listings when one in particular caught my eye: *IOI Intranet Access Passwords, Back Doors, and System Exploits.* The seller claimed to be offering classified proprietary information on IOI's intranet architecture, along with a series of administrative access codes and system exploits that could "give a user carte blanche inside the company network."

I would have assumed the data was bogus had it not been listed on such a respected site. The anonymous seller claimed to be a former IOI contract programmer and one of the lead architects of its company intranet. He was probably a turncoat—a programmer who intentionally coded back doors and security holes into a system he designed, so that he could later sell them on the black market. It allowed him to get paid for the same job twice, and to salve any guilt he felt about working for a demonic multinational corporation like IOI .

The obvious problem, which the seller didn't bother to point out in the auction listing, was that these codes were useless unless you already had access to the company intranet. IOI's intranet was a high-security, stand-alone network with no direct connections to the OASIS. The only way to get access to IOI's intranet was to become one of their legitimate employees (very difficult and time-consuming). Or you could join the company's ever-growing ranks of indentured servants.

I'd decided to bid on the IOI access codes anyway, on the off chance they might come in handy someday. Since there was no way to verify the data's authenticity, the bidding stayed low, and I won the auction for a few thousand credits. The codes arrived in my inbox a few minutes after the auction ended. Once I'd finished decrypting the data, I examined it all thoroughly. Everything looked legit, so I filed the info away for a rainy day and forgot about it—until about six months later, when I saw the Sixer barricade around Castle Anorak. The first thing I thought of was the IOI access codes. Then the wheels in my head began to turn and my ridiculous plan began to take shape.

I would alter the financial records on my bogus Bryce Lynch identity and allow myself to become indentured by IOI. Once I infiltrated the building and got behind the company firewall, I would use the intranet passwords to hack into the Sixers' private database, then figure a way to bring down the shield they'd erected over Anorak's castle.

I didn't think anyone would anticipate this move, because it was so clearly insane.

• • •

I didn't test the IOI passwords until the second night of my indenturement. I was understandably anxious, because if it turned out I'd been sold bogus data and none of the passwords worked, I would have sold myself into lifelong slavery.

Keeping my eargear camera pointed straight ahead, away from the screen, I pulled up the entertainment console's viewer settings menu, which allowed me to make adjustments to the display's audio and video output: volume and balance, brightness and tint. I cranked each option up to its highest setting, then tapped the Apply button at the bottom of the screen three times. I set the volume and brightness controls to their lowest settings and tapped the Apply button again. A small window appeared in the center of the screen, prompting me for a maintenance-tech ID number and access password. I quickly entered the ID number and the long alphanumeric password that I'd memorized. I checked both for errors out of the corner of my eye, then tapped OK. The system paused for what seemed like a very long time. Then, to my great relief, the following message appeared:

MAINTENANCE CONTROL PANEL—ACCESS GRANTED

I now had access to a maintenance service account designed to allow repairmen to test and debug the entertainment unit's various components. I was now logged in as a technician, but my access to the intranet was still pretty limited. Still, it gave me all the elbow room I needed. Using an exploit left by one of the programmers, I was now able to create a bogus admin account. Once that was set up, I had access to just about everything.

My first order of business was to get some privacy.

I quickly navigated through several dozen submenus until I reached the control panel for the Indent Monitoring System. When I entered my employee number my indent profile appeared on the display, along with a mug shot they'd taken of me during my initial processing. The profile listed my indent account balance, pay grade, blood type, current performance review rating—every scrap of data the company had on me. At the top right of my profile were two vidfeed windows, one fed by the camera in my eargear, the other linked to the camera in my hab-unit. My eargear vidfeed was currently aimed at a section of the wall. The hab-unit camera window showed a view of the back of my head, which I'd positioned to block the entertainment center's display screen.

I selected both vidfeed cameras and accessed their configuration settings. Using one of the turncoat's exploits, I performed a quick hack that caused my eargear and hab-unit cameras to display the archived video from my first night of indenturement instead of a live feed. Now, if someone checked my camera feeds, they'd see me lying asleep in my hab-unit, not sitting up all night, furiously hacking my way through the company intranet. Then I programmed the cameras to switch to the prerecorded feeds whenever I shut out the lights in my hab-unit. The split-second jump cut in the feed would be masked by the momentary video distortion that occurred when the cameras switched into night-vision mode.

I kept expecting to be discovered and locked out of the system, but it never happened. My passwords continued to work. I'd spent the past six nights laying siege to the IOI intranet, digging deeper and deeper into the network. I felt like a convict in an old prison movie, returning to my cell each night to tunnel through the wall with a teaspoon.

Then, last night, just before I'd succumbed to exhaustion, I'd finally managed to navigate my way through the intranet's labyrinth of firewalls and into the main Oology Division database. The mother lode. The Sixers' private file pile. And tonight, I would finally be able to explore it.

I knew that I needed to be able to take some of the Sixers' data with me when I escaped, so earlier in the week, I'd used my intranet admin account to submit a bogus hardware requisition form. I had a ten-zettabyte flash drive delivered to a nonexistent employee ("Sam Lowery") in an empty cubicle a few rows away from my own. Making sure to keep my eargear camera pointed in the other direction, I'd ducked into the cube, grabbed the tiny drive, pocketed it, and smuggled it back to my hab-unit. That night, after I shut off the lights and disabled the security cameras, I unlocked my entertainment unit's maintenance access panel and installed the flash drive into an expansion slot used for firmware upgrades. Now I could download data from the intranet directly to that drive.

* * *

I put on the entertainment center's visor and gloves, then stretched out on my mattress. The visor presented me with a three-dimensional view of the Sixers' database, with dozens of overlapping data windows suspended in front of me. Using my gloves, I began to manipulate these windows, navigating my way through the database's file structure. The largest section of the database appeared to be devoted to information on Halliday. The amount of data they had on him was staggering. It made my grail diary look like a set of CliffsNotes. They had things I'd never seen. Things I didn't even know *existed*. Halliday's grade-school report cards, home movies from his childhood, e-mails he'd written to fans. I didn't have time to read over it all, but I copied the really interesting stuff over to my flash drive, to (hopefully) study later.

I focused on isolating the data related to Castle Anorak and the forces the Sixers had positioned in and around it. I copied all of the intel on their weapons, vehicles, gunships, and troop numbers. I also snagged all of the data I could find on the Orb of Osuvox, the artifact they were using to generate the shield around the castle, including exactly where they were keeping it and the employee number of the Sixer wizard they had operating it.

Then I hit the jackpot—a folder containing hundreds of hours of OASIS simcap recordings documenting the Sixers' initial discovery of the Third Gate and their subsequent attempts to open it. As everyone now suspected, the Third Gate was located inside Castle Anorak. Only avatars who possessed a copy of the Crystal Key could cross the threshold of the castle's front entrance. To my disgust, I learned that Sorrento had been the first avatar to set foot inside Castle Anorak since Halliday's death.

The castle entrance led into a massive foyer whose walls, floor, and ceiling were all made of gold. At the north end of the chamber, a large crystal door was set into the wall. It had a small keyhole at its very center.

The moment I saw it, I knew I was looking at the Third Gate.

I fast-forwarded through several other recent simcap files. From what I could tell, the Sixers still hadn't figured out how to open the gate. Simply inserting the Crystal Key into the keyhole had no effect. They'd had their entire team trying to figure out why for several days now, but still hadn't made any progress.

While the data and video on the Third Gate was copying over to my flash drive, I continued to delve deeper into the Sixer database. Eventually, I uncovered a restricted area called the Star Chamber. It was the only area of the database I couldn't seem to access. So I used my admin ID to create a new "test account," then gave that account superuser access and full administrator privileges. It worked and I was granted access. The information inside the restricted area was divided into two folders: *Mission Status* and *Threat Assessments*. I opened the *Threat Assessments* folder first, and when I saw what was inside, I felt the blood drain from my face. There were five file folders, labeled *Parzival, Art3mis, Aech, Shoto,* and *Daito*. Daito's folder had a large red "X" over it.

I opened the Parzival folder first. A detailed dossier appeared, containing all of the information the Sixers had collected on me over the past few years. My birth certificate. My school transcripts. At the bottom there was a link to a simcap of my entire chatlink session with Sorrento, ending with the bomb detonating in my aunt's trailer. After I'd gone into hiding, they'd lost track of me. They had collected thousands of screenshots and vidcaps of my avatar over the past year, and loads of data on my stronghold on Falco, but they didn't know anything about my location in the real world. My current whereabouts were listed as "unknown."

I closed the window, took a deep breath, and opened the file on Art3mis.

At the very top was a school photo of a young girl with a distinctly sad smile. To my surprise, she looked almost identical to her avatar. The same dark hair, the same hazel eyes, and the same beautiful face I knew so well—with one small difference. Most of the left half of her face was covered with a reddish-purple birthmark. I would later learn that these types of birthmark were sometimes referred to as "port wine stains." In the photo, she wore a sweep of her dark hair down over her left eye to try to conceal the mark as much as possible.

Art3mis had led me to believe that in reality she was somehow hideous, but now I saw that nothing could have been further from the truth. To my eyes, the birthmark did absolutely nothing to diminish her beauty. If anything, the face I saw in the photo seemed even more beautiful to me than that of her avatar, because I knew this one was real.

The data below the photo said that her real name was Samantha Evelyn Cook, that she was a twenty-year-old Canadian citizen, five feet and seven inches tall, and that she weighed one hundred and sixty-eight pounds. The file also contained her home address—2206 Greenleaf Lane, Vancouver, British Columbia—along with a lot of other information, including her blood type and her school transcripts going all the way back to kindergarten.

I found an unlabeled video link at the bottom of her dossier, and when I selected it, a live vidfeed of a small suburban house appeared on my display. After a few seconds, I realized I was looking at the house where Art3mis lived.

As I dug further into her file, I learned that they'd had her under surveillance for the past five months. They had her house bugged too, because I found hundreds of hours of audio recordings made while she was logged into the OASIS. They had complete text transcripts of every audible word she'd spoken while clearing the first two gates.

I opened Shoto's file next. They knew his real name, Akihide Karatsu, and they also appeared to have his home address, an apartment building in Osaka, Japan. His file also contained a school photo, showing a thin, stoic boy with a shaved head. Like Daito, he looked nothing like his avatar.

Aech seemed to be the one they knew the least about. His file contained very little information, and no photo—just a screenshot of his avatar. His real name was listed as "Henry Swanson," but that was an alias used by Jack Burton in *Big Trouble in Little China,* so I knew it must be a fake. His address was listed as "mobile," and below it there was a link labeled "Recent Access Points." This turned out to be a list of the wireless node locations Aech had recently used to access his OASIS account. They were all over the place: Boston; Washington, D.C.; New York City; Philadelphia; and most recently, Pittsburgh.

Now I began to understand how the Sixers had been able to locate Art3mis and Shoto. IOI owned hundreds of regional telecom companies, effectively making them the largest Internet service provider in the world.

It was pretty difficult to get online without using a network they owned and operated. From the looks of it, IOI had been illegally eavesdropping on most of the world's Internet traffic in an attempt to locate and identify the handful of gunters they considered to be a threat. The only reason they hadn't been able to locate me was because I'd taken the paranoia-induced precaution of leasing a direct fiber-optic connection to the OASIS from my apartment complex.

I closed Aech's file, then opened the folder labeled *Daito*, already dreading what I might find there. Like the others, they had his real name, Toshiro Yoshiaki, and his home address. Two news articles about his "suicide" were linked at the bottom of his dossier, along with an unlabeled video clip, time-stamped on the day he'd died. I clicked on it. It was hand-held video camera footage showing three large men in black ski masks (one of whom was operating the camera) waiting silently in a hallway. They appeared to receive an order via their radio earpieces, then used a key card to open the door of a tiny one-room apartment. Daito's apartment. I watched in horror as they rushed in, yanked him out of his haptic chair, and threw him off the balcony.

The bastards even filmed him plummeting to his death. Probably at Sorrento's request.

A wave of nausea washed over me. When it finally passed, I copied the contents of all five dossiers over to my flash drive, then opened the *Mission Status* folder. It appeared to contain an archive of the Oology Division's status reports, intended for the Sixers' top brass. The reports were arranged by date, with the most recent one listed first. When I opened it, I saw that it was a directive memo sent from Nolan Sorrento to the IOI Board of Executives. In it, Sorrento proposed sending agents to abduct Art3mis and Shoto from their homes to force them to help IOI open the Third Gate. Once the Sixers had obtained the egg and won the contest, Art3mis and Shoto would "be disposed of."

I sat there in stunned silence. Then I read the memo again, feeling a combination of rage and panic.

According to the time stamp, Sorrento had sent the memo just after eight o'clock, less than five hours ago. So his superiors probably hadn't even seen it yet. When they did, they would still want to meet to discuss Sorrento's suggested course of action. So they probably wouldn't send their agents after Art3mis and Shoto until sometime tomorrow.

I still had time to warn them. But to do that, I would have to drastically alter my escape plan.

Before my arrest, I'd set up a timed funds transfer that would deposit enough money in my IOI credit account to pay off my entire debt, forcing IOI to release me from indenturement. But that transfer wouldn't happen for another five days. By then, the Sixers would probably have Art3mis and Shoto locked in a windowless room somewhere.

I couldn't spend the rest of the week exploring the Sixer database, like I'd planned. I had to grab as much data as I could and make my escape now.

I gave myself until dawn.

I worked frantically for the next four hours. Most of that time was spent copying as much data as possible from the Sixer database to my stolen flash drive. Once that task was completed, I submitted an Executive Oologist Supply Requisition Order. This was an online form that Sixer commanders used to request weapons or equipment inside the OASIS. I selected a very specific item, then scheduled its delivery for noon two days from now.

When I finally finished, it was six thirty in the morning. The next tech-support shift change was now only ninety minutes away, and my hab-unit neighbors would start waking up soon. I was out of time.

I pulled up my indenturement profile, accessed my debt statement, and zeroed out my outstanding balance—money I'd never actually borrowed to begin with. Then I selected the Indentured Servant Observation and Communications Tag control settings submenu, which operated both my eargear and security anklet. Finally, I did something I'd been dying to do for the past week—I disabled the locking mechanisms on both devices.

I felt a sharp pain as the eargear clamps retracted and pulled free of the cartilage on my left ear. The device bounced off my shoulder and landed in my lap. In the same instant, the shackle on my right ankle clicked open and fell off, revealing a band of abraded red skin.

I'd now passed the point of no return. IOI security techs weren't the only ones who had access to my eargear's vidfeed. The Indentured Servant Protection Agency also used it to monitor and record my daily activities, to ensure that my human rights were being observed. Now that I'd re-moved the device, there would be no digital record of what happened to me from this moment forward. If IOI security caught me before I made it out of the building, carrying a stolen flash drive filled with highly in-criminating company data, I was dead. The Sixers could torture and kill me, and no one would ever know.

I performed a few final tasks related to my escape plan, then logged out of the IOI intranet for the last time. I pulled off my visor and gloves and opened the maintenance access panel next to the entertainment center console. There was a small empty space below the entertainment mod-ule, between the prefab wall of my hab-unit and the one adjacent to it. I removed the thin, neatly folded bundle I'd hidden there. It was a vacuum-sealed IOI maintenance-tech uniform, complete with a cap and an ID badge. (Like the flash drive, I'd obtained these items by submitting an intranet requisition form, then had them delivered to an empty cubicle on my floor.) I pulled off my indent jumpsuit and used it to wipe the blood off my ear and neck. Then I removed two Band-Aids from under my mat-tress and slapped them over the holes in my earlobe. Once I was dressed in my new maintenance-tech threads, I carefully removed the flash drive from its expansion slot and pocketed it. Then I picked up my eargear and spoke into it. "I need to use the bathroom," I said.

The hab-unit door irised open at my feet. The hallway was dark and deserted. I stuffed my eargear and indent jumpsuit under the mattress and put the anklet in the pocket of my new uniform. Then, reminding myself to breathe, I crawled outside and descended the ladder.

I passed a few other indents on my way to the elevators, but as usual, none of them made eye contact. This was a huge relief, because I was wor-ried someone might recognize me and notice that I didn't belong in a maintenance-tech uniform. When I stepped in front of the express eleva-tor door, I held my breath as the system scanned my maintenance-tech ID badge. After what felt like an eternity, the doors slid open.

"Good morning, Mr. Tuttle," the elevator said as I stepped inside. "Floor please?"

"Lobby," I said hoarsely, and the elevator began to descend.

"Harry Tuttle" was the name printed on my maintenance tech ID badge. I'd given the fictional Mr. Tuttle complete access to the entire building, then reprogrammed my indent anklet so that it was encoded

with the Tuttle ID, making it function just like one of the security brace-
lets that maintenance techs wore. When the doors and elevators scanned
me to make sure I had the proper security clearance, the anklet in my
pocket told them that yes, I sure did, instead of doing what it was supposed to do, which was zap my ass with a few thousand volts and inca-
pacitate me until the security guards arrived.

I rode the elevator down in silence, trying not to stare at the camera
mounted above the doors. Then I realized the video being shot of me
would be scrutinized when this was all over. Sorrento himself would
probably see it, and so would his superiors. So I looked directly into the
lens of the camera, smiled, and scratched the bridge of my nose with my
middle finger.

The elevator reached the lobby and the doors slid open. I half expected
to find an army of security guards waiting for me outside, their guns leveled at my face. But there was only a crowd of IOI middle-management
drones waiting to get on the elevator. I stared at them blankly for a second, then stepped out of the car. It was like crossing the border into another country.

A steady stream of overcaffeinated office workers scurried across the
lobby and in and out of the elevators and exits. These were regular employees, not indents. They were allowed to go home at the end of their
shifts. They could even *quit* if they wanted to. I wondered if it bothered
any of them, knowing that thousands of indentured slaves lived and toiled
here in the same building, just a few floors away from them.

I spotted two security guards stationed near the reception desk and
gave them a wide berth, weaving my way through the thick crowd, crossing the immense lobby to the long row of automatic glass doors that led
outside, to freedom. I forced myself not to run as I pushed through the
arriving workers. *Just a maintenance tech here, folks, heading home after a
long night of rebooting routers. That's all. I am definitely not an indent making a daring escape with ten zettabytes of stolen company data in his pocket.
Nosiree.*

Halfway to the doors, I noticed an odd sound and glanced down at my
feet. I was still wearing my disposable plastic indent slippers. Each footfall
made a shrill squeak on the waxed marble floor, standing out amid the
rumble of sensible business footwear. Every step I took seemed to scream:
Hey, look! Over here! A guy in the plastic slippers!

But I kept walking. I was almost to the doors when someone placed a hand on my shoulder. I froze. "Sir?" I heard someone say. It was a woman's voice.

I almost bolted out the door, but something about the woman's tone stopped me. I turned and saw the concerned face of a tall woman in her midforties. Dark blue business suit. Briefcase. "Sir, your ear is bleeding." She pointed at it, wincing. "A lot."

I reached up and touched my earlobe, and my hand came away red. At some point, the Band-Aids I'd applied had fallen off.

I was paralyzed for a second, unsure of what to do. I wanted to give her an explanation, but couldn't think of one. So I simply nodded, muttered "thanks," then turned around and, as calmly as possible, walked outside.

The frozen morning wind was so fierce that it nearly knocked me over. When I regained my balance, I bounded down the tiered steps, pausing briefly to drop my anklet into a trash receptacle. I heard it hit the bottom with a satisfying thud.

Once I reached the street, I headed north, walking as fast as my feet would carry me. I was somewhat conspicuous because I was the only person not wearing a coat of some kind. My feet quickly went numb, because I also wasn't wearing socks under my plastic indent slippers.

My entire body was shivering by the time I finally reached the warm confines of the Mailbox, a post office box rental outlet located four blocks from the IOI plaza. The week before my arrest, I'd rented a post office box here online and had a top-of-the-line portable OASIS rig shipped to it. The Mailbox was completely automated, so there were no employees to contend with, and when I walked in there were no customers either. I located my box, punched in the key code, and retrieved the portable OASIS rig. I sat down on the floor and ripped open the package right there. I rubbed my frozen hands together until the feeling returned to my fingers, then put on the gloves and visor and used the rig to log into the OASIS. Gregarious Simulation Systems was located less than a mile away, so I was able to use one of their complimentary wireless access points instead of one of the city nodes owned by IOI.

My heart was pounding as I logged in. I'd been offline for eight whole days—a personal record. As my avatar slowly materialized on my stronghold's observation deck, I looked down at my virtual body, admiring it like a favorite suit I hadn't worn in a while. A window immediately appeared on my display, informing me that I'd received several messages from Aech and Shoto. And, to my surprise, there was even a message from Art3mis. All three of them wanted to know where I was and what the hell had happened to me.

I replied to Art3mis first. I told her that the Sixers knew who she was and where she lived and that they had her under constant surveillance. I also warned her about their plans to abduct her from her home. I pulled a copy of her dossier off the flash drive and attached it to my message as proof. Then I politely suggested that she leave home immediately and get the hell out of Dodge.

Don't stop to pack a suitcase, I wrote. *Don't say good-bye to anyone. Leave right now, and get somewhere safe. Make sure you aren't followed. Then find a secure non-IOI-controlled Internet connection and get back online. I'll meet you in Aech's Basement as soon as I can. Don't worry—I have some good news too.*

At the bottom of the message, I added a short postscript: *PS—I think you look even more beautiful in real life.*

I sent similar e-mails to Shoto and Aech (minus the postscript), along with copies of their Sixer dossiers. Then I pulled up the United States Citizen Registry database and attempted to log in. To my great relief, the passwords I'd purchased still worked, and I was able to access the fake Bryce Lynch citizen profile I'd created. It now contained the ID photo taken during my indent processing, and the words WANTED FUGITIVE were superimposed over my face. IOI had already reported Mr. Lynch as an escaped indent.

It didn't take me very long to completely erase the Bryce Lynch identity and copy my fingerprints and retinal patterns back over to my original citizen profile. When I logged out of the database a few minutes later, Bryce Lynch no longer existed. I was Wade Watts once again.

• • •

I hailed an autocab outside the Mailbox, making sure to select one operated by a local cab company and not a SupraCab, which was a wholly owned subsidiary of IOI.

When I got in, I held my breath as I pressed my thumb to the ID scanner. The display flashed green. The system recognized me as Wade Watts, not as the fugitive indent Bryce Lynch.

"Good morning, Mr. Watts," the autocab said. "Where to?"

I gave the cab the address of a clothing store on High Street, close to the OSU campus. It was a place called Thr3ads, which specialized in "high-tech urban street wear." I ran inside and bought a pair of jeans and a sweater. Both items were "dichotomy wear," meaning they were wired for OASIS use. They didn't have haptics, but the pants and shirt could link up with my portable immersion rig, letting it know what I was doing with my torso, arms, and legs, making it easier to control my avatar than with a gloves-only interface. I also bought a few packs of socks and underwear, a simulated leather jacket, a pair of boots, and a black knit-wool cap to cover my freezing, stubble-covered noggin.

I emerged from the store a few minutes later dressed in my new threads. As the frigid wind enveloped me again I zipped up my new jacket and pulled on the wool cap. Much better. I tossed the maintenance-tech jump-suit and plastic indent shoes in a trash can, then began to walk up High Street, scanning the storefronts. I kept my head down to avoid making eye contact with the stream of sullen university students filing past me.

A few blocks later, I ducked into a Vend-All franchise. Inside there were rows of vending machines that sold everything under the sun. One of them, labeled DEFENSE DISPENSER, offered self-defense equipment: light-weight body armor, chemical repellents, and a wide selection of hand-guns. I tapped the screen set into the front of the machine and scrolled through the catalog. After a moment's deliberation, I purchased a flak vest and a Glock 47C pistol, along with three clips of ammo. I also bought a small canister of mace, then paid for everything by pressing my right palm to a hand scanner. My identity was verified and my criminal record was checked.

NAME: WADE WATTS
OUTSTANDING WARRANTS: NONE
CREDIT RATING: EXCELLENT
PURCHASE RESTRICTIONS: NONE
TRANSACTION APPROVED!
THANK YOU FOR YOUR BUSINESS!

I heard a heavy metallic thunk as my purchases slid into the steel tray near my knees. I pocketed the mace and put the flak vest on underneath my new shirt. Then I removed the Glock from its clear plastic blister packaging. This was the first time I'd ever held a real gun. Even so, the weapon felt familiar in my hands, because I'd fired thousands of virtual firearms in the OASIS. I pressed a small button set into the barrel and the gun emitted a tone. I held the pistol grip firmly for a few seconds, first in my right hand, then my left. The weapon emitted a second tone, letting me know it had finished scanning my handprints. I was now the only person who could fire it. The weapon had a built-in timer that would prevent it from firing for another twelve hours (a "cooling-off period"), but I still felt better having it on me.

I walked to an OASIS parlor located a few blocks away, a franchise outlet called the Plug. The dingy backlit sign, which featured a smiling anthropomorphic fiber-optic cable, promised *Lightning-Fast OASIS Access! Cheap Gear Rental!* and *Private Immersion Bays! Open 24-7-365!* I'd seen a lot of banner ads for the Plug online. They had a reputation for high prices and outdated hardware, but their connections were supposed to be fast, reliable, and lag-free. For me, their major selling point was that they were one of the few OASIS parlor chains not owned by IOI or one of its subsidiaries.

The motion detector emitted a beep as I stepped through the front door. There was a small waiting area off to my right, currently empty. The carpet was stained and worn, and the whole place reeked of industrial-strength disinfectant. A vacant-eyed clerk glanced up at me from behind a bulletproof Plexiglas barrier. He was in his early twenties, with a Mohawk and dozens of facial piercings. He was wearing a bifocal visor, which gave him a semitransparent view of the OASIS while also allowing him to see his real-world surroundings. When he spoke, I saw that his teeth had all been sharpened to points. "Welcome to the Plug," he said in a flat monotone. "We have several bays free, so there's no waiting. Package pricing information is displayed right here." He pointed to the display screen mounted on the counter directly in front of me; then his eyes glazed over as he refocused his attention on the world inside his visor.

I scanned my choices. A dozen immersion rigs were available, of varying quality and price. *Economy, Standard, Deluxe.* I was given detailed specs on each. You could rent by the minute, or pay a flat hourly rate. A visor and a pair of haptic gloves were included in the rental price, but a haptic suit cost extra. The rental contract contained a lot of fine print about the additional charges you would incur if you damaged the equipment, and a lot of legalese stating that the Plug could not be held responsible for *anything* you did, under any circumstances, especially if it was something illegal.

"I'd like to rent one of the deluxe rigs for twelve hours," I said.

The clerk raised his visor. "You have to pay in advance, you realize?"

I nodded. "I also want to rent a fat-pipe connection. I need to upload a large amount of data to my account."

"Uploading costs extra. How much data?"

"Ten zettabytes."

"*Damn*," he whispered. "What you uploading? The Library of Congress?"

I ignored the question. "I also want the Mondo Upgrade Package," I said.

"Sure thing," the clerk replied warily. "Your total comes to eleven thousand big ones. Just put your thumb on the drum and we'll get you all fixed up."

He looked more than a little surprised when the transaction cleared. Then he shrugged and handed me a key card, a visor, and some gloves. "Bay fourteen. Last door on your right. The restroom is at the end of the hall. If you leave any kind of mess in the bay, we'll have to keep your deposit. Vomit, urine, semen, that kinda thing. And I'm the guy who has to clean it up, so do me a solid and show some restraint, will ya?"

"You got it."

"Enjoy."

"Thanks."

Bay fourteen was a soundproofed ten-by-ten room with a late-model haptic rig in the center. I locked the door behind me and climbed into the rig. The vinyl on the haptic chair was worn and cracked. I slid the data drive into a slot on the front of the OASIS console and smiled as it locked into place.

"Max?" I said to the empty air, once I'd logged back in. This booted up a backup of Max that I kept stored in my OASIS account.

Max's smiling face appeared on all of my command center monitors. "H-h-hey there, compadre!" he stuttered. "H-h-how goes it?"

"Things are looking up, pal. Now strap in. We've got a lot of work to do."

I opened up my OASIS account manager and initiated the upload from my flash drive. I paid GSS a monthly fee for unlimited data storage on my account, and I was about to test its limits. Even using the Plug's high-bandwidth fiber-optic connection, the total estimated upload time for ten zettabytes of data was over three hours. I reordered the upload sequence so the files I needed access to right away would get transferred first. As soon as data was uploaded to my OASIS account I had immediate access to it and could also transfer it to other users instantaneously.

First, I e-mailed all of the major newsfeeds a detailed account of how IOI had tried to kill me, how they *had* killed Daito, and how they were planning to kill Art3mis and Shoto. I attached one of the video clips I'd retrieved from the Sixer database to the message—the video camera footage of Daito's execution. I also attached a copy of the memo Sorrento had sent to the IOI board, suggesting that they abduct Art3mis and Shoto. Finally, I attached the simcap of my chatlink session with Sorrento, but I bleeped the part where he said my real name and blurred the image of my school photo. I wasn't yet ready to reveal my true identity to the world. I planned to release the unedited video later, once the rest of my plan had played out. Then it wouldn't matter.

I spent about fifteen minutes composing one last e-mail, which I addressed to every single OASIS user. Once I was happy with the wording, I stored it in my Drafts folder. Then I logged into Aech's Basement.

When my avatar appeared inside the chat room, I saw that Aech, Art3mis, and Shoto were already there waiting for me.

"Z!" Aech shouted as my avatar appeared. "What the hell, man? Where have you been? I've been trying to reach you for over a week!"

"So have I," Shoto added. "Where were you? And how did you get those files from the Sixer database?"

"It's a long story," I said. "First things first." I addressed Shoto and Art3mis. "Have you two left your homes?"

They both nodded.

"And you're each logged in from a safe location?"

"Yes," Shoto said. "I'm in a manga cafe right now."

"And I'm at the Vancouver airport," Art3mis said. It was the first time I'd heard her voice in months. "I'm logged in from a germ-ridden public OASIS booth right now. I ran out of my house with nothing but the clothes on my back, so I hope that Sixer data you sent us is legit."

"It is," I said. "Trust me."

"How can you be sure of that?" Shoto asked.

"Because I hacked into the Sixer Database and downloaded it myself."

They all stared at me in silence. Aech raised an eyebrow. "And how, exactly, did you manage that, Z?"

"I assumed a fake identity and masqueraded as an indentured servant to infiltrate IOI's corporate headquarters. I've been there for the past eight days. I just now escaped."

"Holy shit!" Shoto whispered. "Seriously?"

I nodded.

"Dude, you have balls of solid adamantium," Aech said. "Respect."

"Thanks. I think."

"Let's assume you're not totally bullshitting us," Art3mis said. "How does a lowly indent get access to secret Sixer dossier files and company memos?"

I turned to face her. "Indents have limited access to the company intranet via their hab-unit entertainment system, from behind the IOI firewall. From there, I was able to use a series of back doors and system exploits left by the original programmers to tunnel through the network and hack directly into the Sixers' private database."

Shoto looked at me in awe. "You did that? All by yourself?"

"That is correct, sir."

"It's a miracle they didn't catch you and kill you," Art3mis said. "Why would you take such a stupid risk?"

"Why do you think? To try and find a way to get through their shield and reach the Third Gate." I shrugged. "It was the only plan I could come up with on such short notice."

"Z," Aech said, grinning, "you are one crazy son of a bitch." He walked over and gave me a high five. "But that's why I love you, man!"

Art3mis scowled at me. "Of course, when you found out they had secret files on each of us, you just couldn't resist looking at them, could you?"

"I had to look at them!" I said. "To find out how much they knew about each of us! You would have done the same thing."

She leveled a finger at me. "No, I wouldn't have. I respect other people's privacy!"

"Art3mis, chill out!" Aech interjected. "He probably saved your life, you know."

She seemed to consider this. "Fine," she said. "Forget it." But I could tell she was still pissed off.

I didn't know what to say, so I kept plowing forward.

"I'm sending each of you a copy of all the Sixer data I smuggled out. Ten zettabytes of it. You should have it now." I waited while each of them checked their inbox. "The size of their database on Halliday is unreal. His whole life is in there. They've collected interviews with everyone Halliday ever knew. It could take months to read through them all."

I waited for a few minutes, watching their eyes scan over the data.

"Whoa!" Shoto said. "This is incredible." He looked over at me. "How the hell did you escape from IOI with all of this stuff?"

"By being extra sneaky."

"Aech is right," Art3mis said, shaking her head. "You are certifiably nuts." She hesitated for a second, then added, "Thanks for the warning, Z. I owe you one."

I opened my mouth to say "you're welcome," but no words came out.

"Yes," Shoto said. "So do I. Thanks."

"Don't mention it, guys," I finally managed to say.

"Well?" Aech said. "Hit us with the bad news already. How close are the Sixers to clearing the Third Gate?"

"Dig this," I said, grinning. *"They haven't even figured out how to open it yet."*

Art3mis and Shoto stared at me in disbelief. Aech smiled wide, then began to bob his head and press his palms to the sky, as if dancing to some unheard rave track. "Oh yes! Oh yes!" he sang.

"You're kidding, right?" Shoto asked.

I shook my head.

"You're *not* kidding?" Art3mis said. "How is that possible? Sorrento has the Crystal Key and he knows where the gate is. All he has to do is open the damn thing and step inside, right?"

"That was true for the first two gates," I replied. "But Gate Three is different." I opened a large vidfeed window in the air beside me. "Check this out. It's from the Sixers' video archive. It's a vidcap of their first attempt to open the gate."

I hit Play. The video clip opened with a shot of Sorrento's avatar standing outside the front gates of Castle Anorak. The castle's front entrance, which had been impregnable for so many years, swung open as Sorrento approached, like an automatic door at a supermarket. "The castle entrance will open for an avatar who holds a copy of the Crystal Key," I explained. "If an avatar doesn't have a copy of the key, he can't cross the threshold and enter the castle, even if the doors are already open."

We all watched the vidcap as Sorrento passed through the entrance and into the large gold-lined foyer that lay beyond. Sorrento's avatar crossed the polished floor and approached the large crystal door set into the north wall. There was a keyhole in the very center of the door, and directly above it, three words were etched into the door's glittering, faceted surface: CHARITY. HOPE. FAITH.

Sorrento stepped forward, holding out his copy of the Crystal Key. He slid the key into the keyhole and turned it. Nothing happened.

Sorrento glanced up at the three words printed on the gate. "Charity, hope, faith," he said, reading them aloud. Once again, nothing happened.

Sorrento removed the key, recited the three words again, then reinserted the key and turned it. Still nothing.

I studied Aech, Art3mis, and Shoto as they watched the video. Their excitement and curiosity had already shifted into concentration as they attempted to solve the puzzle before them. I paused the video. "Whenever Sorrento is logged in, he has a team of consultants and researchers watching his every move," I said. "You can hear their voices on some of the vidcaps, feeding him suggestions and advice through his comlink. So far, they haven't been much help. Watch—"

On the video, Sorrento was making another attempt to open the gate. He did everything exactly as before, except this time, when he inserted the Crystal Key, he turned it counterclockwise instead of clockwise.

"They try every asinine thing you can imagine," I said. "Sorrento recites the words on the gate in Latin. And Elvish. And Klingon. Then they get hung up on reciting First Corinthians 13:13, a Bible verse that contains the words 'charity, hope, and faith.' Apparently, 'charity, hope, and faith' are also the names of three martyred Catholic saints. The Sixers have been trying to attach some significance to that for the past few days."

"Morons," Aech said. "Halliday was an atheist."

"They're getting desperate now," I said. "Sorrento has tried everything but genuflecting, doing a little dance, and sticking his pinky finger in the keyhole."

"That's probably next up on his agenda," Shoto said, grinning.

"Charity, hope, faith," Art3mis said, reciting the words slowly. She turned to me. "Where do I know that from?"

"Yeah," Aech said. "Those words *do* sound familiar."

"It took me a while to place them too," I said.

They all looked at me expectantly.

"Say them in reverse order," I suggested. "Better yet, *sing* them in reverse order."

Art3mis's eyes narrowed. *"Faith, hope, charity,"* she said. She repeated them a few times, recognition growing in her face. Then she sang: "Faith *and* hope *and* charity . . ."

Aech picked up the next line: "The heart and the brain and the body . . ."

"Give you three . . . as a magic number!" Shoto finished triumphantly.

"Schoolhouse Rock!" they all shouted in unison.

"See?" I said. "I knew you guys would get it. You're a smart bunch."

"'Three Is a Magic Number,' music and lyrics by Bob Dorough," Art3mis recited, as if pulling the information from a mental encyclopedia. "Written in 1973."

I smiled at her. "I have a theory. I think this might be Halliday's way of telling us how many keys are required to open the Third Gate."

Art3mis grinned, then sang, *"It takes three."*

"No more, no less," continued Shoto.

"You don't have to guess," added Aech.

"Three," I finished, *"is the magic number."* I took out my own copy of the Crystal Key and held it up. The others did the same. "We have four copies of the key. If at least three of us can reach the gate, we can get it open."

"What then?" Aech asked. "Do we all enter the gate at the same time?"

"What if only one of us can enter the gate once it's open?" Art3mis said.

"I doubt Halliday would have set it up like that," I said.

"Who knows what that crazy bastard was thinking?" Art3mis said. "He's toyed with us every step of the way, and now he's doing it again. Why else would he require three copies of the Crystal Key to open the final gate?"

"Maybe because he wanted to force us to work together?" I suggested.

"Or he just wanted the contest to end with a big, dramatic finale," Aech offered. "Think about it. If three avatars enter the Third Gate at the exact same moment, then it becomes a race to see who can clear the gate and reach the egg first."

"Halliday was one crazy, sadistic bastard," Art3mis muttered.

"Yeah," Aech said, nodding. "You got that right."

"Look at it this way," Shoto said. "If Halliday hadn't set up the Third Gate to require three keys . . . the Sixers might have already found the egg by now."

"But the Sixers have a dozen avatars with copies of the Crystal Key," Aech said. "They could open the gate right now, if they were smart enough to figure out how."

"Dilettantes," Art3mis said. "It's their own fault for not knowing all the *Schoolhouse Rock!* lyrics by heart. How did those fools even get this far?"

"By cheating," I said. "Remember?"

"Oh, that's right. I keep forgetting." She grinned at me, and I felt my knees go all rubbery.

"Just because the Sixers haven't opened the gate yet doesn't mean they won't figure it out eventually," Shoto said.

I nodded. "Shoto's right. Sooner or later they'll make the *Schoolhouse Rock!* connection. So we can't waste any more time."

"Well, what are we waiting for?" Shoto said excitedly. "We know where the gate is and how to open it! So let's do it! And may the best gunter win!"

"You're forgetting something, Shoto-san," Aech said. "Parzival here still hasn't told us how we're going to get past that shield, fight our way through the Sixers' army, and get inside the castle." He turned to me. "You *do* have a plan for that, don't you, Z?"

"Of course," I said. "I was just getting to that." I made a sweeping gesture with my right hand, and a three-dimensional hologram of Castle Anorak appeared, floating in the air in front of me. The transparent blue sphere generated by the Orb of Osuvox appeared around the castle, surrounding it both above- and belowground. I pointed to it. "This shield is going to drop on its own, at noon on Monday, about thirty-six hours from now. And then we're going to walk right through the castle's front entrance."

"The shield is going to drop? On its own?" Art3mis repeated. "The clans have been lobbing nukes at that sphere for the past two weeks, and they haven't even scratched it. How are you going to get it to 'drop on its own'?"

"I've already taken care of it," I said. "You guys are gonna have to trust me."

"I trust you, Z," Aech said. "But even if that shield does drop, to reach the castle, we'll still have to fight our way through the largest army in the OASIS." He pointed to the hologram, which showed the Sixer troop positions around the castle, just inside the sphere. "What about these fools? And their tanks? And their gunships?"

"Obviously, we're going to need a little help," I said.

"A lot of help," Art3mis clarified.

"And who, exactly, are we going to convince to help us wage war against the entire Sixer army?" Aech asked.

"Everyone," I said. "Every single gunter on the grid." I opened another window, displaying the brief e-mail I'd composed just before logging into the Basement. "I'm going to send this message out tonight, to every single OASIS user."

Fellow gunters,

It is a dark day. After years of deception, exploitation, and knavery, the Sixers have finally managed to buy and cheat their way to the entrance of the Third Gate.

As you know, IOI has barricaded Castle Anorak in an attempt to prevent anyone else from reaching the egg. We've also learned that they've used illegal methods to uncover the identities of gunters they consider a threat, with the intention of abducting and murdering them.

If gunters around the world don't join forces to stop the Sixers, they will reach the egg and win the contest. And then the OASIS will fall under IOI's imperialist rule.

The time is now. Our assault on the Sixer army will begin tomorrow at noon, OST.

Join us!

Sincerely,

Aech, Art3mis, Parzival, and Shoto

"*Knavery?*" Art3mis said after she'd finished reading it. "Were you using a thesaurus when you wrote this?"

"I was trying to make it sound, you know, grand," I said. "Official."

"Me likey, Z," Aech said. "It really gets the blood stirring."

"Thanks, Aech."

"So that's it? This is your plan?" Art3mis said. "Spam the entire OASIS, asking for help?"

"More or less, yeah. That's the plan."

"And you really think everyone will just show up and help us fight the Sixers?" she said. "Just for the hell of it?"

"Yes," I said. "I do."

Aech nodded. "He's right. No one wants the Sixers to win the contest. And they definitely don't want IOI to take control of the OASIS. People will jump at a chance to help bring the Sixers down. And what gunter is gonna pass up a chance to fight in such an epic, history-making battle?"

"But won't the clans think we're just trying to manipulate them?" Shoto said. "So that *we* can reach the gate ourselves?"

"Of course," I said. "But most of them have already given up. Everyone knows the end of the Hunt is at hand. Don't you think most people would rather see one of us win the contest, instead of Sorrento and the Sixers?"

Art3mis considered it for a moment. "You're right. That e-mail just might work."

"Z," Aech said, slapping me on the back, "you are an evil, sublime genius! When that e-mail goes out, the media will go apeshit! The word will spread like wildfire. By this time tomorrow, every avatar in the OASIS will be headed to Chthonia."

"Let's hope so," I said.

"Oh, they'll show up, all right," Art3mis said. "But how many of them will actually fight, once they see what we're up against? Most of them will probably set up lawn chairs and eat popcorn while they watch us get our asses kicked."

"That's definitely a possibility," I said. "But the clans will help us, for sure. They've got nothing to lose. And we don't have to defeat the entire Sixer army. We just have to punch a hole through it, get inside the castle, and reach the gate."

"*Three* of us have to reach the gate," Aech said. "If only one or two of us make it inside, we're screwed."

"Correct," I said. "So we should all try extremely hard not to get killed."

Art3mis and Aech both laughed nervously. Shoto just shook his head. "Even if we get the gate open, we still have to contend with the gate itself," he said. "It's bound to be harder to clear than the first two."

"Let's worry about the gate later," I said. "Once we reach it."

"Fine," Shoto said. "Let's do this thing."

"I second that," Aech said.

"So, you two are actually gonna go along with this?" Art3mis said.

"You got a better idea, sister?" Aech asked.

She shrugged. "No. Not really."

"OK then," Aech said. "It's settled."

I closed the e-mail. "I'm sending each of you a copy of this message," I said. "Start sending it out tonight, to everyone on your contact list. Post it on your blogs. Broadcast it on your POV channels. We've got thirty-six hours to spread the word. That should be enough time for everyone to gear up and get their avatars to Chthonia."

"As soon as the Sixers catch wind of this, they'll start preparing for an assault," Art3mis said. "They're gonna pull out all the stops."

"They might just laugh it off," I said. "They think their shield is impregnable."

"It *is*," Art3mis said. "So I hope you're right about being able to shut it down."

"Don't worry."

"Why would I be worried?" Art3mis snapped. "Maybe you've forgotten, but I'm homeless and on the run for my life right now! I'm currently logged in from a public terminal at an airport, paying for bandwidth by the minute. I can't fight a war from here, much less try to clear the Third Gate. And I don't have anywhere to go."

Shoto nodded. "I don't think I can stay where I am either. I'm in a rented booth at a public manga cafe in Osaka. I don't have much privacy. And I don't think it's safe for me to stay here if the Sixers have agents out looking for me."

Art3mis looked at me. "Any suggestions?"

"I hate to break it to you guys, but I'm homeless and logged in from a public terminal right now too," I said. "I've been hiding out from the Sixers for over a year, remember?"

"I've got an RV," Aech said. "You're all welcome to crash with me. But I don't think I can make it to Columbus, Vancouver, and Japan in the next thirty-six hours."

"I think I might be able to help you guys out," a deep voice said.

We all jumped and turned around just in time to see a tall, male, gray-haired avatar appear directly behind us. It was the Great and Powerful Og. Ogden Morrow's avatar. And he didn't materialize slowly, the way an avatar normally did when logging into a chat room. He simply popped into existence, as if he had been there all along and had only now decided to make himself visible.

"Have any of you ever been to Oregon?" he said. "It's lovely this time of year."

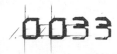

0033

We all stared at Ogden Morrow in stunned silence.

"How did you get in here?" Aech finally asked, once he'd managed to pick his jaw up off the floor. "This is a private chat room."

"Yes, I know," Morrow said, looking a bit embarrassed. "I'm afraid I've been eavesdropping on the four of you for quite some time now. And I hope you'll accept my sincere apologies for invading your privacy. I did it with only the best intentions, I promise you."

"With all due respect, sir," Art3mis said. "You didn't answer his question. How did you gain access to this chat room without an invitation? And without any of us even knowing you were here?"

"Forgive me," he said. "I can see why this might concern you. But you needn't worry. My avatar has many unique powers, including the ability to enter private chat rooms uninvited." As Morrow spoke, he walked over to one of Aech's bookshelves and began to browse through some vintage role-playing game supplements. "Prior to the original launch of the OASIS, when Jim and I created our avatars, we gave ourselves superuser access to the entire simulation. In addition to being immortal and invincible, our avatars could go pretty much anywhere and do pretty much anything. Now that Anorak is gone, my avatar is the only one with these powers." He turned to face the four of us. "No one else has the ability to eavesdrop on you. Especially not the Sixers. OASIS chat-room encryption protocols are rock solid, I assure you." He chuckled lightly. "My presence here notwithstanding."

"He knocked over that stack of comic books!" I said to Aech. "After our first meeting in here, remember? I told you it wasn't a software glitch."

Og nodded and gave us a guilty shrug. "That was me. I can be pretty clumsy at times."

There was another brief silence, during which I finally worked up the courage to speak to Morrow directly. "Mr. Morrow—," I began.

"Please," Morrow said, raising a hand. "Call me Og."

"All right," I said, laughing nervously. Even under the circumstances, I was completely starstruck. I couldn't believe I was actually addressing *the* Ogden Morrow. "*Og.* Would you mind telling us *why* you've been eavesdropping on us?"

"Because I want to help you," he replied. "And from what I heard a moment ago, it sounds as though you could all use my help." We all exchanged nervous looks, and Og seemed to detect our skepticism. "Please, don't misunderstand me," he continued. "I'm not going to give you any clues, or provide you with any information to help you reach the egg. That would ruin all the fun, wouldn't it?" He walked back over to us, and his tone turned serious. "Just before he died, I promised Jim that, in his absence, I would do everything I could to protect the spirit and integrity of his contest. That's why I'm here."

"But, sir—Og," I said. "In your autobiography, you wrote that you and James Halliday didn't speak during the last ten years of his life."

Morrow gave me an amused smile. "Come on, kid," he said. "You can't believe everything you read." He laughed. "Actually, that statement was mostly true. I didn't speak with Jim for the last decade of his life. Not until just a few weeks before he died." He paused, as if calling up the memory. "At the time, I didn't even know he was sick. He just called me up out of the blue, and we met in a private chat room, much like this one. Then he told me about his illness, the contest, and what he had planned. He was worried there might still be a few bugs in the gates. Or that complications might arise after he was gone that would prevent the contest from proceeding as he'd intended."

"You mean like the Sixers?" Shoto asked.

"Exactly," Og said. "Like the Sixers. So Jim asked me to monitor the contest, and to intervene if it ever became necessary." He scratched his beard. "To be honest, I didn't really want the responsibility. But it was the dying wish of my oldest friend, so I agreed. And for the past six years, I've

watched from the sidelines. And even though the Sixers have done everything to stack the odds against you, somehow you four have persevered.
But now, after hearing you describe your current circumstances, I think
the time has finally come for me to take action, to maintain the integrity
of Jim's game."

Art3mis, Shoto, Aech, and I all exchanged looks of amazement, as if
seeking reassurance from one another that this was all really happening.

"I want to offer the four of you sanctuary at my home here in Oregon,"
Og said. "From here, you'll be able to execute your plan and complete
your quest in safety, without having to worry about Sixer agents tracking you down and kicking in your door. I can provide each of you with a
state-of-the-art immersion rig, a fiber-optic connection to the OASIS, and
anything else you might need."

Another stunned silence. "Thank you, sir!" I finally blurted out, resisting the urge to fall to my knees and bow repeatedly.

"It's the least I can do."

"That's an incredibly kind offer, Mr. Morrow," Shoto said. "But I live
in Japan."

"I know, Shoto," Og said. "I've already chartered a private jet for you.
It's waiting at the Osaka airport. If you send me your current location, I'll
arrange for a limo to pick you up and take you to the runway."

Shoto was speechless for a second; then he bowed low. "Arigato,
Morrow-san."

"Don't mention it, kid." He turned to Art3mis. "Young lady, I understand that you're currently at the Vancouver airport? I've made travel ar-
rangements for you, as well. A driver is currently waiting for you in the
baggage claim area, holding a sign with the name 'Benatar' on it. He'll
take you to the plane I've chartered for you."

For a second I thought Art3mis might bow too. But then she ran over
and threw her arms around Og in a bear hug. "Thank you, Og," she said.
"Thank you, thank you, thank you!"

"You're welcome, dear," he said with an embarrassed laugh. When
she finally released him, he turned to Aech and me. "Aech, I understand
that you have a vehicle, and that you're currently in the vicinity of Pittsburgh?" Aech nodded. "If you wouldn't mind driving to Columbus to retrieve your friend Parzival here, I'll arrange for a jet to pick up both of you
at the Columbus airport. That is, if you boys don't mind sharing a ride?"

"No, that sounds perfect," Aech said, glancing at me sideways. "Thanks, Og."

"Yes, thank you," I repeated. "You're a lifesaver."

"I hope so." He gave me a grim smile, then turned to address everyone. "Safe travels, all of you. I'll see you soon." And then he vanished, just as quickly as he'd appeared.

"Well, this blows," I said, turning to Aech. "Art3mis and Shoto get limos, and I have to bum a ride to the airport with your ugly ass? In some shit-heap RV?"

"It's not a shit-heap," Aech said, laughing. "And you're welcome to take a cab, asshole."

"This is gonna be interesting," I said, stealing a quick glance at Art3mis. "The four of us are finally going to meet in person."

"It will be an honor," Shoto said. "I'm looking forward to it."

"Yeah," Art3mis said, locking eyes with me. "I can't wait."

●　●　●

After Shoto and Art3mis logged out, I gave Aech my current location. "It's a Plug franchise. Call me when you get here, and I'll meet you out front."

"Will do," he said. "Listen, I should warn you. I don't look anything like my avatar."

"So? Who does? I'm not really this tall. Or muscular. And my nose is slightly bigger—"

"I'm just warning you. Meeting me might be . . . kind of a shock for you."

"OK. Then why don't you just tell me what you look like right now?"

"I'm already on the road," he said, ignoring my question. "I'll see you in a few hours, OK?"

"OK. Drive safe, amigo."

Despite what I'd said to Aech, knowing that I was about to meet him in person after all these years made me more nervous than I wanted to admit. But it was nothing compared to the apprehension I already felt building inside me at the prospect of meeting Art3mis once we reached Oregon. Trying to picture the actual moment filled me with a mixture of excitement and abject terror. What would she be like in person? Was the photo I'd seen in her file actually a fake? Did I still have any kind of chance with her at all?

With a Herculean effort, I managed to put her out of my mind by forcing myself to focus on the approaching battle.

As soon as I logged out of Aech's Basement, I sent out my "Call to Arms" e-mail as a global announcement to every OASIS user. Knowing most of those e-mails wouldn't get through the spam filters, I also posted it to every gunter message board. Then I made a short vidcap recording of my avatar reading it aloud and set it to run on a continuous loop on my POV channel.

The word spread quickly. Within an hour, our plan to assault Castle Anorak was the top story on every single newsfeed, accompanied by headlines like GUNTERS DECLARE ALL-OUT WAR ON THE SIXERS and TOP GUNTERS ACCUSE IOI OF KIDNAPPING AND MURDER and IS THE HUNT FOR HALLIDAY'S EGG FINALLY OVER?

Some of the newsfeeds were already running the video clip of Daito's murder I'd sent them, along with the text of Sorrento's memo, citing an anonymous source for both. So far, IOI had declined to comment on either. By now, Sorrento would know I'd somehow gained access to the Sixers' private database. I wished I could see his face when he learned how I'd done it—that I'd spent an entire week just a few floors below his office.

I spent the next few hours outfitting my avatar and preparing myself mentally for what was to come. When I could no longer keep my eyes open, I decided to catch a quick nap while I waited for Aech to arrive. I disabled the auto-log-out feature on my account, then drifted off in the haptic chair with my new jacket draped over me as a blanket, clutching in one hand the pistol I'd purchased earlier that day.

• • •

I woke with a start sometime later to the sound of Aech's ringtone. He was calling to let me know he'd arrived outside. I climbed out of the rig, collected my things, and returned the rented gear at the front desk. When I stepped out into the street, I saw that night had fallen. The frozen air hit me like a bucket of ice water.

Aech's tiny RV was just a few yards away, parked at the curb. It was a mocha-colored SunRider, about twenty feet long, and at least two decades old. A patchwork of solar cells covered the RV's roof and most of its body, along with a liberal amount of rust. The windows were tinted black, so I couldn't see inside.

I took a deep breath and crossed the slush-covered sidewalk, feeling a strange combination of dread and excitement. As I approached the RV, a door near the center of the right side slid open and a short stepladder extended to the pavement. I climbed inside and the door slid shut behind me. I found myself in the RV's tiny kitchen. It was dark except for the running lights set into the carpeted floor. To my left, I saw a small bedroom area at the back, wedged into a loft above the RV's battery compartment. I turned and walked slowly across the darkened kitchen, then pulled back the beaded curtain covering the doorway to the cab.

A heavyset African American girl sat in the RV's driver seat, clutching the wheel tightly and staring straight ahead. She was about my age, with short, kinky hair and chocolate-colored skin that appeared iridescent in the soft glow of the dashboard indicators. She was wearing a vintage *Rush 2112* concert T-shirt, and the numbers were warped around her large bosom. She also had on faded black jeans and a pair of studded combat boots. She appeared to be shivering, even though it was nice and warm in the cab.

I stood there for a moment, staring at her in silence, waiting for her to acknowledge my presence. Eventually, she turned and smiled at me, and it was a smile I recognized immediately. That Cheshire grin I'd seen thousands of times before, on the face of Aech's avatar, during the countless nights we'd spent together in the OASIS, telling bad jokes and watching bad movies. And her smile wasn't the only thing I found familiar. I also recognized the set of her eyes and the lines of her face. There was no doubt in my mind. The young woman sitting in front of me was my best friend, Aech.

A wave of emotion washed over me. Shock gave way to a sense of betrayal. How could he—*she*—deceive me all these years? I felt my face flush with embarrassment as I remembered all of the adolescent intimacies I'd shared with Aech. A person I'd trusted implicitly. Someone I thought I knew.

When I didn't say anything, her eyes dropped to her boots and stayed on them. I sat down heavily in the passenger seat, still staring over at her, still unsure of what to say. She kept stealing glances at me; then her eyes would dart away nervously. She was still trembling.

Whatever anger or betrayal I felt quickly evaporated.

I couldn't help myself. I started to laugh. There was no meanness in it, and I knew she could tell that, because her shoulders relaxed a bit and she let out a relieved sigh. Then she started to laugh too. Half laughing and half crying, I thought.

"Hey, Aech," I said, once our laughter subsided. "How goes it?"

"It's going good, Z," she said. "All sunshine and rainbows." Her voice was familiar too. Just not quite as deep as it was online. All this time, she'd been using software to disguise it.

"Well," I said. "Look at us. Here we are."

"Yeah," Aech replied. "Here we are."

An uncomfortable silence descended. I hesitated a moment, unsure of what to do. Then I followed my instincts, crossed the small space between us, and put my arms around her. "It's good to see you, old friend," I said. "Thanks for coming to get me."

She returned the hug. "It's good to see you too," she said. And I could tell she meant it.

I let go of her and stepped back. "Christ, Aech," I said, smiling. "I knew you were hiding something. But I never imagined . . ."

"What?" she said, a bit defensively. "You never imagined what?"

"That the famous Aech, renowned gunter and the most feared and ruthless arena combatant in the entire OASIS, was, in reality, a . . ."

"A fat black chick?"

"I was going to say 'young African American woman.' "

Her expression darkened. "There's a reason I never told you, you know."

"And I'm sure it's a good one," I said. "But it really doesn't matter."

"It doesn't?"

"Of course not. You're my best friend, Aech. My *only* friend, to be honest."

"Well, I still want to explain."

"OK. But can it wait until we're in the air?" I said. "We've got a long way to travel. And I'll feel a lot safer once we've left this city in the dust."

"We're on our way, amigo," she said, putting the RV in gear.

●　　●　　●

Aech followed Og's directions to a private hangar near the Columbus airport, where a small luxury jet was waiting for us. Og had arranged for Aech's RV to be stored in a nearby hangar, but it had been her home for many years, and I could tell she was nervous about leaving it behind.

We both stared at the jet in wonder as we approached it. I'd seen airplanes in the sky before, of course, but I'd never seen one up close. Traveling by jet was something only rich people could afford. That Og could afford to charter three different jets to retrieve us without batting an eyelash was a testament to just how insanely wealthy he must be.

The jet was completely automated, so there was no crew on board. We were all alone. The placid voice of the autopilot welcomed us aboard, then told us to strap in and prepare for takeoff. We were up in the air within minutes.

It was the first time either of us had ever flown, and we both spent the first hour of the flight staring out the windows, overwhelmed by the view, as we hurtled westward through the atmosphere at ten thousand feet, on our way to Oregon. Finally, once some of the novelty had worn off, I could tell that Aech was ready to talk.

"OK, Aech," I said. "Tell me your story."

She flashed her Cheshire grin and took a deep breath. "The whole thing was originally my mother's idea," she said. Then she launched into an abbreviated version of her life story. Her real name, she said, was Helen Harris, and she was only a few months older than I was. She'd grown up in Atlanta, raised by a single mother. Her father had died in Afghanistan when she was still a baby. Her mother, Marie, worked from home, in an online data-processing center. In Marie's opinion, the OASIS was the best thing that had ever happened to both women and people of color. From the very start, Marie had used a white male avatar to conduct all of her online business, because of the marked difference it made in how she was treated and the opportunities she was given.

When Aech first logged into the OASIS, she followed her mother's advice and created a Caucasian male avatar. "H" had been her mother's nickname for her since she was a baby, so she'd decided to use it as the name of her online persona. A few years later, when she started attending school online, her mother lied about her daughter's race and gender on the application. Aech was required to provide a photo for her school profile, so she'd submitted a photorealistic rendering of her male avatar's face, which she'd modeled after her own features.

Aech told me that she hadn't seen or spoken to her mother since leaving home on her eighteenth birthday. That was the day Aech had finally come out to her mother about her sexuality. At first, her mother refused to believe she was gay. But then Helen revealed that she'd been dating a girl she met online for nearly a year.

As Aech explained all of this, I could tell she was studying my reaction. I wasn't all that surprised, really. Over the past few years, Aech and I had discussed our mutual admiration for the female form on numerous occasions. I was actually relieved to know that Aech hadn't been deceiving me, at least not on that account.

"How did your mother react when she found out you had a girlfriend?" I asked.

"Well, it turns out that my mother had her own set of deep-seated prejudices," Aech said. "She kicked me out of the house and said she never wanted to see me again. I was homeless for a little while. I lived in a series of shelters. But eventually I earned enough competing in the OASIS arena leagues to buy my RV, and I've been living in it ever since. I usually only stop moving when the RV's batteries need to recharge."

As we continued to talk, going through the motions of getting to know each other, I realized that we already *did* know each other, as well as any two people could. We'd known each other for years, in the most intimate way possible. We'd connected on a purely mental level. I understood her, trusted her, and loved her as a dear friend. None of that had changed, or could be changed by anything as inconsequential as her gender, or skin color, or sexual orientation.

The rest of the flight seemed to go by in a blink. Aech and I quickly fell into our old familiar rhythm, and before long it was like we were back in the Basement, trash-talking each other over a game of Quake or Joust. Any fears I had about the resiliency of our friendship in the real world had vanished by the time our jet touched down on Og's private runway in Oregon.

We'd been flying west across the country, just a few hours ahead of the sunrise, so it was still dark when we landed. Aech and I both froze in our tracks as we stepped off the plane, gazing in wonder at the scene around us. Even in the dim moonlight, the view was breathtaking. The dark, towering silhouettes of the Wallowa Mountains surrounded us on all sides. Rows of blue runway lights stretched out along the valley floor behind us, delineating Og's private landing strip. Directly ahead, a steep cobblestone staircase at the edge of the runway led up to a grand, floodlit mansion constructed on a plateau near the base of the mountain range. Several waterfalls were visible in the distance, spilling off the peaks beyond Morrow's mansion.

"It looks just like Rivendell," Aech said, taking the words right out of my mouth.

I nodded. "It looks exactly like Rivendell in the *Lord of the Rings* movies," I said, still staring up at it in awe. "Og's wife was a big Tolkien fan, remember? He built this place for her."

We heard an electric hum behind us as the jet's staircase retracted and the hatch closed. The engines powered back up and the jet rotated, preparing to take off again. We stood and watched it launch back up into the clear, starry sky. Then we turned and began to mount the staircase leading up to the house. When we finally reached the top, Ogden Morrow was there waiting for us.

"Welcome, my friends!" Og bellowed, extending both his hands in greeting. He was dressed in a plaid bathrobe and bunny slippers. "Welcome to my home!"

"Thank you, sir," Aech said. "Thanks for inviting us here."

"Ah, you must be Aech," he replied, clasping her hand. If he was surprised by her appearance, he didn't show it. "I recognize your voice." He gave her a wink, followed by a bear hug. Then he turned and hugged me, too. "And you must be Wade—I mean, Parzival! Welcome! Welcome! It's truly an honor to meet you both!"

"The honor is ours," I said. "We really can't thank you enough for helping us."

"You've already thanked me enough, so stop it!" he said. He turned and led us across an expansive green lawn, toward his enormous house. "I can't tell you how good it is to have visitors. Sad to say, I've been all alone here since Kira died." He was silent a moment; then he laughed. "Alone except for my cooks, maids, and gardeners, of course. But they all live here too, so they don't really count as visitors."

Neither I nor Aech knew how to reply, so we just kept smiling and nodding. Eventually, I worked up the courage to speak. "Have the others arrived yet? Shoto and Art3mis?"

Something about the way I said "Art3mis" made Morrow chuckle, long and loud. After a few seconds, I realized Aech was laughing at me too.

"What?" I said. "What's so funny?"

"Yes," Og said, grinning. "Art3mis arrived first, several hours ago, and Shoto's plane got here about thirty minutes before you arrived."

"Are we going to meet them now?" I asked, doing an extremely poor job of hiding my apprehension.

Og shook his head. "Art3mis felt that meeting you two right now would be an unnecessary distraction. She wanted to wait until after the 'big event.' And Shoto seemed to agree." He studied me for a moment. "It probably *is* for the best, you know. You've all got a big day ahead of you."

I nodded, feeling a strange combination of relief and disappointment.

"Where are they now?" Aech asked.

Og raised a fist triumphantly in the air. "They're already logged in, preparing for your assault on the Sixers!" His voice echoed across the grounds and off the high stone walls of his mansion. "Follow me! The hour draws near!"

Og's enthusiasm pulled me back into the moment, and I felt a nervous knot form in the pit of my stomach. We followed our bathrobed benefactor across the expansive moonlit courtyard. As we approached the main house, we passed a small gated-in garden filled with flowers. The garden was in a strange location, and I couldn't figure out its purpose until I saw the large tombstone at its center. Then I realized it must be Kira Morrow's grave. But even in the bright moonlight, it was still too dark for me to make out the inscription on the headstone.

Og led us through the mansion's lavish front entrance. The lights were off inside, but instead of turning them on, Morrow took an honest-to-God *torch* off the wall and used it to illuminate our way. Even in dim torchlight, the grandeur of the place amazed me. Giant tapestries and a huge collection of fantasy artwork covered the walls, while gargoyle statues and suits of armor lined the hallways.

As we followed Og, I worked up enough courage to speak to him. "Listen, I know this probably isn't the time," I said. "But I'm a huge fan of your work. I grew up playing Halcydonia Interactive's educational games. They taught me how to read, write, do math, solve puzzles . . ." I proceeded to ramble on as we walked, raving about all of my favorite Halcydonia titles and geeking out on Og in a classically embarrassing fashion.

Aech must have thought I was brown-nosing, because she snickered throughout my stammering monologue, but Og was very cool about it. "That's wonderful to hear," he said, seeming genuinely pleased. "My wife and I were very proud of those games. I'm so glad you have fond memories of them."

We rounded a corner, and Aech and I both froze before the entrance of a giant room filled with row after row of old videogames. We both knew it must be James Halliday's classic videogame collection—the collection he'd willed to Morrow after his death. Og glanced around and saw us lingering by the entrance, then hurried back to retrieve us.

"I promise to give you a tour later, when all the excitement is over," Og said, his breathing a bit labored. He was moving quickly for a man his age and size. He led us down a spiral stone staircase to an elevator that carried us down several more floors to Og's basement. The decor here was much more modern. We followed Og through a maze of carpeted hallways until we reached a row of seven circular doorways, each numbered.

"And here we are!" Morrow said, gesturing with the torch. "These are my OASIS immersion bays. They're all top-of-the-line Habashaw rigs. OIR-Ninety-four hundreds."

"Ninety-four hundreds? No kidding?" Aech let out a low whistle. "Wicked."

"Where are the others?" I asked, looking around nervously.

"Art3mis and Shoto are already in bays two and three," he said. "Bay one is mine. You two can take your pick of the others."

I stared at the doors, wondering which one Art3mis was behind.

Og motioned to the end of the hall. "You'll find haptic suits of all sizes in the dressing rooms. Now, get yourselves suited and booted!"

He smiled wide when Aech and I emerged from the dressing rooms a few minutes later, each dressed in brand-new haptic suits and gloves.

"Excellent!" Og said. "Now grab a bay and log in. The clock is ticking!"

Aech turned to face me. I could tell she wanted to say something, but words seemed to fail her. After a few seconds she stuck out her gloved hand. I took it.

"Good luck, Aech," I said.

"Good luck, Z," she replied. Then she turned to Og and said, "Thanks again, Og." Before he could respond, she stood on her tiptoes and kissed him on the cheek. Then she disappeared through the door to bay four and it hissed shut behind her.

Og grinned after her, then turned to face me. "The whole world is rooting for the four of you. Try not to let them down."

"We'll do our best."

"I know you will." He offered me his hand and I shook it.

I took a step toward my immersion bay, then turned back. "Og, can I ask you one question?" I said.

He raised an eyebrow. "If you're going to ask me what's inside the Third Gate, I have no idea," he said. "And even if I did, I wouldn't tell you. You should know that. . . ."

I shook my head. "No, that's not it. I wanted to ask what it was that ended your friendship with Halliday. In all the research I've done, I've never been able to find out. What happened?"

Morrow studied me for a moment. He'd been asked this question in interviews many times before and had always ignored it. I don't know why he decided to tell me. Maybe he'd been waiting all these years to tell someone.

"It was because of Kira. My wife." He paused a moment, then cleared his throat and continued. "Like me, he'd been in love with her since high school. Of course, he never had the courage to act on it. So she never knew how he felt about her. And neither did I. He didn't tell me about it until the last time I spoke to him, right before he died. Even then, it was hard for him to communicate with me. Jim was never very good with people, or with expressing his emotions."

I nodded silently and waited for him to continue.

"Even after Kira and I got engaged, I think Jim still harbored some fantasy of stealing her away from me. But once we got married, he abandoned that notion. He told me he'd stopped speaking to me because of the overwhelming jealousy he felt. Kira was the only woman he ever loved." Morrow's voice caught in his throat. "I can understand why Jim felt that way. Kira was very special. It was impossible not to fall in love with her." He smiled at me. "You know what it's like to meet someone like that, don't you?"

"I do," I said. Then, when I realized he had no more to say on the subject, I said, "Thank you, Mr. Morrow. Thank you for telling me all of that."

"You're quite welcome," he said. Then he walked over to his immersion bay, and the door irised open. Inside, I could see that his rig had been modified to include several strange components, including an OASIS console modified to look like a vintage Commodore 64. He glanced back at me. "Good luck, Parzival. You're going to need it."

"What are you going to do?" I asked. "During the fight?"

"Sit back and watch, of course!" he said. "This looks to be the most epic battle in videogame history." He grinned at me one last time, then stepped through the door and was gone, leaving me alone in the dimly lit hallway.

I spent a few minutes thinking about everything Morrow had told me. Then I walked over to my own immersion bay and stepped inside.

It was a small spherical room. A gleaming haptic chair was suspended on a jointed hydraulic arm attached to the ceiling. There was no omni-directional treadmill, because the room itself served that function. While you were logged in, you could walk or run in any direction and the sphere would rotate around and beneath you, preventing you from ever touching the wall. It was like being inside a giant hamster ball.

I climbed into the chair and felt it adjust to fit the contours of my body. A robotic arm extended from the chair and slipped a brand-new Ocu-lance visor onto my face. It, too, adjusted so that it fit perfectly. The visor scanned my retinas and the system prompted me to speak my new pass phrase: "Reindeer Flotilla Setec Astronomy."

I took a deep breath as the system logged me in.

I was ready to rock.

My avatar was buffed to the eyeballs and armed to the teeth. I was packing as many magic items and as much firepower as I could squeeze into my inventory.

Everything was in place. Our plan was in motion. It was time to go.

I entered my stronghold's hangar and pressed a button on the wall to open the launch doors. They slid back, slowly revealing the launch tunnel leading up to Falco's surface. I walked to the end of the runway, past my X-wing and the *Vonnegut*. I wouldn't be taking either of them today. They were both good ships, with formidable weapons and defenses, but neither craft would offer much protection in the epic shitstorm that was about to unfold on Chthonia. Fortunately, I now had a new mode of transportation.

I removed the twelve-inch Leopardon robot from my avatar's inventory and set it down gently on the runway. Shortly before I'd been arrested by IOI, I'd taken some time to examine the toy Leopardon robot and ascertain its powers. As I suspected, the robot was actually a powerful magical item. It hadn't taken me long to figure out the command word required to activate it. Just like in Toei's original *Supaidaman* TV series, you summoned the robot simply by shouting its name. I did this now, taking the precaution of backing away from the robot a good distance before shouting "Leopardon!"

I heard a piercing shriek that sounded like rending metal. A second later, the once-tiny robot had grown to a height of almost a hundred meters. The top of the robot's head now protruded through the open launch doors in the hangar ceiling.

I gazed up at the towering robot, admiring the attention to detail Halliday had put into coding it. Every feature of the original Japanese mech had been re-created, including its giant gleaming sword and spiderweb-embossed shield. A tiny access door was set into the robot's massive left foot, and it opened as I approached, revealing a small elevator inside. It carried me up through the interior of the robot's leg and torso, to the cockpit located inside its armored chest. As I seated myself in the captain's chair, I spotted a silver control bracelet in a clear case on the wall. I took it out and snapped it onto my avatar's wrist. The bracelet would allow me to use voice commands to control the robot while I was outside it.

Several rows of buttons were set into the command console in front of me, all labeled in Japanese. I pressed one of them and the engines roared to life. Then I hit the throttle and the twin rocket boosters in each of the robot's feet ignited, launching it upward, out of my stronghold and into Falco's star-filled sky.

I noticed that Halliday had added an old eight-track tape player to the cockpit control panel. There was also a rack of eight-track tapes mounted over my right shoulder. I grabbed one and slapped it into the deck. *Dirty Deeds Done Dirt Cheap* by AC/DC began to blast out of the robot's internal and external speakers, so loud it made my chair vibrate.

As soon as the robot was clear of my hangar, I shouted "Change *Marveller!*" into the control bracelet (the voice commands appeared to work only if you shouted them). The robot's legs, arms, and head folded inward and locked into new positions, transforming the robot into a starship known as the *Marveller.* Once the transformation was complete, I left Falco's orbit and set a course for the nearest stargate.

When I emerged from the stargate in Sector Ten, my radar screen lit up like a Christmas tree. Thousands of space vehicles of every make and model were crawling through the starry blackness around me, everything from single-seater craft to giant moon-sized freighters. I'd never seen so many starships in one place. A steady stream of them poured out of the stargate, while others converged on the area from every direction in the sky. All of the ships gradually funneled together, forming a long, haphazard caravan of vessels stretching toward Chthonia, a tiny blue-brown orb floating in the distance. It looked like every single person in the OASIS was headed for Castle Anorak. I felt a brief surge of exhilaration, even though I knew Art3mis's warning might still prove true—there was a chance most of these avatars were here only to watch the show and had no intention of actually risking their lives to fight the Sixers.

Art3mis. After all this time, she was now in a room just a few feet away from me. We would actually be meeting in person as soon as this fight was over. The thought should have terrified me, but instead I felt a zen calm wash over me: Whatever was going to happen down on Chthonia, everything I'd risked had already been worth it.

I transformed the *Marveller* back into its robot configuration, then joined the long parade of spacecraft. My ship stood out in the vast array of vessels, since it was the only giant robot. A cloud of smaller ships quickly formed around me, piloted by curious avatars zooming in for a closer look at Leopardon. I had to mute my comlink because so many different people were trying to hail me, asking who the hell I was and where I'd picked up such a sweet ride.

As the planet Chthonia grew larger in my cockpit window, the density and number of ships around me seemed to increase exponentially. When I finally entered the planet's atmosphere and began to descend toward the surface, it was like flying through a swarm of metal insects. When I reached the area around Castle Anorak, I had a hard time believing my eyes. A concentrated, pulsing mass of ships and avatars covered the ground and filled the air. It was like some otherworldly Woodstock. Shoulder-to-shoulder avatars stretched to the horizon in all directions. Thousands more floated and flew through the air above, dodging the constant influx of ships. And at the center of all this insanity stood Castle Anorak itself, an onyx jewel gleaming beneath the Sixers' transparent spherical shield. Every few seconds some hapless avatar or ship would inadvertently fly or careen into the shield and get vaporized, like a fly hitting a bug zapper.

When I got closer, I spotted an open patch of ground directly in front of the castle's entrance, just outside the shield wall. Three giant figures stood side by side at the center of the clearing. The crowd around them was continuously surging inward and then receding as avatars pushed back against each other to try to keep a respectful distance from Aech, Art3mis, and Shoto, who each sat inside their own gleaming giant robot.

This was my first opportunity to see which robots Aech, Art3mis, and

Shoto had selected after clearing the Second Gate, and it took me a moment to place the towering female robot Art3mis was piloting. It was black and chrome in color, with elaborate boomerang-shaped headgear and symmetrical red breastplates that made it look like a female version of Tranzor Z. Then I realized it *was* the female version of Tranzor Z, an obscure character from the original *Mazinger Z* anime series known as Minerva X.

Aech had selected an RX-78 Gundam mech from the original *Mobile Suit Gundam* anime series, one of his longtime favorites. (Even though I now knew Aech was actually a female in real life, her avatar was still male, so I decided to continue to refer to him as such.)

Shoto stood several heads taller than both of them, concealed inside the cockpit of Raideen, the enormous red-and-blue robot from the mid-'70s *Brave Raideen* anime series. The massive mech clutched his signature golden bow in one hand and had a large spiked shield strapped to the other.

A roar swept through the crowd as I flew in low over the shield and rocketed to a halt above the others. I rotated my orientation so that Leopardon was upright, then cut the engines and dropped the remaining distance to the surface. My robot landed on one knee, and the impact shook the ground. As I stood it upright, the sea of onlookers began to chant my avatar's name. *Par-zi-val! Par-zi-val!*

As the chanting faded back to a dull roar, I turned to face my companions.

"Nice entrance, ya big show-off," Art3mis said, using our private comlink channel. "Did you show up late on purpose?"

"Not my fault, I swear," I said, trying to play it cool. "There was a long line at the stargate."

Aech nodded his mech's massive head. "Every transport terminal on the planet has been spitting out avatars since last night," he said, motioning to the scene around us with his Gundam's massive hand. "This is unreal. I've never seen so many ships or avatars in one place."

"Me neither," Art3mis said. "I'm surprised the GSS servers can handle the load, with so much activity in one sector. But there doesn't seem to be any lag at all."

I took a long look at the sea of avatars around us, then shifted my attention to the castle. Thousands of flying avatars and ships continued to buzz around the shield, occasionally firing bullets, lasers, missiles, and other projectiles at it, all of which impacted harmlessly on the surface. Inside the sphere, thousands of power-armored Sixer avatars stood in silent formation, completely encircling the castle. Interspersed through their ranks were rows of hover tanks and gunships. In any other setting, the Sixer army would have appeared formidable. Maybe even unstoppable. But in the face of the endless mob that now surrounded them, the Sixers looked woefully outnumbered and outmatched.

"So, Parzival," said Shoto, turning his robot's huge head in my direction. "It's showtime, old friend. If that sphere doesn't come down like you promised, this is going to be pretty embarrassing."

"'Han will have that shield down,'" Aech quoted. "'We've got to give him more time!'"

I laughed, then used my robot's right hand to tap the back of its left wrist, indicating the time. "Aech is right. It's still six minutes to noon."

The end of my sentence was drowned out by another roar from the crowd. Directly in front of us, inside the sphere, the massive front doors of Castle Anorak had just swung open, and now a single Sixer avatar was emerging from within.

Sorrento.

Grinning at the din of booing and hissing that greeted his arrival, Sorrento waved his hand at the Sixer troops stationed directly in front of the castle and they immediately scattered, clearing a large open space. Sorrento stepped forward into it, positioning himself directly opposite us, just a few dozen yards away, on the other side of the shield. Ten other Sixer avatars emerged from the castle and positioned themselves behind Sorrento, each of them standing a good distance apart.

"I have a bad feeling about this," Art3mis muttered into her headset.

"Yeah," Aech whispered. "Me too."

Sorrento surveyed the scene, then smiled up at us. When he spoke, his voice was amplified through powerful speakers mounted on the Sixer gunships and hover tanks, allowing him to be heard by everyone in the area. And since there were cameras and reporters from every major newsfeed outlet present, I knew his words were being broadcast to the entire world.

"Welcome to Castle Anorak," Sorrento said. "We've been expecting you." He made a sweeping gesture, indicating the angry mob that surrounded him. "I must say, we are a bit surprised so many of you showed up here today. By now it must be obvious, to even the most ignorant among you, that nothing can get past our shield."

His proclamation was met with a deafening roar of shouted threats, insults, and colorful profanity. I waited a moment, then raised both of my robot's hands, calling for quiet. Once a semblance of silence had descended, I got on the public comm channel, which had the same effect as turning on a giant PA system. I dialed my headset volume down to kill the feedback, then said, "You're wrong, Sorrento. We're coming in. At noon. All of us."

A roar of approval erupted from the assembled gunters. Sorrento didn't bother waiting for it to die down. "You're welcome to try," he said, still grinning. Then he produced an item from his inventory and placed it on the ground in front of him. I zoomed in for a closer look and felt the muscles in my jaw tighten. It was a toy robot. A bipedal dinosaur with armor-plated skin and a pair of large cannons mounted on its shoulder blades. I recognized it immediately, from several turn-of-the-century Japanese monster flicks.

It was Mechagodzilla.

"Kiryu!" Sorrento shouted, his voice still amplified. At the sound of the command word, his tiny robot instantly grew in size until it stood almost as tall as Castle Anorak itself, twice the height of the "giant" robots that Aech, Shoto, Art3mis, and I piloted. The mechanical lizard's armored head almost touched the top of the spherical shield.

An awestruck silence fell over the crowd, followed by a rumble of fearful recognition from the thousands of gunters present. They all recognized this giant metal behemoth. And they all knew it was nearly indestructible.

Sorrento entered the mech through an access door in one of its massive heels. A few seconds later, the beast's eyes began to glow bright yellow. Then it threw back its head, opened its jagged maw, and let out a piercing metallic roar.

On cue, the ten Sixer avatars standing behind Sorrento pulled out their toy robots and activated them, too. Five of them had the huge robotic lions that could form Voltron. The other five had giant mechs from *Robotech* and *Neon Genesis Evangelion*.

"Oh shit," I heard Art3mis and Aech whisper in unison.

"Come on!" Sorrento shouted defiantly. His challenge echoed across the crowded landscape.

Many of the gunters on the front lines took an involuntary step backward. A few others turned and ran for their lives. But Aech, Shoto, Art3mis, and I held our ground.

I checked the time on my display. Less than a minute to go now. I pressed a button on Leopardon's control panel, and my giant robot drew its gleaming sword.

● ● ●

I didn't witness it firsthand, but I can tell you with some certainty that this is what happened next:

The Sixers had erected a large armored bunker behind Castle Anorak, filled with pallets of weapons and battle gear that had been teleported in by the Sixers before they activated their shield. There was also a long rack of thirty Supply Droids, which had been installed along the bunker's eastern wall. Due to a lack of imagination on the part of the Supply Droids' original designer, they all looked exactly like the robot Johnny Five from the 1986 film *Short Circuit.* The Sixers used these droids primarily as gofers, to run errands and fill equipment and ammo requisitions for the troops stationed outside.

At exactly one minute to noon, one of the Supply Droids, designation SD-03, powered itself on and disengaged from its charging dock. Then it rolled forward on its tank treads, across the bunker floor, to the armory cage at its opposite end. Two robotic sentries stood outside the armory's entrance. SD-03 transmitted its equipment requisition order to them—an order that I myself had submitted on the Sixer intranet two days earlier. The sentries verified the requisition and stepped aside, permitting SD-03 to roll into the cage. It continued past long storage racks that held a wide array of weaponry: magic swords, shields, powered armor suits, plasma rifles, railguns, and countless other weapons. Finally, the droid rolled to a stop. The rack in front of it held five large octahedron-shaped devices, each roughly the size of a soccer ball. Each device had a small control panel set into one of its eight sides, along with a serial number. SD-03 found the serial number that matched the one on my requisition form. Then, following a set of instructions I'd programmed into it, the little droid used its clawlike index finger to enter a series of commands on the device's control panel. When it finished, a small light above the keypad turned from green to red. Then SD-03 lifted the octahedron in its arms. As it exited the armory, one antimatter friction-induction bomb was subtracted from the Sixers' computerized inventory.

SD-03 then rolled out of the bunker and began to climb a series of ramps and staircases the Sixers had built onto the castle's outer walls to provide access to the upper levels. Along the way, the droid rolled through several security checkpoints. Each time, robotic sentries scanned its security clearance and found that the droid was allowed to go anywhere it damn well pleased. When SD-03 reached Castle Anorak's uppermost level, it rolled out onto a large observation platform located there.

At this point, SD-03 may have drawn a few curious looks from the squadron of elite Sixer avatars guarding the platform. I have no way of knowing. But even if the guards somehow anticipated what was about to happen and opened fire on the little droid, it was too late for them to stop it now.

SD-03 continued rolling directly to the center of the roof, where a high-level Sixer wizard sat holding the Orb of Osuvox—the artifact generating the spherical shield around the castle.

Then, executing the last of the instructions I'd programmed into it two days earlier, SD-03 lifted the antimatter friction-induction bomb up over its head and detonated it.

The explosion vaporized the supply droid, along with all the avatars stationed on the platform, including the Sixer wizard who was operating the Orb of Osuvox. The moment he died, the artifact deactivated and fell to the now-empty platform.

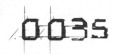

0035

A brilliant flash of light accompanied the detonation, momentarily blinding me. When it receded, my eyes focused back on the castle. The shield was down. Now, nothing separated the mighty Sixer and gunter armies but open ground and empty space.

For about five seconds, nothing happened. Time seemed to stop and everything was silent and still. Then all hell broke loose.

Sitting alone in the cockpit of my mech, I let out a silent cheer. Incredibly, my plan had worked. But I had no time to celebrate, because I was now standing smack-dab in the middle of the largest battle in the history of the OASIS.

I don't know what I expected to happen next. I'd hoped maybe a tenth of the gunters present would join our assault on the Sixers. But in seconds it was clear that every single one of them intended to join the fight. A fierce battle cry rose from the sea of avatars around us and they all surged forward, converging on the Sixer army from every direction. Their total lack of hesitation astounded me, because it was obvious many of them were rushing toward certain death.

I watched in amazement as the two mighty forces clashed all around me, on the ground and in the sky. It was a chaotic, breathtaking scene, like several beehives and wasp nests had been smashed together and then dropped onto a giant anthill.

Art3mis, Aech, Shoto, and I stood at the center of it all. At first, I didn't even move for fear of crushing the wave of gunters swarming around and over my robot's feet. Sorrento, however, didn't wait for anyone to get out of his way. He crushed several dozen avatars (including a few of his own troops) under his mech's titanic feet as he lumbered toward us, each of his footfalls creating a small crater in the rocky surface.

"Uh-oh," I heard Shoto mutter as his mech assumed a defensive posture. "Here he comes."

The Sixer mechs were already taking an immense amount of fire from all directions. Sorrento was getting hit more than anyone, because his mech was the biggest target on the battlefield, and no gunter with a ranged weapon could seem to resist taking a shot at him. The intense barrage of projectiles, fireballs, magic missiles, and laser bolts quickly destroyed or disabled the other Sixer mechs (who never even got a chance to form Voltron). But Sorrento's robot somehow remained undamaged. Every projectile that hit him seemed to ricochet harmlessly off his mech's armored body. Dozens of spacecraft swooped and buzzed around him, peppering his mech with rocket fire, but their attacks also seemed to have little effect.

"It is *on!*" Aech shouted into his comlink. "It is *on* like *Red Dawn!*" And with that, he unleashed all of his Gundam's considerable firepower at Sorrento. At the same moment, Shoto began firing Raideen's bow, while Art3mis's mech fired some sort of red energy beam that appeared to originate from Minerva X's giant metal breasts. Not wanting to be left out, I fired Leopardon's Arc Turn weapon, a gold boomerang that launched from the mech's forehead.

All of our attacks were direct hits, but Art3mis's beam weapon was the only one that seemed to do any real damage to Sorrento. She blasted a chunk out of the metal lizard's right shoulder blade and disabled the cannon mounted there. But Sorrento didn't pause in his approach. As he continued to close in on us, the Mechagodzilla's eyes began to glow a bright blue. Then Sorrento opened its mouth, and a cascading bolt of blue lightning shot outward from the mech's open maw. The beam struck the ground directly in front of us, then cut a deep smoking furrow in the earth as it continued to sweep forward, vaporizing every avatar and ship in its path. All four of us managed to leap out of the way by launching our robots skyward, though I nearly took a direct hit. The lightning weapon shut down a second later, but Sorrento continued to trudge forward. I noticed that his mech's eyes were no longer glowing blue. Apparently, his lightning weapon had to recharge.

"I think we've reached the final boss," Aech joked over the comlink. The four of us were now spread out and circling above Sorrento, making ourselves moving targets.

"Screw this, guys," I said. "I don't think we can destroy that thing."

"Astute observation, Z," Art3mis said. "Got any bright ideas?"

I thought for a second. "How about I distract him while the three of you cut around and head for the castle entrance?"

"Sounds like a plan," Shoto replied. But instead of heading for the castle, he banked and flew straight at Sorrento, closing the distance between them in the space of a few seconds.

"Go!" he shouted into his comlink. "This bastard is all mine!"

Aech cut across Sorrento's right flank and Art3mis banked left, while I rocketed upward and over him. Below me, I could see Shoto facing off against Sorrento, and the difference in the size of their mechs was disturbing. Shoto's robot looked like an action figure next to Sorrento's massive metal dragon. Nevertheless, Shoto cut his thrusters and dropped to the ground directly in front of the Mechagodzilla.

"Hurry," I heard Aech shout. "The castle entrance is wide open!"

From my vantage point in the sky above, I could see that the Sixer forces surrounding the castle were already being overrun by the endless mob of enemy avatars. The Sixers' lines were broken, and hundreds of gunters were streaming past them now, running up to the open castle entrance only to discover once they reached it that they couldn't cross the threshold because they didn't possess a copy of the Crystal Key.

Aech swung around directly in front of me. Still a hundred feet off the ground, he popped the hatch of his Gundam's cockpit and leapt out, whispering the robot's command word in the same instant. As the giant robot shrank back to its original size, he snatched it out of the air and stowed it in his inventory. Now flying by some magical means, Aech's avatar swooped down, passed over the bottleneck of gunters clustered at the castle entrance, and disappeared through the open double doors. A second later, Art3mis executed a similar maneuver, stowing her own mech in midair and then flying into the castle right behind Aech.

I dropped Leopardon into a sharp dive and prepared to follow them.

"Shoto," I shouted into my comm. "We're going inside now! Let's go!"

"Go ahead," Shoto replied. "I'll be right behind you." But something about the tone of his voice bothered me, and I pulled out of my dive and swung my mech back around. Shoto was hovering above Sorrento, near his right flank. Sorrento slowly turned his mech around and began to stomp back toward the castle. I could see now that his mech's weakness was its lack of speed. The Mechagodzilla's slow movement and attacks counterbalanced its seeming invulnerability.

"Shoto!" I shouted. "What are you waiting for? Let's go!"

"Go on without me," Shoto said. "I owe this son of a bitch some payback."

Before I could reply, Shoto dove at Sorrento, swinging a giant sword in each of his mech's hands. The blades both cut into Sorrento's right side, creating a shower of sparks, and to my surprise, they actually did some damage. When the smoke cleared I saw that the Mechagodzilla's right arm now hung limp. It was nearly severed at the elbow.

"Looks like you'll be wiping with your left hand now, Sorrento!" Shoto shouted triumphantly. Then he fired Raideen's boosters and headed in my direction, toward the castle. But Sorrento had already swiveled his mech's head around and was now taking a bead on Shoto with two glowing blue eyes.

"Shoto!" I shouted. "Look out!" But my voice was drowned out by the sound of the lightning weapon firing out of the metal dragon's mouth. It nailed Shoto's mech directly in the center of its back. The robot exploded in an orange ball of fire.

I heard a brief screech of static on the comm channel. I called out Shoto's name again, but he didn't reply. Then a message flashed on my display, informing me that Shoto's name had just disappeared from the Scoreboard.

He was dead.

This realization momentarily stunned me, which was unfortunate, because Sorrento's lightning weapon was still firing, moving in a fast sweeping arc, cutting across the ground, then diagonally up the castle wall, toward me. I finally reacted—too late—and Sorrento nailed my mech in the lower torso, just a split second before the beam cut off.

I looked down to discover that the bottom half of my robot had just been blasted away. Every warning indicator in my cockpit started to flash as my mech began to fall out of the sky in two smoking, burning halves.

Somehow, I had the presence of mind to reach up and yank the ejection handle above my seat. The cockpit canopy popped off, and I jumped free of the falling mech a split second before it impacted on the castle steps, killing several dozen of the avatars crowded there.

I fired my avatar's jet boots just before I hit the ground, then quickly adjusted my immersion rig's control setup, because I was now controlling my avatar instead of a giant robot. I managed to land on my feet in front of the castle, just clear of Leopardon's flaming wreckage. A second after I landed, a shadow spilled over me, and I turned around to see Sorrento's mech blotting out the sky. He raised its massive left foot, preparing to crush me.

I took three running steps and jumped, firing my jet boots in midleap. The thrust threw me clear just as the Mechagodzilla's huge clawed foot slammed down, forming a crater in the spot where I'd stood a second before. The metal beast let out another earsplitting shriek, followed by hollow, booming laughter. Sorrento's laughter.

I cut my jet-boot thrusters and tucked my avatar into a ball. I hit the ground rolling, tumbled forward, then came up on my feet. I squinted up at the metal lizard's head. Its eyes weren't glowing again—not yet. I could fire my jet boots again now and make it inside the castle before Sorrento could fire on me again. He wouldn't be able to follow me inside—not without getting out of his oversize mech.

I could hear Art3mis and Aech shouting at me on my comlink. They were already inside, standing in front of the gate, waiting for me.

All I had to do was fly into the castle and join them. The three of us could open and enter the gate before Sorrento caught up with us. I was sure of it.

But I didn't move. Instead, I took out the Beta Capsule and held the small metal cylinder in the palm of my avatar's hand.

Sorrento had tried to kill me. And in the process, he'd murdered my aunt, along with several of my neighbors, including sweet old Mrs. Gilmore, who had never hurt a soul. He'd also had Daito killed, and even though I'd never met him, Daito had been my friend.

And now Sorrento had just killed Shoto's avatar, robbing him of his chance to enter the Third Gate. Sorrento didn't deserve his power or his position. What he deserved, I decided in that moment, was public humiliation and defeat. He deserved to have his ass kicked while the whole world watched.

I held the Beta Capsule high over my head and pressed its activation button.

There was a blinding flash of light, and the sky turned crimson as my avatar changed, growing and morphing into a gigantic red-and-silver-skinned humanoid alien with glowing egg-shaped eyes, a strange finned head, and a glowing light embedded in the center of my chest. For the next three minutes, I was Ultraman.

The Mechagodzilla stopped shrieking and thrashing. Its gaze had been pointed down at the ground, where my avatar had stood a second earlier. Now its head slowly tilted up, taking in the size of its new opponent, until our glowing eyes finally met. I now stood face-to-face with Sorrento's mech, matching its height and size almost exactly.

Sorrento's mech took several awkward steps backward. Its eyes began to glow again.

I crouched slightly and struck an offensive pose, noticing that a timer now appeared in the corner of my display, counting down from three minutes.

2:59. 2:58. 2:57.

Below the timer there was a menu listing Ultraman's various energy attacks in Japanese. I quickly selected SPECIUM RAY and then held my arms up in front of me, one horizontal and the other vertical, forming a cross. A pulsing beam of white energy shot out of my forearms, striking the Mechagodzilla in its chest and knocking it backward. Thrown off balance, Sorrento lost control and tripped over his own mammoth feet. His mech tumbled to the ground, landing on its side.

A cheer went up from the thousands of avatars watching from the chaotic battlefield around us.

I launched myself into the air and flew half a kilometer straight upward. Then I dropped back down, feet first, aiming my heels directly at the Mechagodzilla's curved spine. When my feet hit, I heard something inside the metal beast snap under my crushing weight. Smoke began to pour out of its mouth, and the blue glow in its eyes quickly dissipated.

I executed a backflip and landed behind the supine mech in a crouch. Its single functioning arm flailed wildly while its tail and legs thrashed about. Sorrento appeared to be struggling with the controls in an effort to get the beast back on its feet.

I selected YATSUAKI KOHRIN from my weapon menu: *Ultra-Slice.* A glowing circular saw blade of electric-blue energy appeared in my right hand, spinning fiercely. I hurled it at Sorrento, releasing it with a snap of my wrist, like a Frisbee. It whirred through the air and struck the Mechagodzilla in its stomach. The energy blade cut into its metal skin as if it were tofu, slicing the mech into two halves. Just before the entire machine exploded, the head detached and blasted away from the neck. Sorrento had ejected. But since the mech was lying flat, the head shot out on a trajectory parallel to the ground. Sorrento quickly adjusted for this, and the rockets sprouting from the head began to tilt it skyward. Before it could get very far, I crossed my arms again and fired another specium ray, nailing the retreating head like a clay pigeon. It disintegrated in an immensely satisfying explosion.

The crowd went wild.

I checked the Scoreboard and confirmed that Sorrento's employee number had vanished. His avatar was dead. I couldn't take too much satisfaction from this, though, because I knew he was probably already kicking one of his underlings out of a haptic chair so he could take control of a new avatar.

The counter on my display had only fifteen seconds remaining when I deactivated the Beta Capsule. My avatar instantly shrank back to normal size, and my appearance returned to normal. Then I spun around, powered on my jet boots, and flew into the castle.

When I reached the opposite end of the huge foyer, I found Aech and Art3mis standing in front of the crystal door, waiting for me. The smoking, bloodied bodies of over a dozen recently slain Sixer avatars lay scattered on the stone floor around them, slowly fading out of existence. Apparently, there had been a brief and decisive skirmish and I'd just missed it.

"No fair," I said, cutting my jet boots and dropping to the floor beside Aech. "You could have saved at least one of them for me."

Art3mis didn't reply. She just gave me the finger.

"Congrats on wasting Sorrento," Aech said. "It was an epic throwdown, for sure. But you're still a complete idiot. You know that, right?

"Yeah." I shrugged. "I know."

"You're such a selfish asshole!" Art3mis shouted. "What if you'd gotten yourself killed too?"

"I didn't, though. Did I?" I said, stepping around her to examine the crystal door. "So chill out and let's open this thing."

I examined the keyhole in the center of the door, then looked at the words printed directly above it, etched into the door's faceted surface. *Charity. Hope. Faith.*

I took out my copy of the Crystal Key and held it up. Aech and Art3mis followed suit and held up their keys too.

Nothing happened.

We all exchanged concerned looks. Then an idea occurred to me, and I cleared my throat. " 'Three is a magic number,' " I said, reciting the first line of the *Schoolhouse Rock!* song. As soon as I spoke the words, the crystal door began to glow, and two additional keyholes appeared, on either side of the first.

"That did it!" Aech whispered. "Holy shit. I can't believe this. We're really here. Standing in front of the Third Gate."

Art3mis nodded. "Finally."

I inserted my key in the center keyhole. Aech inserted his into the keyhole on the left, and Art3mis placed hers in the keyhole on the right.

"Clockwise?" Art3mis said. "On the count of three?"

Aech and I nodded. Art3mis counted to three, and we turned our keys in unison. There was a brief flash of blue light, during which all of our keys and the crystal door itself vanished. And then the Third Gate stood open in front of us, a crystal doorway leading into a spinning whirlpool of stars.

"Wow," I heard Art3mis whisper beside me. "Here we go."

As the three of us stepped forward, preparing to enter the gate, I heard an earsplitting boom. It sounded like the entire universe was cracking in half.

And then we all died.

0036

When your avatar gets killed, your screen doesn't fade to black right away. Instead, your point of view automatically shifts to a third-person perspective, treating you to a brief out-of-body replay of your avatar's final fate.

A split second after we heard the thunderous boom, my perspective shifted, and I found myself looking at our three avatars, standing there frozen in front of the open gate. Then an incinerating white light filled the world, accompanied by an earsplitting wall of sound. It was what I'd always pictured being fried in a nuclear blast would be like.

For a brief moment, I saw our avatars' skeletons suspended inside the transparent outlines of our motionless bodies. Then my avatar's hit-point counter dropped to zero.

The blast wave arrived a second later, disintegrating everything in its path—our avatars, the floor, the walls, the castle itself, and the thousands of avatars gathered around it. Everything was turned to a fine, atomized dust that hung suspended in the air for a second before slowly settling to earth.

The entire surface of the planet had been wiped clean. The area around Castle Anorak, which had been crowded with warring avatars a split second before, was now a desolate and barren wasteland. Everyone and everything had been destroyed. Only the Third Gate remained, a crystal doorway floating in the air above the crater where the castle had stood a moment before.

My initial shock quickly turned to dread as I realized what had just happened.

The Sixers had detonated the Cataclyst.

It was the only explanation. Only that incredibly powerful artifact could have done this. Not only had it killed every avatar in the sector, it had even destroyed Castle Anorak, a fortress that, until now, had proven itself to be indestructible.

I stared at the open gate, floating in the empty air, and waited for the inevitable, final message to appear in the center of my display, the words I knew every other avatar in the sector must be seeing at this very moment: GAME OVER.

But when words finally did appear on my display, it was another message entirely: CONGRATULATIONS! YOU HAVE AN EXTRA LIFE!

Then, as I watched in amazement, my avatar reappeared, fading back into existence in the exact same location where I'd died a few seconds earlier. I was standing in front of the open gate again. But the gate was now floating in midair, suspended several dozen meters above the planet's surface, over the crater that had been created by the destruction of the castle. As my avatar finished materializing, I looked down and realized that the floor I'd been standing on earlier was now gone. So were my jet boots, and everything else I'd been carrying.

I seemed to hover in midair for a moment, like Wile E. Coyote in the old Roadrunner cartoons. Then I plummeted straight down. I made a desperate grab for the open gate in front of me, but it was well out of reach.

I hit the ground hard and lost a third of my hit points from the impact. Then I slowly got to my feet and looked around. I was standing in a vast cube-shaped crater—the space where the foundation and lower basement levels of Castle Anorak had stood. It was completely barren and eerily silent. There was no rubble from the destroyed castle, and no wreckage from the thousands of spaceships and aircraft that had filled the sky a few moments ago. In fact, there was no sign at all of the grand battle that had just been fought here. The Cataclyst had vaporized everything.

I looked down at my avatar and saw that I was now wearing a black T-shirt and blue jeans, the default outfit that appeared on every newly created avatar. Then I pulled up my stats and item inventory. My avatar had the same level and ability scores I'd had previously, but my inventory was completely empty except for one item—the quarter I'd obtained after playing my perfect game of Pac-Man on Archaide. Once I'd placed the quarter in my inventory, I hadn't been able to remove it, so I'd never been able to have any divination or identification spells cast on it. I'd had no way of ascertaining the quarter's true purpose or powers. During the tumultuous events of the past few months, I'd forgotten I even had the damn thing.

But now I knew what the quarter was—a single-use artifact that gave my avatar an extra life. Until that moment, I hadn't even known such a thing was possible. In the history of the OASIS, there was no record of any avatar ever acquiring an extra life.

I selected the quarter in my inventory and tried again to remove it. This time, I was able to take it out and hold it in the palm of my avatar's hand. Now that the artifact's sole power had been used, it no longer possessed any magical properties. Now it was just a quarter.

I looked straight up at the crystal gate floating twenty meters above me. It was still sitting there, wide open. But I had no idea how I was going to get up there to enter it. I had no jet boots, no ship, and no magic items or memorized spells. Nothing that would allow me to fly or levitate. And there wasn't a single stepladder in sight.

There I was, standing a stone's throw from the Third Gate, but unable to reach it.

"Hey, Z?" I heard a voice say. "Can you hear me?"

It was Aech, but her voice was no longer altered to sound male. I could hear her perfectly, as if she were talking to me via comlink. But that didn't make sense, because my avatar no longer *had* a comlink. And Aech's avatar was dead.

"Where are you?" I asked the empty air.

"I'm dead, like everyone else," Aech said. "Everyone but you."

"Then how can I hear you?"

"Og patched all of us into your audio and video feeds," she said. "So we can see what you see and hear what you hear."

"Oh," I said.

"Is that all right with you, Parzival?" I heard Og ask. "If it isn't, just say so."

I thought about it for a moment. "No, it's fine with me," I said. "Shoto and Art3mis are listening in too?"

"Yes," Shoto said. "I'm here."

"Yeah, we're here, all right," Art3mis said, and I could hear the barely contained rage in her voice. "And we're all dead as doornails. The question is, why aren't you dead too, Parzival?"

"Yeah, Z," Aech said. "We *are* a bit curious about that. What happened?"

I took out the quarter and held it up in front of my eyes. "I was awarded this quarter on Archaide a few months ago, for playing a perfect game of Pac-Man. It was an artifact, but I never knew its purpose. Not until now. Turns out it gave me an extra life."

I heard only silence for a moment; then Aech began to laugh. "You lucky son of a bitch!" she said. "The newsfeeds are reporting that every single avatar in the sector was just killed. Over half the population of the OASIS."

"Was it the Cataclyst?" I asked.

"It had to be," Art3mis said. "The Sixers must have bought it when it went up for auction a few years ago. And they've been sitting on it all this time, waiting for the perfect moment to detonate it."

"But they just killed off all of their own troops, too," Shoto said. "Why would they do that?"

"I think most of them were already dead," Art3mis said.

"The Sixers had no choice," I said. "It was the only way they could stop us. We'd already opened the Third Gate and were about to step inside when they detonated that thing—" I paused, realizing something. "How did they know we'd opened it? Unless—"

"They were watching us," Aech said. "The Sixers probably had remote surveillance cameras hidden all around the gate."

"So they saw us open it," Art3mis said. "Which means they know how to open it now too."

"Who cares?" Shoto interjected. "Sorrento's avatar is dead. And so are all of the other Sixers."

"Wrong," Art3mis said. "Check the Scoreboard. There are still twenty Sixer avatars listed there, below Parzival. And their scores indicate that every single one of them has a copy of the Crystal Key."

"Shit!" Aech and Shoto said in unison.

"The Sixers knew they might have to detonate the Cataclyst," I said. "So they must have taken the precaution of moving some of their avatars outside of Sector Ten. They were probably waiting in a gunship just across the sector border, where it was safe."

"You're right," Aech said. "Which means there are twenty more Sixers headed your way right now, Z. So you need to get your ass moving and get inside that gate. This is probably going to be your only chance to clear it." I heard her let out a defeated sigh. "It's over for us. So we're all rooting for you now, amigo. Good luck."

"Thanks, Aech."

"*Gokouun o inorimasu*," Shoto said. "Do your best."

"I will," I said. Then I waited for Art3mis to give me her blessing too.

"Good luck, Parzival," she said after a long pause. "Aech is right, you know. You're never going to get another shot at this. And neither will any other gunter." I heard her voice catch, as if she were choking back tears. Then she took a deep breath and said, "Don't screw this up."

"I won't," I said. "No pressure, right?"

I glanced back up at the open gate, suspended in the air above me, so far out of reach. Then I dropped my gaze and began to scan the area, desperately trying to figure out how I was going to get up there. Something caught my eye—just a few flickering pixels in the distance, near the opposite end of the crater. I ran toward them.

"Uh, not to be a backseat driver or anything," Aech said. "But where the hell are you going?"

"All of my avatar's items were destroyed by the Cataclyst," I said. "So now I have no way to fly up there and reach the gate."

"You've got to be kidding me!" Aech sighed. "Man, the hits just keep on coming!"

As I approached the object in the distance, it became gradually clearer. It was the Beta Capsule, floating just a few centimeters above the ground, spinning clockwise. The Cataclyst had destroyed everything in the sector that could be destroyed, but artifacts were indestructible. Just like the gate.

"It's the Beta Capsule!" Shoto shouted. "It must have been thrown over here by the force of the blast. You can use it to become Ultraman and fly up to the gate!"

I nodded, raised the capsule over my head, then pressed the button on the side to activate it. But nothing happened. "Shit!" I muttered, realizing why. "It won't work. It can only be used once a day." I stowed the Beta Capsule and started to scan the ground around me. "There must be other artifacts scattered around here," I said. I began to run along the perimeter of the castle foundation, still scanning the ground. "Were any of you guys carrying artifacts? One that would give me the ability to fly? Or levitate? Or teleport?"

"No," answered Shoto. "I didn't have any artifacts."

"My Sword of the Ba'Heer was an artifact," Aech said. "But it won't help you reach the gate."

"But my Chucks will," Art3mis said.

"Your 'Chucks'?" I repeated.

"My shoes. Black Chuck Taylor All Stars. They bestow their wearer with both speed and flight."

"Great! Perfect!" I said. "Now I just have to find them." I continued to run forward, eyes sweeping the ground. I found Aech's sword a minute later and added it to my inventory, but it took me another five minutes of searching before I found Art3mis's magic sneakers, near the south end of the crater. I put them on, and they adjusted to fit my avatar's feet perfectly. "I'll get these back to you, Arty," I said, just as I finished lacing them up. "Promise."

"You better," she said. "They were my favorites."

I took three running steps, leapt into the air, and then I was flying. I swooped up and around, then turned back toward the gate, aiming straight for it. But at the last moment, I banked to the right, then arced back around. I stopped to hover in front of the open gate. The crystal doorway hung in the air directly ahead, just a few yards away. It reminded me of the floating door in the opening credits of the original *Twilight Zone*.

"What are you waiting for?" Aech shouted. "The Sixers could show up any minute now!"

"I know," I said. "But there's something I need to say to all of you before I go in."

"Well?" Art3mis said. "Spit it out! The clock is ticking, fool!"

"OK, OK!" I said. "I just wanted to say that I know how the three of you must feel right now. It isn't fair, the way this has played out. We should all be entering the gate together. So before I go in, I want you guys to know something. If I reach the egg, I'm going to split the prize money equally among the four of us."

Stunned silence.

"Hello?" I said after a few seconds. "Did you guys hear me?"

"Are you insane?" Aech asked. "Why would you do that, Z?"

"Because it's the only honorable thing to do," I said. "Because I never would have gotten this far on my own. Because all four of us deserve to see what's inside that gate and find out how the game ends. And because I need your help."

"Could you repeat that last bit, please?" Art3mis asked.

"I need your help," I said. "You guys are right. This is my only shot at clearing the Third Gate. There won't be any second chances, for anyone. The Sixers will be here soon, and they'll enter the gate as soon as they arrive. So I have to clear it before they do, on my first attempt. The odds of me pulling that off will increase drastically if the three of you are backing me up. So . . . what do you say?"

"Count me in, Z," Aech said. "I was planning to coach your dumb ass anyway."

"Count me in too," said Shoto. "I've got nothing left to lose."

"Let me get this straight," Art3mis said. "We help you clear the gate, and in return, you agree to split the prize money with us?"

"Wrong," I said. "If I win, I'm going to split the prize money with you guys, regardless of whether you help me or not. So helping me is probably in your best interest."

"I don't suppose we have time to get that in writing?" Art3mis said.

I thought for a moment, then accessed my POV channel's control menu. I initiated a live broadcast, so everyone watching my channel (my ratings counter said I currently had more than two hundred million viewers) could hear what I was about to say. "Greetings," I said. "This is Wade Watts, also known as Parzival. I want to let the whole world know that if and when I find Halliday's Easter egg, I hereby vow to split my winnings equally with Art3mis, Aech, and Shoto. Cross my heart and hope to die. Gunter's honor. Pinky swear. All of that crap. If I'm lying, I should be forever branded as a gutless Sixer-fellating punk."

As I finished the broadcast, I heard Art3mis say, "Dude, are you nuts? I was kidding!"

"Oh," I said. "Right. I knew that."

I cracked my knuckles, then flew forward into the gate, and my avatar vanished into the whirlpool of stars.

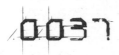

I found myself standing in a vast, dark, empty space. I couldn't
see the walls or ceiling, but there appeared to be a floor, because I was
standing on something. I waited a few seconds, unsure of what to do.
Then a booming electronic voice echoed through the void. It sounded as if
it were being generated by a primitive speech synthesizer, like those used
in Q*Bert and Gorf. *"Beat the high score or be destroyed!"* the voice announced. A shaft of light appeared, shining down from somewhere high
above. There, in front of me, at the base of this long pillar of light, stood
an old coin-operated arcade game. I recognized its distinctive, angular
cabinet immediately. Tempest. Atari. 1980.

I closed my eyes and dropped my head. *"Crap,"* I muttered. "This is not
my best game, gang."

"Come on," I heard Art3mis whisper. "You *had* to know Tempest was
going to factor into the Third Gate somehow. It was so obvious!"

"Oh really?" I said. "Why?"

"Because of the quote on the last page of the *Almanac*," she replied. "'I
must uneasy make, lest too light winning make the prize light.'"

"I *know* the quote," I said, annoyed. "It's from Shakespeare. But I figured it was just Halliday's way of letting us know how difficult he was
going to make the Hunt."

"It was," Art3mis said. "But it was also a clue. That quote was taken
from Shakespeare's final play, *The Tempest*."

"Shit!" I hissed. "How the hell did I miss that?"

"I never made that connection either," Aech confessed. "Bravo, Art3mis."

"The game Tempest also appears briefly in the music video for the song 'Subdivisions' by Rush," she added. "One of Halliday's favorites. Pretty hard to miss."

"Whoa," Shoto said. "She's good."

"OK!" I shouted. "It should have been obvious. No need to rub it in!"

"I take it you've haven't had much practice at this game, Z?" Aech said.

"A little, a long time ago," I said. "But not nearly enough. Look at the high score." I pointed at the monitor. The high score was 728,329. The initials next to it were JDH—James Donovan Halliday. And, as I feared, the credit counter at the bottom of the screen had a numeral one in front of it.

"Yikes," Aech said. "Only one credit. Just like Black Tiger."

I remembered the now-useless extra life quarter in my inventory and took it out. But when I dropped it into the coin slot, it fell right through into the coin return. I reached down to remove it and saw a sticker on the coin mechanism: TOKENS ONLY.

"So much for that idea," I said. "And I don't see a token machine anywhere around here."

"Looks like you only get one game," Aech said. "All or nothing."

"Guys, I haven't played Tempest in years," I said. "I'm screwed. There's no way I'm going to beat Halliday's high score on my first attempt."

"You don't have to," Art3mis said. "Look at the copyright year."

I glanced at the bottom of the screen: ©MCMLXXX ATARI.

"Nineteen eighty?" Aech said. "How does that help him?"

"Yeah," I said. "How does that help me?"

"That means this is the very first version of Tempest," Art3mis said. "The version that shipped with a bug in the game code. When Tempest first hit the arcades, kids discovered that if you died with a certain score, the machine would give you a bunch of free credits."

"Oh," I said, somewhat ashamed. "I didn't know that."

"You would," Art3mis said, "if you'd researched the game as much as I did."

"Damn, girl," Aech said. "You've got some serious knowledge."

"Thanks," she said. "It helps to be an obsessive-compulsive geek. With no life." Everyone laughed at that, except me. I was much too nervous.

"OK, Arty," I said. "What do I need to do to get those free games?"

"I'm looking it up in my quest journal right now," she said. I could hear paper rustling. It sounded like she was flipping through the pages of an actual book.

"You just happen to have a hard copy of your journal with you?" I asked.

"I've always kept my journal longhand, in spiral notebooks," she said. "Good thing, too, since my OASIS account and everything in it was just erased." More flipping of pages. "Here it is! First, you need to rack up over one hundred eighty thousand points. Once you've done that, make sure you end the game with a score where the last two digits are oh six, eleven, or twelve. If you do that, you'll get forty free credits."

"You're absolutely positive?"

"Positively absolutely."

"OK," I said. "Here goes."

I began to run through my pregame ritual. Stretching, cracking my knuckles, rolling my head and neck left and right.

"Christ, will you *get on with it*?" Aech said. "The suspense is killing me here!"

"Quiet!" Shoto said. "Give the man some room to breathe, will you?"

Everyone remained silent while I finished psyching myself up. "Here goes nothing," I said. Then I hit the flashing Player One button.

Tempest used old-school vector graphics, so the game's images were created from glowing neon lines drawn against a pitch-black screen. You're given a top-down view of a three-dimensional tunnel, and you use a spinning rotary dial to control a "shooter" that travels around the rim of the tunnel. The object of the game is to shoot the enemies crawling up out of the tunnel toward you while dodging their fire and avoiding other obstacles. As you proceed from one level to the next, the tunnels take on gradually more complex geometric shapes, and the number of enemies and obstacles crawling up toward you multiplies drastically.

Halliday had put this Tempest machine on Tournament settings, so I couldn't start the game any higher than level nine. It took me about fifteen minutes to get my score up above 180,000, and I lost two lives in the process. I was even rustier than I thought. When my score hit 189,412, I intentionally impaled my shooter on a spike, using up my last remaining life. The game prompted me to enter my initials, and I nervously tapped them in: W-O-W.

When I finished, the game's credit counter jumped from zero up to forty.

The sound of my friends' wild cheers filled my ears, nearly giving me a heart attack. "Art3mis, you're a genius," I said, once the noise died down.

"I know."

I tapped the Player One button again and began a second game, now focused on beating Halliday's high score. I still felt anxious, but considerably less so. If I didn't manage to get the high score this time, I had thirty-nine more chances.

During a break between waves, Art3mis spoke up. "So, your initials are W-O-W? What does the O stand for?"

"Obtuse," I said.

She laughed. "No, seriously."

"Owen."

"Owen," she repeated. "Wade Owen Watts. That's nice." Then she fell silent again as the next wave began. I finished my second game a few minutes later, with a score of 219,584. Not horrible, but a far cry from my goal.

"Not bad," Aech said.

"Yeah, but not that good, either," Shoto observed. Then he seemed to remember that I could hear him. "I mean—much better, Parzival. You're doing great."

"Thanks for the vote of confidence, Shoto."

"Hey, check this out," Art3mis said, reading from her journal. "The creator of Tempest, Dave Theurer, originally got the idea for the game from a nightmare he had about monsters crawling up out of a hole in the ground and chasing after him." She laughed her little musical laugh, which I hadn't heard in so long. "Isn't that cool, Z?" she said.

"That *is* cool," I replied. Somehow, just hearing her voice set me at ease. I think she knew this, and that was why she kept talking to me. I felt re-energized. I hit the Player One button again and began my third game.

They all watched me play in complete silence. Nearly an hour later, I lost my last man. My final score was 437,977.

As soon as the game ended, Aech's voice cut in. "Bad news, amigo," she said.

"What?"

"We were right. When the Cataclyst went off, the Sixers had a group of avatars in reserve, waiting just outside the sector. Right after the detonation, they reentered the sector and headed straight for Chthonia. They . . ." Her voice trailed off.

"They *what?*"

"They just entered the gate, about five minutes ago," Art3mis answered. "The gate closed after you went in, but when the Sixers arrived, they used three of their own keys to reopen it."

"You mean the Sixers are already inside the gate? Right now?"

"Eighteen of them," Aech said. "When they stepped through the gate, each one entered a stand-alone simulation. A separate instance of the gate. All eighteen of them are playing Tempest right now, just like you. Trying to beat Halliday's high score. And all of them used the exploit to get forty free credits. Most of them aren't doing that well, but one of them has some serious skill. We think Sorrento is probably operating that avatar. He just started his second game—"

"Wait a second!" I interrupted. "How can you possibly know all this?"

"Because we can see them," Shoto said. "Everyone logged into the OASIS right now can see them. They can see you, too."

"What the hell are you talking about?"

"The moment someone enters the Third Gate, a live vidfeed of their avatar appears at the top of the Scoreboard," Art3mis said. "Apparently, Halliday wanted clearing the final gate to be a spectator sport."

"Wait," I said. "You mean to tell me that the entire world has been watching me play Tempest for the past hour?"

"Correct," Art3mis said. "And they're watching you stand there and jabber back at us right now too. So watch what you say."

"Why didn't you guys tell me?" I shouted.

"We didn't want to make you nervous," Aech said. "Or distract you."

"Oh, great! Perfect! Thank you!" I was shouting, somewhat hysterically.

"Calm down, Parzival," Art3mis said. "Get your head back in the game. This a race now. There are eighteen Sixer avatars right behind you. So you need to make this next game count. Understand?"

"Yeah," I said, exhaling slowly. "I understand." I took another deep breath and pressed the Player One button once again.

As usual, competition brought out the best in me. This time, I managed to slip into the zone. Spinner, zapper, super-zapper, clear a level, avoid the spikes. My hands began to work the controls without my even having to think about it. I forgot about what was at stake, and I forgot about the millions of people watching me. I lost myself in the game.

I'd been playing just over an hour and had just cleared level 81 when

I heard another wild burst of cheering in my ears. "You did it, man!" I heard Shoto shout.

My eyes darted up to the top of the screen. My score was 802,488.

I kept playing, instinctively wanting to get the highest score possible. But then I heard Art3mis loudly clear her throat, and I realized there was no need to go any further. In fact, I was now wasting valuable seconds, burning away whatever lead I still had on the Sixers. I quickly depleted my two extra lives, and GAME OVER flashed on the screen. I entered my initials again, and they appeared at the top of the list, just above Halliday's high score. Then the monitor went blank, and a message appeared in the center of the screen:

WELL DONE, PARZIVAL!
PREPARE FOR STAGE 2!

Then the game cabinet vanished, and my avatar vanished with it.

• • •

I found myself galloping across a fog-covered hillside. I assumed I was riding a horse, because I was bobbing up and down and I heard the sound of hoofbeats. Directly ahead, a familiar-looking castle had just appeared out of the fog.

But when I looked down at my avatar's body, I saw that I wasn't riding a horse at all. I was walking on the ground. My avatar was now dressed in a suit of chain-mail armor, and my hands were held out in front of my body, as though I were clutching a set of reins. But I wasn't holding anything. My hands were completely empty.

I stopped moving forward and the sound of hoofbeats also ceased, but not until a few seconds later. I turned around and saw the source of the sound. It wasn't a horse. It was a man banging two coconut halves together.

Then I knew where I was. Inside the first scene of *Monty Python and the Holy Grail.* Another of Halliday's favorite films, and perhaps the most-beloved geek film of all time.

It appeared to be another Flicksync, like the *WarGames* simulation inside Gate One.

I was playing King Arthur, I realized. I wore the same costume Graham

Chapman had worn in the film. And the man with the coconuts was my trusty manservant, Patsy, as played by Terry Gilliam.

Patsy bowed and groveled a bit when I turned to face him, but said nothing.

"It's Python's *Holy Grail*!" I heard Shoto whisper excitedly.

"Duh," I said, forgetting myself for a second. "I know that, Shoto."

A warning flashed on my display: INCORRECT DIALOGUE! A score of –100 points appeared in the corner of my display.

"Smooth move, Ex-lax," I heard Art3mis say.

"Just let us know if you need any help, Z," Aech said. "Wave your hands or something, and we'll feed you the next line."

I nodded and gave a thumbs-up. But I didn't think I was going to need much help. Over the past six years, I'd watched *Holy Grail* exactly 157 times. I knew every word by heart.

I glanced back up at the castle ahead of me, already aware of what was waiting for me there. I began to "gallop" again, holding my invisible reins as I pretended to ride forward. Once again, Patsy began to bang his coconut halves together, galloping along behind me. When we reached the entrance of the castle, I pulled back on my "reins" and brought my "steed" to a halt.

"Whoa there!" I shouted.

My score increased by 100 points, bringing it back up to zero.

On cue, two soldiers appeared up above, leaning over the castle wall. "Who goes there?" one of them shouted down at us.

"It is I, Arthur, son of Uther Pendragon, from the castle of Camelot," I recited. "King of the Britons! Defeater of the Saxons! Sovereign of all England!"

My score jumped another 500 points, and a message informed me that I'd received a bonus for my accent and inflection. I felt myself relax, and I realized I was already having fun.

"Pull the other one!" the soldier replied.

"I am," I continued. "And this is my trusty servant Patsy. We have ridden the length and breadth of the land in search of knights who will join me in my court at Camelot. I must speak with your lord and master!"

Another 500 points. In my ear, I could hear my friends giggling and applauding.

"What?" the other soldier replied. "Ridden on a horse?"

"Yes!" I said. 100 points.

"You're using coconuts!"

"What?" I said. 100 points.

"You've got two empty halves of coconut and you're bangin' 'em together!"

"So? We have ridden since the snows of winter covered this land, through the kingdom of Mercia, through—" Another 500 points.

"Where'd you get the coconuts?"

And so it went. The character I was playing changed from one scene to the next, switching to whomever had the most dialogue. Incredibly, I flubbed only six or seven lines. Each time I got stumped, all I had to do was shrug and hold out my hands, palms up—my signal that I needed some help—and Aech, Art3mis, and Shoto would all gleefully feed me the correct line. The rest of the time they remained silent except for the occasional giggle fit or burst of laughter. The only really difficult part was not laughing myself, especially when Art3mis started doing note-perfect recitations of all of Carol Cleveland's lines in the Castle Anthrax scene. I cracked up a few times and got hit with score penalties for it. Otherwise, it was smooth sailing.

Reenacting the film wasn't just easy—it was a total blast.

About halfway through the movie, right after my confrontation with the Knights of Ni, I opened up a text window on my display and typed STATUS ON THE SIXERS?

"Fifteen of them are still playing Tempest," I heard Aech reply. "But three of them beat Halliday's score and are now inside the *Grail* simulation." A brief pause. "And the leader—Sorrento, we think—is running just nine minutes behind you."

"And so far, he hasn't missed a single line of dialogue," Shoto added.

I nearly cursed out loud, then caught myself and typed SHIT!

"Exactly," Art3mis said.

I took a deep breath and returned my attention to the next scene ("The Tale of Sir Launcelot"). Aech continued to give me updates on the Sixers whenever I asked for them.

When I reached the film's final scene (the assault on the French Castle), I grew anxious again, wondering what would happen next. The First Gate had required me to reenact a movie (*WarGames*), and the Second Gate had contained a videogame challenge (Black Tiger). So far, the Third

Gate had contained both. I knew there must be a third stage, but I had no idea what it might be.

I got my answer a few minutes later. As soon as I completed *Holy Grail*'s final scene, my display went black while the silly organ music that ends the film played for a few minutes. When the music stopped, the following appeared on my display:

CONGRATULATIONS!
YOU HAVE REACHED THE END!
READY PLAYER 1

And then, as the text faded away, I found myself standing in a huge oak-paneled room as big as a warehouse, with a high vaulted ceiling and a polished hardwood floor. The room had no windows, and only one exit— large double doors set into one of the four bare walls. An older high-end OASIS immersion rig stood in the absolute center of the expansive room. Over a hundred glass tables surrounded the rig, arranged in a large oval around it. On each table there was a different classic home computer or videogame system, accompanied by tiered racks that appeared to hold a complete collection of its peripherals, controllers, software, and games. All of it was arranged perfectly, like a museum exhibit. Looking around the circle, from one system to the next, I saw that the computers seemed to be arranged roughly by year of origin. A PDP-1. An Altair 8800. An IMSAI 8080. An Apple I, right next to an Apple II. An Atari 2600. A Commodore PET. An Intellivision. Several different TRS-80 models. An Atari 400 and 800. A ColecoVision. A TI-99/4. A Sinclair ZX80. A Commodore 64. Various Nintendo and Sega game systems. The entire lineage of Macs and PCs, PlayStations and Xboxes. Finally, completing the circle, was an OASIS console—connected to the immersion rig in the center of the room.

I realized that I was standing in a re-creation of James Halliday's office, the room in his mansion where he'd spent most of the last fifteen years of his life. The place where he'd coded his last and greatest game. The one I was now playing.

I'd never seen any photos of this room, but its layout and contents had been described in great detail by the movers hired to clear the place out after Halliday's death.

I looked down at my avatar and saw that I no longer appeared as one of the Monty Python knights. I was Parzival once again.

First, I did the obvious and tried the exit. The doors wouldn't budge.

I turned back and took another long look around the room, surveying the long line of monuments to the history of computing and videogames.

That was when I realized that the oval-shaped ring in which they were arranged actually formed the outline of an egg.

In my head, I recited the words of Halliday's first riddle, the one in *Anorak's Invitation:*

> *Three hidden keys open three secret gates*
> *Wherein the errant will be tested for worthy traits*
> *And those with the skill to survive these straits*
> *Will reach The End where the prize awaits*

I'd reached the end. This was it. Halliday's Easter egg must be hidden somewhere in this room.

"Do you guys see this?" I whispered.

There was no reply.

"Hello? Aech? Art3mis? Shoto? Are you guys still there?"

Still no reply. Either Og had cut their voice links to me, or Halliday had coded this final stage of the gate so that no outside communication was possible. I was pretty sure it was the latter.

I stood there in silence for a minute, unsure of what to do. Then I followed my first instinct and walked over to the Atari 2600. It was hooked up to a 1977 Zenith Color TV. I turned on the TV, but nothing happened. Then I switched on the Atari. Still nothing. There was no power, even though both the TV and the Atari were plugged into electrical outlets set into the floor.

I tried the Apple II on the table beside it. It wouldn't switch on either.

After a few minutes of experimentation, I discovered that the only computer that would power on was one of the oldest, the IMSAI 8080, the same model of computer Matthew Broderick owned in *WarGames*.

When I booted it up, the screen was completely blank, save for one word.

LOGIN:

I typed in ANORAK and hit Enter.

IDENTIFICATION NOT RECOGNIZED—CONNECTION TERMINATED.

Then the computer shut itself off and I had to power it back on to get the LOGIN prompt again.

I tried HALLIDAY. No dice.

In *WarGames,* the backdoor password that had granted access to the WOPR supercomputer was "Joshua." Professor Falken, the creator of the WOPR, had used the name of his son for the password. The person he'd loved most in the world.

I typed in OG. It didn't work. OGDEN didn't work either.

I typed in KIRA and hit the Enter key.

IDENTIFICATION NOT RECOGNIZED—CONNECTION TERMINATED.

I tried each of his parents' first names. I tried ZAPHOD, the name of his pet fish. Then TIBERIUS, the name of a ferret he'd once owned.

None of them worked.

I checked the time. I'd been in this room for over ten minutes now. Which meant that Sorrento had caught up with me. So he would now be inside his own separate copy of this room, probably with a team of Halliday scholars whispering suggestions in his ear, thanks to his hacked immersion rig. They were probably already working from a prioritized list of possibilities, entering them as fast as Sorrento could type.

I was out of time.

I clenched my teeth in frustration. I had no idea what to try next.

Then I remembered a line from Ogden Morrow's biography: *The opposite sex made Jim extremely nervous, and Kira was the only girl that I ever saw him speak to in a relaxed manner. But even then, it was only in-character, as Anorak, during the course of our gaming sessions, and he would only address her as Leucosia, the name of her D&D character.*

I rebooted the computer again. When the LOGIN prompt reappeared, I typed in LEUCOSIA. Then I hit the Enter key.

Every system in the room powered itself on. The sounds of whirring disk drives, self-test beeps, and other boot-up sounds echoed off the vaulted ceiling.

I ran back over to the Atari 2600 and searched through the giant rack of alphabetized game cartridges beside it until I found the one I was looking for: Adventure. I shoved it into the Atari and turned the system on, then hit the Reset switch to start the game.

It took me only a few minutes to reach the Secret Room.

I grabbed the sword and used it to slay all three of the dragons. Then I found the black key, opened the gates of the Black Castle, and ventured into its labyrinth. The gray dot was hidden right where it was supposed to be. I picked it up and carried it back across the tiny 8-bit kingdom, then used it to pass through the magic barrier and enter the Secret Room. But unlike the original Atari game, this Secret Room didn't contain the name of Warren Robinett, Adventure's original programmer. Instead, at the very center of the screen, there was a large white oval with pixelated edges. An egg.

The egg.

I stared at the TV screen in stunned silence for a moment. Then I pulled the Atari joystick to the right, moving my tiny square avatar across the flickering screen. The TV's mono speaker emitted a brief electronic *bip* sound as I dropped the gray dot and picked up the egg. As I did, there was a brilliant flash of light, and then I saw that my avatar was no longer holding a joystick. Now, cupped in both of my hands, was a large silver egg. I could see my avatar's warped reflection on its curved surface.

When I finally managed to stop staring at it, I looked up and saw that the double doors on the other side of the room had been replaced with the gate exit—a crystal-edged portal leading back into the foyer of Castle Anorak. The castle appeared to have been completely restored, even though the OASIS server still wouldn't reset for several more hours.

I took one last look around Halliday's office; then, still clutching the egg in my hands, I walked across the room and stepped through the exit.

As soon as I was through it, I turned around just in time to see the Crystal Gate transform into a large wooden door set into the castle wall.

I opened the wooden door. Beyond it there was a spiral staircase that led up to the top of Castle Anorak's tallest tower. There, I found Anorak's study. Towering shelves lined the room, filled with ancient scrolls and dusty spellbooks.

I walked over to the window and looked out on a stunning view of the surrounding landscape. It was no longer barren. The effects of the Cataclyst had been undone, and all of Chthonia appeared to be have been restored along with the castle.

I looked around the room. Directly beneath the familiar black dragon painting there was an ornate crystal pedestal on which rested a gold chalice encrusted with tiny jewels. Its diameter matched that of the silver egg I held in my hands.

I placed the egg in the chalice, and it fit perfectly.

In the distance, I heard a fanfare of trumpets, and the egg began to glow.

"You win," I heard a voice say. I turned and saw that Anorak was standing right behind me. His obsidian black robes seemed to pull most of the sunlight out of the room. "Congratulations," he said, stretching out his long-fingered hand.

I hesitated, wondering if this was another trick. Or perhaps one final test . . .

"The game is over," Anorak said, as if he'd read my mind. "It's time for you to receive your prize."

I looked down at his outstretched hand. Then, after a moment's hesitation, I took it.

Cascading bolts of blue lightning erupted in the space between us, and their spiderweb tines enveloped us both, as if a surge of power were passing from his avatar into mine. When the lightning subsided, I saw that Anorak was no longer dressed in his black wizard's robes. In fact, he no longer looked like Anorak at all. He was shorter, thinner, and somewhat less handsome. Now he looked like James Halliday. Pale. Middle-aged. He was dressed in worn jeans and a faded Space Invaders T-shirt.

I looked down at my own avatar and discovered that I was now wearing Anorak's robes. Then I realized that the icons and readouts around the edge of my display had also changed. My stats were all completely maxxed out, and I now had a list of spells, inherent powers, and magic items that seemed to scroll on forever.

My avatar's level and hit-point counters both had infinity symbols in front of them.

And my credit readout now displayed a number twelve digits long. I was a multibillionaire.

"I'm entrusting the care of the OASIS to you now, Parzival," Halliday said. "Your avatar is immortal and all-powerful. Whatever you want, all you have to do is wish for it. Pretty sweet, eh?" He leaned toward me and lowered his voice. "Do me a favor. Try and use your powers only for good. OK?"

"OK," I said, in a voice that was barely a whisper.

Halliday smiled, then gestured around us. "This is your castle now. I've coded this room so that only your avatar can enter it. I did this to ensure that you alone have access to this." He walked over to a bookshelf against the wall and pulled on the spine of one of the volumes it held. I heard a click; then the bookshelf slid aside, revealing a square metal plate set into the wall. In the center of the plate there was a comically large red button embossed with a single word: OFF.

"I call this the Big Red Button," Halliday said. "If you press it, it will shut off the entire OASIS and launch a worm that will delete everything stored on the GSS servers, including all of the OASIS source code. It will shut down the OASIS forever." He smirked. "So don't press it unless you're absolutely positive it's the right thing to do, OK?" He gave me an odd smile. "I trust your judgment."

Halliday slid the bookshelf back into place, concealing the button once again. Then he startled me by putting his arm around my shoulders. "Listen," he said, adopting a confidential tone. "I need to tell you one last thing before I go. Something I didn't figure out for myself until it was already too late." He led me over to the window and motioned out at the landscape stretching out beyond it. "I created the OASIS because I never felt at home in the real world. I didn't know how to connect with the people there. I was afraid, for all of my life. Right up until I knew it was ending. That was when I realized, as terrifying and painful as reality can be, it's also the only place where you can find true happiness. Because reality is *real*. Do you understand?"

"Yes," I said. "I think I do."

"Good," he said, giving me a wink. "Don't make the same mistake I did. Don't hide in here forever."

He smiled and took a few steps away from me. "All right. I think that covers everything. It's time for me to blow this pop stand."

Then Halliday began to disappear. He smiled and waved good-bye as his avatar slowly faded out of existence.

"Good luck, Parzival," he said. "And thanks. Thanks for playing my game."

Then he was completely gone.

* * *

"Are you guys there?" I said to the empty air a few minutes later.

"Yes!" Aech said excitedly. "Can you hear us?"

"Yeah. I can now. What happened?"

"The system cut off our voice links to you as soon as you entered Halliday's office, so we couldn't talk to you."

"Luckily, you didn't need our help anyway," Shoto said. "Good job, man."

"Congratulations, Wade," I heard Art3mis say. And I could tell she meant it too.

"Thanks," I said. "But I couldn't have done it without you guys."

"You're right," Art3mis said. "Remember to mention that when you talk to the media. Og says there are a few hundred reporters on their way here right now."

I glanced back over at the bookshelf that concealed the Big Red Button. "Did you guys see everything Halliday said to me before he vanished?" I asked.

"No," Art3mis said. "We saw everything up until he told you to 'try and use your powers only for good.' Then your vidfeed cut out. What happened after that?"

"Nothing much," I said. "I'll tell you about it later."

"Dude," Aech said. "You've got to check the Scoreboard."

I opened a window and pulled up the Scoreboard. The list of high scores was gone. Now the only thing displayed on Halliday's website was an image of my avatar, dressed in Anorak's robes, holding the silver egg, along with the words PARZIVAL WINS!

"What happened to the Sixers?" I asked. "The ones who were still inside the gate?"

"We're not sure," Aech said. "Their vidfeeds vanished when the Scoreboard changed."

"Maybe their avatars were killed," Shoto said. "Or maybe . . ."

"Maybe they were just ejected from the gate," I said.

I pulled up my map of Chthonia and saw that I could now teleport anywhere in the OASIS simply by selecting my desired destination in the atlas. I zoomed in on Castle Anorak and tapped a spot just outside the front entrance, and in a blink, my avatar was standing there.

I was right. When I'd cleared the Third Gate, the eighteen Sixer avatars who were still inside had been ejected from the gate and deposited in front of the castle. They were all standing there with confused looks on their faces when I appeared in front of them, resplendent in my new threads.

They all stared at me in silence for a few seconds, then pulled out guns and swords, preparing to attack. They all looked identical, so I couldn't tell which one was being controlled by Sorrento. But at this point, I didn't really care.

Using my avatar's new superuser interface, I made a sweeping gesture with my hand, selecting all of the Sixer avatars on my display. Their outlines began to glow red. Then I tapped the skull-and-crossbones icon that now appeared on my avatar's toolbar. All eighteen Sixer avatars instantly dropped dead. Their bodies slowly faded out of existence, each leaving behind a tiny pile of weapons and loot.

"Holy shit!" I heard Shoto say over the comlink. "How did you do that?"

"You heard Halliday," Aech said. "His avatar is immortal and all-powerful."

"Yeah," I said. "He wasn't kidding, either."

"Halliday also said you could wish for whatever you wanted," Aech said. "What are you gonna wish for first?"

I thought about that for a second; then I tapped the new Command icon that now appeared at the edge of my display and said, "I wish for Aech, Art3mis, and Shoto to be resurrected."

A dialog window popped up, asking me to confirm the spelling of each of their avatar names. Once I did, the system asked me if, in addition to resurrecting their avatars, I wanted to restore all of their lost items, too. I tapped the Yes icon. Then a message appeared in the center of my display: RESURRECTION COMPLETE. AVATARS RESTORED.

"Guys?" I said. "You might want to try logging back into your accounts now."

"We're already on our way!" Aech shouted.

A few seconds later, Shoto logged back into his account, and his avatar materialized a short distance in front of me, in the exact spot where he'd been killed a few hours earlier. He ran over to me, grinning from ear to ear. "*Arigato*, Parzival-san," he said, bowing low.

I returned the bow, then threw my arms around him. "Welcome back," I said. A moment later, Aech emerged from the castle entrance and ran over to join us.

"Good as new," he said, grinning down at his restored avatar. "Thanks, Z."

"*De nada.*" I glanced back through the castle's open entrance. "Where's Art3mis? She should have reappeared right next to you—"

"She didn't log back in," Aech said. "She said she wanted to go outside and get some fresh air."

"You saw her? What—?" I searched for the right words. "How did she look?"

They both just smiled at me; then Aech rested a hand on my shoulder. "She said she'd be outside waiting for you. Whenever you're ready to meet her."

I nodded. I was about to tap my Log-out icon when Aech held up her—his—hand. "Wait a second! Before you log out, you've got to see something," he said, opening a window in front of me. "This is airing on all of the newsfeeds right now. The feds just took Sorrento in for questioning. They stormed into IOI headquarters and yanked him right out of his haptic chair!"

A video clip began to play. Handheld camera footage showed a team of federal agents leading Sorrento across the lobby of the IOI corporate headquarters. He was still wearing his haptic suit and was shadowed by a gray-haired man in a suit who I assumed was his attorney. Sorrento looked annoyed more than anything, as if this were all just a mild inconvenience. The caption along the bottom of the window read: *Top IOI Executive Sorrento Accused of Murder.*

"The newsfeeds have been playing clips from the simcap of your chatlink session with Sorrento all day," Aech said, pausing the clip. "Especially the part where he threatens to kill you and then blows up your aunt's trailer."

Aech hit Play, and the news clip continued. The federal agents continued to usher Sorrento through the lobby, which was packed with reporters, all pushing against one another and shouting questions. The reporter shooting the video we were watching lunged forward and jammed the camera in Sorrento's face. "Did you give the order to kill Wade Watts personally?" the reporter shouted. "How does it feel to know you just lost the contest?"

Sorrento smiled, but didn't reply. Then his attorney stepped in front of the camera and addressed the reporters. "The charges leveled against my client are preposterous," he said. "The simcap being circulated is clearly a doctored fake. We have no other comment at this time."

Sorrento nodded. He continued to smile as the feds led him out of the building.

"The bastard will probably get off scot-free," I said. "IOI can afford to hire the best lawyers in the world."

"Yes, they can," Aech said. Then he flashed his Cheshire grin. *"But now so can we."*

When I stepped out of the immersion bay, Og was standing there waiting for me. "Well done, Wade!" he said, pulling me into a crushing bear hug. "Well done!"

"Thanks, Og." I was still dazed and felt unsteady on my feet.

"Several chief executives from GSS arrived while you were logged in," Og said. "Along with all of Jim's lawyers. They're all waiting upstairs. As you can imagine, they're anxious to speak with you."

"Do I have to talk to them right now?"

"No, of course not!" He laughed. "They all work for you now, remember? Make the bastards wait as long as you like!" He leaned forward. "My lawyer is up there too. He's a good guy. A real pit bull. He'll make sure that no one messes with you, OK?"

"Thanks, Og," I said. "I really owe you."

"Nonsense!" he said. "I should be thanking you. I haven't had this much fun in decades! You did good, kid."

I glanced around uncertainly. Aech and Shoto were still in their immersion bays, holding an impromptu online press conference. But Art3mis's bay was empty. I turned back to Og.

"Do you know which way Art3mis went?"

Og grinned at me, then pointed. "Up those stairs and out the first door you see," he said. "She said she'd wait for you at the center of my hedge maze." He smiled. "It's an easy maze. It shouldn't take you very long to find her."

I stepped outside and squinted as my eyes adjusted to the light. The air was warm, and the sun was already high overheard. There wasn't a cloud in the sky.

It was a beautiful day.

The hedge maze covered several acres of land behind the mansion. The entrance was designed to look like the facade of a castle, and you entered the maze through its open gates. The dense hedge walls that comprised the maze were ten feet tall, making it impossible to peek over them, even if you stood on top of one of the benches placed throughout the labyrinth.

I entered the maze and wandered around in circles for a few minutes, confused. Eventually, I realized that the maze's layout was identical to the labyrinth in Adventure.

After that, it took me only a few more minutes to find my way to the large open area at the maze's center. A large fountain stood there, with a detailed stone sculpture of Adventure's three duck-shaped dragons. Each dragon was spitting a stream of water instead of breathing fire.

And then I saw her.

She was sitting on a stone bench, staring into the fountain. She had her back to me, and her head was tilted down. Her long black hair spilled down over her right shoulder. I could see that she was kneading her hands in her lap.

I was afraid to move any closer. Finally, I worked up the courage to speak. "Hello," I said.

She lifted her head at the sound of my voice, but didn't turn around.

"Hello," I heard her say. And it was her voice. Art3mis's voice. The voice I'd spent so many hours listening to. And that gave me the courage to step forward.

I walked around the fountain and stopped once I was standing directly in front of her. As she heard me approach, she turned her head away, averting her eyes and keeping me out of her field of vision.

But I could see her.

She looked just as she had in the photo I'd seen. She had the same Rubenesque body. The same pale, freckled skin. The same hazel eyes and raven hair. The same beautiful round face, with the same reddish birthmark. But unlike in that photo, she wasn't trying to hide the birthmark with a sweep of her hair. She had her hair brushed back, so I could see it.

I waited in silence. But she still wouldn't look up at me.

"You look just like I always pictured you," I said. "Beautiful."

"Really?" she said softly. Slowly, she turned to face me, taking in my appearance a little at a time, starting with my feet and then gradually working her way up to my face. When our eyes finally met, she smiled at me nervously. "Well, what do you know? You look just like I always thought you would too," she said. "Butt ugly."

We both laughed, and most of the tension in the air dissipated. Then we stared into each other's eyes for what seemed like a long time. It was, I realized, also the very first time.

"We haven't been formally introduced," she said. "I'm Samantha."

"Hello, Samantha. I'm Wade."

"It's nice to finally meet you in person, Wade."

She patted the bench beside her, and I sat down.

After a long silence, she said, "So what happens now?"

I smiled. "We're going to use all of the moolah we just won to feed everyone on the planet. We're going to make the world a better place, right?"

She grinned. "Don't you want to build a huge interstellar spaceship, load it full of videogames, junk food, and comfy couches, and then get the hell out of here?"

"I'm up for that, too," I said. "If it means I get to spend the rest of my life with you."

She gave me a shy smile. "We'll have to see," she said. "We just met, you know."

"I'm in love with you."

Her lower lip started to tremble. "You're sure about that?"

"Yes. I am. Because it's true."

She smiled at me, but I also saw that she was crying. "I'm sorry for breaking things off with you," she said. "For disappearing from your life. I just—"

"It's OK," I said. "I understand why you did it now."

She looked relieved. "You do?"

I nodded. "You did the right thing."

"You think so?"

"We won, didn't we?"

She smiled at me, and I smiled back.

"Listen," I said. "We can take things as slow as you like. I'm really a nice guy, once you get to know me. I swear."

She laughed and wiped away a few of her tears, but she didn't say anything.

"Did I mention that I'm also extremely rich?" I said. "Of course, so are you, so I don't suppose that's a big selling point."

"You don't need to sell me on anything, Wade," she said. "You're my best friend. My favorite person." With what appeared to be some effort, she looked me in the eye. "I've really missed you, you know that?"

My heart felt like it was on fire. I took a moment to work up my courage; then I reached out and took her hand. We sat there awhile, holding hands, reveling in the strange new sensation of actually touching one another.

Some time later, she leaned over and kissed me. It felt just like all those songs and poems had promised it would. It felt wonderful. Like being struck by lightning.

It occurred to me then that for the first time in as long as I could remember, I had absolutely no desire to log back into the OASIS.

Acknowledgments

Many of my favorite people were subjected to early drafts of this book, and each of them gave me invaluable feedback and encouragement. My sincere thanks to Eric Cline, Susan Somers-Willett, Chris Beaver, Harry Knowles, Amber Bird, Ingrid Richter, Sara Sutterfield Winn, Jeff Knight, Hilary Thomas, Anne Miano, Tonie Knight, Nichole Cook, Cristin O'Keefe Aptowicz, Jay Smith, Mike Henry, Jed Strahm, Andy Howell, and Chris Fry.

I'm also indebted to Yfat Reiss Gendell, the Coolest Agent in the Known Universe, who managed to make several of my lifelong dreams come true just a few months after I met her. Thanks also to Stéphanie Abou, Hannah Brown Gordon, Cecilia Campbell-Westlind, and all of the awesome folks at Foundry Literary and Media.

A huge shout-out to the amazing Dan Farah, my friend, manager, and Hollywood partner in crime. My gratitude also goes out to Donald De Line, Andrew Haas, and Jesse Ehrman at Warner Bros., for believing that this book will make a great movie.

Thanks to the incredibly talented and supportive team at Crown, including Patty Berg, Sarah Breivogel, Jacob Bronstein, David Drake, Jill Flaxman, Jacqui Lebow, Rachelle Mandik, Maya Mavjee, Seth Morris, Michael Palgon, Tina Pohlman, Annsley Rosner, and Molly Stern. And to my fantastic copyeditor, Deanna Hoak, who found the Secret Room in Adventure back in the day.

I owe a special debt of gratitude to Julian Pavia, my brilliant editor, who believed in my ability as a writer long before I finished this book. Julian's startling intelligence, insight, and relentless attention to detail helped me shape *Ready Player One* into the book I'd always wanted it to be, and he made me a better writer in the process.

Finally, I want to thank all of the writers, filmmakers, actors, artists, musicians, programmers, game designers, and geeks whose work I've paid tribute to in this story. These people have all entertained and enlightened me, and I hope that—like Halliday's hunt—this book will inspire others to seek out their creations.

ABOUT THE AUTHOR

Ernest Cline lives in Austin, Texas,
where he devotes a large portion of his time
to geeking out. This is his first novel.

For more information please visit:
www.ernestcline.com